RANDOM HOUSE

LARGE PRINT

ALSO AVAILABLE FROM RANDOM HOUSE LARGE PRINT

TOM CLANCY

COMMAND
AND
CONTROL

★

MARC CAMERON

RANDOM HOUSE
LARGE PRINT

Copyright © 2023 by The Estate of Thomas L. Clancy, Jr.; Rubicon, Inc.; Jack Ryan Enterprises, Ltd.; and Jack Ryan Limited Partnership

All rights reserved. Published in the United States of America by Random House Large Print in association with G. P. Putnam's Sons, an imprint of Penguin Random House LLC.

Cover design and art: Eric Fuentecilla
Cover image: (radar) Makhnach_s/ Shutterstock
Maps by Jeffrey L. Ward

The Library of Congress has established a Cataloging-in-Publication record for this title.

ISBN: 978-0-593-79267-4

www.penguinrandomhouse.com/large-print-format-books

FIRST LARGE PRINT EDITION

Printed in the United States of America

1st Printing

If the highest aim of a captain were to preserve his ship, he would keep it in port forever.

Thomas Aquinas

The nation that will insist upon drawing a broad line of demarcation between the fighting man and the thinking man is liable to find its fighting done by fools and its thinking by cowards.

Sir William F. Butler

PRINCIPAL CHARACTERS

Jack Ryan, Sr.: President of the United States
Cathy Ryan: First Lady
Mark Dehart: Vice president of the United States
Arnie van Damm: White House chief of staff
Mary Pat Foley: Director of national intelligence
Dan Murray: Attorney general
Jay Canfield: Director of the CIA
Scott Adler: Secretary of state
Bob Burgess: Secretary of defense

WINDWARD STATION CIA OPERATIONS OFFICERS

Adam Yao
Eric "Ripper" Ward
James "Sal" Salazar
Myrna Chaman
Chris Nestor
Al Lopez
Ben "Boomer" Ramos
Adrian Hernandez

UNITED STATES SECRET SERVICE

Gary Montgomery: Special agent in charge, presidential detail
Maureen "Mo" Richardson: Special agent in charge, FLOTUS detail
Keenan Mulvaney: Special agent in charge, vice presidential detail
Brett Johnson: Special agent in charge, director of national intelligence detail

THE CAMPUS

John Clark: Director of operations
Domingo "Ding" Chavez: Assistant director of operations
Dominic "Dom" Caruso: Operator
Jack Ryan, Jr.: Operator
Lisanne Robertson: Operator
Adara Sherman: Operator
Bartosz "Midas" Jankowski: Operator
Steven "Chilly" Edwards: Operator
Amanda "Mandy" Cobb: Operator

PANAMA

Rafael Botero: President of Panama
Lionel Carré: Vice president of Panama
Gabriella Canto: Major, National Police of Panama (PNP)
Alfredo "Fredi" Perez: Canto's driver (PNP)

OTHER CHARACTERS

Javier Guerra: Commissioner, National Police of Panama (PNP)

Fabian Pinto: Guerra's driver (PNP)

Felix Moncada: Botero's trusted economic adviser

Joaquín Fernando Gorshkov: Venezuelan-Russian assassin

Sabine Gorshkova: Joaquín's older sister

Blanca Gorshkova, aka Blanca Pakulova: Joaquín's younger sister

Hector Alonso: Joaquin's adopted guardian

Admiral Kozlov: Commander, Northern Fleet, Russian Navy

Alejandro Berugatte: Indigenous Emberá Panama Canal pilot

Vladimir Rykov: Captain of the Russian destroyer **Admiral Chabanenko**

Pagodin: Captain of the Russian landing vessel **Ivan Gren**

Commander Rick "Seldom" Wright: MH-6 Little Bird pilot

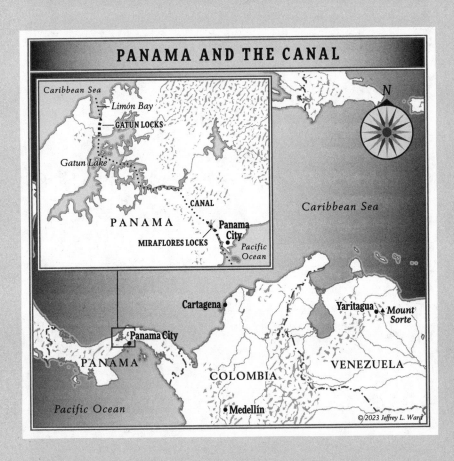

1

A hushed commotion fluttered outside Vice President Mark Dehart's ceremonial office—like birds escaping the path of an oncoming truck. Dehart glanced toward the door, smiling broadly to show the young reporter who was sitting on the other side of the Roosevelt desk that he was still paying attention to her questions. Fresh out of Penn State journalism school with a new job at the **Philadelphia Inquirer,** she was still unjaded enough to be a little starry-eyed about Washington politics.

Poor kid.

Cub reporter or not, she'd had enough moxie to ask her editor if she could try for an interview with the vice president. That alone was enough to earn her points with Dehart.

He was tall and trim with just enough silver at the temples of his dark hair to make him look like that favorite uncle who showed up with interesting stories at Thanksgiving. His deep farmer's tan must have been hereditary because he hadn't had more than a few moments on his old John Deere for over a decade. Dehart wasn't crazy about it, but being the kind of politician that journalists loved to photograph worked well for the man who held the office that was often described as the "spare tire" of the United States government.

Still smiling at the reporter, he cocked an ear toward the sounds outside—sotto voce whispers that virtually screamed to be heard, the telltale squeak of his secretary's chair as she got to her feet to race whomever it was to the door.

The Eisenhower Executive Office Building was normally a sleepy place compared to the frenetic atmosphere of the West Wing just a short walk away across the White House campus. The wide tiled halls had a way of swallowing up the building's inhabitants, where the White House felt as if it were about to burst at the seams.

Dehart pushed away from the Roosevelt desk. He'd signed his name inside the lap drawer like every vice president since Lyndon Johnson. And like every VPOTUS since the 1940s, he used his ceremonial digs in the EEOB when he needed a more picturesque backdrop than his utilitarian office in the West Wing for photo ops, greeting foreign officials, interviews with journalists, etc. As far as he could tell, this was going to be a complimentary piece from his home-state paper, easy, but devoid of much substance. Unlike most politicians, Dehart despised talking about himself and, frankly, would welcome the interruption.

He'd never wanted the job of vice president—or the one he'd had before it, for that matter. He and his wife, Dee, had lived in blissful happiness when he served as the senior United States senator from Pennsylvania, that is until Jack Ryan swooped in and asked him to be the secretary of homeland security.

Dehart liked to be ahead of the curve, so he stood abruptly as the noise at the door grew louder.

Startled, the reporter dropped her pen. "Is everything—"

Keenan Mulvaney, the special agent in charge of Dehart's Secret Service detail, cut her off mid-sentence, bursting in with three other agents hot on his heels.

Dehart groaned. The Secret Service whisked him away to a secure location more frequently than he would have imagined before he got the job. Drones, inbound unidentified aircraft, crazy people with guns on Seventeenth Street—any number of "trip wires" triggered the arrival of a cadre of armed agents.

This time, they brought someone with them.

Arnie van Damm, President Ryan's ever-rumpled chief of staff, trooped in with the agents.

Dehart offered the reporter an apologetic smile.

"Please excuse me. I'm afraid I have to go." He started around the desk, but Mulvaney raised a hand.

"I apologize, Mr. Vice President, but she'll have to go. I'd ask you to stay put, sir."

Van Damm said nothing, instead pacing back and forth in a tiny piece of real estate by the door. Eyes flashing, his jaw clenched like a trapped animal about to gnaw his own leg off.

Dehart's secretary ushered the reporter out, promising to reschedule as soon as possible.

"The PEA-YOC?" Dehart asked as soon as they were gone, meaning, **Are you taking me to the Presidential Emergency Operations Center?** The PEOC was an underground bunker that served as a secure if starkly utilitarian situation room during a threat. Any visit there was a shock to the system, but some were worse than others. The look on van Damm's face said this was going to be one of the latter.

Mulvaney nodded grimly. "We'll go via the underground, Mr. Vice President."

The area beneath the White House and the Eisenhower Executive Office Building had enough tunnels to stoke more than a few conspiracy theories, many of them Dehart had yet to explore.

Van Damm finished with the hangnail he'd been chewing on and flicked a hand toward the door. "We'll take a breath here while your secretary clears the outer office."

"Okay . . ." Dehart gave a shrug. "You want to fill me in, Arnie?"

"Panama is turning to shit as we speak," van Damm said. "And at this moment, President Ryan is unaccounted for. The principals are coming in now."

The "principals" were the principal members of the NSC, the National Security Council.

Mulvaney raised a hand, signaling that he was getting a message on his earpiece from an agent posted outside.

"We're clear to move, sir," he said.

Dehart stood fast, staring down the chief of staff. "What does that mean exactly, 'unaccounted for'?"

"It means what it means," van Damm snapped. A pained look creased his face, like he was nursing a bad tooth. "The Secret Service can't find the President. Incommunicado? Injured? Kidnapped . . ." He waved off the next logical thought. That was unimaginable. "It means that you are acting POTUS until we find Jack Ryan."

2

VENEZUELA
FOUR DAYS EARLIER

The Ground Branch operators tasked with hunting down and killing Joaquín Fernando Gorshkov were known as WINDWARD STATION.

The Office of the Director of National Intelligence at Liberty Crossing called this operation SUDDEN SQUALL. Whomever came up with the code names was apparently a weather buff. Maybe a sailor, CIA operations officer Adam Yao thought as he looked out the grimy bus window at the Venezuelan jungle and mulled over how he and his team had gotten to this spot.

Barely forty, Yao was clean-shaven with a thick head of black hair that looked forever windblown unless he gooped it up with pomade—which he did not do. As well as English, he spoke Mandarin, Cantonese, and Spanish like a native, but he listened more than he spoke. Tall, but not overly so, he had the body of a decathlete—well muscled like a sprinter, but a shade on the lean side for endurance work. Had he worn a tank top or gone shirtless like half the men crammed on the creaking bus, his defined physique would have been apparent, but an Asian man dressed in chinos, desert boots, and a loose gray linen shirt was unremarkable—and, more important to him surviving the night, forgettable. As the saying went, if you were one in a million in China, there were three thousand more just like you. Yao didn't exactly blend in with the local population, but Chinese, Japanese, and Middle Eastern surnames were not at all uncommon across South America. Yao wasn't Latin, but he didn't look like a **yanqui,** and in the broken nation of Venezuela, that was what mattered.

When boiled down to the basics, he and his team only had two objectives: Kill Joaquín Gorshkov and stay alive while they were doing it.

Having someone killed, Yao had learned over his fifteen years in the Agency, was a surprisingly complex endeavor. The same U.S. Code Title 50 that made his team covert and deniable gave the President and the National Security Council the authority to act as a sort of "star chamber," deeming certain people a clear and present danger to the well-being of the United States and its citizens. At least that's the way the lawyers interpreted it.

For the time being.

Contrary to spy novels and Hollywood action flicks, CIA officers didn't make a habit of going around whacking their enemies. Intelligence work was, for the most part, mundane and plodding, playing the long game of winning hearts and minds by convincing people that your dogma was better than their dogma—or at the very least your dogma paid better. If anyone died on either side, something had gone terribly wrong. That said, such "active measures" weren't unheard of, either, especially not lately. The threat board was chock-full of hostiles who wanted nothing more than to make Americans bleed. They had to be stopped.

Targeted killings made the news, but in reality, they were rarer than honest politicians. Such action required lengthy investigations, days of back-and-forth debate by the principals of the National Security Council, meticulously researched legal "spins" from White House lawyers—and a nod from the Commander in Chief.

After all that, the bureaucratic machine spat out a death warrant—though Yao had never heard it called that. Lawyers used all manner of obfuscation. Past administrations had called it by all sorts of different names—the A List, Remedies, Disposition Matrix, or even Kill List (though the last was only spoken and rarely written down). Everyone steered well away from anything remotely close to **assassination**—which remained illegal under U.S. law, no matter the spins.

In the psyche of American jurisprudence there was a bright line between assassination and targeted killing. But in the field, each required the one pulling the trigger to do things that normal, well-adjusted members of society found abhorrent—backstabbing, poisoning, or, as the Russians seemed to prefer, defenestration—throwing someone out a high window. An instructor at the Farm had told Adam Yao's class that the Russians had learned through trial and error that six stories was the absolute minimum to get the job done. Yao had never pushed anyone out a window, but six stories sounded about right.

This would be his third tasking with a capture or kill order. Operations officers didn't routinely get emails from the lofty realms of the director of national intelligence—essentially his boss's boss's boss—so when Mary Pat Foley put him on a secure video conference call with the President of the United States, Yao wasn't about to say no. He was trusted, and in an agency where layers of lies and subterfuge obscured the truth, trust was a pearl to be guarded with great care. He had accepted the assignment to lead WINDWARD STATION on the spot—every bloody aspect of it.

And this guy was one of the bloodiest Adam Yao had ever heard of.

Yao and his team referred to their target as FRIAR, a nod to Gorshkov's self-styled nickname, "Torquemada." A Spanish priest, Tomás de

Torquemada was a Dominican friar and the first grand inquisitor who oversaw the brutal torture and murder of thousands in both the Old and New Worlds. Few people realized it, but when they thought of the fifteenth-century Spanish Inquisition—iron maidens, breast rippers, joint-destroying racks—they were imagining the work of Tomás de Torquemada. Yao considered "FRIAR" too polite a code name, but they needed to call the bastard something when they referred to him on the radio. Whispering "murdering son of a bitch" out among the public would draw too much attention.

Yao's handpicked team was comprised mainly of former military from Ground Branch—the pipe hitters of the Agency. WINDWARD STATION wasn't made of the "pale and Yale" personnel stereo-typical of the CIA. Almost all of them were from Latin-American families.

At this point, WINDWARD STATION had been in operation for eleven slogging months, two weeks, and six days. Before them, FBI, CIA, USSOCOM, and a half-dozen foreign intelligence services had been on the hunt for the elusive fugi-tive for over two years. Their target slinked back and forth between secret hidey-holes, eluding so much as a sighting, much less capture.

Three and a half years earlier, a liquid explo-sive bomb had detonated in the cafeteria of a Department of Defense elementary school on Aviano Air Base in northeastern Italy. The death toll would have been much worse but for an alert elementary school teacher who spotted a telltale wire protruding from under one of the tables. The twenty-six-year-old mother of two had time to usher most of her students to safety, but died along with a teacher's aide and three second graders when the device detonated during the evacuation.

An unidentified subject known as Torquemada— a faceless "UNSUB" black silhouette in official reports up to this point—was already a person of interest to the FBI for the firebrand manifestos he posted online. His white-hot hatred for the United States boiled over in every vehement diatribe. Torquemada's words carried the fervor of a religious zealot—his religion based on little but a burning hatred for capitalism, the hottest part of that reserved for the United States.

Analysts pointed out that phrases like "we reject and condemn human rights as Yankee imperialist bourgeois" and "we annihilate to create a vacuum" evoked the wording of similarly brutal manifestos written by leaders of the Shining Path two decades before—or a Guns N' Roses song.

FBI agents traveled to Peru and conducted dozens of interviews. They opened old investigations into the militant movement and put together photo boards of every known member of the violent organization, including a thin stack of stapled papers from a Catholic orphanage that was supposed to have been a favorite cause of certain vocal Shining

Path guerrillas. A yearbook of sorts, the papers contained given names and photographs of nineteen children, both girls and boys, from toddlers to their early teens. No particulars beyond their names were provided. Investigators found nothing noteworthy about any of the names.

Then Torquemada posted another rant in which he fervently justified the Aviano school bombing. Like before, the IP address was spoofed and bounced all over the world, leaving it untraceable. But the contents provided a lead. He posted details, like where the device had been placed, that had never been released by law enforcement. He was clearly involved.

Authorities felt reasonably certain they had their man—they just had no idea who he was or how to find him.

Security video from the Aviano bombing showed a dark male leaving the base behind the wheel of a maintenance van five minutes before the bomb went off. The van had been stolen and the photo was so grainy, facial recognition was a bust.

Then a new FBI analyst decided to feed the nineteen photos from the Peruvian orphanage book into his computer and ask an AI program to "age" them and see what they would look like in present day. The idea got traction with the analyst's supervisors. Rather than relying on just their own program, they asked the CIA to have a go at it, independent of the Bureau. Both agencies came up with remarkably similar renderings.

One of the photos showed a handsome boy with a bright smile and wide eyes, as if startled by the flash of the camera. His computer-aged photo bore a striking resemblance to the UNSUB in the van leaving the Aviano school bombing.

According to the orphanage book, his name was Joaquín.

It took almost a year of records searches and plodding interviews to piece together the evidence that the smiling young man in the photograph was a Venezuelan-Russian citizen named Joaquín Fernando Gorshkov and that he and the writer who called himself Torquemada could be one and the same person.

Eight months after the school bombing, a seven-member medical team from a U.S. NGO were brutally murdered outside the mountainous Bolivian village of Camargo. Eleven women and children who were waiting to receive care met the same fate. The brutality of the killings led Bolivian authorities to first believe the medical team had had a run-in with local narcos, until Torquemada, not knowing that he'd been identified, boasted of the attack in an online manifesto. Two months later, he attacked again at a Peruvian clinic funded by American missionaries, murdering everyone and then burning the building to the ground.

Nothing of value was stolen, no political target had been present. The thread that tied the incidents together was that all the victims were American or had received assistance from the United States. For that, volunteers, women, and children in both Bolivia and Peru had been killed with hatchets and claw hammers.

Torquemada struck and then melted into the ether, his manifestos rolling out like news releases shortly after each bloody act. Russia and Venezuela provided the perfect briar patches for him to hide in and remain anonymous. One of Yao's in-place assets, an officer in the SVR (Sluzhba Vneshney Razvedki), Russia's counterpart to the CIA, believed Gorshkov acted from time to time as a contracted thug for the Kremlin. The asset's code name was VICAR. The Russians had a file complete with contact information to be sure, but VICAR was unable to get his hands on it. As long as Gorshkov proved to be a useful thug, the people employing him kept it tucked away. Venezuela's Bolivarian National Intelligence Service would rather see every WINDWARD STATION operative rotting in prison than catch a man who was essentially a serial killer hiding behind a political agenda. Yao's team ran up against little but roadblocks and dead ends.

Then the terrorist-hunting gods smiled on WINDWARD STATION, as if they had finally paid their dues.

The new development came from VICAR.

Yao's SVR asset provided a cell-phone number belonging to a Russian sushi chef, who was said to accompany Gorshkov virtually everywhere he went. For a man who hated capitalism, Torquemada/Gorshkov certainly enjoyed the finer things in life. The cell number was new and would likely only be active for a few days, but they used that window to trace it.

That was the thing about burner phones. The people who utilized them were paranoid, but the act of tossing a prepaid every two or three days gave them a false sense of security. Dimitri Chernoff was a sushi chef, not a trained intelligence operative. Once WINDWARD STATION knew the number of his burner, they were able to learn where he and his sushi-eating employer were within that two- or three-day window he kept the phone.

But time was of the essence.

A couple of CIA mandarins up the food chain at Langley balked at Yao's "dangerous, spur-of-the-moment plan" for an incursion into a failed state like Venezuela. In their stolid estimation, a more measured approach was advised. They would wait, put locates out with border crossings and friendly intelligence organizations. Facial recognition and biometric readers would be a safer way to follow the sushi chef, catching him and Gorshkov somewhere between Venezuela and Russia.

Yao was a patient man, but waiting when a target

clearly presented itself was not in his DNA. Too much could go haywire. The sushi chef might choke on a gob of rice. He might die in a car wreck. For that matter, Joaquín Gorshkov appeared to be just unstable enough to end the sushi chef with a claw hammer if he messed up on a crunch roll. No, it was better to strike at the first possible opportunity rather than bank on measured approaches.

Fortunately, the director of national intelligence shared Yao's feelings.

Maybes were horseshit.

3

With Director Foley's blessing, WINDWARD STATION operatives stuffed their gear into inconspicuous backpacks and hustled off to Colombia. From there, they hitched rides across the border with Venezuelans who'd driven over with full tanks of cheap gasoline to sell, keeping just enough to return to their own country. Colombian border guards kept a watchful eye on who came in, but cared little about who left. The only papers Venezuelan guards appeared to be interested in were U.S. dollars.

Once across the border, it was a nine-hour bus ride to Barquisimeto, a city of just over a million souls in the northwestern state of Yaracuy. The team spent every endless mile hoping against hope that they'd arrive in time to find Joaquín Gorshkov at the Hotel Tiffany—the location where the sushi chef's phone was last active before it went dark five hours earlier.

No joy.

Gorshkov had been at the Hotel Tiffany the night before, or, at least, someone important had, according to a prostitute who plied her trade out of a dusty eight-stool bar half a block down from the hotel.

Yao guessed the woman to be in her mid- to late thirties, but that was a difficult bet with someone who lived her life on the edge. Lourdes Ortiz might well have been anywhere between twenty-five and forty-five. Her thick black hair was pulled back in a plastic band, giving her face a tight, Botoxed look. Bright crimson lipstick did a poor job of covering an angry cold sore that crusted the corner of pouty lips. Not exactly the best advertisement for a date, but Yao supposed men who paid this woman for her services weren't overly focused on a weeping mouth scab.

Besides being a close talker, which set Yao's teeth on edge, Lourdes gestured wildly as she spoke, pointing with nicotine-stained fingers and tossing her head with such verve Yao thought she might pop out of her stretchy blue polyester tube top. He bought her a bottle of Solera beer in hopes of calming her down.

It did not, but it did get her talking. She insisted that Yao join her at a small table in the back corner of the bar and in a voice that held all the charm of a rusty straight razor, explained there had been quite a fuss at the hotel the night before. A parade of fancy vehicles and angry-looking men with guns had scared away even her most devoted customers.

She leaned forward to impart a secret, driving her point home by brandishing the neck of the Solera bottle inches from Yao's nose.

"Piratas," she whispered. "Pirates. Narcos. Bad men." A splash of beer ran down her hand, dripping onto doughy breasts where they mashed against the tabletop. She tilted her head to lick her hand without spilling any more beer and then fell back against her chair. Peering down her nose, as if to take a measure of what Yao was made of, she patted the table. "You should be careful. A pretty man like you does not look dangerous enough to go to war with pirates." She finished off the beer in one long pull, never taking her eyes off Yao, then wiped her mouth with a forearm, wincing when she was too rough on the cold sore . . . or whatever the thing was. Still locked on, she slammed the empty bottle down on the table and gave a sleepy wag of her head, chest heaving. Yao wasn't sure if she was flirting or throwing down a gauntlet in challenge. Probably both.

"So, my love." She drummed her fingers on the table. For the first time, Yao noticed another weeping sore the size of a quarter where her thumb met the back of her hand. She'd tried to cover it with makeup. "Are you?"

Yao glanced quickly away from the sore. He affected a chuckle to hide a reflexive gag and then waved at the bartender. "Am I what?"

"A dangerous man."

"Nothing like that." He explained himself no further. This woman wouldn't believe him anyway. Spies often employed prostitutes in the course of their duties. Life had jaded these women so completely that little in the world surprised them. They could spot a lie before a man even knew he was going to tell it.

The bartender sidled up to the table, apparently used to men ordering things for Lourdes. Yao bought her another beer and a shredded pork sandwich called a **pepito.** Needing to keep his head clear, he ordered himself a Pony Malta soft drink.

She leaned in close again after the bartender had gone. Mouth set in a tight line, she rested a hand on top of Yao's—the hand with the weeping sore. He stilled himself, resisting the urge to pull away, and let her keep it there, meeting her eyes. Intelligence work had much more to do with social engineering than it did with capture or kill orders. If Hollywood gave an accurate portrayal of spies, Bond would have spent a lot more time in shabby bars chatting up poor souls like Lourdes than he did watching Ursula Andress emerge from a Caribbean lagoon. Though Yao had to admit, that image of Andress in a white bikini had a hell of a lot to do with him wanting to join the Central Intelligence Agency.

Lourdes studied his face for a time, head cocked

to one side, and then stroked his hand as if she'd reached an important conclusion.

"I have changed my mind," she said at length. "Maybe you **are** dangerous enough."

"For . . . ?"

"For me to tell you that the men you are looking for have gone to Montaña de Sorte. Tonight is the festival of the blessed queen Santa Maria de la Onza. I would go, but I have to work."

Lourdes spent half an hour giving Yao a quick tutorial, speaking reverently over her beer and sandwich. In the end, she admitted that it was too much for her to tell in one night. He would just have to see for himself.

She leaned over the table and gave his hand a slow pat, fluttering her lashes—surely not realizing that it made her look like she was about to pass out.

"You have some time before the bus departs," she said. "If you wanted to, you know . . . have a serious date . . ."

"It is my loss," Yao said. "But sadly, I have too much to do."

He gave her forty dollars, twice what she normally made on a "date."

She took it, and then fell against the back of her chair with a resigned sigh, eyeing Yao down the neck of her beer. "Be careful, my pretty man. Montaña de Sorte is full of spirits . . . and some of those spirits will surely side with the pirates."

4

A dusky haze settled over the countryside as the bus rattled away from the sleepy lights of Yaritagua for the twenty-mile trip to the jungles of Mount Sorte and the festival celebrating the cult of Maria Lionza.

According to legend, sometime around 1535, an Indigenous chief had a beautiful daughter named Yara, who was born with blue eyes. Light eyes were a bad omen, and according to the shaman, she had to be killed. Unable to murder his own daughter, the chief sent her to the jungle to hide—where she was promptly eaten by a giant anaconda. Yara was so pure that Mount Sorte took pity on her and caused the snake to swell and explode, freeing the young maiden. The mountain absorbed her into its very essence, where she began to act as intermediary between the living and spirits of the dead. Devotees held or attended channeling rituals throughout the year, but their main gathering occurred tonight, on the twelfth of October.

Venezuela was a Catholic nation, but an over-whelming majority—including the late president—also professed some level of belief in the cult of Maria Lionza, a mixture of Indigenous, African, and Catholic religions. A heroic statue near the Central University of Venezuela in Caracas de-picted a twenty-foot-tall Maria Lionza, naked and extremely muscular, riding on a giant tapir, arms stretched aloft, holding a female pelvis. Few outside Venezuela had even heard of the "blessed queen." Inside the country, Maria Lionza was considered by many to be a saint.

Yao and five of his team got the last seats on the bus. The remaining two WINDWARD STATION operators would follow as soon as they'd worked out how to procure some vehicles. Rental cars were impossible to come by in Yaritagua. The place wasn't exactly a tourist mecca.

The bus rumbled along a rough dirt road, squeak-ing in concert with a shirtless man pounding a skin drum in the back. The passengers—there were easily fifty of them—listened intently to a young woman chanting and moaning two seats ahead of Yao. Without warning, the woman shot to her feet, eyes rolled back, head tilted skyward, elbows drawn against her sides, winglike.

Lourdes had explained that these **las materias,** or "oracles," channeled the spirits who were in commu-nication with the Indigenous goddess. Yao hadn't ex-pected it to happen until they reached the mountain.

A low growl escaped the woman's chest. She began to speak in short, barked sentences Yao took for one of Venezuela's many Indigenous languages—or possibly some sort of tongue brought on by religious fervor.

The grandma sitting in the seat beside him gave a rattling whimper and crossed herself, clutching a set of beads against her belly with her free hand. Wanting to blend, he nodded in time with the beating drum. He pulled the backpack on his lap away from the swooning grandma to keep her from crushing its precious contents as she listed sideways.

Ahead, a man sprang from his seat to teeter and sway in the aisle behind the barking woman. He opened his hands behind her in case she toppled over on the swaying bus. Another man pulled a long knife and drew it across his chest, causing a superficial—but bloody—cut. He began to chant along with the drums.

This was going to be an interesting night.

No one on WINDWARD STATION was the sort to get spooked by a knife. All were experienced operators—former Special Forces, Delta, SEALs, Air Force Pararescue, and two females who, though they hadn't held SOCOM positions, had served frontline tours in the CIA and proven themselves to be capable and steady under fire. The women certainly helped the team blend in, but they were far from just arm candy. Yao made certain of that. Neither was small, particularly shapely, or, for that matter, likely to win any beauty contest. They were, like the rest of the team members, fluent in Spanish and otherwise unremarkable. He needed a team of eight, not a team of six with two more whom everyone else would have to carry if things went to shit.

The Israelis put the optimum size of a hit team at eleven. Some operators preferred to work alone.

Yao thought eight was the Goldilocks number.

Eight allowed for contingencies, variables, the unknown unknowns that inevitably threatened to derail virtually every mission: commo that went tits up at the most inopportune moment, a weapon that malfed when the bad guy was smack in the crosshairs, or some kid that wandered into the field of fire to pick up a forgotten baby doll. Eight allowed for the human element if someone got the runs from drinking bad water or lost focus because of the death of a loved one at home. Operators were human, and a team of eight made it easier to complete the mission and still get all those humans home alive.

The bus hit a tire-eating pothole, throwing Yao against the window and the grandma against Yao. The chanting woman staggered forward while the driver chewed his way through the transmission searching for a lower gear. A collective groan ran through the passengers until the bus lurched forward again. It only had a short way to go up the mountain before they turned in to a wide gravel parking lot full of cars, motorbikes, and a half-dozen other buses. Hundreds of Maria Lionza devotees from all walks of life streamed like ants at a picnic toward a gap in the jungle that formed the trailhead. There were couples, families, farmers in dirt-stained shirts, people in pressed khaki shorts and breezy linen blouses. Some, like Yao and his team, carried only small daypacks, while others lugged bulky foam bedrolls, intending to make several nights of it.

Every devotee approaching the sacred mountain had to pass a motorcade of three dark Suburbans and a charcoal-gray BMW 7 Series sedan that was parked near the trailhead. Dressed in chinos and dark polo shirts, stone-faced men stood watch over the vehicles, all armed with holstered Glock pistols. At least one carried an SMG. Yao couldn't make out the type because the shooter had it parked on a sling hanging over his right kidney.

"Pros," he said to himself. "Pirates . . ."

5

Yao followed the procession to the trailhead, drawn forward by the drums and rhythmic chants moaning from the dark tangle of trees and vines. He and the rest of his team had taken care to dress down, shorts and loose shirts against the heat. Nothing, not even his daypack, stood out.

Early in his career he'd learned it was important to **be** tactical rather than **look** tactical. Skill at your job could save your life. Acting a role—even one you were good at—put you first in line for a bullet. His powder-blue backpack had no MOLLE webbing or hanging carabiners. It looked like a book bag because it was a book bag, something a tourist might carry. There was certainly a place to wear web riggers' belts or tactical khaki operator pants with integral magazine pouches—but that place was not Venezuela, nor anywhere in South America for that matter. Even a plain vanilla G-Shock wristwatch could earn an unpleasant encounter with Venezuela's Bolivarian secret police. A 007 dive watch—an even cheaper brand that looked like a Rolex—simply drew too much attention. Yao went with an understated Timex Ironman on this kind of op—and left his Submariner at home.

He loved cool gear as much as the next guy, but in his line of work, EDC—everyday carry—was a couple hundred dollars in small bills and an open credit card.

A small footbridge lay just inside the tree line, some fifty feet from the parking lot. Stalls and carts peddled everything from fried plantains to wooden cross pendants and blue candles to show devotion to the goddess. A withered cob of a man stood at the end of the bridge, blowing cigar smoke in the devotees' faces as they shuffled by. More smoke from campfires and tobacco rose through a forest canopy mingling with the blue evening haze. Periodic shrieks spilled through the foliage. At first, Yao took the cries to be human, but soon realized the racket came from a pair of black and yellow troupials over the restrooms in the clearing beyond the bridge. The national bird of Venezuela, troupials were brood parasitic, using nests built by other birds, often eating the eggs or young of the host before laying their own eggs.

The deeper Yao went into the trees, the more intense the drumbeats and chanting. A tiny device on his upper right rear molar buzzed slightly, sending the voice of Ben Ramos, the former Air Force

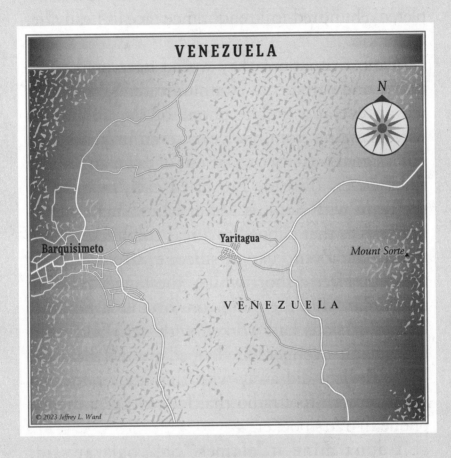

VENEZUELA

N

Barquisimeto

Yaritagua

Mount Sorte

VENEZUELA

© 2023 Jeffrey L. Ward

PJ on the team, vibrating through his jawbone and into his ear. Yao felt as well as heard the message.

"Well, this is all creepy as hell," Ramos said. The oldest member at forty-seven, he'd only just completed a hundred-mile endurance race in Leadville, Colorado.

In most situations they would have used a cell phone and earbuds to communicate. No one batted an eye at a mobile phone or the ubiquitous wires hanging from one's ears, even in Venezuela, but a signal was iffy this far out of town and under thick cover. Instead, Yao fitted each member of the team with Sonitus Molar Mics, small vibrating devices that clipped to a rear tooth like a dental bridge. Even custom silicone earpieces grew tiresome after a short while. The longer he wore the Molar Mic, the more comfortable it became. Earlier versions had worked with near-field technology and a copper wire looped around the neck. These devices did away with that and connected via Bluetooth to a radio that looked like a mobile phone in Yao's pocket.

"I don't mind it," James "Sal" Salazar said. "Where else do we get paid to smoke fine Cuban cigars in order to blend in?" Sal came to Ground Branch from the Marine Corps. Not a Tier 1 operator like many on WINDWARD STATION, his Devil Dog tenacity and natural athleticism made him every bit as proficient as the others. Beyond that, the man was a beast, benching his body weight of a buck ninety until Yao's arms got tired.

"I'm with Boomer," a female voice said. "No matter how much you read about this, it is some whacked-out voodoo shit."

It was Myrna Chaman, a seasoned case officer who'd spent most of her eleven years in the CIA bouncing back and forth between hot spots in Mexico and her parents' home country of Peru. She called Ramos by the nickname the team had given him.

Yao used his tongue to flip a tiny switch on the device from receive to transmit.

"Cut them some slack," Yao said. "Any religion can look odd if you start looking at it under a microscope."

"No shit." Eric "Ripper" Ward's voice carried over the net. "My auntie was Pentecostal," he said. "One of the finest women I ever met, but Sundays with her scared the hell out of me . . ."

New to Ground Branch, Ward had come over from Special Forces, the team sergeant with Operational Detachment Alpha (ODA) 0312, based in Fort Carson, Colorado. Apart from Yao, he was the only other non-Latin member of WINDWARD STATION. Ward's father was Black and his mother a tall blond German, giving him the ambiguous ethnicity to work in any part of the world. His Spanish was flawless.

Yao stepped off the trail for a moment, checking out a group of men and women smoking cigars. They ignored him completely. Nothing Lourdes had said prepared Yao for the rituals that mixed cigar smoke, fire walking, and communing with the dead.

"How about we just focus on locating FRIAR," he said, continuing up the trail.

The entire mountain was a hive of activity. A shirtless man squatted over three middle-aged women, their bodies outlined by dozens of votive candles like flaming crime scene chalk. Lourdes had warned that the mountains were so full of spirits that the roots of the trees were said to glow. The sea of lights flickering through the hanging vines made it easy to believe her.

The team spread out, looking interested without becoming too engrossed, searching for their target. Myrna Chaman sang out first, her voice coming in loud and clear inside Yao's head.

"Tallyho," she said. "If you head east, you'll reach a small stream. FRIAR and his entourage are standing fifty feet to the north in front of a little tin hut along the water's edge. Just follow the sound of the dude trying to cough up a chicken bone . . ."

Hyperalert, Yao picked his way through the trees, following the frenzied sounds of spits and coughs.

The Viking, or as some followers of Maria Lionza called him, Mr. Barbaro, was supposed to be the spirit of Erik the Red. Tonight, his **la materia** happened to be a shirtless, balding man with the oil-stained hands of a mechanic. This oracle staggered back and forth between a crowd of onlookers and a small lean-to hut made of rusted, corrugated tin. Two camp lanterns and countless candles threw eerie shadows across the dirt and against the surrounding jungle.

Yao stopped short at the edge of the trees, forcing himself not to stare. A subtle shift in the whites of the eyes could earn a man a slap for his wandering gaze—or a bullet in more dire circumstances.

Across the clearing, Joaquín Gorshkov, the man Yao had been hunting for months, stood in the flesh. A fat cigar clenched in a sadistic sneer. A short, boxy woman stood beside him in rapt concentration on the Viking. Her sleeveless white blouse seemed to glow against the inky backdrop of snaking vines and thick foliage. Her arms were folded over her belly. A moonish face glistened in candlelight. Though she was on the heavier side and erect to Gorshkov's slender and slightly stooped frame, the woman shared the same piggish nose and deep-set eyes. There was little doubt that they were related, probably siblings, though Yao's team had no intelligence indicating Gorshkov had a sister.

Yao counted six frowning members of the security team. A tall blond man stood behind and slightly to the left of the moonfaced woman. A scowling security man with a close-cropped black beard took up a similar spot behind Gorshkov.

The entire team wore khaki slacks and navy-blue muscle-mapping polo shirts, displaying their physiques as a first-line intimidation tactic like a lion's mane or a bull elk's antlers.

Myrna Chaman's voice came over the net. "Anyone else notice these shitbirds are running a diamond formation? Principal, flankers, right and left rear, advance, the works."

Yao gave an inward groan. "Yeah, they're professionals," he said. "That's apparent."

"It gets worse," Ward said from the shadows to Yao's left. "Looks like our guy's running a second team around the inner diamond, plugging any gaps. I've counted four for sure, but I'd bet on at least six or seven if they continue the same pattern on the side I can't see through the trees."

"I hear you." Yao cursed under his breath. He avoided military-sounding words and phrases like **copy, negative,** or **roger that.** Too many listening ears.

He'd expected Gorshkov's security to be a bunch of goons, hired by the pound and easily distracted by annoyances like drums and chanting spirit-talkers. These men were disciplined and well-armed hitters who saw the Maria Lionza devotees not as attractions but as threats. They were good—no, they were better than good. Absent a full-on assault that threatened to harm bystanders, the protective ring was virtually impenetrable. Gorshkov's security made no attempt to cover holstered Glocks or the HK MP7s that hung on shoulder harnesses.

Another voice, this one deeply Southern, filled Yao's head. It was Chris Nestor, a wiry former Delta operator from Brownsville, Texas. "Kind of alarming that all these guys are packing the same kit. My experience, these **sicario** types like their fancy pistols and **cuerno de chivo,** gold-plated AKs. They don't normally give a shit about interoperability of their weapons."

"Some of 'em look Slavic . . . like they could be Russian," Myrna Chaman offered.

Yao felt a flutter of dread in his gut. Gorshkov's entire team moved with a surety that said they were all pros. Gorshkov had no need to be covert, so it made sense that some of his team wasn't Latin.

"More bad news," Nestor said from his vantage point on the far side of the Viking's candlelit clearing. "I recognize the guy with the dark beard directly behind FRIAR. Chilean Special Forces, or at least he was three years ago. Manny Ramirez. That guy knows his shit."

"Manuel Ramirez?" Chaman said. "We got a cable on him last month. He's supposed to be affiliated with the Camarilla?"

"Right," Yao said.

The Camarilla was a mystery, much of what the CIA knew about it little more than a theory. They were thought to be a small but well-funded private army with intelligence capability that was for sale to the highest bidder. As ruthless as Russia's Wagner Group, they were thought to be comprised of more elite former operators and therefore much more lethal. A group of Camarilla employed by an Indian billionaire had kidnapped the First Lady and murdered her Secret Service protection detail in San Antonio. All but one of them had been killed during the First Lady's rescue. The FBI and Secret Service Protective Intelligence Division had worked together to build a thumbnail profile from the dead operatives, eventually using link analysis to connect them to seven other former special operators. Their connections with the dead Texas operators and the fact that these seven had dropped completely off the grid after separating from the military was prima facie evidence that they'd been folded into the Camarilla.

Yao scanned the thick foliage, looking for escape routes. If one of Gorshkov's team was Camarilla, there was a better-than-average chance all of them were.

"Would Ramirez recognize you?" he asked Nestor.

"We had a few beers together," Nestor said. "But we weren't buds or anything."

"Stay back so he doesn't see you."

"He may already have. He just hasn't figured out how he knows me yet."

"Okay." Yao said what everyone else was thinking. "Listen up. We need to get as many of this security team on camera as possible. Sal, you and I will deploy on my mark. Nestor, fade back and cover Sal. Chaman, get ready with the sat link."

After collective **okay**s over his Molar Mic, Yao drifted behind a vine-covered tree and unzipped his pack.

"I've got your back, brother," Boomer said.

"As do I," Ward added.

"Many thanks," Yao said. "This Viking dude is working up to a crescendo. Hopefully that'll give us enough of a diversion that Sal and I can deploy our little honeybees . . ."

The Viking **la materia** held a bottle of rum by the neck in one hand and a small razor blade in the other. A man from the crowd sat upright in a chair in front of him, listening intently. Groaning, the oracle staggered, channeling a resonant voice, at first in broken English—as if that were the language of Erik the Red, and then in Spanish. In a flash of movement, he reached up and sliced his own tongue with the blade. A fresh splash of crimson arced across a chest that was already glistening with alcohol and sweat. Blood and spittle hung in ropy lines from his sagging lips. He gagged, as Myrna described it, like he was coughing up a chicken bone, before coughing answers to questions that apparently had to do with the seated man's dead father. Hacking and gagging, he took a swig of rum and then spewed it into the air, as if to put an exclamation point on the Viking's words.

Even most of Gorshkov's security detail appeared transfixed by the smoky, bloody, contorted spectacle of it all.

"Set!" Yao said.

Salazar responded instantly from beyond the thick foliage to Yao's right. "Set."

"Lift!" Yao said.

The "honeybee" rose from Yao's open palm with a whispered whir less than five seconds after he'd removed it from his daypack.

The micro drone's cameras fed video not only to the operators' cell phones but to a satellite link Myrna Chaman had retrieved from her daypack and set up in the shadows.

The coded transmission gave a front-row seat to those gathered in the White House and a secure anteroom at Buckingham Palace.

6

LONDON

President of the United States Jack Ryan leaned forward in a nineteenth-century mahogany library chair and studied the glowing green images on the open laptop on the table in front of him. His director of national intelligence, Mary Pat Foley, sat in a matching chair beside him, hunched over, blue reading glasses perched on the end of her nose as she watched the same video.

It was late, a few minutes before midnight, and Ryan's hair was mussed in front as if he'd just sat through the LSAT. A black wool suit jacket hung over the back of the chair. A matching silk tie was slightly crooked and loose along with the top button of a once crisp white shirt. He was tall and runner-fit, some might even say gaunt, with more salt in his hair than pepper these days. His longish face held the resigned expression of someone who had predicted doom and was now deeply saddened to be proven right.

A video conference this sensitive should have taken place in the SCIF at Winfield House, the U.S. ambassador's home in Regent's Park. If he'd been newer in this job, or slightly less patient, Ryan might have groused about the timing of it all. He'd been around the block enough to know that field operations could rarely be scheduled. And even when they were, it was for safety's sake, not to coincide with his visit to Buckingham Palace. The royal family had befriended him decades before and he'd come to London to pay his respects after the recent passing of Her Majesty the Queen.

Mary Pat had approached Ryan during brandy and cigars with news of the pending action in Venezuela. With no time to make the trip to the U.S. embassy or the ambassador's residence, the king's private secretary had worked with a butler to secure a small anteroom adjacent to the Blue Drawing Room. United States Navy Commander Robert Forrestal, the deputy national security adviser traveling with Ryan, worked with Mary Pat's people to do a quick TSCM (technical surveillance countermeasures) sweep as unobtrusive as possible so as not to offend.

The U.S. and the UK enjoyed a special relationship when it came to intelligence matters, meaning (in theory) that they shared everything. Still, even trusted friends kept tabs on one another. Ryan routinely received intelligence reports regarding Britain, Canada, Germany, and a host of friendly nations during the President's Daily Brief. He was certain they got reports on him as well. It was expected as long as no one got caught doing it.

The prime minister had come with him to the palace, so Ryan invited him to take part in the observation. When he found out exactly what sort of operation they planned to observe, the PM opted to wait outside.

It was probably for the best.

Ryan marveled at the clarity of the images on the laptop. Modern technology rendered them incredibly vivid, even in low light. Too vivid, Ryan often thought when he woke up in the middle of the night and replayed past scenes he'd watched over and over in his mind.

He took a deep breath, memorizing the frenetic details on the screen—a woman's smile that revealed a missing front tooth, the rip in the neck of a man's Nike T-shirt, as if someone had grabbed him by the collar. People milled in small groups, bathed in firelight, transfixed by someone or something off-screen, oblivious to the fact that a man was about to die in front of their noses.

Ryan glanced sideways, lowering his reading glasses to catch the eye of his most trusted adviser. He and Mary Pat Foley went back further than either of them cared to admit.

Arnie van Damm, Ryan's chief of staff, along

with most of the principals of the National Security Council, were on a secure line, watching the same video feed from the White House Situation Room. Van Damm sounded rumpled and exhausted, though it was not even seven p.m. where he was.

"Walk me through what we're seeing here, Mary Pat," Ryan said.

She'd briefed Ryan daily on the generalities of WINDWARD STATION, specifically Operation SUDDEN SQUALL, but events in Venezuela were unfolding faster than anyone had expected. He was getting this latest information in real time, just like everyone else.

Foley rested her elbows on the thighs of a worsted wool skirt, dark like Ryan's suit to match the occasion. Chin balanced on her fists, she nodded slightly at the screen as she explained.

"The images are coming from a micro drone we call Arista," Foley said. "Actually, a pair of them. The drone with the lower angle is primary. It will take the shot. The one providing us the higher-angle view provides redundancy. Two is one and one is none . . . We may not get another chance at Torquemada/Gorshkov for some time."

"Good thinking," Ryan said. "Arista. Short for Aristaeus, Greek god of beekeepers."

Foley shook her head in dismay. "Jack, if only they allowed presidents to be on **Jeopardy!** . . ."

The two had bled together and were dear enough

friends that Foley called him by his given name when they were outside the Oval Office.

"At any rate," Foley continued, "you are correct. We call this little bird Arista because, like the venerable honeybee, she has a sting, but in order to use that sting, she herself dies."

"Got it," van Damm said over the phone line. "A kamikaze."

Ryan pushed up his glasses again, following the images as both micro drones scanned the crowd face by face, hunting. Another quick side-eye to Foley and then back to the screen.

"Hell of a lot of Slavic-looking people for Venezuela," van Damm offered.

"Well spotted," Foley said. "The team suspects FRIAR's security detail is a grab bag of former Russian Spetsnaz and special forces from various Latin America countries."

"That makes sense," Ryan said, "considering his movements." He cocked his head, mesmerized. "Arista must be awfully quiet to get this close and not be heard."

The image settled on a round female face, Arista hovering slightly above and out of her eyeline.

"They are extremely quiet," Foley said. She paused and bit her bottom lip, the way she did when she was nervous—a rare occurrence.

Ryan glanced from his friend to the screen, then back to his friend again. "What is it?"

"Nothing," Foley said. "Probably that woman in the frame is a new actor . . . The one standing beside Gorshkov. She's someone we've not seen until now."

"No matches with the age-enhanced photos from the Peruvian orphanage?" Ryan asked.

"I don't believe so, sir," Foley said, throwing him a little smile, happy he'd waded that deeply into the reports.

Lexi Glazier, the CIA's Latin America division chief, spoke up, introducing herself before she said, "We're comparing the data in real time, Mr. President. Eleven of the nine children in the photographs are female, but none of them appear to be a match for this woman."

Van Damm gave a low grunt, barely audible over the phone connection. "Does Gorshkov have a sister?"

"That's my guess," Foley whispered. "She shares so many similarities, there is an outside chance Arista's facial recognition system will mistake the two."

Ryan frowned at that. "Might the weapon take her out instead?"

Foley shook her head, as if coming out of a trance. "Highly doubtful," she said. "I've seen the tests on this bird in person—and I trust the tech. If Arista believed this was FRIAR she would have already deployed her weapon. Gorshkov is probably lined up behind one of his security men. The drone is just loitering, waiting for a clear shot. The biggest danger here is that Arista may not reacquire before someone notices and takes measures to avoid her. Beyond that, she's small, so battery life is just shy of a half hour."

The lower image wobbled slightly, as if Arista was attempting to make a decision.

Foley continued her play-by-play.

"The EFP, or explosively formed penetrator, in Arista's nose is extremely small, a copper disk shaped into an inverted cone . . . with the open end toward the enemy. Once the target is acquired and confirmed, three grams of explosive in a tube behind the point of the cone will detonate, turning the copper inside out and into a molten stream of metal able to penetrate a quarter inch of steel plating—or more depending on the angle and standoff from the target. The body of the device is frangible polymer, just heavy enough to counter the weight of the copper projectile and send it downrange. The electric motor, batteries, and rotors will likely remain intact, but the fuselage will all but disintegrate. When one Arista makes a clean shot, the other unit will destroy itself. There will be theories, but no identifying markers to tie the honeybee to us."

"Frangible . . ." Ryan mused.

"Yes, Mr. President," Foley said. "This is about as surgical as one of these operations can get, but someone may well end up with debris in their eyes."

Ryan nodded, taking it all in. EFPs made of

copper disks were not uncommon in U.S. ordnance. Iraqi insurgents used the principle with great effect in their IEDs.

A balding Latin man with a wide jaw crossed the camera view. The scowl on his face was clearly visible, even in the ghostly green of the display. Arista rotated a hair to the left as the man passed—bringing a new face to center screen. Foley's assumption had been correct. Joaquín Fernando Gorshkov—FRIAR—stood slightly behind his twin's left shoulder, nearly eclipsed from view until Arista moved into the correct angle.

If this was going to happen, it would be now.

Ryan held his breath.

"Well, shit," Foley whispered.

The woman, Joaquín Gorshkov's twin, suddenly glanced up and peered directly at the screen, as if, there in the jungles of Venezuela, she'd locked eyes with the President of the United States.

7

Sweat poured down Adam Yao's spine. His thumb hovered over the controls of his cell phone. The woman in white looked straight at the camera a half breath before a staccato crack creased the dark canopy above her. Few in the crowd were likely to have noticed the pop or the tiny flash of light amid the pounding drums and rhythmic chanting.

But the woman noticed.

Yao's stomach convulsed, as if he'd been gut punched.

The woman canted her head, trying to make sense of what had just happened. Beside her, Joaquín Gorshkov slumped, arms suddenly devoid of muscle tone, dead on his feet as the fiery jet of molten copper pierced his forehead above the left eye. He teetered there for what seemed an eternity before crumpling to the forest floor. To Yao's surprise, the glaring Chilean operator behind Gorshkov slumped to his knees and then pitched forward, his jowl wedged against his dead boss's shoulder.

The molten copper had evidently pierced Gorshkov's skull and then kept going, taking out his bodyguard in the process.

Primary target down, Sal's Arista detonated in a split-second flash and crack.

The woman in white touched her face, likely spattered by debris from an all but vaporized micro drone. Her eyes flew wide as she looked at the two dead men at her feet.

"We're heading your way, Adrian," Yao said to his team member with the cars.

"I hear you, boss," Hernandez responded immediately. That was a relief. "Ready to roll when you get here."

Gorshkov and his guard were down, but no one outside his inner circle paid any attention. Countless **lionceros**—Maria Lionza devotees—smoked cigars and swayed, overcome with religious fervor. In the adjoining clearing, a man walked over a bed of glowing coals. The Viking oracle continued his guttural communion, while a crowd stood gape-jawed.

"Everyone take it easy," Yao reminded his team. "Fade into the jungle. Slow is fast."

The outer ring of Gorshkov's security detail raised their MP7s, scanning for secondary attacks, while the inner perimeter closed ranks. Astonishingly, only one stooped to check on Gorshkov. Everyone else moved to surround the woman in white. The blond Slavic man stayed glued to her side.

Yao had no experience doing formal protective

work, but he understood the standard response to a threat. Unlike law enforcement officers, protective agents were not immediately concerned with arresting the aggressor. Their job was to get their principal out of danger. If they saw a threat, they would neutralize it with extreme prejudice during the heat of an attack, but more important, they needed to get their protectee the hell out of Dodge. They were trained to **sound off, cover, and evacuate.**

The blond security officer beside Gorshkov's twin grabbed at her shoulder, attempting to turn her toward the parking lot, and, no doubt, hustle her to safety. The woman yanked her arm away, dropping to her knees beside a motionless Gorshkov.

She cradled the dead man's head, studying the wound, then looked up suddenly, peering into the trees as if she'd heard something.

Yao followed her gaze, watching in horror as Sal lunged from his hiding spot toward a teenage boy who was apparently attempting to steal his day-pack. It was instinctive to try to protect his gear, but the movement drew too much attention—and left him exposed holding his phone—a piece of incriminating electronics mere moments after a device from the sky had killed Joaquín Gorshkov.

"Sal!" Yao hissed. "Let it go! She's looking right at—"

Adrian, still in the parking lot, bonked over the radio, cutting him off. His voice crackled with urgency.

"Two cops just un-assed a sedan behind the buses—and the target's motorcade is saddling up to move."

Everyone on Yao's team was a type A personality, a critical thinker capable of making complex decisions on the fly, but they were also team players, fully prepared to take orders from a single leader. They all stayed silent, waiting for him to speak.

The woman in white barked orders over her shoulder as the main protection detail hustled her down the mountain toward the parking lot.

Yao stood rooted beside his tree. If his team ran now, they'd reach the parking lot at the same time as the woman and her detail, drawing more unwanted attention. If they stayed, they ran the risk of being rounded up for questioning as Venezuelan police swarmed the mountain.

Sal's voice broke squelch. "This ain't good, boys and girls . . . Afraid I'm burned."

The woman in white pulled away and stopped mid-trail, staring hard at Sal. She screamed an unintelligible order. Yao didn't understand it, but her team certainly did. Two of them broke away from the main detail and now moved straight for Salazar, weapons trained at his chest. Rhythmic drumming sifted through the trees, but the men's shouted orders were clear.

If Salazar so much as twitched, they would shoot him.

Yao groaned softly as a wide grin spread across his friend's face.

Sal spoke like a ventriloquist, whispering over the Molar Mic through tight lips as he locked eyes with the approaching gunmen. "You guys haul ass when the crowd starts to run!"

"Negative!" Yao snapped. "There are only two—"

"There's more of them in the trees, buddy," Sal whispered. "You know that." Then, "Well, hell . . . This is gonna hurt . . ."

Sal dropped the phone, turning suddenly to shove his hand into the open bag. It didn't matter if he had a gun or not. The men leaned into their weapons, cutting him down in a hail of bullets.

Myrna, close enough to witness firsthand what had happened, gave a muted cry over the radio.

Yao thought he might vomit.

The sudden gunfire produced the exact result that Sal had intended. The drumming abruptly stopped. Terrified shrieks rose from those who'd been close enough to see the carnage, rippling through the crowd and infecting people all across the mountainside. The oracle bit through his cigar and dropped the Viking affect completely as he made a mad dash toward the trailhead.

"Go," Yao barked to the rest of his team, swimming in despair. "Stick with the crowd—"

Myrna's voice. "We can't just leave him."

"Get to the cars," Yao said. "Sal did this for us."

8

The left side of the screen in front of Ryan flashed and then went dark as the primary Arista sent the jet of molten copper into her target. Seconds later, both screens were blank, but not before Ryan realized there had been an unintended victim.

"Signal from the team says the primary target is neutralized, Mr. President," Lexi Glazier, the CIA's Latin America division chief, said.

"Confirming we have two down?" Foley said.

"That's correct, Madam Director," Glazier said. "One of our Ground Branch operators identified the second man as Manuel Ramirez, formerly of Chilean Special Forces. Looks as though he was Gorshkov's primary bodyguard."

"Poor bastard picked the wrong person to protect," van Damm said. "Still, it's good we built in a layer of deniability for you, Mr. President, in the event the Chilean government gets their hackles up."

Ryan frowned. "You know better than to use that word, Arnie. I'm not one for deniability." Then, to Foley. "So the other guy was a Chilean named Ramirez?"

Foley gave a tight-lipped shrug. "Manuel Ramirez is on our list of seven."

Ryan gave a contemplative nod. "Camarilla, then," he said.

Jay Canfield, the director of the CIA, came across the speaker. "We're confirming that it's the same Manuel Ramirez now, Mr. President, but with the Chilean Special Forces connection . . . I like the odds."

Foley stood, arms folded across her chest. "Thanks to WINDWARD STATION, we have a treasure trove of video, faces we can feed into link analysis and give us a better picture of this group."

"Good," Ryan said. "I want all available assets working on this."

"Yes, Mr. President," Foley said, beating those on the other end of the line to the punch.

"From what I saw in that video this woman in white wasn't just some hanger-on," Ryan said. "It looked to me like that was her security detail as much as Gorshkov's. Maybe more so. They closed ranks around her PDQ and all but ignored him when he went down. Let's get into exactly who she is."

"Glazier is on that as we speak, Mr. President," Director Canfield said.

Ryan took a deep breath, held it, then exhaled slowly. "Thank you, Jay," he said at length.

"You okay?" van Damm asked, hearing the pause over the phone.

"I'm fine," Ryan said. "What **do** we know about the woman at this point?"

"Nothing," Glazier said. "Still no match on the orphanage photos. We're getting nothing from the facial recognition crawlers we have out on the Web. So far, we're unable to find any other photographs of this individual."

"It's a starting point, Mr. President," Foley added. "We'll build on it."

"Very well," Ryan said. "Jay, be ready to brief me on whatever you've got while I'm on the plane home tomorrow morning. Air Force One is wheels up at . . ." He glanced sideways at Foley.

"Eight a.m. London."

Ryan looked at his watch. "That's three a.m. your time, so . . . shall we say six eastern time? I'll be in the air."

"You'll have what we have by five thirty, Mr. President," Canfield said. "Chief Glazier and I will be on the line at five minutes before six."

"Okay," Ryan said. "It goes without saying that I want these Camarilla assholes run to ground. It looks as though this woman may be the key." He paused, willing himself to calm down. "Thank you all for your work."

Ryan reached to end the call, but van Damm spoke up and stopped him. "One more thing before you go."

Ryan yawned. "Very well." Van Damm knew his job, and more important, he knew Ryan's schedule. If he felt a matter important enough to bring up at midnight London time, then Ryan paid attention.

"President Botero of Panama has reached out three times in as many hours."

"Three?" Ryan shot a glance at Foley, then turned back to the speaker. "In reference to . . . ?"

"His office didn't share that," van Damm said.

"Thank you," Ryan said. "I'll give him a call. He's under a great deal of pressure from within."

"That's putting it mildly, Mr. President." The vice president's rich voice came across the speaker. A recent appointment after the untimely death of the previous VP, Anthony Hargrave, Mark Dehart was a welcome addition to the small cadre of steady voices in Ryan's orbit. The fact that Dehart had no designs on Ryan's job meant he valued hard truths over political vagaries. His counsel was especially valuable.

"Panamanian teachers are on strike again, protesting inflation, government corruption, the usual suspects. There's a mob of them camped out blocking the Pan-American Highway. Internal problems, but many of those problems appear to have merit."

Canfield spoke next. "Those internal problems provide the socialist side of Panama's government with a broad target to rail against."

Secretary of Defense Robert Burgess spoke up for the first time in the meeting. "Not to mention the Russians are running their own version of a Chinese charm offensive in the region. Two of their warships are steaming toward the canal as we speak, on their way to joint maneuvers off the coast of Cuba and Venezuela."

"True," Foley said. "It's probably too late to talk about it tonight, but—"

"Don't even go there," van Damm snapped. "I don't see President Botero calling about that Panama problem."

As tired as he was, Ryan perked up at the mystery. He knew there were countless things his advisers didn't bother him with, but if Mary Pat thought it important . . .

He gave her a nod. "Go ahead. What sort of Panama problem?"

"Hear me out," she said. "I wouldn't be surprised if President Botero wants to talk about his favorite social media influencer."

Ryan rubbed a hand across his face, feeling the stubble of a very long day chatter against his hand.

"This is ridiculous," van Damm said. "An influencer? Seriously?"

Foley shrugged, comfortable enough in her own

skin to put up with a little pushback. She knew the debate was with Ryan, not Arnie van Damm.

"Propaganda is propaganda, Mr. President," she said. "Russian internet troll or influential blogger . . . both have the potential to sway public opinion in substantial—and sometimes dangerous—ways."

"And some political blogger has come out with an opinion against Panama?"

"Not a political blogger per se . . ." Foley gave her own exhausted sigh. "A fashion blogger."

Ryan started to speak, but she held up her hand to show she wasn't finished.

"A fashion **influencer** with a hundred and seventeen million followers," Foley said.

"The entire population of Panama is only four million," Dehart mused.

"The point," Foley said, "is that a very large swath of the population listens to Keidra Noyes. And she's throwing out rhetorical questions like grenades."

"Noyes . . . noise . . ." Ryan said, unable to believe he was getting briefed on a social media personality. "Give me an example of her questions?"

"Her catchphrase, sir," Director Canfield said, joining team Foley, "'I'm just askin',' gives her wiggle room to toss whatever incendiary accusations she pleases and then, hand to chest, act indignant if anyone has the audacity to fact-check her."

"Keeps her hands clean," Foley said. "Only yesterday she posted a photo of an Indigenous

Panamanian child wearing a USA shirt somewhere along the Mosquito Gulf next to a puddle of murky water and then asks, 'Hey, Botero, you ever think about the Indian kids who don't have clean water? Just askin'.' It's always something incendiary that speaks of U.S. imperialism or the sitting government's ambivalence."

Foley pulled up Keidra Noyes's latest social media reel and turned her tablet toward Ryan.

A blond woman who couldn't have been more than twenty-one spoke into her camera as she walked along a beach. The angle of the shot looked as though she were filming herself. While exuberant, the poor kid sounded more like a middle schooler than someone fit to be dishing out advice to over a hundred million followers.

"Check this out, y'all," she said. "I just heard about this little thing called the Monroe Doctrine, where President James Monroe warned the Europeans to keep their greedy paws off the Western Hemisphere. Ya think President Botero has thought of saying the same thing to us? Just askin'."

"Shit like this makes it appear to her millions of followers that the U.S. is trying to recolonize Panama—generously seasoned with posts about how Panama is stomping on Indigenous rights and using too much water."

"Yes," Vice President Dehart said. "But who are those followers? A bunch of teens wanting fashion advice and fifteen-year-old boys mesmerized by her yoga pants?"

"There's that," Foley said. "But oddly, she's gained real traction as a media darling in both China and Russia. Look at any protest in either country and you'll see a forest of picket signs with her latest selfie and '#justasking.'"

"What's her connection to Panama?" Ryan asked.

"At the risk of sounding like we're spying on our own citizens," Director Canfield said, "her boyfriend is Panamanian."

Ryan groaned. Gone were the days when all he had to worry about were lost Soviet submarines.

"And there's a little more to our fashion blogger than meets the eye," Foley said. "Somebody taught her how to file Freedom of Information Act requests. She's caught wind of the possibility of a larger joint counter-narcotics training base on old Fort Sherman at Toro Point. She's now demanding to know the wheres and wherefores from the Pentagon."

"Okay," Ryan said with a sigh. "What did we tell her?"

"Secretary Burgess's office Glomared her," van Damm said. "That'll just feed the conspiracy theories, but it's the best we have until we paper the deal for the base with President Botero."

"True enough," Ryan said.

To "Glomar" stemmed from the CIA's 1974

answer to media questions regarding the **Hughes Glomar Explorer.** A salvage ship mission-built by the CIA's Special Activities Division to clandestinely retrieve a sunken Soviet diesel-electric submarine three miles beneath the surface of the Pacific Ocean right under the nose of the Soviets.

After the fact, the media smelled something fishy and submitted a FOIA request. Even admitting that there had been a salvage effort would have torpedoed what little goodwill there was between the U.S. and the Soviet Union. So the CIA issued what came to be known as the Glomar response— **We can neither confirm nor deny the existence of the information requested.**

Ryan suspected that ninety percent of bureaucrats in government who regularly "Glomared" the media had no idea of the term's origin. It was the kind of stuff he used to quiz his children about when they were growing up.

"So, we're thinking someone put our fashion blogger up to submitting a FOIA," Ryan mused. "Which means she's likely a pawn."

"That's my guess, Mr. President," Foley said.

"My niece follows her," Secretary of State Scott Adler jumped in on the call. "It's all beyond shallow content, but it has impact. This might be what's giving Botero heartburn."

"Well," van Damm said. "Whatever it is, his office called less than an hour ago, saying he needs to speak with you about matters, and I quote, 'of grave import to both the United States and Panama.'"

"Suppose it's not our influencer's propaganda?" Ryan asked.

"It may be both, Mr. President," Lexi Glazier offered. "Her Panamanian boyfriend could be working for someone else. Not a stretch to see Moscow doing everything they can to get their hooks into Latin America. The Russian propaganda news site RT has Spanish bureaus in Miami, Los Angeles, Madrid, Havana, Buenos Aires, Managua, and Caracas."

Ryan folded his arms. "Troll farms and fashion bloggers."

Glazier continued. "Moscow has sent twice the usual number of warships through the canal into the Caribbean over the past three months. As Secretary Burgess mentioned, joint exercises with the Nicaraguan, Venezuelan, and Cuban navies—saber-rattling. Besides this blogger, there are a lot of people who would love for us to have less influence in Latin America—especially in a strategic place like Panama. Some of them see our people assisting with anti-corruption, money-laundering investigations, and narco-trafficking enforcement as a second invasion. The Kremlin openly call all our efforts 'Operation JUST 'CAUSE WE FEEL LIKE IT.'"

Panamanians loved the American dollar, but were still bruised from the 1989 invasion. Even those who had no use for Manuel Noriega, their drug-dealing, money-laundering military dictator, viewed Operation JUST CAUSE as blatant Yankee imperialism. After all, it was no secret that he'd been in the pocket of the American CIA for years.

History made it easier to swallow the new propaganda.

Ryan checked his watch, a Rolex Explorer II that Cathy had given him. It had a second hour hand that he left set to eastern standard time when he traveled.

"Panama is in the same time zone as D.C.," he said. "Right?"

Foley nodded.

"Very well," Ryan said. "Arnie, have the switchboard set up a call with President Botero at his earliest convenience. I'll be on my cell."

Ryan thanked the members of the NSC and ended the call. He arched his back, looking up at the ceiling.

"You good, Jack?" Foley asked.

"Just tired," he said. "Aren't you? Having someone killed after a day of mourning with friends is about the most exhausting activity I know."

"I hear you," Foley said. "What I mean is—"

Ryan's cell began to buzz. "Hold that thought," he said, and then picked up.

"Ryan."

It was the White House operator. According to his office, President Rafael Botero was "unavailable at present."

Ryan told the switchboard he would try again tomorrow and slipped the cell into his pocket. "Guess the matter of great import to our nations will have to wait." He'd been friends with Foley long enough to know exactly where she'd been headed. "And I'm fine by the way. I just don't much care for it when Arnie talks about my having deniability."

"We're all responsible, Jack," Foley said. "CIA and the Bureau put together the intel. I took it to the NSC, who brought it to you."

"I get all that," Ryan said. "I'm not saying we're in the wrong. I will sleep fine tonight, even with the death of the bodyguard. Stand by a man like Joaquín Gorshkov long enough and you'll eventually get bloody—maybe with your own blood. What I don't like is hiding behind the Washington two-step. I gave the kill order."

Foley pursed her lips in thought. "Two things, if I may."

"Of course."

"First," she said, "when someone tells me they will sleep fine, they are usually trying to convince themselves. And you know what? It's okay if you . . . if we need a minute to process taking the life of another human being. I've lost count over the years of the deaths I've been responsible for . . ."

Ryan gave an exhausted smile. "You are right, my friend," he said. "And what is that second thing?"

"Gorshkov was an extremely bad man."

Ryan stood and grabbed his coat. "If that were the

only criterion to send a jet of molten copper through someone's brain, Mary Pat, we'd have a hell of a lot fewer enemies on the threat board. If I've learned anything during my years as a decision-maker, it is that people don't die in a vacuum. Every death has consequences and some of those consequences are larger than others."

"True enough," Foley said.

"The woman in white, for instance," Ryan said. "She looked directly at the camera . . . right at me. Do we really think someone with ties to an organization with the reach of the Camarilla is the kind of person to let a brother's death go unanswered?"

Foley gave a sober nod at the thought. "We don't know anything about her, Jack."

"Right," Ryan said. "Well, I have an uneasy feeling that we are about to learn a hell of a lot."

9

Joaquín's blood spattered the front of Sabine Gorshkova's white blouse. She stripped down to her bra the moment she walked through the door of the safe house her uncle had found. It was too dangerous to return to the hotel Joaquín had chosen and its unwashed prostitutes with layered mascara and skin that shone like varnished mahogany. Joaquín could be so stupid . . .

A sob caught hard in her throat, dying there.

Joaquín . . .

Sabine was two years older than her brother, almost to the day. They could have been twins but for their disparate builds. He was tall and slender, where she was short and . . . not. She'd inherited their late mother's propensity to prepare for some coming famine by packing a good portion of everything she ate around her tummy and hips.

Sabine's uncle Hector rose quickly from the tufted leather couch. He set the white rum he'd been drinking on the glass table in front of him and came to her, patting her bare shoulder with a slender hand. If he was bothered by her state of undress, he didn't act it. Sabine didn't care.

Hector Alonso was a small man, shoulders stooped from his sixty-eight years, many of them spent hiding in austere jungle encampments. Withered like a raisin with a wispy silver mustache and goatee, he could have been a jolly-looking man but for the flint-hard look in his eyes. They had seen a great deal of death—the lion's share of it inflicted by Uncle Hector himself.

Sabine's eyes held the same look, as if it were genetic, though he was not her uncle by blood. The stooped Peruvian had been a dear friend of her father's—inasmuch as a leader in Peru's Shining Path could have a friendship with anyone. Friendship and devotion could be looked at as bourgeois. The collective was what mattered. One sacrificed for the group, not another individual. Shining Path manifestos were clear in that regard. But when it came to Sabine's family, tiny, hate-filled Hector Alonso gave up everything to take care of Sabine and her family after her parents' deaths. They became the children he never had—if not by blood, with blood.

"You should rest," the old man whispered.

She pulled away.

"Rest?" Sabine hooked a thumb toward her chest and wagged her head. "Look at me! I am fine. Untouched. While, in the meantime, poor, stupid

Joaquín has a hole in his head. I am not even sure how it got there."

"A bullet from a suppressed rifle?"

Her face screwed up in a scoff. "You and I both have much experience with what a rifle bullet does to a human skull." She clenched her eyes shut, racking her brain for all the possibilities. "No, I could see the entry wound steaming before De Bruk dragged me away."

She stood dutifully while Hector reached to wipe a spatter of blood off her chin with his thumb.

"A small caliber pistol, then," he said.

"No." She wheeled and walked to the window, peeking outside to make sure her security detail was where they were supposed to be. "This was not a pistol. I saw something in the air just before he was killed."

Working herself into a frenzy again, she spat on the floor. Someone else would clean it up.

"Something in the air?" her uncle prodded. Accustomed to her temper, he always looked coiled when she got like this, as if he might have to spring out of the way to keep from getting crushed underfoot.

"It was a drone of some kind," she said. "I thought it was a bird or a bat at first glance. Before I could see what it really was, the thing spat fire at Joaquín . . . and then exploded—"

"Exploded?"

"Exactly that," she said, gearing up to spit again.

"A drone. Someone murdered my brother and I want to know who!"

"You left people behind to check the scene—"

"You think me an imbecile?" she snapped. "Of course I have people checking the scene. I would still be there if not for De Bruk. Flaco will bring down the bodies."

The old man poured her a drink, clucking softly in thought.

She took the glass and tossed it back greedily. The government of Venezuela had collapsed into a smoldering dung heap of corruption and poverty, but it somehow still managed to produce excellent rum.

"You should sit before you fall," he said, attempting to guide her toward the couch.

She'd just put the tumbler to her lips a second time when there was a knock at the door.

It was Gregor. The Russian was one of the two men who had shot the assassin. Impossibly large biceps glistened in the lamplight like the top of his bald head.

"Why are you not still on the mountain?" Sabine demanded the moment he stepped through the door. "You could not have done a proper search in such a short time!"

"The others are still searching," he said. "Forgive me, **patrona,** but there is something you must see." If he was nervous, he did not show it. That was good. Sabine demanded respect from her employees, but she could not stomach weakness. Quivering servants did not survive long around her.

Gregor held a small plastic and wire device between his thumb and forefinger.

Rum in hand, she leaned forward to study it.

"A piece of a small drone?"

The Russian shook his head. "The others are collecting pieces of a drone to be sure, but this is something much different. I found it inside the assassin's mouth."

"Is that so?" Uncle Hector moved closer. "In the man's mouth?"

"Yes, **patrón**," Gregor said. "The device was clipped to his back tooth. I believe he was using it to communicate."

Sabine scoffed. "He had a phone in his hand that he was using to control the drone. This is nothing but dental work."

"If you would allow me, please." Gregor took the tiny device in his palm and demonstrated. "A small switch, which is probably activated with the tongue."

The Russian flipped the switch back and forth with his thumb and forefinger.

She glared at him, losing patience.

"Show me how one would activate that with their tongue."

"Just so." Gregor used the tip of his finger to flip the tiny plastic switch again.

"Put it in your mouth."

Gregor made a face as if he'd just sucked the juice from a bitter lemon.

"Grow some balls or find another job!" Sabine snapped. She snatched the device out of Gregor's hands and dropped it into her rum.

"Patrona!" he all but yelped. "It may become damaged—"

"Perhaps you will discover some brains while you search for your balls!" Sabine swished the device around in the glass. "The man carried this in his mouth. I doubt a little alcohol will do it any harm."

She put the device in her own mouth, situating it as best she could over a back molar, toying at the switch with her tongue. Vibrations rippled through her jaw, transferring to the bones in her ear as hissing static as it searched for a signal.

"You are right," she said at length. "A communication device of some sort." She spit it into her palm and showed it to Hector. He took the saliva-covered thing without a second thought and held it up to the light.

"No markings," he said. "I suspect it links to a covert radio or mobile device."

"So, there were more of them," Sabine said, more to herself than to either of the men in the room. "Who was he talking to?" She looked up from the device, meeting Gregor's eye. "Who was this assassin?"

"There was nothing on the body to identify

him," Gregor said. "No tattoos. He was Latin. Venezuelan, maybe? A rebel?"

"I do not think so," Sabine said. "This has a certain degree of sophistication . . . Venezuelans still rely on two tin cans and a length of string for communication." She took the device back from Hector and turned it over in her hand, studying it carefully. "Joaquín was murdered by a tiny drone, stealthy and almost invisible. All extremely high-tech . . ."

It suddenly occurred to her that the dead assassin's device might be capable of listening in. She dropped it back into the rum and handed the glass to Gregor.

"I will look into this," he said. "Do not worry, **patrona.** We will find out who killed Joaquín."

Gorshkova's lips drew back in a snarl. "I know exactly who is behind my brother's murder. And I feel sure they are after me now."

Hector raised an open hand. "My dear," he said, "the Americans did not even know you existed before tonight. If they did, they would have killed you as well—"

She snatched the glass from Gregor and drank most of the rum, leaving just enough to cover the electronics. Eyes blazing, lips glistening, she glared at the two men.

"Leaving me alive is an oversight they will soon come to regret."

10

The special agent in charge of the PPD—
the Secret Service's Presidential Protective
Division—Gary Montgomery had managed
Jack Ryan's security long enough that he'd become
something of a confidant, an unofficial adviser to
the President. The former University of Michigan
boxer's wide face twisted as if he had an abscessed
tooth, unable to contain his disgust at the British
prime minister's minuscule three-car detail. He
noted under his breath to his fellow PPD agents
that the PM's limo driver got out and opened the
door for their protectee rather than staying at the
ready behind the wheel. Montgomery was as fair-
minded as they came, but he could not abide slip-
shod security.

Ryan couldn't blame the man. Moist earth still
covered the freshly turned graves of eleven United
States Secret Service agents who'd been tasked with
protecting Ryan's wife. Eleven of Montgomery's

friends and coworkers. The Service had a zero tolerance policy for failure. It didn't matter to them that the attack had been extremely well planned and flawlessly executed. The First Lady was taken, so they had failed.

As the special agent in charge, Montgomery had tendered his resignation. Maureen "Mo" Richardson, the special agent in charge of the FLOTUS detail, had been on leave the day of the attack, leaving Cathy in the care of her friend and detail whip, Special Agent Karen Sato. Sato died in the initial assault, shielding Cathy Ryan's body as she attempted to get Cathy to safety.

Mo Richardson, too, had turned in her papers.

Ryan understood taking responsibility, but he also knew how hard Montgomery worked to keep PPD in top form. He'd refused to accept either resignation. Asking instead that the Service redouble their already herculean efforts to investigate the events in San Antonio and work closely with the FBI to bring the power brokers of the army of private contractors known as the Camarilla to justice. Montgomery stayed on as requested, but had grown even more quiet than usual, as if he were embarrassed to be around the President.

He shut the limo door and sat down in the front passenger seat, massive shoulders visible above the top of the open privacy screen.

Ryan wanted someone like Montgomery protecting

him, so he kept it light, hoping the man would someday stop taking the blame for something that was not his fault in any way.

"Gary, you look as though you've had a bad glass of milk," Ryan noted as he settled himself in the back of the presidential limo across from Mary Pat Foley. "Everything okay?"

Montgomery craned his head around. "All good, Mr. President. Just noting that some organizations appear to run dignitary protection with concentric rings of hope and prayer."

"But not us?" Ryan said, raising a brow at the agent, who would gladly throw himself between Ryan and a bullet.

"No, sir," Montgomery said. "Not by a long shot." The burly agent turned to face forward and said something into the mic pinned under the collar of his shirt. Almost immediately, the honor guard of four Metropolitan Police motorcycles and two marked squad cars rolled out, lights flashing, sirens yelping. The armored Cadillac presidential limo known as the Beast followed, then an identical decoy/spare limo, two Secret Service follow SUVs, two armored Chevy Suburbans packed with heavily armed operators of the Secret Service Counter Assault Team, and a snaking line of vehicles full of staff.

As director of national intelligence, Mary Pat Foley warranted her own Secret Service detail, albeit exponentially smaller than the President's.

Inside the Beltway this normally consisted of a limo and follow car. She now sat across from Ryan in the Beast, her back to the driver's compartment in the vis-à-vis seating. Her protective-detail agents followed in the seventeen-car monstrosity that made up the President's motorcade.

It was late, but as usual, Foley was scrolling through her tablet, trying to keep up with the endless waterfall of reports and briefs that came her way from the eighteen intelligence agencies in her purview. Ryan looked out the tinted window at the quiet, hedge-lined road.

Foley lowered her device and peered over the top. "You ever think about the old days?"

"I feel old every day, Mary Pat," Ryan said.

She chuckled. "I know what you mean. I'm talking about those ops you and I ran here in Europe."

"Sometimes," Ryan said. "I suppose. Cathy thinks about them all the time, especially lately. She uses a piece of fabric from my old overcoat as a bookmark."

"You guys are adorable," Foley said.

"It's got a bullet hole in it," Ryan said.

"Ah," Foley said. "That overcoat."

"I suppose she kept the damned thing to remind her how fickle life can be . . . and how dangerous. Lord knows she doesn't need that reminder anymore . . ."

Ryan felt certain his wife still hadn't told him everything about her time in the captivity of Camarilla operatives. With the unimaginable loss of life in her Secret Service detail came an equally unimaginable loss of confidence on Cathy's part. If a group of armed men could get past the layers of security guarding the First Lady of the United States, how could she ever be safe? How could anyone?

Foley took a deep breath and held it, as if deciding whether or not to give some piece of unsolicited advice.

"Are you going to tell her about this new lead on the Camarilla?" she asked at length. "This kind of thing has the potential to—"

"Oh, hell no," Ryan said. "She's already uncomfortable staying in the White House without me there."

"That's the most fortified place in the country."

Ryan shrugged. "She knows that. Intellectually, anyway. Emotionally, I'm pretty sure she sees it as a big white bull's-eye in the middle of a manicured lawn. She hates to stay home, but this trip has been difficult on her. I'm afraid she's going to shatter her teeth."

Foley gave him a soft smile. "Seems natural that she'd want to stick close, considering the hell she's just been through. Reality shifts in a big way when we come face-to-face with our own mortality. I know from experience, after a traumatic event nowhere near as awful as Cathy's, and I still spent weeks crawling out of my skin expecting the next bad thing at any second . . ."

Ryan fished the secure cell phone out of his

jacket. "Speaking of that, I should call her and warn her we're on the way back to Winfield House. She doesn't like surprises."

"Jack." Foley caught his eye as he put the phone to his ear. "We'll get these bastards. I promise."

Ryan lowered the phone to his lap and met her gaze. It was difficult to imagine a look that held more intensity and righteous indignation. He was glad this woman's sword was on his side.

"You look like you have a plan," he said.

She nodded slowly through another deep breath. "We're hunting a shadowy group of former special operators who work outside the bounds of the law. We have our own organization made up of operators with similar training, who work outside the bounds of bureaucracy. They've been on this from the start. I'll make sure they know to take the gloves off."

Ryan gave a sardonic chuckle. "I don't know if taking the gloves off Clark is the safest course of action."

"You're hilarious, Jack," Foley said. "I'm pretty sure Clark doesn't even know what gloves are. He's augmenting the team now, as you know, but I'll make sure he's getting all the help he needs. We'll catch these bastards, Jack. I promise."

Cathy was in bed when Ryan got back to their room at the ambassador's residence. It was well after midnight, so that made perfect sense. Blond hair splayed across her pillows, but instead of her usual gown or shorts, she'd switched to a loose Marine Corps T-shirt and gray sweatpants for sleepwear. Rather than her customary medical journals on ophthalmic surgery, she flipped through some mindless tabloid about the royal family. Her chest rose and fell in a deep sigh when she saw him.

"Everything go okay?"

"Swimmingly," Ryan said, as if he needed to convince himself. He left out the gory details of the deaths of Joaquín Gorshkov and his bodyguard. Losses had been limited to one CIA case officer, but that was hardly anything to celebrate. He gave his wife of over forty years a wan smile while he pulled off his tie and began to unbutton his shirt. "It's late. I thought you might be asleep."

She chuckled, as ever, reading what he meant not what he said. "Yeah, right . . ."

Ryan brushed his teeth, then stripped down to his shorts and put on a clean T-shirt. Exhausted to the point of delirium, he picked up a fat and well-worn copy of **The Complete Works of Saki** from the bedside table. Though he'd grown up solidly middle class as the son of a Baltimore police detective, Jack Ryan had made some intelligent (and some would say lucky) investments on Wall Street by the time he'd met Cathy Mueller. They'd never had the experience of being poor newlyweds living in a tiny apartment with a black-and-white television and a dedicated pair of pliers to change the channel. It didn't matter what they could afford. Neither of them was a big TV watcher, so it took them a while to get around to buying one. Instead, they'd spent their evenings and weekends lounging in bed in various stages of undress, reading to each other. Anything by Ken Follett or Frederick Forsyth went to the top of their pile. But their all-time favorites were the short stories of H. H. Munro, a British author who wrote under the pen name Saki.

A busy life of growing kids, time-consuming careers, and social obligations had seen them set the habit aside, but the shock of Cathy's kidnapping had sent them running to the comfort of their books. It was Cathy who'd dragged the tattered copy out of the bookcase in their bedroom.

Jack hopped in bed beside her, book in hand. "You up for a little witty prose before we fall asleep?"

She dropped the tabloid over the side of the bed and turned to face him, smoothing a lock of salt-and-pepper hair out of his eyes. "You look like you may be asleep already."

"I'm wide-awake," he lied. "I'll read first."

Cathy nestled deeper in the covers next to him and gave an almost imperceptible nod. "Okay . . ."

Ryan thumbed to the page he was looking for, then adjusted his reading glasses and cleared his throat.

"'The Open Window,'" he said.

"I love this one," she whispered, snuggling even closer, her breath warm against his neck.

He had to contort his arms in order to hold the book and turn the pages with her draped on top of him. He didn't care.

He was a paragraph from the end, when she rolled away to face the ceiling.

He lowered the book to his chest. "You okay?"

"I'm fine," she said. "Just thinking of how much I wish we could do more of this."

"Someday," Ryan said.

"I guess," she said. "But what if someday doesn't come?"

"It will—"

"It may not, Jack," she said. "Every Secret Service agent on my detail had a significant other. They had plans, dreams . . . someone waiting at home to read with them . . ."

Ryan gave a somber nod, but said nothing.

Cathy stayed locked in, staring at the ceiling. "They're still out there, aren't they?"

"'They'?"

"Those men," she said, her face darkening in thought. "The Camarilla. I know you got the ones who took me, but I heard them talking after they dragged me into the van. It's not a small organization. I'd always thought men who could kill like they did would be consummate evil. Like animals . . . like . . . I don't know . . . feral. These men were professionals, Jack, doing a job—and I was that job."

It was all Ryan could do to keep his voice steady. "That's my definition of evil, sweetheart," he said.

"They were after us then," she whispered. "I can't shake the feeling that they still are. And they have an army to do it."

"They were hired for a specific assignment," Ryan said. "And the man who hired them is dead."

Cathy was too smart. She knew full well when he was lying to protect her, and she usually let him get away with it. This was not one of those times. He didn't even try. The FBI had taken a detailed statement from her after she'd been freed. All the Camarilla operatives but for one had been killed during the rescue. The survivor had apparently been trying to help Cathy escape. He was completely cooperative, but suffered from a traumatic brain injury that left him unable to focus. The Bureau described it like interviewing a preoccupied four-year-old. Ryan had read the after-action reports of the FBI, the Secret Service—and Domingo Chavez. The Camarilla appeared to be a group of private contractors. No one in U.S. intelligence had been able to find where they were headquartered or learn much of anything about their organizational structure. Whoever led them was a black silhouette on a scant organizational chart.

"You're right," Ryan said. He waited a beat, started to say something about the future, but decided it was too cliché. Instead, he said, "Love you."

She lifted her head and looked at him, cheeks flushed and moist with tears. "I'll get through this, Jack," she said. "I promise."

"I'm sure of it," Ryan said. "You know what you are . . . ?" He thought of something Saki wrote and flipped through the pages until he found the story to illustrate his point. "Here it is. 'Confront a child, a puppy, and a kitten with a sudden danger; the child will turn instinctively for assistance, the puppy will grovel in abject submission to the impending visitation, the kitten will brace its tiny body for a frantic resistance.'"

"I like that," Cathy said, wedging herself closer, as if that were even physically possible. "So, I'm a kitten?"

"Oh, there's no doubt." He maneuvered his arm under her neck and pulled her close, so she was lying on his chest again.

"I wonder what Steven is up to," she said out of the blue.

"Who?" Ryan asked.

"Steven Edwards," she said. "You know, Chilly, that young Abilene police officer who saved my life. It seems like we should do more for him than a thank-you call."

"I can check on him again if you'd like," he said. The truth was, Ryan had no idea where Chilly Edwards was at that moment, but he knew exactly where he'd be tomorrow.

"We should have him for dinner at the White

House," she said, smiling at the thought of it. "Anyway, yes. Please check on him again."

"I will," Ryan said. "And inviting Chilly Edwards for dinner at the White House is an excellent idea." Cathy didn't press the issue, so he changed the subject, turning back to where he'd left off in "The Open Window." "Shall I read the rest?"

She sighed and then kissed him softly on the neck. "No," she said. "I have the last line memorized." She affected an impish British accent and lifted her head so she was looking up at him, eyes wide, before kissing him again. Her words fluttered against his neck.

"'Romance at short notice was her specialty.'"

11

ABILENE, TEXAS

I've got movement!" Steven "Chilly" Edwards
said into the mic on the collar of his Crye G3
shirt. Most of the SWAT team was close enough
to hear him, but he put the information out over
the radio anyway. It was good to keep command
staff aware of the situation in real time.

The baby-faced SWAT operator came across as
much more mature than his thirty-one years.

He was supposed to turn in his gear that evening, along with his badge. He'd already turned in
his Accuracy International sniper rifle to the guy
taking his place on the team, which put him as a
regular operator on the hostage rescue that would
be his last callout.

The entire Abilene PD SWAT team had been at
Chilly's going-away party at Perini Ranch Steak-
house eighteen miles south of town in Buffalo Gap
when the call came in. Chilly had just "popped

smoke," deploying a Maximum HC white smoke grenade behind the restaurant. A tradition when separating from the SWAT team. Chilly had balked when the call first came in, thinking he was already "out." The SWAT team leader, Sergeant Johnson had looked at him like he'd grown a third eye, said, "Bullshit. Get your gear."

The Perinis were dear friends of Abilene's thin blue line. Lisa promised to keep the lights on and the team's steaks warm until they finished with their callout.

It was taking much longer than expected.

"Number one window on the two side," Chilly continued, his voice direct and precise. "Hold fire. Hold fire. Female hostage coming out."

The other members of the team observed the split-level house from behind their armored BearCat. They understood exactly what Chilly meant. The team assigned numbers to the sides of a building for clear communication. **One** was the front, continuing clockwise around, in this case, a simple four-sided, split-level dwelling. Windows were numbered counterclockwise and started over on each new side. The downstairs one window on the two side meant the lower first window from the left side of the house.

Two Sierra Units—the snipers, part of Chilly's old cadre—stood overwatch on the roof across the street, ready to send a 168-grain, 30-caliber MatchKing into the brain of Donald Volente the moment he showed himself, in order to save the two women he'd taken hostage. Now one of the women was coming out. She was covered with blood and gore, but alive—and sobbing uncontrollably. Chilly parked his Colt M4 short-barreled rifle on a sling behind his hip for easy access in case the suspect decided to come out guns blazing. He beckoned the frazzled woman to come to him behind the cover of the BearCat, while the rest of the eight-man team covered the residence with their M4s. K9 Brutus, the team's Belgian Malinois, whined at the woman's approach, but stuck by his handler, a tall soft-spoken operator called Oats.

"Leila's dead!" the woman sobbed. She was young, nineteen or twenty, gaunt and hollow-eyed with lifeless, rust-colored hair. "Donnie stabbed her to death! He wasn't supposed to hurt her. I swear." Chilly recognized her as a local prostitute named Tina Tyson, who went by the street name Tee Tee.

Sergeant Johnson adjusted his Kevlar helmet and took his eyes off the dwelling long enough to shoot a glance at the trembling woman. "Who is **she,** Tee Tee? Who you talking about?"

"My sister," Tee Tee sobbed. "She's not even in the life, you know. She's got a job at Costco, a nice home, and everything. I thought she might loan me some money."

"House comes back belonging to Leila Tyson," Chilly said.

"That's what I said!" Tee Tee screeched. She

nodded to the lower windows. "She's down there, in the hall . . . I can't believe that bastard stabbed her. We were just supposed to borrow some money . . ."

"Where was Volente when you last saw him?"

"Crawling around in the living room," Tee Tee said. "He's smart enough to know y'all will shoot him if he stands up. I sneaked away when his head was down."

"Is he armed?"

"Hell yes, he's armed," she scoffed. "A bonin' knife from the kitchen and a Glock. The Glock's got one of those long-ass clip things with fifty bullets or something."

"Any other weapons?"

"Leila keeps our dad's old double barrel in her bedroom closet down in the basement." Tee Tee sniffed back the tears. "Kept . . ." She dropped to her knees and began to shake, crying again until she could no longer breathe.

Sergeant Johnson waved up a tactical medic to accompany the shattered woman back to the outer perimeter and a waiting ambulance. He relayed the information she'd given him over the radio so everyone including the brass a half block away in the mobile command post had the whole picture. Johnson had a good enough reputation that the commander just listened and let him lead.

"Witness says the suspect was upstairs crawling on hands and knees to avoid being seen when she escaped. He's armed with a knife and a Glock pistol with extended magazine. Witness Tyson reports suspect has killed the other hostage. Units in back, stand by with the 9-Bang. Sending breachers up to rig the front door now. We have time if the hostage is dead. We'll set the breaching charge and then decide when to go in."

Johnson gave Ike and Winslow a nod. "Barth, you're on lethal cover. Chilly, cover that two window to the right of the door." His lip curled in disgust under a bristle-brush mustache. "I hate split-levels."

"Copy that," Chilly said. He fell in behind Barth and the two breachers, while the remainder of the team covered their advance.

Pelkey, one of the two Sierra Units across the street, crackled over the radio in Chilly's earpiece.

"I'm seeing shadowed movement through the upper two window. Dining room area, I think. Suspect is not presenting a target, but I believe he is upstairs, staying low."

The breachers moved quickly and quietly, taping their pre-rigged charge on the hinge side of the front door. It took mere seconds. Barth stood at the door, weapon up during the process, giving them lethal cover.

Chilly took up a position to the left of the lower two window. Dim light from down the hall filtered into the carpeted room. Chilly took in the details while still watching the door and keeping the big picture. The closet was open and stacked high with cardboard boxes. An insane number of throw pillows covered the double bed. More boxes and plastic coat hangers were stacked in a forgotten pile on a treadmill in the corner—a combination guest bedroom and convenient spot to shove things and get them out of the way.

But no Donald Volente in sight.

Finished, the breachers unspooled a line of non-electrical fuse known as NONEL and trailed it as they retreated to the rest of the emergency response team behind the armored BearCat thirty feet away. Barth followed. Chilly was about to turn, when a flash of movement in the hall caused him to pause and bring his rifle up to eye level. It took him a moment to understand what it was in the scant light.

A female foot. Leila.

Chilly's fist shot up.

"Hold!"

Closer inspection revealed a blood trail in the carpet where she'd dragged herself down the hall. A lot of blood. The foot moved again, coming up on its toes in Leila's feeble attempt to propel herself, maybe toward the shotgun she had in the back bedroom.

Atta girl, Chilly thought. He hustled the ten steps back to the rest of the team. "I see the victim on the ground. She's alive. On the floor in the hallway. In the basement, two window on the one side. She's moving, but it looks like she's bleeding out fast."

A wounded hostage sped up the timeline exponentially. Events unfolded from there at lightning speed.

"Copy," Sergeant Johnson said, voice ice calm despite the circumstances. "Let's initiate a deliberate assault. Units in the back, stand by with the bang. Barth, take the Break-N-Rake and move in with Chilly. Initiate! Initiate! Initiate!"

The eight team members were close enough to make quick entry, but far enough away to avoid the blast. All of them, including Chilly, faced their ballistic plates to the blast with their heads down, mouths open to equalize the pressure in their ears.

"Copy," Winslow, the assistant breacher, said over the radio, equally calm. "Initiate on the breach. Stand by . . ."

Ike, the lead breacher, held the triggering cone in one hand, his other hand open and poised above the plunger. When he heard the **b** of the first **breach** he would drive the plunger sharply downward, striking a primer that would ignite the explosive in the NONEL's hollow core, sending a wave of energy down the plastic tube at 6,500 feet per second that would detonate the breaching charge taped to the hinges of the front door.

Winslow unkeyed the radio for a moment, giving anyone with last-minute traffic the opportunity to chime in.

No one did.

At the same moment, Ike nodded and Winslow gave the command to blow the door.

"Breach! Breach! Breach!"

A percussive wave hit Chilly in the chest, not painful at all, but he felt it.

The 9-Bang went off simultaneously at the back of the house, popping in erratic intervals and, hopefully, drawing Volente's attention in that direction.

Short-barrel M4 pressed to his shoulder, Chilly moved with purpose to the window, where he visually cleared the room and covered the hall, while Barth moved up with the Break-N-Rake. Like the name implied, the tool was a hooked rake-like device fixed to a long metal pole that officers could use to break the window and then rake out or sweep aside shards of broken glass, curtains, or miniblinds. In this case, the curtains were open. Barth bashed in the window, then ran the rake around the edges of the frame, attempting to clear away the jagged shards that threatened to shred the operators as they made entry through the new opening.

A string of curses rose from the stack of SWAT operators lined up at the front door.

Johnson barked, "Failed breach!"

K9 Brutus voiced his frustration with a whining yowl from the edge of the BearCat.

Chilly glanced sideways just long enough to see the front door laying at an odd angle, wedged into the threshold like a ramp. The breaching charge had blown it off its hinges, but there was less than two feet between the door and the frame for the team to make entry, leaving them vulnerable to gunfire from Volente.

"Son of a bitch," Ike said. "Bastard's thrown all the furniture down the stairs and piled it against the door." He used a Halligan tool to try to break through the door.

Movement in the hall drew Chilly's attention away from the shitshow at the front entry. Leila Tyson's head poked tentatively around the threshold, low, hugging the carpet.

"Victim in sight," Chilly said. Barth had seen her, too. He thrust the Break-N-Rake through the window and yanked at an upright portion of the frame, trying to pull it free to enlarge the portal.

In a perfect world, he would have dropped the Break-N-Rake and gone in first while Chilly provided cover with his M4, following Barth after he got set inside. But shit happened and the upright wasn't as tough as Barth expected. He gave it a harder yank than he needed to and staggered backward to land flat on his tailbone.

The team practiced constantly for just such real-world eventualities. Chilly was now closer to the window. Rather than trying to regroup, Barth simply said, "Go" and took up a position of cover with his rifle while Chilly dropped inside. Eyes on the doorway, he managed to gash his left forearm from elbow to wrist during the process. A quick assessment told him it was dripping not gushing, so he pushed on. He watched the door while Barth came in behind him.

"Inside," Chilly said over the radio.

"I have the door," Barth whispered, moments after his boots hit the carpet.

They cleared the room with a quick scan, a simple matter since the closet was open and they could see under the bed. Without another word, both men went straight for the wounded hostage.

The rest of the team had abandoned the failed breach and poured through the window behind them. Winslow, the last to leave, shouted out over the radio.

"I've got movement past the front door! Suspect's headed downstairs."

The team's priorities for safety were hostages first, other officers, then the suspect—but that didn't mean they ignored the danger and got fixated on the "eye candy" of the wounded hostage.

Still, they moved quickly, both men eager to put their ballistic plates between the hostage and the bad guy's bullets.

Barth posted to the left of the doorframe, while Chilly took a position to the right. He had the better angle to toss a bang and get it far enough away from the hostage.

Both operators hooked around the doorframe at the sound of the bang, Barth facing the direction of the suspect, while Chilly squatted to grab

Leila Tyson by both shoulders and drag her into the room. An onlooker would have sworn that the officers never paused, but tossed the bang at the same time they rounded the corner.

Fueled with adrenaline the men careened off each other as they went through the narrow doorway.

Pistol shots cracked down the hall, wild and un-aimed. But wild shots could be plenty fatal. Barth returned fire. He hopped sideways, accidentally slamming a boot into Chilly's kidney.

Chilly stumbled forward, wobbled by the sudden blow to his back. He caught himself, then wasted no time snatching up the wounded woman under her arms, mopping the floor with her blood as he hauled her into the bedroom behind a wall of plate-wearing SWAT officers.

Barth shouted, broadcasting over the radio, "Suspect going out the east side."

An otherworldly scream rose from outside the house an instant later, followed by a flurry of growls and the high-pitched bark of a Belgian Malinois.

The landing to the door was blocked by an up-ended couch thrown down the stairs, so Chilly and half the team passed Leila Tyson through the broken window to the waiting medics, while the others cleared the remainder of the house for un-known threats. Outside, Volente got acquainted with K9 Brutus.

SOP dictated the operators perform a blood sweep on one another after they were exposed to gunfire. Chilly was closest and bleeding from the gash on his left arm, so Sergeant Johnson started with him.

"Did either of you get hit?" he asked, lifting Chilly's arms above his head to check his torso.

Blood dripped from the elbow of Chilly's olive-green tactical shirt. "I'm fine, Sarge, but I should probably get a couple of stitches . . ." He arched his back and shot a glance at Barth. "I know we were moving fast, but you kicked the shit out of me getting into position in the hall."

"Not me." Barth shook his head. "I never touched you."

Johnson took Chilly by the shoulder and spun him around.

"Holy shit, kid!"

"What?"

"It looks like a bullet smacked you in the rifle plate just above your kidney. Lucky for you your soft body armor hangs down lower than the plates. Spalling and bullet fragments ripped the hell out of the Kevlar, probably while you were stooped over picking up the victim."

Barth took a look at the damage and gave a low whistle.

"Chilly, you are one lucky son of a bitch. If you'd been bending over a little farther, you woulda taken one straight up Main Street."

Johnson shot a glance at Barth, then performed a blood sweep on him as well.

"You good?"

"No problems, boss," Barth said. "I'm ten-two!"

Outside, the ambulance yelped, lights flashing as it pulled away with Leila Tyson.

Sergeant Johnson waved his index finger in a circle above his head, rallying the troops. "Let's get you to the hospital." He put a hand on Chilly's shoulder. "Then we'll have to go back to the PD. We have some stuff we need to take care of."

"Figured," Chilly said.

Sergeant Johnson didn't say it, but that "stuff" to take care of was collecting the rest of Chilly's gear, including his badge.

12

Chilly ended up with nineteen tell-your-grandkids-the-kickass-story sutures on his forearm. The stitches didn't take long, but he'd picked a busy night at the hospital to take a bullet to the body armor. Glancing shot though it was, city policy required him to get an X-ray. He'd brought his MDT into the hospital and was able to bang out his report during the interminable wait for the X-ray tech.

Finally finished at the hospital, Chilly made the slow drive back to the PD, a converted grocery store in a strip mall on South First Street. He couldn't decide if the short hike from employee parking to the secure door was the beginning of a fantastic new adventure or a walk to the gallows. He checked his watch—a Tudor Ranger the team had given him before they'd all had to bug out for the SWAT callout. Five past midnight. His resignation papers listed yesterday as his last day of employment with the city of Abilene. For all practical purposes, he wasn't a cop anymore.

Chilly didn't like to dwell on it, but he had damned few details about what came next. His fellow officers thought he'd lost his mind when he told them he'd decided to leave law enforcement for a job at a financial arbitrage firm called Hendley Associates in Alexandria, Virginia.

Chilly kept the real details of his new job to himself. He told everyone that he wasn't sure yet what the firm would have him doing. They apparently felt a short stint in the Army along with a history major and four accounting classes made him a good fit. Oh, yeah, and he'd saved the First Lady's life. That was a pretty good résumé booster.

His father took it in stride. "You're young," the old man said. "You have time to change your course a couple of times after you get this nonsense out of your system."

His older brother, an operator with the FBI's Hostage Rescue Team, was less circumspect. "You're an idiot to give up on the Bureau when you're as good as in. The FBI's not gonna hang around and wait for you to pull your head out of your ass."

Maybe his brother was right, but the Bureau hadn't seemed all that excited to bring him aboard. For some reason, the shot that had saved Mrs. Ryan had somehow put his application on a slow roll. He'd heard "Just be patient" one too many times, when two strangers in a black pickup he'd pulled over for speeding called him by name and offered him what sounded like a very interesting job. At least from what few details he could piece together.

Every time Chilly spoke with Ding Chavez, he came away excited about future prospects, but filled with more questions than he'd had going in.

"We'll get to that" appeared to be the man's favorite phrase.

It wasn't that Chilly was uneasy about the new job. Police work had taught him to be cynical, but for some reason, he found himself trusting Chavez and the scary-as-shit older guy named Clark more than he'd ever trusted anyone in his life but his own father. The personal call from President Ryan had helped. He'd been able to tell his buds about that—just not all of it.

More than anything, Chilly wanted to be part of something bigger, and this new gig seemed to fit the bill. What he knew of it anyway. Most of it was still shrouded in mystery . . . But he loved mysteries.

He punched his code into the cipher lock on the back door. Luckily, IT hadn't set it to expire at midnight. The smell of cooked steaks rolled out and hit him in the face as soon as he stepped inside. Lisa Perini had arrived an hour before with sixteen freshly cooked rib eyes, jalapeño bites, and baked potatoes. A friend to law enforcement indeed.

The building was a hive of activity despite the late hour. Detectives and brass all the way up to the chief interviewed, pecked at keyboards, or sat in on after-action debriefs. Officer Barth had hit Donald Volente once in the left thigh and K9 Brutus had apparently eaten a sizable chunk of his biceps. Those were the least of his problems. Leila was still in surgery. This was Texas. If she died on the operating table, Volente was looking at the death penalty.

Sergeant Johnson waved Chilly into his office after the top brass left and the team had tucked into their midnight snack of steak and baked potato.

"Got a minute?"

"Of course," Chilly said. "A bunch of us are going out for drinks after. Are you coming?"

"Wouldn't miss it," Johnson said. "Sorry again about your party."

Chilly chuckled. "What are you talking about? It's like y'all planned it. Hostage rescue, gunfire, and felony arrest. Hell, Sarge, that's the best send-off I've ever even heard of."

Johnson gave an almost imperceptible nod. His eyes narrowed, as if sizing Chilly up.

"Most of my gear is squared away," Chilly said. "I turned in the rifle this morning. It's after one a.m. I'll get the rest done and drag it in here before we head out. My flight's early, so I'm not planning on getting any sleep tonight anyhow." He took a deep breath and then, steeling himself, slid his badge across the desk. "Might as well go ahead and turn this in now since I'm not on the books anymore."

Johnson took the badge and spun it like a top on the desk, thinking for a moment. He spoke without looking up. "A guy who rides his Harley into a shopping mall in the middle of a gunfight stays on the books forever."

The incident had been weeks before, but Chilly still took a lot of good-natured guff about his bravado—and a lot of silent nods of approval, too.

He wasn't much of a weeper, but the knot in his throat made it difficult to get the words out. "It's been an honor to work with you, Sarge—"

"About that." Johnson cut him off. "I just don't get it, son. You love the hell out of this stuff." He shook his head, eyes at half squint, as if seized by a fleeting pain. "And you're so damned good at it. I can't do anything about the money here. Abilene pays what Abilene pays, but holy shit . . . At least hold out for the FBI. They're almost cops."

Chilly sighed, humbled. A call into the boss's office usually meant you were trying to keep your job, not being asked to stay.

"Did my brother put you up to this?"

Sergeant Johnson gave the badge another spin on the desk, mesmerized by it. "Nope. This is all me. I just can't see a future where you're happy sittin' on your ass in front of a computer at some financial arbitrage firm." He looked up. "The thing is, Chilly, I've seen this before. The jump-the-fence-for-greener-pastures syndrome. A guy gets it into his head that some girl has a prettier mouth or better ass or whatever than the one they're with."

"Are we still talking about my new job?"

"I'm saying you're gonna find the same people and some level of boredom pretty much everywhere you go. They may have different names and different faces, but the grass on the other side of the fence is still just grass. Nine times outta ten, guys your age regret their decision a day or two after they jump. They're just too damned proud to admit it . . . or they've torched all the bridges behind them." The sergeant stood and shook Chilly's hand, drawing him close and slapping his back in a brotherhood embrace before stepping away.

"How about this?" he said. "I'll hold your gear in my office. We'll call this next two weeks annual leave for . . . I don't know . . . almost getting shot in the ass. If you decide your new job is the stuff of lollipops and rainbows, then Godspeed. Continue on your merry way. Drop the badge in the mail and I'll process your separation papers. Until then, you still have a rifle to come back to."

13

CIA operations officer Colleen Vance turned her dark blue Toyota Corolla left off George Washington Memorial Parkway, following a long line of morning commuters onto the campus of the George Bush Center for Intelligence, commonly known as Langley. Both hands gripping the top of the wheel, she tapped her thumbs in time with the heavy bass beat of "Workhorse" by All Them Witches. Taillights cast red shadows on wet pavement in the morning twilight. Windshield wipers thumped frantically against a cold fall downpour, and she craned forward, chest to the steering wheel, squinting through the darkness like her mother did when she drove, as if the extra few inches would help her see better.

A cable had come in the day before—with questions about a female subject believed to be named Sabine Gorshkova. Eager to check on the hooks she'd baited yesterday, Vance had come in to work early. Unfortunately, so had everyone else, from the looks of all the traffic.

She passed the small guard shack on her right, its windows covered with one-way film making it impossible to see the machine-gun-carrying CIA Security Protective Service officers inside. In 1993 Pakistani terrorist Mir Aimal Kansi got out of his car in this very spot and opened fire, killing CIA employees Lansing Bennett and Frank Darling and wounding three others who were on their way to work. The CIA had added the shack at the entry point shortly after. Vance nodded subconsciously. There were far too many stars on the Memorial Wall at Langley—but there was no job on earth she'd rather have.

The secrecy was a hassle. All her siblings thought she worked for the U.S. Geological Survey. Only her parents knew what she did for a living. That part of it had seemed way cooler than it was before she came aboard. But the job. That was amazing. The dark arts of human behavior—analyzing the mysteries—that was her thing.

Yesterday's priority cable came directly from Liberty Crossing—ODNI—the Office of the Director of National Intelligence. High priority, what Vance and her colleagues called a "short-fuse" tasking: locate the round-faced woman in white depicted in the attached photographs and confirm her identity. The cable had gone out worldwide to all stations and bases with special attention to Latin

America and Russia desks. Simple and unambiguous, but with few details other than the woman was believed to be one Sabine Gorshkova, a citizen of both Venezuela and Russia. Anyone with information was to push it up the chain without delay.

Vance had gotten the familiar flush of adrenaline when she read the name, like when she scored tickets to see a good band, or when a particular blond guy on the Eastern Europe desk said hello in the cafeteria.

One look at social media showed that most names were shared by dozens of people, but there couldn't be more than a couple of Sabine Gorshkovas in the world.

Prior to joining the Agency, Vance had attended a year at the University of Cartagena. It had been a good way to practice her Spanish and she'd met a lot of cool people. One of those people was a shy Venezuelan student named Blanca Pakulova. Considering Venezuela's communist leanings, Russian surnames were not uncommon. Blanca came from money, enough to send her to a good school in Colombia. She rarely spoke of her family, but when she did, it was of her crazy siblings—going so far as to remark that her sister would probably murder her one day. Only once, when she'd been very drunk, had Blanca mentioned this sister's name.

Sabine.

It was a long shot. "Pakulova" was a far cry from "Gorshkova," but it was enough to dig further. And

Vance did, sending cables to a classmate from the Farm whose first tour was in Bogotá. She could get Blanca's records from the university, pin down her particulars, family members, etc.

There was something there. Vance could feel it in her bones. If she could just find a parking place and make it to her desk without drowning in the rain.

She slowed to show her ID badge—blue as a CIA employee (as opposed to green for contractors)—to a uniformed security police officer. He nodded and she kept right, skirting the Old Headquarters Building—the iconic one with the giant CIA seal and Memorial Wall of stars in the foyer. The statue of Nathan Hale was on her left, just visible near the OHB. There was a statue of Harriet Tubman as well, but Vance couldn't see it from the road. She passed the Mi-17 chopper used to insert Gary Schroen's CIA JAWBREAKER team into Afghanistan just days after 9/11, and the A-12 spy plane that her father had mistakenly called an SR-71 Blackbird when he'd come in for family day.

She stopped to swipe her card at the parking gate and punched in her code to raise the entry arm. Parking for junior employees at the CIA was first come, first served. Even if you got there early it could be a hike. Newbies often joked that most of their parking spots were in West Virginia. To make matters worse, she'd forgotten her umbrella. Jason Bourne she was not.

Cell phones were verboten inside the building,

so she left hers in the glove box, gathered the plastic bag with her good shoes, and stepped into the rain with the latest issue of the **Economist** over her head.

She squished with every step by the time she made it inside, but so did most everyone else. Like the Farm, the shared hardship of things like far-flung parking bonded junior officers and analysts together.

Hannah Jensen, a slightly senior operations officer from Idaho, also on the South America desk, had a spare blouse in her cubby. It was distractingly tight across the bust and had a high collar and bow that looked like something one of Colleen's friends' mothers would have worn in the early eighties. But it was dry, so she kept her mouth shut and accepted the favor. Her own blouse would be fine by lunchtime. Hopefully she could keep the buttons from popping off Hannah's until then.

It was not uncommon to have a half-dozen tasks waiting when Vance logged in and this morning was no exception. The first three were mundane, NSA traces the branch chief wanted her to follow up.

The fourth was from her friend at Bogotá Station.

Vance read the information in the cable and then spent the morning dotting her i's and crossing her t's, conducting address and flight-manifest checks of her own before she banged out a BLUF (bottom line up front) report distilling what she'd discovered. As a junior officer, she didn't have the authority to share intelligence information directly, but forwarded her report instead to her branch chief, James Canterbury, for approval.

With no idea why the ODNI was so interested in Sabine Gorshkova, Vance decided to grab an early lunch before Mr. Canterbury found something she needed to flesh out or correct in her report. Her blouse still wasn't dry, so she wore Hannah's too-tight 1980s getup and hoped she didn't run into the hunky blond guy from the Eastern Europe desk.

The rain had stopped, and the sun had come out, so she took her salad and Dr Pepper to the court-yard to eat by the Kryptos cipher sculpture. She'd no sooner sat down than Mr. Canterbury poked his head out the door and waved her over. The lack of cell phones inside CIA facilities made it necessary for him to physically hunt her down. He was an avuncular man with salt-and-pepper hair, match-ing short-cropped beard, and a hypnotically reso-nant voice that had pitched and recruited countless foreign assets in his previous stations. Though he was Vance's boss, he acted more like her cheer-leader, offering her opportunities to shine and then pointing her acumen out to the other bosses when she did.

"I thought I might find you here," he said.

She stood the moment she saw him. If he'd made the effort to come looking for her, it must be something important.

It was.

"You'll have to eat lunch later," he said. "Dump that and come with me."

He offered no other explanation, just his normally taciturn self. Maybe a hair more tense.

"Everything okay?"

"All good," Canterbury said. "Division chief wants to see us in reference to your report." He waited for her to drop her salad in the trash and then held the door open. "Excellent work, by the way."

She thanked him. The division chief . . . Her boss's boss. That was interesting.

Alexis Glazier, chief of the division, met them in the hallway. She was a tall, slender woman, about the same age as Canterbury, but with slightly more time on the job. Her dark hair was pulled back in a businesslike updo. If central casting was seeking a sexy lady spy, Lexi Glazier would get the part. Her look could have been seen as severe but for the hint of a grin that always seemed to hang on the corners of her mouth, as if she knew a good joke that she'd decided to keep to herself.

She eyed Vance up and down for a quick moment, then said, "Colleen, right?"

"Yes, ma'am," Vance said.

Glazier's brow arched up a hair. Her grin grew wider. "Interesting choice of wardrobe."

"I got soaked coming in this morning," Vance said. "I had to borrow—"

"It's fine." Glazier turned to walk toward the

elevators, no doubt expecting Vance and Canterbury to follow. "Excellent report," she said over her shoulder.

"Thank you." Vance rocked back and forth and looked nervously at the branch chief, who smiled and motioned for her to get a little fleck of salad off her teeth as they boarded the elevator. Glazier pretended not to notice. Vance shot Canterbury a more-than-terrified grimace when Glazier swiped her ID badge and pushed the button for the seventh floor.

The division chief clocked the look and gave Vance a wink. "I got us an appointment with the DDO. He's reading your report as we speak. I'm sure he'll have questions. Just be honest. Remember, he likes color commentary, the nitty-gritty. How you came to these particular conclusions and the like."

The idea of briefing the deputy director for operations—the number two spy in the Agency—made Vance queasy enough that she swayed in place. She'd only been to the seventh floor once, and that was with a group right after she'd onboarded with her original Clandestine Service Trainee cohort.

DDO Gary Berryhill met them at the elevator, shaking each of their hands in turn. He eyed Vance's high-collared blouse with an amused chuckle and shake of his head.

"Director Canfield says to go on in," he said.

They'd no sooner entered the director's suite,

when Canfield walked out of his inner office, leather folio in hand. He acknowledged them, but spoke to his secretary.

"Becky," he said. "Do me a favor and let the detail know we're on our way down." He turned and extended his hand. "Officer Colleen Vance?"

"Yes, sir . . ."

"Absolutely stellar work," Canfield said. "Finding Sabine Gorshkova's sister and using her to pinpoint a possible location. I mean, seriously, that is a damned good job." He started toward the elevator. "You're with me."

"With you, sir?"

Canfield gave her a knowing nod. "Not all bosses at this agency would be quite so magnanimous, but Canterbury and Glazier both insisted on giving credit where credit is due and taking you with us."

"Thank you," Vance said. She looked at the branch and division chiefs in dismay. "But . . . Take me where with you?"

"The White House," Canfield said, as if it were obvious. "DNI Foley and President Ryan are both alumni of these halls. POTUS enjoys being briefed by the Agency's new blood."

Vance barely heard anything past "the White House."

"Balls . . ." she said under her breath, light-headed.

Canterbury leaned sideways, whispering to her. "Not a bad deal, getting to brief the President this early in your career."

"Can I change my clothes?" Vance felt sure she was about to throw up, or, at the very least, pop a button.

"You're fine," Chief Glazier said, nodding at the absurd blouse. "I'm sure the President won't even notice."

14

PANAMA CITY

The tip came into the San Miguelito Area B Substation while Commissioner Javier Guerra of the Policía Nacional de Panamá was locked in the muscular embrace of his mistress. Normally, his second in command, Major Gabriella Canto, would have called his driver, a junior officer named Pinto, had she wanted to reach him. Pinto customarily waited in the car during Guerra's trysts with Josefina. Today he'd been called away, so Canto had apparently decided to bother Guerra directly.

He let the phone ring.

Major Canto was a pert little pigeon. Pinto made no secret of the fact that he wouldn't mind a few minutes alone with her. Guerra was more taciturn, but pictured her often when he took his wife to bed and, on rare occasion, when he was with Josefina. The problem with Gabriella Canto was that she was forever pecking around where she did not belong. And that was making Guerra's life extraordinarily difficult.

It was always something with that woman, but never what he wanted it to be. Guerra had tried desperately to take her to bed from the moment she'd transferred to San Miguelito. Each and every time, she laughed off his advances as if he were making some hilarious joke. Anger would have been preferable to such laughter. Worse than the rebuffs, her zeal routinely got the better of her and she launched some ill-conceived investigation into businessmen or politicians who paid large sums of money to be off-limits from such scrutiny. Troublesome yes, but he **was** the commissioner and therefore had the power to quash investigations before they went anywhere.

Guerra's phone danced across the bedside table for the third time, and he rolled over quickly to turn the damned thing off. A woman as spirited as Josefina required his full concentration. He could not be bothered with work.

There were three voice messages from Canto by the time he'd finished, but Guerra didn't bother to listen to them then. She knew where he spent his siestas. If anything had been that important, she would have sent someone to come and get him—or better yet, come herself. The thought of her showing up in the same place as Josefina made him gloriously light-headed.

The commissioner was what Panamanians called

rabiblanco. Literally "white buttocks," the term referred to people with a decidedly European look. Guerra had inherited his athletic build and chiseled looks from his Spanish grandfather, a square-jawed man who had achieved some minor fame as a model in Barcelona during the 1960s. A lock of sandy hair habitually fell across his forehead, that and his ruddy complexion made him look as though he'd just been in a wrestling match. Women said he looked playful, boyish despite a thick mustache. Most women, anyway. Just not Gabriella Canto.

Guerra noted the phalanx of police sedans and Ford F-150 pickup trucks as he nosed his Lexus into his reserved parking spot.

"Gabriella Canto, you handsome little bitch . . ." he said under his breath. "What have you gotten us into now?" He called Fabian Pinto before he climbed out of the car, but got his voicemail.

He left a message. "Something's happening," he said. "You should come in."

It was standing room only inside the normally quiet San Miguelito Station. All of those gathered were dressed in tactical gear—elbow pads, ballistic rifle plates, Kevlar helmets—as if they were heading off to battle. Some of them worked for him. The majority did not.

The officers from San Miguelito jumped out of the way and let him through the moment they saw him coming. The ones from other stations moved as well. They just took their time.

Guerra shook his head at the crowd of young faces all in tactical gear when he walked into the office. Most of them had only one or two stripes, corporals. A few were slick-sleeved, with no rank. The newest, freshest faces. In Panama these enlisted personnel without rank were called **agentes**— "agents." Guerra marveled at how young they all were. And so much work in the middle of the day. This new generation seemed to have little use for a siesta. Such a loss, Guerra thought. They would probably die of stress before their time.

Major Canto and her assistant, Sergeant Alfredo "Fredi" Perez, met him at the door. Like the others, they were both dressed in tactical kit. Major Canto's hair was pulled back into a shining blue-black ponytail so she'd be able to wear a ballistic helmet. A healthy five feet seven, she was much comelier than the tactical vest and green BDUs indicated. The sight of such a beautiful piece of ass dressed like all the boys made Guerra want to spit. **Such a waste.**

The youthful Sergeant Perez, with his broad shoulders and Superman curl of black hair hanging above his eyes, stood next to her like a guard dog. Perez was Canto's assistant and principal staff officer. Like Guerra's driver, Fabian Pinto, the British police would have called Sergeant Perez Canto's driver and personal aide a bagman. Guerra hated the boy for all the time he was able to spend with Canto. Though Perez had three stripes on his collar, he seemed no older than the others who milled around the squad room. It probably took him all of ten seconds to shave.

Guerra scanned the room, frowning. "What are all these men from Rolando Martinez Station doing here? And why is everyone dressed to go out?" He gave her a lecherous grin. **"¿Vamos pal war?"**

It was Spanish for "Are we going to war?" but in Panama, it euphemistically meant "Are we going to have sex?"

Fredi Perez glowered, venturing very close to the line of insubordination with his frown of disapproval. Canto patted the sergeant's arm and let the joke slide off, shaking her head. "Not war, **patrón,**" she said. "We are going to raid some arms traffickers. They are said to be bringing weapons up from Colombia through the Darien Gap. I took the liberty of getting a warrant."

It came as no surprise to Guerra that she had drawn up the affidavit, paid a visit to the judge, and assembled the squad. She'd even recruited additional staff from Rolando Martinez, a PNP substation to the west—all without his advice or permission.

He would have to work on her more slowly, like breaking a spirited horse. Carefully. One did not force himself on a woman who carried a gun and knew how to use it as well as Gabriella Canto. Perez would be a problem, but when the time was right, Guerra would simply have him transferred to the Mosquito Gulf or some other out-of-the-way posting—or have Fabian Pinto put a knife in his belly. The hatred between the two men was palpable. In the meantime, Guerra would shower the woman with praise and heap on more and more responsibility. He would help her career, while her zeal for catching criminals would help his. If she got too close to one of his political untouchables, he would nudge her toward something more productive. One day she would come around and realize she owed him a favor.

"Well done, Major." He started for his office, summoning Canto to follow with a flick of his hand. The rest of the unit waited in the squad room, champing at the bit like racehorses, joking, and swapping stories, as young policemen do the world over. There was much talk in Panama about **botellas**—employees of a bloated government who were on the payroll but had no real assignments. These men in the squad room, dressed in ballistic vests, armed with Glock pistols and CZ Scorpion rifles, were far from "empty bottles." Along with Major Canto, their statistics made him look good.

Guerra held up an open hand for Sergeant Perez to wait outside, shut the door, and then sat down behind his desk. He thumb-typed a quick text to Pinto, telling him to come in right away, then waved at a chair when he looked up and saw Canto remained on her feet. She stayed standing, rocking slightly, shoulders moving, a boxer impatient to get in the ring.

"You look to have gathered yourself a small army, Gabriella," the commissioner said. "Are you going up against some kind of invasion?"

He retrieved two bottles of cold water from the minifridge behind him and offered one to her. She declined, instead briefing him quickly, as if he would be just as eager as she was to get moving when he had the information.

"One of my informants, **patrón**," Canto said. "She personally saw the stockpile of weapons and ammunition inside the residence less than two hours ago."

"Very well," Guerra said. He took another drink. Afternoons with Josefina always left him feeling dehydrated. He wiped his mustache with the back of his arm.

Trafficking of all kinds—guns, drugs, and humans—was a constant problem in a country that was quite literally the gateway between two oceans. It never stopped. It was no surprise that Major Canto with all her bullheaded determination had rooted out a smuggling operation. He flicked his hand toward the door, dismissing her.

"I'll be along in a few minutes."

"Of course, **patrón**." Canto turned to go. "I'll leave the address with your secretary."

"Where is it?"

"Your old patrol area," she said. "A run-down slum house on Avenue X."

Guerra felt as if a cold hand had gripped him by the throat. He sat up a little straighter.

"Rolando Martinez Station should be the ones to handle that area."

"That's why they are here, **patrón,**" Canto said. "It is my informant, but in their zone. Now, if you will excuse me . . ."

Guerra clenched his fists, out of sight behind the desk, resisting the urge to strangle this woman.

He nearly turned over his chair scrambling to his feet. "On second thought," he said. "I should come along with you. I know the alleys and apartments of these slums like the back of my hand."

"Very good, sir," Canto said, though if she was happy, her face did not show it.

"One moment," he said, clearing his husky voice. "Who issued the warrant?"

"Judge Vasquez."

Guerra hid his curse under a concerned smile. The fool Vasquez was unbribable, which caused no end of headaches for Guerra's friends—and extra legwork for Guerra when he had to sort things out.

"Who is this informant of yours?"

"A local prostitute," Canto said. "She has always been reliable."

Guerra rubbed his chin, racking his brain for some way around this.

"Perhaps we should get her back inside the residence one more time. You and I both know what a stickler for details Judge Vasquez can be."

"With all due respect, **patrón,** this poor girl was afraid they were going to kill her the first time.

Prostitutes do not return unbidden to the . . . scene of the crime, so to speak. At least not unless they are called."

"Then we should wait for them to call her again."

"We have the warrant now, **patrón.**"

"I am curious as to why they did not kill this woman the first time?"

"The weapons were covered," Canto said. "They were not aware she saw them."

"Even so," Guerra said. "According to you, two hours have passed since she glimpsed these supposed weapons. They could have been moved. I do not want to burst into an empty house and make an enemy of Judge Vasquez—"

"All good, Commissioner," Canto said. "We had agents watching the residence fifteen minutes after my informant came out. They have kept the place under constant surveillance. There has been no movement."

Guerra forced a smile. "Good work," he mumbled.

He thought briefly of calling ahead with a warning, but that left too much to chance. Gabriella Canto was a dog with a bone when it came to investigations. The men inside the residence were better armed and better trained than the agents outside. Apart from the monumental mistake of not killing the prostitute after she'd been inside the apartment, their operation was near flawless. Any attempt to raid them would be a bloodbath with heavy losses to Major Canto and her men.

Still, PNP agents were no slouches when it came to armed confrontation. There was too great a chance they would bring down one or more of the men inside. It was possible they might even take one into custody. If that happened, Major Canto would pull phone records.

He tried Pinto again. He had a burner phone with which he could call ahead. Still nothing but voicemail.

Guerra cursed under his breath. It was far too late to call off the operation without raising Canto's suspicion. Deep in his gut he felt a familiar flutter that told him something was about to go terribly wrong.

"Gabriella," he said. "I am impressed with how you lead from the front."

"Always, **patrón,**" she said.

Guerra gave a sad smile. These people did not play games. Gabriella Canto would be one of the first in the door—and one of the first to die. He glanced up at Sergeant Fredi Perez, who waited outside the door for his master like a lapdog. With any luck that son of a whore would eat some lead.

Jorge Arias smelled the woman as soon as he entered the apartment. He'd been out, checking on the other cells, making certain they had what they needed before returning to this self-imposed hellhole to finish what he had started—making the bombs needed for this operation. This place was a pigsty, a far cry from his regular accommodations with most of the others. It was a wonder he could smell anything beyond stale cigarettes and the **hojaldre**—Panamanian fried dough—the men cooked up and ate with every meal.

One more day of this shit and he could return to the hotel and shower in a tub without anything growing in it.

He drew the Browning Hi-Power from beneath the tail of his loose cotton shirt and held it low at his side. These were not men at whom you brandished a weapon unless you intended to pull the trigger—quickly.

Gustavo, from El Salvador, slumped sullenly in the corner and gestured toward the front door with a sweating brown bottle of Balboa beer.

"La puta se fue," he mumbled. The whore went away. He shook his head as if he was just as upset about her visit as Arias.

That was doubtful. Arias would have shot them all if the noise wouldn't have drawn so much attention.

"And you let her walk out of here? Alive?"

The men nodded.

Santiago, one of the two Guatemalans, gave a resigned shrug. "She saw nothing, boss."

Arias scanned the room. There was nothing incriminating in view, if you did not count the squalor these men lived in.

"You had better hope you are right," he said.

He sat down at the table, shoving a plastic plate of half-eaten arepa and fried plantain onto the floor with his forearm—to show his displeasure as much as to clear a space for him to work.

His skills were what had gotten him here. That, and the fact that he was in charge of all the Camarilla men on the ground in Panama and he believed wholeheartedly in leading from the front.

A former explosive ordnance technician, Arias had deployed twice to Iraq with the Plus Ultra Brigade representing Spain in the coalition forces. He was accustomed to working in austere conditions, but this was ridiculous. Four grown men crowded into a small apartment with no air-conditioning and damned little ventilation, all sharing the same filthy bathroom. Tomás and Santiago, the big Guatemalans, did everything as a set, like book-ends. Gustavo kept to himself. The man hardly said a word, leaving Arias with his own bloody thoughts during most of each visit. Arias preferred it that way.

The men were all outsiders, mercenaries in a country that seemed overrun with police who did the job of civilian law enforcement and protecting the border.

What kind of shithole country didn't even have an army?

He looked forward to the day when Operation JAMAICA was behind him.

The fourth man living in the apartment was a

local from the slums of San Miguelito. Arias didn't know his real name. Everyone called him Changa because his big head and shortish arms made him look like a South American mole cricket. He knew the streets and, more important, the habits of the cops who patrolled them. A mechanic by trade, Changa now found himself making more money than he'd ever made in his life, just for watching and keeping quiet. Unbeknownst to the odd little mole cricket, his severance package would be a one-way trip to the bottom of Panama Bay, but so far, he was as blissfully unaware as a puppy—and just as devoted. It was a shame, Arias thought, but hard decisions were the brother of war—and war was exactly where they were.

Arias wiped the perspiration off his brow with a handkerchief and leaned back, lighting a Fortuna cigarette. It was a guilty pleasure—but in his line of work he was certain the tar and nicotine would never have an opportunity to kill him.

Soon, this would all be over. Shit, as the Americans liked to say, was about to get real.

Arias took a satisfying drag on the Fortuna and then gingerly rubbed his bum knee, knocking a bit of ash onto his jeans. Years of heavy-ruck marches and too many fistfights had beaten the hell out of his body. He'd risen from logistics and transport to a leadership role within the organization, doing double duty manufacturing the most important explosive devices. The promotion was an opportunity, yes, but an opportunity fraught with danger. If JAMAICA were to fail, like the captain of a ship, he would shoulder the blame. Someone else might be at fault for, say, inviting a prostitute inside an apartment filled with weapons and bombs . . . But that did not matter. Arias would bear the responsibility. The Spaniard did not accept failure. There was no doubt in Arias's mind that if he or anyone on his team failed, he would end up like Changa, at the bottom of someplace dark.

Arias chuckled to himself. Sooner or later, everyone ended up someplace dark. He'd vowed long ago to enjoy himself on the way there.

He felt a sudden chill run up his spine despite the oppressive heat. The air grew suddenly heavy. The squeal of bicycles and chatter of pedestrians on the street below fell quiet.

He stubbed out his cigarette on the wooden table, scarred from others who'd done the same thing a thousand times before him, then drew his Hi-Power again and set it on the blackened wood.

Across the small room, Changa knelt on the threadbare couch peering out the dusty curtains like a curious dog.

He reached for the short Kalashnikov on the cushion beside him, at the same time whispering a warning.

"Babylon! Babylon!"

Police.

A half a breath later the flimsy apartment door flew off its hinges, slamming into Tomás and knocking him backward. The Guatemalan crawled for his rifle. A flash-bang rolled through the glaringly bright opening and landed beside the man's head.

Arias had just enough time to open his mouth and close his eyes before it went off.

Uniformed officers in full body armor poured into the room, shouting, weapons up, heavy boots tromping on the wooden floor, all surreally backlit in the smoky room by the open door behind them.

Blinded by the explosive flash, Changa ducked his head, but foolishly hung on to his rifle. He sent a convulsive and useless burst into the wall. The neighbor screamed, probably hit by one of the rounds, but Changa, cut to ribbons by the first two officers through the door, never heard it.

Tomás, probably unconscious from the concussion of the grenade going off so close to his head, flapped his hand weakly toward his rifle. The movement was enough to earn him a half-dozen bullets to the center of his chest.

Santiago dropped to his knees, one hand clamped to his ear. A Glock pistol dangled from the other. The officers gunned him down as well.

Gustavo tried to run for the back stairs, Uzi in hand. A nine-millimeter bullet from a PNP Scorpion tore away a chunk of his calf, causing him to stumble and spin mid-step. He fell on his back, firing a rattling burst from the Uzi as he went down.

One of the officers caught a round in the center vest. Another got a glancing round off his Kevlar helmet. It wobbled him, but didn't take him down.

A withering hail of return fire turned Gustavo into burger.

All the while, three of the officers, one of them female, kept their weapons trained on Arias, who raised both hands high over his head. He'd attempted to sweep the Browning Hi-Power off the table with his elbow as he'd lifted his arms, but missed. From the look in the young officers' eyes, the proximity of that pistol was going to be a problem. Gunfire inevitably spawned more gunfire, especially with the young and inexperienced.

Fortunately for Jorge Arias, these young officers were led by an experienced commander, the third one in the stack of eight that entered the apartment. The insignia of a PNP major in the center of her helmet along with her blood type.

CZ Scorpion to her shoulder, she aimed directly at Arias's face and ordered him in no uncertain terms to move away from the pistol with his hands up. She was steady but direct, showing no hint of nerves or room for negotiation.

After the dust had settled, a man in perfectly bloused boots and the camouflage uniform of a police commissioner strode through the bright light of the demolished doorway—like a guardian angel.

Arias kept his hands up, but shifted his gaze to the new arrival and relaxed by degree with every step closer the man took. His savior had arrived. He mouthed the name in relief.

"PULGA . . ."

15

Commissioner Guerra caught the glint of recognition in Jorge Arias's eyes. Idiot. Canto was sure to have noticed. One of the men on the ground choked, surely dead judging from the blood and gore spilling from the side of his neck. Agonal breathing. It was enough to draw the other officers' attention away—only for a split second, but long enough for Guerra to shoot Arias twice above the bridge of his nose. Dirty cop or not, he was an excellent marksman with his Glock.

Major Canto jumped at the report, deafening in the enclosed space. She stayed aimed in, trying to work out what had just happened.

"The man moved for his pistol," Guerra snapped. "Frankly, Gabriella, I'm surprised at you for not firing on the man yourself."

"I . . ."

"That is quite all right, my dear," Guerra said. "Do not scold yourself. You will learn over time.

But remember, it only takes a blink for an evil man like this to pick up a gun and kill you."

Sergeant Perez helped other officers clear and search the rest of the tiny apartment, calling out when they found the Uzis and what they believed to be two explosive devices. Major Canto ordered everyone to stay off their radios rather than risk detonation and had two junior officers handcuff the downed men. Smart, Guerra thought. Far too many good agents had been killed by outlaws who were not quite dead enough.

A senior sergeant from Rolando Martinez Station called up from the bottom of the stairs.

"The basement appears to be clear, but there are more connecting doors. This place is a rat's nest . . ."

Canto started to speak, but Guerra cut her off.

"That's enough, Sergeant!" he snapped. "There are bombs here. It is time to back out and bring in explosive ordnance disposal."

Guerra had to fight to keep from sighing with relief when the sergeant and the men with him trooped back up the stairs.

Canto nodded. "Yes, **patrón,** that is wise." She gave the order, then stooped next to the dead man nearest the door. Shirtless and handcuffed behind his back, he lay on his face. Canto nodded to the tattoo above his left biceps—a flaming sword and maroon beret.

"Kaibiles," Sergeant Perez whispered.

The RM sergeant nudged another of the dead with the toe of his boot. "This one as well."

"Guatemalan Special Forces?" Canto said. "Who are these people—"

A string of curses came from the back bedroom. A baby-faced agent came out carrying a coffee-stained manila file folder.

"What is it?" Guerra asked, though he suspicioned he already knew.

Major Canto crowded in to look at the folder. She, too, cursed, then she looked up at Guerra with a pained expression. "It is a map, **patrón,** of the Palacio de las Garzas. The home of His Excellency."

Perez took the folder from the young agent and flipped through the contents. "Look at this, Major," he said. "There are photographs of President Botero's limousine . . . Do you think—"

"Stop it!" Guerra snapped. "Do not jump to conclusions."

Canto looked up at him, incredulous. "Machine guns, bombs, and photographs of the target. This is not a jump, **patrón.** This is evidence of a plot." She glared hard, daring him to say otherwise.

"Relax, Gabriella," Guerra said. "This is most excellent work. We will get this information to the director general of SPI."

SPI was Servicio de Protección Institucional— the Institutional Protection Service—an umbrella organization that oversaw, among other things, the Presidential Protection Group.

Guerra continued. "I would not be surprised if His Excellency President Botero commends you personally."

"Thank you, **patrón,**" Canto said, waving away the compliment. "But I do not care about credit."

"This I know," Guerra said. "Now, it is dangerous here. Pull our people out at once."

She braced. This was the second time he'd given the order and men still milled about the room.

"You heard Commissioner Guerra," she barked, finally appearing to see the wisdom of his thinking. She turned as if to go, but paused to stoop down and study the man with two bullet holes above what was left of his nose.

"Who is this man?" she asked.

Guerra bristled, maybe a little too much.

"How should I know. Some idiot gun smuggler with a wish to die at the hands of the police."

"And an assassin," Perez chimed in.

Canto froze in place, transfixed, as she studied the corpse. "It is only that . . ."

"What is it, Major?" Again, Guerra found himself being much too defensive for the situation. He took a deep calming breath. "I trust your judgment. What is on your mind, my dear?"

"Did it not seem as though this man recognized you, **patrón**?"

Guerra's stomach lurched, but he gave what he hoped was a disinterested shrug.

"He must have thought I was someone else. I've

never seen him before. Now, as much as I commend you for this investigation, I am ordering you for the final time, get everyone out of here at once!" Then, loud enough for everyone to hear, "Remember, this is extremely sensitive. Do not speak of it to your friends, your families, or the press. Lives are at stake. If information on this matter leaks, I will find out who did it and I will have your balls. Understood?"

A murmur of consent went around the apartment.

"Now," Guerra ordered. "Out! All of you. I will call in the bomb technicians to disable these explosives."

A river of sweat dripped down the commissioner's spine. What a flaming bag of shit this had all turned into! His job was to prevent this very thing, and now an overzealous bitch had probably gotten him killed. He took another deep breath, steadying himself. He knew there was a truck full of explosives parked in a garage through the door downstairs. If he could get word up the chain, then they could come and drive it out the back. The sergeant from Rolando Martinez Station was correct. This entire place was a rat's nest of interconnected shanties, garages, and warehouses. If he saved the truck and its contents, perhaps that would atone for his oversight.

Canto cleared her throat as she moved toward the door, clicking her canine teeth the way she did when she was trying to solve some riddle.

"And what did that one mean by **'pulga'**?" she asked Perez.

Guerra interrupted before the sergeant could answer.

"It did sound like **pulga**," he said, doing everything but physically shoving her out the door to get her to leave. "But that makes no sense. Perhaps we are mistaken, and it was something else."

"No," Canto said matter-of-factly. "I heard him clearly. That is exactly what he said. **'Pulga . . .'**"

Guerra shrugged. "Perhaps," he said. "But a strange thing to say at such a moment. Please tell me when you figure out the mystery."

Guerra knew, of course. While not actually a member of the Camarilla, he was an inside man. He and Pinto and a handful of others like him were being well compensated by their employers. Very well compensated. Unfortunately, they'd given Guerra the odd code name LA PULGA.

The Flea.

He raised an eyebrow and gave Canto a wan smile that he hoped said he was as fascinated by her mystery as she was. This little bitch was going to stick her nose somewhere that would get her killed. The Spaniard would probably make him do it— if they didn't kill him first.

16

CIA operations officer Colleen Vance dug a thumbnail into the palm of her hand in an attempt to stave off her growing panic. Director Canfield's limo pulled past the North Portico toward another door near the Press Briefing Room.

This was really happening.

A uniformed Secret Service officer at a podium inside the entrance greeted Director Canfield with a smile, but looked at Glazier, Canterbury, and Vance like they owed her money until she found their names on her list. She issued **A** visitor badges and then, with a nod to Canfield, said, "They're expecting you."

Vance shuffled along the narrow hallways, at once overwhelmed by the grandeur of actually being in the White House and struck by how small the building seemed inside.

The furnishings were plush and ornate, but the ceilings hung much lower than they appeared on television or in movies. Historic paintings of the likes of Theodore Roosevelt and Dwight Eisenhower adorned the walls, along with large photographs of military helicopters and fighter jets. There was a bend toward the Marine Corps—which made sense considering the President's past service. What Vance did not see were numerous hero shots of President Ryan.

A twenty-by-twenty-four photograph of Ryan approaching Marine One on the South Lawn struck her in particular. The President was not the focus of the photo. That honor went to the straight-backed young Marine crew chief braced at attention in front of his gleaming white-top helicopter. The fact that President Ryan didn't have to be the center of the universe made Vance like the man all the more.

And made her exponentially more nervous to meet him.

Canfield led the way down the steps past the nondescript door marked W-16—the Secret Service offices directly underneath the Oval. He hung a right and then a left to take them down another set of steps past the Navy Mess to the Situation Room. Here, another Secret Service agent checked yet another list before keying them inside.

If Vance had been overwhelmed before, setting foot in the rarified air of the CEMENT MIXER made it hard to breathe. Everyone who was anyone in the executive branch of the United States government sat at the long oval table under an array of video monitors and world clocks. The vice president; Director Foley; Secretaries Adler and Burgess;

the national security adviser; the chairman of the Joint Chiefs, General Vogel; the attorney general; the director of the FBI . . .

Director Canfield took a seat at the table.

Chief Glazier nodded to the chairs along the wall behind Canfield. "We're in the number two seats," she said.

"That puts me in the number four or five seat," Vance said, working hard to keep her face from twitching.

"Don't sell yourself short," Canterbury said.

Her nerves turned to dread. "Wait," she whispered. "I thought we were going to brief . . . I mean . . . Is this entire meeting just for my information?"

Chief Glazier put a hand on Vance's forearm. "No," she said. "We've been summoned to an already scheduled meeting, but you're definitely on the agenda."

"When the President calls on you," Canterbury said, "speak clearly and give your honest assessment. Don't be afraid to stick to your guns. Our job is to give him intelligence, so he can make informed decisions."

Vance heard "When the President calls on you . . ." After that, it was nothing but the whoosh of blood in her ears. She'd just sat down, when a commotion drew her attention toward the door. Everyone stood as President Ryan came in and took his spot at the head of the table.

He was tall and slender with an easy walk that said he was comfortable in his own skin. There was a surety about him that said, **I know what I'm doing. Follow me.**

It would have been calming had Vance not been so terrified.

"Be seated," Ryan said. Then, to Canfield, "Jay, I understand you have some new information."

"We do, Mr. President," the director said. "Colleen Vance, one of our newer ops officers, attended a year of university in Colombia. She's—"

"Is she here?" Ryan craned his head around the room.

"She is, sir," Canfield said.

"Let's hear it from her, then," Ryan said.

A prodding elbow in the ribs from Glazier and Vance got to her feet.

"Thank you, Mr. President," she said.

Ryan leaned back in his chair, hands folded together at his chest as he listened intently to the beginning of her brief, like a father hearing about a good report card or a school project gone well.

"So I understand," Ryan said at length, "you've met this Blanca Pakulova?"

"Yes, Mr. President."

"And she mentioned a 'crazy' sister named Sabine?"

"I only heard her use the name once," Vance said. "When she was intoxicated."

"But you've not been able to find any official records stating Blanca has a sister?"

"Yes, sir," Vance said. "I mean, no, sir. I mean, there aren't any records to that effect."

"So your hypothesis hinges on . . . erasures?"

"Yes." Vance swallowed hard. "A Cyrillic **G** looks like an upside-down **L,** which is easy enough to turn into a **P,** which looks like a pi symbol."

Ryan nodded. **"Vy gavareete pa russki?"**

"What?" Vance stammered. "I mean, no, I don't speak Russian. I had to look up the Cyrillic online."

"I see," Ryan said, nodding again. "Please continue."

Vance felt every eye in the room boring holes in her, laughing silently at her foolish grasping at straws, not to mention her 1980s mom-blouse.

She dug the thumbnail into her palm again.

"An online search revealed the **o** and **r** in **Gorshkova** are more difficult to change into the **a** and **k** of **Pakulova.** My counterpart at Bogotá Station got me a trove of scanned university records, some of them from when Blanca was first admitted to the school, two years before I met her. I found a rental receipt for racquetball gear at the university gym that shows an erasure that I believe is a Cyrillic **G** that was overwritten as a roman **P.** An application for a parking pass that same year shows an instance where Blanca apparently started to write what looks like another surname beginning with Cyrillic **G-o** and then overwrote it with her pen to read **P-a-kulova** in roman letters."

Ryan tapped his fingers on the table while he scanned the report in front of him.

"So that's it?" he asked.

"Yes," Vance said. "But it's—"

Canterbury cleared his throat behind her.

"Yes," she said again. "That's it."

Ryan looked up suddenly and turned to Director Canfield. "I have a feeling we'll be seeing more of Officer Vance's work in the future." Then to Vance, smiling broadly. "Excellent work, Colleen . . ."

He said other things, too, but none of it registered.

The President of the United States had complimented her effort, called her by her first name in front of a Situation Room crammed with political notables, and hadn't said a word about her ludicrous blouse.

17

It was a wonderful thing, freedom of the press. In his own country, the man wearing the backward Washington Nationals ball cap would surely have been approached by the secret police, but here in the United States of America he could stand at the iron fence with a telephoto lens all day long and photograph the comings and goings of White House visitors. The President rarely showed his face out front, keeping out of the eye—and sight picture—of the general public by leaving via Marine One from the South Lawn. Visitors like Director of National Intelligence Mary Pat Foley were more visible.

The man in the backward cap took photos of Foley leaving the building. Her Secret Service protection detail was relatively small, consisting of a limo and a follow Suburban. Fewer than ten agents. There were other vehicles, too, behind Foley's, but the man recognized one of the men as the CIA director. That meant all of them were spooks, including the girl with big boobs whose clothes looked like she bought them from Goodwill. The man took photos of them as well. It never hurt to have a list of CIA bastards on file.

Foley's motorcade left first, coming through the E Street barricades onto Seventeenth about the time the man in the backward cap made it to his car, a retired taxi that blended in with traffic.

He fell in four car lengths behind the motorcade, watching, taking notes on the way they maneuvered, obeying traffic lights, driving the speed limit. Still, the agents looked capable, missing little as they kept a keen eye on everyone around them. They knew they were a small detail and seemed to compensate by being overly aware. If they were running any countersurveillance agents, the man in the hat didn't see them.

He fell back another car length and punched a number into his encrypted phone.

Sabine Gorshkova picked up on the second ring. "Talk to me!" she demanded in Spanish, her voice husky, forced. She always sounded that way, like she was bracing herself to take a punch in the stomach or trying to make her voice deeper than it naturally was.

"What you want me to do is possible," the man in the hat said in English. He spoke passable Spanish, but lengthy conversations in anything but Russian or English gave him a headache. "She has a great deal of security—"

"My brother had security!" Gorshkova snapped, switching to English. "And yet Mary Pat Foley was able to order his murder."

"Yes, of course," the man said. "There is no question that I can get to her, but—"

"I do not want you to merely get to her," Gorshkova said. "I want her to suffer. What I want is for her to know that this order to end her is from me, the sister of Joaquín Fernando Gorshkov."

"I understand," the man said. "And I **can** do that, but it will take significantly more planning, more time."

The line fell silent for a moment, then, "She is married, no?"

"She is." The Russian glanced at the file folder on the seat beside him. It was empty now, the contents burned in a hotel parking lot, but he'd memorized the information. "Her husband was once the director of the CIA, but he is an old man now. He kisses her goodbye in the mornings wearing a ratty robe and then greets her at the door when she returns home."

"How sweet," Gorshkova spat. "Perhaps you can shoot him in the heart while he is in the bathrobe."

"I suppose," the Russian said. "But your message would be—"

"Never mind," Gorshkova said. "That would be too quick."

"I am sure they have an alarm system," the Russian said. "But that will not pose a problem . . . And, as I said, he is an old man. He will not pose a problem, either."

"Excellent," Gorshkova said. "I don't much care how you do it, but kill him in such a way that when she finds his body, she will feel his pain. I would prefer you use a hammer."

"Very well," the Russian said. "I'll work up an entry plan and let you know before I go in." He turned right on Twenty-Third, letting Mary Pat Foley's motorcade continue on toward Highway 66 and her home in Leesburg unmolested . . . for now.

"I want photographs of his body when you are done," Gorshkova said.

"Of course. They will be in your inbox within the week."

The man in the Washington Nationals cap gave a silent chuckle. A hammer . . . photographs . . . Sabine Gorshkova was insane, but she paid well. To the Russian, that was all that mattered.

18

Chilly Edwards's iPhone first alerted him to the possibility of a tail while he was waiting in baggage claim on the lower level of Terminal 2 at Washington's Reagan National Airport.

He would have preferred to travel with just a carry-on, but since he didn't know what he was getting into, he decided to bring his pistol. A Texas cop to the bone, if he was wearing pants there was a one hundred percent chance he'd have a knife and ninety-nine he'd have a handgun—except when he flew. Though technically still an Abilene police officer, he'd wanted to bring his favorite sidearm, a Colt Combat Commander. The Texas Ranger assigned to Taylor County was fond of saying that God made that little hollow in the small of a man's back because it fit a .45 so perfectly.

When Mr. Chavez learned he carried a Glock 43X as a BUG, or backup gun, on duty, he politely but firmly suggested Chilly bring that.

Cop or not, Chilly wasn't a Fed, so he couldn't

fly armed without a written pre-authorization letter from the chief of his department, which he did not have. Still, checking a firearm at the airport was a straightforward affair, especially in Texas, where airport staff was accustomed to the paperwork. The hardest part was leaving his handgun to the baggage handlers, even though it was locked in a hard case inside his luggage.

Oddly, after all the security checks getting it turned in, his bag popped up on the regular carousel with all the non-gun-bearing luggage when he arrived at Washington National.

He'd just spotted his suitcase on the carousel, when his iPhone sent him a message—the same set of Apple AirPods had been nearby since his layover in Dallas. The phone wanted to know if he would like to pair with this device.

Weird.

Then he saw the girl.

White female, mid- to late twenties—about Chilly's age—forest-green fleece, brunette ponytail spilling out the back of a nondescript faded green ball cap. A pair of Randolph aviators hid her eyes against the low sun blasting through the windows to the west. He'd first spotted her in Dallas.

The Hendley Associates' travel office had made his reservations and inexplicably put him in Dallas for a five-hour layover. He'd had the chance to spot a lot of people. It was given as gospel among his brethren at the Abilene Police Department that

God had blessed Dallas, Texas, with more than its fair share of handsome women—and this one in the green fleece and ball cap bore witness to that truth. She was the kind of interesting-cute that made guys notice her.

There were plenty of other flights leaving for D.C., but Mr. Chavez had given strict, if sparse, instructions not to deviate from the flights assigned by the travel office. Everything seemed normal, until the last moment of the call, when Chavez had casually reminded him to make certain he wasn't followed at any point of this trip.

Countersurveillance wasn't high on the training priorities for Abilene PD, but his new boss's cryptic warning had sent Chilly to the internet for two solid weeks, attempting to learn everything he could about the subject. He was smart enough to know a bunch of YouTube videos weren't going to make him a surveillance expert, but in the end, he made peace with it. He **was** a sniper, and snipers paid attention to the smallest details—like the intensity of this young woman's blue eyes while she ate her sandwich in the DFW terminal. She'd not paid attention to him then, which was no surprise. They'd boarded the same flight, so of course she'd have baggage to pick up.

He put her out of his mind, but ducked into a stall in the men's room to retrieve the slimline Glock and an inside-the-pants holster from his bag.

He reloaded the magazine, slipped it quietly into the gun, then broke a cardinal rule when running a semiauto and "rode" the slide forward, easing it into battery. There was no mistaking the sound of a round being chambered the correct way, and he didn't want any attention from airport police. The pistol and the holster went inside his waistband over his right kidney—right where it was supposed to be. Only the grip protruded above the waist of his khakis. He covered the whole shebang with a brown Schott 530 leather jacket.

The process took a few minutes inside the cramped stall. Even so, Green Fleece and her AirPods somehow ended up behind him on the escalator to the Metro platform across from the terminal.

They waited together, ignoring each other on the breezy train platform, both apparently going the same direction, north, toward Crystal City, the Pentagon, and Arlington Cemetery. She paid little attention to Chilly, but he caught her shooting a furtive glance at a fit middle-aged dude studying an area map at the other end of the platform.

This guy had been on their flight as well. Chilly put him around six foot and a buck ninety, wiry like a distance runner, but old enough to be someone's dad. He wore a black canvas vest over a checked flannel shirt. A dark wool beanie hid most of his hair, but he had a closely cropped beard. He had only a rolling carry-on. When Green Fleece glanced at the guy, he met her eye for a fleeting moment, then shifted his gaze to study Chilly, overtly, as if sizing him up.

Chilly returned the look, but only for a moment. He'd decided a long time ago that there were some opponents he could take hand to hand, others he'd prefer not to face without a baseball bat, and still others that would require his .308 from two hundred yards. The challenge in this guy's eyes said he'd been in more than one life-or-death situation, and probably enjoyed them.

Chilly's law enforcement training told him to make contact with a threat, shine the bright light of day on it. He had a feeling that tactic wasn't going to work in this new gig. He found himself happy he'd taken the time to retrieve the handgun—and now resisted the urge to touch it, just to make sure it was still there. The look between Black Beanie and Green Fleece was momentary, but there seemed little doubt that they were working together.

Shit. There had been a lot of stuff in the training videos about the benefits of male-female surveillance teams.

Chilly told himself this was just a test. Right? Mr. Chavez had been clear that the work they did was dangerous and that Chilly would likely make a fair number of enemies along the way—but there hadn't been time for that.

He checked his watch for the third time in five

minutes, closed his eyes, and took a deep breath, willing himself to calm down.

Flat melon-sized lights flush with the platform began to flash and the Yellow Line train screamed in from the south, squealing to a stop. Apart from a handful of people getting off with their luggage, the train was virtually empty. There were plenty of empty seats, but Chilly got on and stood with his back to the opposite set of doors. He only had one stop.

The guy in the black beanie got on the next car back. Green Fleece walked down the platform toward the escalators. For a moment Chilly thought she'd decided to wait for another train. Instead, she boarded farther up, putting Chilly in between her and Black Beanie.

Well, hell . . . They **were** working together.

Chilly briefly entertained the thought of staying aboard the train past his stop. Trouble was, he'd only studied maps of the area around Crystal City, where his hotel and the meeting were located. This was his first time to D.C. If he continued toward downtown, he'd be putting himself in an un-familiar area—and these two would know he was onto them.

The next stop was the Crystal City underground, which, according to Chilly's study, led to assorted shops, eateries, and several hotels, including the Gateway Marriott, where the travel office had him staying for the next two weeks until he found a place to live. Mr. Chavez had warned him that in addition to Amazon employees that had all but taken over this area of Virginia, the Marriott would be chock-full of federal agents from myriad bureaus and departments and beaucoup military folks detailed to the Pentagon, which was only two Metro stops away. It was a safe hotel as far as petty crime, but all the government clientele meant that he was highly surveilled by foreign intelligence services. Mr. Clark had said little during any of their meetings, but had warned Chilly in all seriousness to keep his curtains drawn and not to engage in any activities in his room that he would not want an enemy government to get on video.

That was comforting.

Now Green Fleece and Black Beanie had him pinched in the train car between them. This was probably a gut check. Spies? Really? No way.

Moments after the train ducked below ground level, a garbled voice that sounded like it was talking into a wall announced Crystal City Station.

Chilly stepped off the car without looking back, took the escalator up a level, and swiped his Metro card to get through the turnstile. He didn't know if it was the stuff they used on the trains or the high percentage of crisp business suits, but the whole place smelled like the inside of a dry cleaner's. What he did know was that Green Fleece and Black Beanie were still behind him.

Another much longer escalator took him up to the

mall level, past a couple of buskers playing violins and an assortment of posters advertising weapons systems from Raytheon and other defense contractors. Chilly paused for a split second at the top. The Gateway was to the right through the doors and down the hall to the left. He took the double doors, holding them open for an elderly couple behind him. No sense in letting his Texas upbringing slip, even if he was being pursued by foreign agents. He caught a glance of Green Fleece thirty feet back. He thought of holding the door for her, but decided to draw the line there.

A set of three steps just inside the double doors led him up to Dunkin' Donuts level. He decided to stop at a small six-stool sushi shop on his right for a quick bite and see if his tails continued past or waited. This was new and he needed a minute to figure out his next move.

Green Fleece came by first. She'd taken off her aviators and her eyes focused straight ahead as she walked, lost in thought. Chilly relaxed by a degree. Maybe she wasn't following him after all. Black Beanie passed next, scanning, covering a lot of ground with his long legs. He registered the girl, nodded to himself, and then kept looking until he saw Chilly. He spoke into the mic on a pair of white earbuds dangling from his ears, and then picked up his pace for a few yards, ducking into a small art shop. He obviously planned to browse until Chilly passed him again.

What the hell . . . ?

Chilly told the chef he'd decided on boxed sushi instead and bought a California roll for the road, stuffing it in the pocket of his jacket to keep his hands free.

He passed the art shop, watching every reflective surface he could for Black Beanie. The hallway ended in a T, where Chilly made a left, going through another set of double doors toward the Gateway. It was a long, ramp-like tiled hall lined with mirrors and devoid of any shops. A sterile area prior to entering the Marriott hotel. He caught sight of Green Fleece again when he made another left, past a rental car kiosk and into the spacious hotel lobby. She stood by one of the thick pillars in front of the registration desk. Maybe she was waiting for someone. Maybe that someone was Black Beanie.

Green Fleece caught his reflection in a glass information sign alongside the pillar. She waited until he passed before heading straight for the main entrance, ducking past the valet stand to disappear around the corner, heading north on the sidewalk.

Chilly glanced behind him. Black Beanie was nowhere to be seen. Was that good or bad? Chilly was a newbie at this. For all he knew, Black Beanie was still out there, just wearing some kickass **Mission Impossible** disguise. He checked his watch, then cursed under his breath. He seriously needed to stop doing that. He knew what time it was.

After ten minutes of second-guessing every decision and possible outcome, he went ahead and checked in at registration. Rather than going to his room, he left the bag with the bellman, and then retraced his steps into the Crystal City underground, falling in behind a half-dozen Air Force officers in blue Class A uniforms.

He made his way past the underground shops, winding through the river of commuters moving between office and Metro. It was still relatively early, well before rush hour. He popped out on street level to the buzz of traffic and early-evening joggers. It was easy to get turned around in the maze beneath the city and he paused for a moment to get his bearings. This was Crystal Drive. A commercial airliner landing from the north above the trees told him the airport was across the road to his right.

There was no sign of either Green Fleece or Black Beanie.

The Hyatt Regency, where he was supposed to meet Mr. Chavez, was fifteen blocks south. He had twenty minutes. Doable if he picked up the pace—and everything went perfectly.

It did not.

Five blocks later, just past Ted's Montana Grill, he nearly ran into Green Fleece as she came around the corner where Twenty-Third Street met Crystal Drive.

Chilly Edwards, the unflappable APD sniper who

could shoot the nuts off a horsefly at two hundred yards, stutter-stepped—and looked at his watch.

Instead of trying to avoid contact, Green Fleece marched straight to him, blue eyes locked on like a laser-guided missile.

Her voice was much huskier than he'd expected. "Listen up, asshole," she said.

He didn't have to feign surprise.

"Yeah, I'm talking to you," she said, a touch of the South in her words. Not a twang, but buttery and smooth. Sexy voice or not, she was still a threat.

Chilly shot a quick glance behind him, searching for an escape. This woman looked like she might have a bag o' blades or some other weapon hidden somewhere in her suitcase, which still roared behind her as she dragged it along the sidewalk. He'd lost sight of her since she left the hotel and there was no telling how many compatriots she was working with.

He braced for a physical attack, but she stopped ten feet out. She let go of the carry-on, stepping sideways so it wasn't directly behind her. Left hand up slightly as if making a point, right hand at her side, she stepped back on her right foot, body bladed relative to Chilly. A fighting stance. Her voice was low, resonant, just loud enough to hear over the passing cars.

"You got some kind of problem with me?" she said.

"I don't even know you," Chilly said. He had to concentrate to keep her hands in view and not get sucked into focusing on her eyes.

"Damned right you don't know me," she said. "Since we are not acquainted, then why do I see you every time I turn around?"

"I—"

"Get lost!" She stomped her foot like she was scaring off a dog. "I mean it. Beat feet or I'll call the cops."

Chilly shrugged, doing his best to conceal his nerves. He looked at his watch again (damn it!) and then started south on Crystal.

"Nope!" Green Fleece said. "I'm headed that way. You go back the way you came."

"Whatever." Chilly waved her off. He was already late. Mr. Chavez had warned him about surveillance. He'd understand. Maybe.

Chilly ducked into an ice cream shop up the street that looked like it led back into the underground and got a small sweet cream and Heath to bide his time while he watched for anyone else on Green Fleece's team. This had to be a test. Nobody knew he was coming but the people who set up the travel. A mole in Hendley Associates? On the other hand, Mr. Clark looked like the kind of dude who would tell Chilly to keep an eye out for surveillance and then send a team to follow him . . .

Whatever this was, he had a meeting to get to.

He tossed the half-eaten ice cream in the trash and then headed south with no sign of Green Fleece or Black Beanie.

Fifteen minutes later—ten minutes after he should have arrived, he bounded up seven flights of stairs at the Hyatt Regency. He was just beginning to catch his breath, when the door to Room 722 swung open before he had a chance to knock.

Mr. Chavez gave a flick of his hand, motioning Chilly inside.

"You're late."

"Yes, sir," Chilly said. "I picked up tail at the . . ."

His voice trailed off when he rounded the corner and saw not only Mr. Clark, but Black Beanie and Green Fleece sitting at a small table.

"So, it was a test," he said.

"Of sorts," Chavez said, clearly suppressing a grin.

Green Fleece gave a dejected sigh. "For all of us. I clocked you as following me. You thought I was your tail."

Black Beanie's chair was tipped back against the wall. He let it fall forward so his arms rested on the table. "Dom Caruso," he said. "I was following both of you, but you were doing such a good job of creeping each other out, I just stepped back and let you do your own heavy lifting."

"Great way to start off," Green Fleece said. "Looking like idiots in front of our new bosses."

"Not at all," Mr. Clark said. He was tall and weathered with thinning silver hair and big hands that looked like they might grab you and not let go. He gave what Chilly took to be a rare smile and said, "Don't beat yourselves up. This is day one. You recognized each other as repeatedly popping up." He scanned the room now, eyeing them both in turn, measuring their mettle. "The question is, did anyone see me?"

"Where?" Green Fleece raised a brow in disbelief.

Clark shrugged. "Eating a donut at the airport . . . Having a coffee in the underground mall." He shot an amused look at Chavez. "Ding was behind the counter at the hotel."

"Nope," Green Fleece whispered.

Chilly groaned. He'd met Domingo Chavez in person twice and should have recognized him.

Chavez smiled. "Like Mr. C said, this is day one. Learn from it, then move on. You'll all be doing a lot of that over the next few months."

"So, you're acquainted with Dom," Clark said. "You'll meet the rest of the team later. For now, let's get to know one another."

19

Chilly took a chair beside Green Fleece, whose name turned out to be Amanda "Mandy" Cobb. She gave him a polite nod. If she was embarrassed about their earlier confrontation, she didn't show it. Her scary vibe toned down a little now that she knew everyone in the room was on the same team. Taciturn and still—two traits Chilly admired.

Mr. Clark spent five minutes explaining that "The Campus" was a private intelligence group that worked independently from, but in conjunction with, the Office of the Director of National Intelligence. Funded by its cover identity, the financial arbitrage firm Hendley Associates, they were able to fly under the radar and off the books, giving the DNI another arrow in her quiver than the litany of other private military and intelligence contractors who were sometimes folded into the payroll. It was a small and extremely tight-knit group. Skill was second only to trust. You didn't

apply to come aboard The Campus. You were invited if you had the requisite skills and aptitude to
learn more.

From the sound of things, the organization didn't
have many operatives. Hence the need to bring two
more into the fold.

"Don't get me wrong, sir," Mandy Cobb said.
"But I'm still trying to find out how you settled on
the two of us. I mean, I've got some law enforcement and my time at Quantico, but that puts me
on par with about twenty thousand other candi-
dates. Two months ago, I didn't even know what a
financial arbitrage firm was."

Chilly gave an embarrassed shrug. He'd pretended to know the term over dinner with Clark
and Chavez when they'd first met in Abilene, and
then looked it up on his phone when he got back
to his truck.

"Not a problem," Clark said. "None of us are
here because of our stock-trading acumen. We have
people for that.

"They'd already begun the pre-vetting process
before the FBI director happened to mention you
to me. Organizations like The Campus have always faced the difficulty of remaining in the shadows while conducting background investigations
on potential operatives. We do credit checks and
financial histories, of course. But we don't have
the luxury of coming out of the woodwork to do
lengthy interviews with neighbors or seventh-grade

English teachers. By the time you appear on our radar, some other entity has done the legwork. Skills are important, but we're looking for character on top of a clean background. You will eventually be given an incredible amount of latitude in your decisions. It's imperative that Campus operators have a clear definition of right and wrong, while periodically allowing themselves to step outside the confines of written law, especially outside the U.S."

Chilly drummed his fingers on the table. "A rule-keeper who is willing to break the rules."

"About the size of it," Clark said, stone-faced. "Difficult for most, impossible for some." He nodded to Chavez.

"This is a good time to do introductions," Chavez said. "And since you are all quiet professionals, I'll take care of it."

Mandy Cobb was thirty-three. John Clark had plucked her out of a group of new agent trainees during her seventeenth week at the FBI Academy in Quantico, where she had routinely scored at the top of her class. Prior to the Bureau, Cobb had been a deputy with the Wake County Sheriff's Office in North Carolina. Before that, she'd done a stint in Army Intelligence, learning Russian—which made her an asset Chilly was sure the FBI was none too happy to lose. Oh, and she ran ultramarathons in her off-hours.

Chilly wanted to fade into the wallpaper as Mr. Chavez briefed everyone on his background.

Cobb was an Army Intelligence–trained Russian linguist with law enforcement and FBI training. How was a country boy from Abilene PD supposed to compete with that? The only thing he seemed to have on Cobb was that he'd taken out the guys who'd kidnapped the First Lady. The APD badge still in his pocket was beginning to feel pretty good.

". . . and he's conversant in Spanish," Chavez said, rounding out Chilly's short introduction.

Mr. Clark, who'd been leaning against the desk by the television, stood up as if on cue.

"I'm sure you both have questions. We'll cover most of them this evening. Grab some dinner. Get to know each other. Then get back here for a mission brief in"—he checked his Seiko—"ninety minutes."

Mandy Cobb cocked her head. "Mission brief? Like a scenario?"

"Nope," Chavez said. "This'll be about as real as it gets."

20

The horrific narco-violence of Reynosa, Mexico, crept north into Texas like a plague. But the decapitations, burnings, and rapes paled in comparison to the Mexican side of the border, much of it fueled by the presence of the notorious Gulf Cartel. The Reynosa State Prison in the state of Tamaulipas was what Ian Doyle's old man would have called a **wee dooter** from the good old USA—a jaunt, not even a hike.

Doyle parked his car, a beat-up Ford Taurus he'd bought used at a lot in Pharr, Texas, east of McAllen. It was unremarkable, and therefore less likely to be stolen or impounded by Mexican law enforcement—which was exactly the same thing. The morning had brought a patter of rain. It did little to cool things off, but was enough to speckle stones and pock the yellow dirt with little craters. Enough to beat back the ever-present dust.

Doyle rolled down the window a crack—a necessity in the heat that would come later. A flash of light glinted from the tower as he unfolded himself from the car. One of the rifle-wielding guards was wearing sunglasses. They were eyeing him, maybe even looking at him through a scope. They did that kind of shit. He could feel it. They knew he was coming, though—or at least their boss did. Probably their boss's boss. Doyle wasn't about to let their glares and guns hurry him any faster than he wanted to go. He leaned against the car and decided to take a minute and enjoy the pleasant ozone smell of moist earth before he ventured into the stench of piss and fear common to every hellhole prison he'd ever been in. And he'd been in many.

Anyone who described Ian Doyle might skip the fact that he was six feet tall and simply say he was wide. He wasn't fat, not by a long shot, but he was thick, with broad shoulders and a waist like a tree trunk. Shovel-like hands, wrists like two-by-fours balanced the frame that his last commanding officer had described as an aircraft carrier with eyes. Such bulk usually came with lumbering movements, but Doyle was whip fast and even able to run if the need arose—and it often did in his line of work. Thick straw-colored hair hung sullenly over a high forehead, covering at least a few of the scars there. His old man had always encouraged him to use his head, mainly to butt some opponent in the nose. It took some trial and error, but Ian had perfected the move.

He shook out a Carrolls Number 1, figuring

he'd have to give up the rest of the pack to someone once he got inside. Cigarettes and ramen were coin of the realm in lockups the world over. He lit his, finding pleasure in the click of the Zippo his old man had gifted him decades before. A piece of work his old man was.

Here's a lighter for when you start to smoke, boyo.

C'mere to me, son, and I'll show you just how much we gotta stomp on this heroin to make money and still give our customers enough of a rush to keep them coming back.

Oh, an' how about you come with me to the States and visit with my old narco mate Berto Cárdenas . . .

Oh, yeah, a piece of work, to be sure.

Twenty-five years earlier, when Doyle was still in his teens, he'd made the trip to Texas with his old man to meet with Cárdenas, a lieutenant in the Gulf Cartel, or CDG, about some black tar heroin business in Ireland. Cárdenas was in his early twenties at the time and looked to young Ian like pictures he'd seen of a fierce Aztec warrior. He'd taken them across the border into Reynosa and treated them to the best food and music they had ever partaken of and made introductions with people who could not be seen in the United States.

It was much simpler, the cartel lieutenant had said, if they crossed by foot. The authorities were far less likely to believe they were smugglers if they walked. Mobs of bedraggled children, snot-nosed and smudged, thronged them from the moment they set foot on Mexican soil, hawking tiny packets of chicle chewing gum. It made him sad at first, then angry when the kids would not leave them alone. Even then, Ian had sensed the danger of the border. There were killers here, rival cartels vying for primacy, wild-eyed **sicarios** exacting revenge for some misdeed or slight against their **patrón,** and people who just felt life was cheap and would as soon stab you as ask you to kindly move out of the way. There were, of course, good, God-fearing people, too. Ian was just too young to notice them. He thought only of whores and all the bloody violence he'd spent the last month and a half reading about.

Oh, yeah, there were killers, and he'd found himself thinking he and his old man were probably walking around Reynosa with one of them.

Considering that his father planned to go into business with the Gulf Cartel, teenage Ian had studied everything in the Dublin Central Library about drug cartels, drawing a clucked disapproval from the old bag of a librarian when he checked out so many violent books and studied so many bloody periodicals. Even at fourteen, he was big enough to break her in half, so she snooted off and left him to his research.

He'd read of the 1989 murder of American college student Mark Kilroy, abducted during spring break in Matamoros only an hour to the east.

Kilroy was tortured and killed as a human sacrifice, his body dismembered by a group the media dubbed narco-satanists. And then there was Kiki Camarena, the American DEA agent who'd been abducted by corrupt Mexican officials on the payroll of the Guadalajara Cartel. Camarena had been shot in both legs and tortured with an electric drill to the point that they had to bring in a doctor to keep him awake for further torture. He lasted thirty hours.

Ian's old man had taken him to lunch with men who did such things and more on a routine basis. It was no wonder he turned out like he did. Doyle knew his father wasn't much better. Ian had never seen it, but he'd heard the old man was also keen on electric drills to make his point.

One of his enemies had been keen on .303 British rifles, and the old man had soon taken one through the ear, leaving Ian an orphan at the age of fifteen.

With competitors fast gobbling up his father's business and no prospects on the horizon, Doyle did what any boy in his shoes would do and joined the Royal Marines the day he turned sixteen. His size gave him a leg up with Marines much older than he was. He proved to be an excellent shooter and soon found a home in Brigade Reconnaissance Force, 3 Commando, though his upbringing with a grandmother from Belfast gave him latent tendencies toward the Ulster Liberation Army. Now, a quarter of a century and a hell of a lot of bad decisions later, the younger Doyle found himself going into Reynosa State Prison to recruit yet another shit-bag for his unit. Seven out of ten guys they got from the regular lockup were either too sociopathic to do the job, or dumb as a box of rocks—guys with military backgrounds like this one usually fared better.

But higher command had a spot to fill, and Doyle followed orders, so he was here to make certain this was the man to fill it.

He dropped the butt of his cigarette to the gravel and ground it out with the toe of his boot—Lowa Renegades, not the shitkicker cowboy boots everyone seemed to wear down here. He needed to be able to run if the need arose.

The guards waved him into the small sally-port enclosure. The outer gate swung shut behind him before the inner gate was opened. He lifted the tail of his jacket without being told and turned so the guard could see he didn't have anything in his waistband. They patted him down anyway, mainly to show him they were very much in charge. One of them, a fat asshole with a droopy eye, kept his pack of Carrolls.

Doyle shrugged it off and waited until the captain in charge of the unit came to meet him. Prisoners milled in the courtyard and rusted fence enclosures that looked like dog runs, apparently meant to keep certain groups of prisoners separated from others.

Over three-quarters of the men incarcerated here were members of the Gulf Cartel.

An electronic lock buzzed, and a steel door rattled open. Doyle stood where he was, waiting. This was, after all, a prison. When no one came through, he peeked around to find a potbellied guard. The man took a long drag from the cigarette dangling between his lips and then cocked his head to consider Doyle for a moment. His name was Sanchez and he served as a scout for the Camarilla, watching for prospective assets with military, law enforcement, or even gang experience. Men with such backgrounds who solved most problems with their fists were especially valuable.

Sanchez got paid when he found a prospect, and a bonus when he made introductions to someone of a high-enough caliber to meet the standards of the Camarilla.

At length, Sanchez gave a what-are-you-waiting-for flick of his hand and turned to waddle down a dimly lit hall.

The place smelled like piss and dead dreams.

"Through there," he said, pointing at a rusted door with his chin. "He's been here less than a month. I doubt he will make it another week."

Motivated, Doyle thought. **Good.**

Maybe.

"Why do you say that?" he asked.

"We are supposed to keep him away from the Gulf Cartel men," the guard said. "But many of the guards are Gulf. So you see, keeping him separate is impossible."

"He's a fighter?"

Doyle looked through the one-way glass. The guy looked all right. Well-muscled, alert. He wasn't tweaking like the last prospect.

"Oh, yeah," Sanchez said. "Likes to use his teeth."

"A problem solver." Doyle gestured to the door. "Give me ten minutes with him."

"As you wish, **señor,**" Sanchez said, preoccupied, no doubt thinking of the twenty-five-thousand-dollar bonus he'd been paid to facilitate this deal. It was a relatively large sum for such a transaction, but everyone had expenses. Big facilitators had to make enough so that they could afford to pay off subordinates to alter paperwork and keep quiet.

Sanchez waved down the hall, and central control opened the door. Doyle stood at the threshold for a few seconds, getting used to the odor. The cell smelled worse than the hall, if such a thing was even possible.

Martin Flores stood and braced to attention as soon as Doyle entered the room, greeting him in English. Respectful. A promising sign. He stood just under six feet tall. Fit, with what Doyle called "prison traps"—thick neck muscles that seemed to go from ear to shoulder. Muscles like that tended to make smaller men look more imposing and warlike, an important consideration in prison.

Doyle ordered Flores to sit and then took a metal stool across from him at the three-by-three metal table. He took a notebook from his pocket and got straight to business.

"Ten years Naval Infantry Corps," Doyle said, eyeing his notebook.

"Yes, sir," Flores said. "Second Battalion, Fifth Brigade . . ."

"Hmmm," Doyle said, jotting a note in his book. "Regular infantry . . ."

Flores squirmed, ever so slightly. "I spent six years in FESGO. Fuerzas Especiales del Golfo."

"Gulf Special Forces?" Doyle said. "You made no mention of that in your email." He leaned across the table to make a point. "Remember what our original solicitation said about lying. We can bring you aboard with almost any crime, but you must not lie. Let's start again. Why didn't you mention special forces in your paperwork?"

Flores opened his mouth to speak, but Doyle stopped him.

"Most people embellish some when they tell stories. You know, build themselves up with a bunch of shit to impress. You left it out. Either way, it's a lie. Up to now is a free pass. I admonish you one last time. From this point on, if you lie to me, I give you my word, I will shoot you in the head."

"I did not know if I should include it," Flores said, squirming a little more now. "It was a special unit."

"So you're sticking with that story?"

"I am," Flores said. "There was much secrecy

within the Navy. I thought I should talk to you in person rather than committing it to email."

Doyle peered over the top his notebook. "How's that working out for you?"

"What do you mean, sir?"

"The Naval Infantry Corps are essentially Mexican Marines."

"We are," Flores said.

"Mexico uses its Marine Special Forces to fight the drug war."

"Correct . . ." Flores said.

"Eighty percent of the people you're locked up with are Gulf Cartel," Doyle said. "See where I'm going with this? To them you might as well be a cop."

Flores gave a resigned shrug. "I was on their payroll," he said.

Doyle tossed his notebook on the metal table. "These narcos need rats, to be sure, but in my experience, they don't much trust them."

Doyle reviewed the man's shooting and physical aptitude scores, which were all in the ninetieth percentile. He was impressive, but for his tendency to play ball for the highest bidder.

"Have you discussed our meeting or the Camarilla with anyone else inside or outside this facility?"

"Your solicitation told me not to," Flores said.

"That's not an answer."

"No, sir," Flores said. "The guards know of the

meeting, of course. If they know anything of the Camarilla, they did not hear it from me."

"Why are you locked up?" Doyle asked.

"Murder," Flores said, squirming in his seat again. "Surely you know this already."

"What sort of murder?" Doyle asked.

Flores took a long pause, then exhaled and whispered, "Beating a man to death after he touched my twelve-year-old niece. Inappropriately."

"That's understandable," Doyle said. He closed the notebook and then sat back for a time, staring at the other man in silence.

A hell of a lot of confessions came gushing out during awkward moments of quiet.

At length, Doyle slammed both palms on the table, causing the other man to jump.

"In exchange for purchasing the remainder of your ten-year sentence, along with a yearly salary of one hundred and fifty thousand dollars plus bonuses, depending on the job, you agree to fight alongside us whenever and wherever for a contracted term of ten years."

"I say that sounds amazing," Flores said.

"As long as you don't lie."

"I am not lying, **señor.** My service record is easy enough to check."

It was almost but not quite a whine. In Doyle's book, whining was just one notch above lying.

"Very well," he said. "Give me a minute. You wait here."

Flores stood and waved his hand at the concrete walls. "I promise not to go anywhere."

A little flippant, Doyle thought. The training cadre would beat that out of him in the first hour. Doyle pounded on the door with a fist, sending a cascade of dust down the concrete wall. Sanchez opened it immediately. His eyes shifted from Flores to Doyle, and then back to Flores. He secured the door and motioned Doyle down the hall toward the glassed control booth.

Something had clearly changed while he'd been in the cell. If this prick wanted more money . . .

Doyle ground his teeth and took a deep breath. "What is it?"

"I know you value honesty, **señor,**" Sanchez said, "above all else."

"I do," Doyle said. "So be honest with me."

"Of course," Sanchez said. "This prisoner, Flores. I had no idea when I sent you his name."

Doyle darkened. "No idea about what?"

"This man is imprisoned for murder."

"That's perfectly fine," Doyle said. He did not mention that ninety percent of the men in the Camarilla had criminal records for murder—and every last one of them rightfully should have.

"He told me." Doyle shrugged. "He killed a man who molested his niece. Pretty shitty of the cops to charge him with murder for that."

Sanchez sucked in his bottom lip. "That is the thing, **señor.** New information has come to light.

Flores did not kill the man who was molesting his niece. He killed the man who caught **him** molesting his niece. She came forward after she knew he was locked away and could not hurt her."

"I see," Doyle said. "She has proof?"

The man nodded quickly, as if he wanted to be done with all of this. "There is apparently a mobile-phone video." He rocked back and forth, a pinched look of concern crossing his face. "He will still be of use to you. No?"

"No," Doyle said. "We've got no place for a man like that in my organization. You can keep him."

He turned to go, but Sanchez grabbed his shoulder. Had they not been in the locked confines of a prison it would have been the last thing Sanchez ever did.

"But, **señor,**" the guard said. "I cannot keep him. Paperwork on his release has already been filed and approved. You have bought him fair and square. He is yours. No returns."

Doyle frowned, clenching his fists enough to make the guards in the control center stand and attempt their best menacing glares. Pretty damned courageous when they were behind their glass fortress.

"Just throw him in with the cartels. They'll take care of him—"

"Impossible," Sanchez said. "Every death must be explained. Even here. Flores goes out the gate with you. Leave him in a culvert. I do not care. As I said, he is yours. You paid for him."

Flores bounced on the balls of his feet as Doyle escorted him out the sally-port gate to his beater Ford. If Doyle had planned to keep the car, he never would have let the prick near it. But he couldn't very well take care of him in the parking lot of Reynosa State Prison. He had no idea that Doyle knew the real situation with his niece.

Giddy at his new freedom, Flores grew chatty, harping away about the recent rain as he buckled in.

"Don't ruin the rain for me, asshole," Doyle snapped.

Flores's expression fell. **"Señor?"**

"Recruits don't speak unless spoken to. Think of me as your new drill instructor."

The idiot braced in his seat, relieved. Liars were always waiting for the other shoe to drop.

"Sí, señor."

Doyle hadn't had time to put the car in gear before his phone rang. He checked the caller ID. This couldn't be good.

"I have to take this outside," he said. "Keep your ass planted where it is."

Doyle killed the engine and took the keys with him.

"Request permission to lower a wind—"

"Request denied," Doyle said, stone-faced. "I don't give two shits if you get a little warm."

He slammed the door and stepped far enough away from the Taurus that Flores couldn't hear him.

"What is it?"

The phones were end-to-end encrypted, but the men kept it vague anyway.

"JAMAICA," the voice said, clipped. It was a South African named De Bruk.

"What now?" Doyle said.

The operation in Panama had been a delicate one from the start. A coup was one thing, but this Rube Goldberg plan that was Operation JAMAICA had far too many moving parts for Doyle's taste. You wanted someone out of office, you shot them in the face, simple as that.

"A local cop we had on the payroll screwed us with his intel," De Bruk said. "We are now four men down. The guys in San Miguelito."

Shit! That wasn't good. Jorge Arias was a decent guy. They'd worked together on more than one assignment. He didn't deserve to rot in prison.

"Who has them?"

De Bruk sighed. "That's the thing, mate. Panamanian National Police shot all our guys—and their lookout. They're done for."

Doyle rubbed his face. "All of them? The PNP?"

"Afraid so," De Bruk said. "Sad loss. We are now minus an ops leader and two very important noisemakers."

"The large noisemaker?" Doyle asked, ignoring the first observation. He'd seen the ops plans. The truck bombs were crucial to JAMAICA's success. He'd grieve over the loss of his friend later.

"Nah," De Bruk said. "That's our only bit of good news. Our dirty cop saved us on that one. Lucky for him, too. Kept the boss from sending someone to cut his nuts off. Losing one of the big items would have delayed us for a month. Sounds like our cop has a problem underling making him jump through hoops. The boss is losing her mind."

"And you're calling me to take care of this problem?"

"Nah," De Bruk said. "We have someone taking care of her."

Her. A hard-charging lady cop. That made things interesting.

"If the bitch had anything to do with Jorge's death, tell the boss I'm happy to do her myself," Doyle said.

"It's being handled," De Bruk said. "I promise."

Doyle patted his pocket, hunting for a cigarette, then cursed under his breath when he remembered that the prison dick had kept them. "I thought we were relying on agents in place for most of this one."

"We were," De Bruk said. "And we are. But everyone there was a crucial part of the operation. And your mate Arias was running the local show for our client. And that's not counting the two missing noisemakers. The boss wants you down there—as explosives guy and ops commander."

"I'm on my way," Doyle said.

"Outstanding, mate." De Bruk let out a relieved groan. "That's the only acceptable answer. You can bring that new guy along. He's with you now, right?"

"He is." Doyle shot a glance toward the Taurus.

"Good," De Bruk said. "I'm glad he worked out."

"He didn't work out."

"Bollocks," De Bruk said. "I won't even ask why. Those shitheels made you take him anyway, didn't they?"

"They did," Doyle said.

"Ah," De Bruk said. "Make it quick, but don't get caught. She wants in you Panama, like, yesterday."

21

As usual when speaking to another world leader, Jack Ryan had an interpreter listening in from a chair beside the Resolute desk. Commander Robby Forrestal the deputy national security adviser, Mary Pat Foley, D/CIA Jay Canfield, and Arnie van Damm, along with the secretaries of state and defense, Scott Adler and Bob Burgess, perched in various locations around the Oval Office, nursing cups of coffee and listening in. Private conversations didn't happen very often in this job—and even when they did, they were almost always recorded. Ryan had invited Special Agent in Charge Gary Montgomery to the meeting as well. He sat next to the fireplace. He'd declined any coffee. Ryan rarely ever saw the man without his gun hand free.

Ryan's longtime secretary came over the intercom. "We have President Botero of Panama on the line for you, Mr. President."

"Thank you, Betty." Ryan pushed the flashing

button on his desk phone. "Your Excellency," he said.

"Mr. President," Botero said. "I beg you, do not weigh me down with that title. It is bad enough when my own countrymen do it. 'Doctor' is title enough. Don't you think?"

Ryan smiled, though the other man could not see him. "I understand completely," he said. "'Doctor' looks better on you than me. My eldest daughter is fond of pointing out that a medical doctor is much more useful than a doctor of history."

"Daughters," Botero said. "What is one to do? I thank you for taking my call. I know you are very busy . . ."

"My pleasure, Rafael," Ryan said. "I know your English is flawless, but I have a White House interpreter on the line."

"I understand, Jack," Botero said. "It is only myself and Vice President Carré on my end. This matter is quite sensitive, and though I trust my staff . . . it is much easier to speak without wondering which of them I might offend . . ."

The conversation moved through Ryan's least favorite phase, the diplomatic version of two dogs sniffing each other. The niceties taken care of, Ryan got to the point.

"To what do I owe this pleasure, my old friend?"

"I hesitate to bring this up at your level, but—"

"Please, Rafael," Ryan said. "We are here to talk. So talk."

"Thank you, Jack. To be candid, one of your bloggers is causing us no small number of problems."

D/CIA Canfield gave a silent nod to Mary Pat Foley for getting the intel correct.

"She's not **my** blogger, Rafael," Ryan said.

"This I know," Botero said. "But she is a U.S. citizen and the things she says are quite troubling, not to mention blatantly untrue. Our protesting teachers have embraced her as their patron saint!"

Ryan sighed, settling deeper in his chair. "You know I can't stop her. So . . ."

"Of course not," Botero said. "And I would never suggest it. What I propose is a bit of good press to counter the bad. There are many here who love our relationship with the United States. But I have to tell you, Russia is fighting hard for our hearts and minds. A recent editorial made a point of saying that though the canal is supposed to be neutral, the U.S. is a bully big brother who allows Panama the perception of control. Our Russian ambassador is quick to tell anyone who will listen that it need not always be thus. Even now, Russian warships come through at five times their normal frequency. And their promises . . . Oh, my friend. Socialists make such promises. If they had their way we would nationalize everything and . . ."

"And become like Venezuela," Ryan said.

"Inevitably," Botero said. "But it is not difficult to convince the poor that cheap gasoline is a good thing. As I said, there are many people who love the United States. But you are getting much bad press lately. Calling you a failed state. Our morning paper accuses you of an assassination in the mountains of Venezuela. I am sure your people had nothing to do with that, but you are getting blamed for it in any case."

"Thank you for letting me know," Ryan said.

"Jack, I'm saying I . . . we . . . need to give the people something to root for. Perhaps a joint appearance where you and I discuss our partnership in the rural school initiative."

"A photo op and short presser while we're in Argentina," Ryan mused. "Of course."

Botero came back immediately. "I had hoped for something before that. Here in Panama. Everyone in my country knows that I am friendly with the U.S. It would be very beneficial if they could see the U.S. is friendly with us without considering us your lapdog. Please remember, this is not about reelection. Even if I wanted to, I could not run again without a five-year break. The memory of the people is short. The things I say during my term will be forgotten. Only the things I **do** have a chance of living on. My friend, this is about getting the obstacles out of the road so that I have enough political capital to drive this country forward during the years I have left in office."

"A brief stopover while we're en route to Argentina?" Ryan said.

"That is exactly what I planned to suggest," Botero said. "I would be willing to make the announcement about the joint training base at Fort Sherman. Get it out in the open for healthy debate rather than sneaking around. A stop in Panama would be, as you say, a win-win."

Montgomery leaned forward and stared at the floor, giving an almost imperceptible shake of his head, as if he were trying to conceal a sudden pain.

Ryan had anticipated Botero's request. It made sense to do a little show of solidarity on his way to the summit. He'd not mentioned it to anyone, not Mary Pat, not the Secret Service, and certainly not to Cathy, but he'd known in his gut that it was coming. That's why he'd asked Gary Montgomery to be present for the call.

"No doubt," Ryan said. "That said, this may not be feasible. Even a short visit requires a tremendous amount of planning and coordination, not an easy task on short notice. Considering the time frame, the Secret Service would insist that my schedule be kept secret until I was there. Your most trusted security personnel would need to coordinate with the U.S. Secret Service. No one else could be told. Even your closest advisers should be kept in the dark until the last minute. In other words, if you want to schedule a press conference, that's fine. My participation will not be known until I am on-site."

"Of course," Botero said. "But I must tell you,

Jack, Panama is not a war-torn nation. Our government has some level of—"

"I'm not being judgmental as to Panama, Rafael," Ryan said. "A short-notice trip like this would be kept confidential wherever it was."

"I understand. My Institutional Protection Service will do anything you require on this end."

"And the protesters?" Ryan asked.

"A few fistfights here and there," Botero said. "They have made no moves toward real violence . . ." He paused, as if gathering up his courage, then said, "The protests are only problematic for travel because they block roadways, but there is a matter about which I need to be honest."

Ryan shot a glance at Montgomery and then Foley. "And what is that, Rafael?"

Botero exhaled sharply. "Our police in Panama City have uncovered a plot, apparently targeting me for assassination."

He gave a quick thumbnail of the raid in San Miguelito, running down the number of weapons and explosive devices and where found, then added, "The conspirators decided to put up a fight during the arrest and were all killed."

"Any reason to believe they were part of a larger plot?" Ryan asked.

"None at all," Botero said. "At least two of the dead appear to have been former Kaibiles. Guatemalan Special Forces are very well trained. They are sometimes recruited by drug traffickers when they leave the military. This was surely something to do with my stand on narco-trafficking."

"Well," Ryan said, "I appreciate your honesty."

He didn't mention to Botero that U.S. intelligence sources already knew of the San Miguelito raid. If Botero hadn't mentioned it, Ryan would never have even considered a stopover.

"I realize such an event causes concerns for your Secret Service."

Special Agent Montgomery gave a distinct nod.

Botero continued. "Concerns can be mitigated by doing as you said. A handful of my most trusted Presidential Guard would coordinate with your people, necessarily keeping most in the dark until the moment of your arrival. We will have made our appearance and moved on to Mar del Plata before any protests have time to form."

"Give me a chance to discuss this with my senior staff."

"Excellent," Botero said. "I will leave you with something my mother always said. 'The politics of trade will win out over the politics of politics every day of the week.'"

"Smart woman, your mother," Ryan said.

"She was indeed," Botero said. "Now you and I must give my people some trade to root for. I will stand by for a call with your specifics."

"No promises," Ryan said.

"Of course, my friend," Botero said, clearly taking the **maybe** as a **yes.**

He makes good points," Ryan said. He looked around the Oval Office at his team. "Thoughts?"

Jay Canfield looked at Montgomery and then back to Ryan. "I'd advise you to pass, Mr. President. The foiled plot against President Botero alone is a good enough reason to take a breath and check political temperatures in Argentina."

"I have to agree with Jay," Foley said. "The assassination plot is so recent our people are kicking up new intel daily. We're not exactly sure what we have yet."

"Right," Canfield said. "And Panamanian media already has the story on SUDDEN SQUALL. It's only a matter of time before someone finds a pic of James Salazar on the Web and plasters photos of a dead CIA operator over every news outlet there is. I'm sure the Russians are frothing at the mouth."

"And we can't forget the Russian ships," Commander Forrestal said. "The missile destroyer **Admiral Chabanenko** and the landing ship **Ivan Gren.** They're sailing past Costa Rica as we speak, apparently on the way to the canal."

The SecDef spoke up now. "That might be just the occasion for a short surprise visit," Burgess said. "The Russians are strutting. Would it be a bad thing if we postured a little ourselves? And what better way to do that than sending the Commander in Chief to put boots on the ground. Hell, sir, the fact that you'd be coming in with a smaller-than-usual contingent of security would show them you . . ." His voice trailed off when he caught Foley's eye.

She finished his sentence. "What Bob is trying to say is that if you show up in Panama on a short-notice trip, then even the Russians will say you have brass balls."

Ryan scoffed. "What do they say now?"

Scott Adler pursed his lips in thought. An expert poker player, he was a hard man to read, which made him an excellent secretary of state.

"Mr. President," Adler said at length, "there are many people in the world who hate you, some who even see you as the head of the Great Satan. That said, I doubt any leader on the planet doubts your integrity or your chutzpah. But they may doubt President Botero. I mean this as a compliment, sir, but Jack Ryan is the kind of man who creates his own weather."

Arnie van Damm jumped on the bandwagon. "Scott makes a valid argument," the CoS said. "If Rafael Botero is wobbling, your standing beside him may be enough to prop him up."

"Right," Adler said. "The same sun shining on your face shines on his."

Gary Montgomery got up and walked to the fireplace, where he stood with his hands at his sides, still as a statue, while he waited for the others to give their counsel.

Canfield spoke up again, rebutting the diplomatic

and political reasons to go, adding a few last-minute thoughts to his doomsday scenarios, including a strong sense from the Panama City station chief that there was more to the assassination plot than they knew at the moment.

"And the Secret Service?" Ryan asked.

"We have a large number of agents already posted in Argentina in advance of your visit to the summit," Montgomery said. His jaw tensed with every word, building up a head of steam as he spoke. "I strongly advise you to skip this one, sir. Street protests are living things. Seemingly peaceful groups can go from holding cardboard signs to beating you with the pickets in a matter of seconds. I'd not be doing my job if I didn't bring up Caracas in 1958. Vice President Nixon's motorcade was surrounded and stopped by an angry mob. Local police just stood by."

"Speaking of brass balls," Foley said. "Those Secret Service agents with Nixon had some **huevos.**"

"They did indeed, ma'am," Montgomery said. "Twelve men prepared to engage a crowd of hundreds."

"If I remember correctly," Ryan said, "Nixon coolly told the agents not to fire without his order."

"Due respect to former president Nixon," Montgomery said, "that wouldn't happen today. My agents would engage a threat before you had time to speak, let alone order us not to shoot."

Ryan gave a contemplative nod. He was glad this hulking agent was on his side.

"Social media makes it even worse now," Canfield said, bolstering Montgomery's argument. "Groups coordinate movements, allowing violence to materialize out of thin air on routes thought to be secured."

Ryan put both hands flat on his desk, palms down. "I'm not blind to the dangers," he said. "But there are protests outside the White House every day. Marches. Bullhorns. The works. The Secret Service does a tremendous job keeping track of dozens of threats on me, my family, and scores of other people under their protection. This visit has the possibility of not only helping President Botero, but demonstrating a little goodwill that could sway public opinion toward the United States instead of Russia."

Foley sighed. "Still—"

"Heaven knows I'm not numb to what happened in San Antonio," Ryan said. "My family . . . hell, the entire country is on edge. If anything, that's another reason to carry on."

"Or not to," Canfield said.

"Gary," Ryan said. "Have Protective Intelligence get me everything they can find on the situation down there. Jay, you do the same with your sources at the CIA. This meeting in Panama has value. If that value outweighs the risk, then we'll go. If it doesn't, we'll meet President Botero at the Mar del Plata summit." He stood, prompting everyone in the Oval Office to do the same. "I don't plan to be irrational, but I don't plan to hide behind the curtains forever, either."

22

When he was eleven years old, Rafael Botero's mother had warned him what kind of life he had in store. **You are too small and too plain for anyone on earth to respect you because of your looks. A boy of your stature should be content with any number of noble professions—taxi driver, market clerk, even teacher.**

Her words were harsh, but they were true. He did not want to drive a taxi and his mother knew it. She also knew he was stubborn and that her pronouncements of his future had only made him work harder to prove her wrong—and gotten him where he was today, sitting in the Palacio de las Garzas at the polished oak desk under a life-sized portrait of Simón Bolívar.

"Do you think he'll do it?" Vice President Lionel Carré asked as soon as the call with Ryan ended. Still in his early forties, the bright-eyed and rosy-cheeked man seemed much too young and earnest to hold the second-highest office in the country.

Elbows on his desk, chin resting against his hands, Botero glanced up at the question. "I hope so," he said. "But I cannot stress enough the importance of secrecy if he does decide to visit. Advance agents of the Secret Service can seem like an invading army. They will need to have a plausible cover story as they prepare for his arrival."

"Perhaps we let it leak that there will be a visit **after** the summit," Carré offered.

Botero nodded, thinking through the political ramifications of deceiving his own cabinet. "That would work," Botero said. "With the wrong timing, any protesters would be caught flat—"

A sudden knock at the door caused him to fall silent.

Felix Moncada, Botero's economic adviser, strode into the office, leather folio in hand. Botero had never gotten a good look inside the folio, but the man was never without it, so it was obviously important.

Moncada was everything Botero was not. Tall, athletic, the life of the party. He preferred expensive suits and fine watches, where Botero, a surgeon by training, wore off-the-rack and a Timex. Botero was balding. Moncada's straw-colored hair and light complexion meant he was often referred to as **gringo** or **rabiblanco** not only by people who did not know him, but by political opponents and sometimes even the media.

Moncada shot a dismissive glance at Carré, darkening when he met Botero's eye, seemingly annoyed that any meeting would take place without him, especially one that included the vice president.

Botero ignored the silent chastening.

"What's the news?" he asked.

Moncada pursed his lips. "SPI is still following up, of course, Mr. President. But they have found no evidence of a larger plot."

"What of the smaller plot, then?" Botero asked. "Bombs, Guatemalan Special Forces . . . Who is behind all this?"

"A matter for the SPI and PNP," Moncada said. "I am sure Commissioner Guerra will have more information very soon."

"There is always someone who wants to kill the person who sits beneath this portrait." Botero nodded at the painting of Bolívar, and then waved the idea away. "We have more important things to worry about. No?" He put both hands on the desk and took a deep breath. "What of the Russian ship?"

"Ships," Moncada said. "Missile destroyer **Admiral Chabanenko** and troop-landing ship **Ivan Gren.**"

"**Admiral Chabanenko,**" the vice president mused.

"She was the first Russian warship to pass through the canal since World War II. She's thirty miles off the coast of Managua as we speak, conducting exercises with the Nicaraguan Navy. They are scheduled to transit Miraflores Locks in two days' time, presumably on their way to continue their exercises with Venezuela and Cuba."

"Good, they won't be staying," the vice president said.

Moncada ignored him, standing silently, peering into his open folio. He mentioned no reason for his visit, but didn't leave, either. It was as if he were waiting to be briefed on what had just occurred in the closed-door meeting.

"Are you all right, my friend?" Botero asked.

Moncada's head snapped up, his top lip quivering just a hair, as if surprised by the question.

"Me?" he said. "I am fine, but I must admit this plot the police uncovered is disturbing. Would it not be wise to forego the trip to Mar del Plata?"

"Nonsense," Vice President Carré said. "You have only just told us the plot appeared to be contained."

Moncada focused his efforts on the president. "I urge you to take precautions, sir."

"Was the assassination plot contained or was it not?" Carré asked.

"At least allow me to speak with Commissioner Guerra," Moncada said. "SPI are handling the investigation of the plot against you, but the National Police had the original case. I am sure he will have more information soon."

"Fine," Botero said. "I mean, of course I want him to do his job. But you do not need to bother with it."

Moncada put a hand to his chest. "I know I am merely your economic adviser, but you know I have your best interests at heart. If nothing else, we should augment the numbers of your security."

"Of course."

"Very good," Moncada said. Then, offhandedly, "Your call with the U.S. President. Did he agree to a bilateral meeting in Argentina?"

Botero considered mentioning his invitation for Ryan to visit Panama prior to the summit in Mar del Plata, but thought better of it. Moncada was deeply patriotic, but his mother had been killed by a stray bullet during the invasion of 1989. How could such a tragedy not have shaped his feelings for the United States?

"Foreign Minister Popov has asked for some time as well," Moncada said.

"Popov?" Carré said, taken aback. "What business does Russia have at a summit of the Americas?"

Botero raised his hand. "Let him finish, please, Lionel."

"The same as the United States, I would imagine," Moncada said matter-of-factly. "Wielding their might and money to exert influence in Central and South America. The labor unions would not be upset with a bit more socialist influence."

"Summit of the **Americas,**" Carré said, emphasizing the last.

Moncada wheeled. "You forget, Lionel, that you represent the people—"

The vice president came half out of his seat. "'Lionel'?"

Botero raised his hand again. "Gentlemen, please!"

"Excuse me, Mr. President." Moncada's lip began to quiver in earnest. "I will take my leave."

He shut the folio with a snap and strode out the door as purposefully as he'd come in.

"The balls on that man," Carré said. "He talks as if he were running the country."

"He and many others," Botero said. "But his economic advice has been sound."

"Someone was trying to kill you," Carré said. "It is a given you have enemies. Please tell me you do not trust that one."

Botero looked at the vice president with a sad smile. "I did not mention President Ryan's visit," he said. "That should tell you what you need to know."

23

Hugo Sandoval had worn a tank top and gym shorts to pick up the truck in San Miguelito. His girlfriend, Valeria, drove him, bitching the whole way about how he looked like a slob and asking if he was allergic to sleeves. He'd been in her house binge-watching episodes of **Escándalos,** a popular television show about real scandals, when he got the call. It sounded urgent, like someone was about to die if he didn't move his ass.

Valeria was as sexy as they came, but her volume knob rose to level ten if she became the least bit annoyed—which happened a little too often lately. There was a limit to sexy. By the time they reached San Miguelito, Hugo wished he'd taken one of the city's crowded chicken buses rather than listening to her squawk all the way.

Why the hurry, Hugo? They are paying that much to move a truck, Hugo? Woooo, Hugito, you are some secret squirrel . . . It was like an electric blender on high speed. She had beautiful hair, or he probably would have left her a long time ago.

She was also right.

There had to be something **vago**—sketchy— about this whole thing. Five hundred U.S. dollars to move a truck twenty minutes away from where it was parked. That was okay. He could do sketchy for five hundred dollars. Hugo didn't even know who hired him, just a deep voice over the phone who said they had mutual friends. Talk about **vago.**

The instructions had been clear. Hugo would make five hundred dollars if he could get to San Miguelito in the next ten minutes, take the truck out the rear door of the garage, and drive it to his house, where he should store it until he received another phone call. No one told him not to look in the back. They did not have to. Whatever it was, it had to be contraband. Illegal shit. Guns, drugs, hell, maybe women. He'd once seen a shipping container come in from China with ventilation fans, food and water, and bucket toilets. He guessed someone could do the same to a ten-foot box truck.

As far as Valeria knew, Hugo made his living as a **camarón.** The word meant "shrimp" in Spanish, but came from the days when rich Americans living in the canal zone would ask locals to "come aroun'" and do odd jobs. Some of the jobs were odder than others. He knew better than to look inside anything he moved for the people who hired him, let alone the back of a truck some unknown guy was paying him five hundred dollars to hold.

Valeria was not so careful.

Hugo was standing in the kitchen shirtless, opening himself a cold Balboa, when he heard the screen door leading from the enclosed backyard squeak open, then slam shut. Valeria was pissed about something. Her feet shuffled on the tile floor behind him. He barely had time to set down the beer before she slapped him hard across the face, ringing his ear and bloodying his nose with one swipe.

He covered up, ready for one of her full-blown thundersqualls. They were rough, but they blew over quickly. He just wished she'd tell him what she was so pissed about. He had to grab the counter to keep from dropping to his knees by the time she finally got around to telling him why she was so mad.

"What an egg you are!" she screamed, swiping at him over and over, her manicured nails drawing blood on his face and unprotected chest. "An idiot! What are you thinking bringing that truck to my house?"

"Oh, no, no, no," he groaned, dabbing a hand to his face and checking it for blood as he retreated. "Please tell me you did not look inside."

She barreled on. "It is a bomb, Hugo! Did you know you parked a bomb in my courtyard? What is your plan here?"

Hugo staggered backward to a chair and collapsed. "I did not know what it was. But now that we do, we have to leave."

Valeria nodded fiercely, comprehending the danger, but furious over the implications.

He looked up. "What kind of bomb?"

"Really?" she demanded. "I know nothing of bombs, Hugo! I only know that this is a big one."

"This is bad, Valli," he whispered. "Very bad. These people will know that you opened the truck."

Her face fell. "How?"

"Trust me," Hugo said. "They will know. Come. I need to see what we are dealing with."

There did not appear to be any sort of seal on the door, but that didn't mean anything. It was a simple matter to install an electronic switch that would tell them remotely if the door had been tampered with. For all he knew, they had cameras inside. In truth, he had no idea who "they" were. He just knew they were dangerous. Honest people did not pay five hundred dollars for twenty minutes' work.

Once he swung the door open, it took him all of two seconds to realize this was more than a bomb. This was eighteen stacked plastic barrels of fertilizer, each fitted with a sausage-like tube that was connected to a thick white wire running to a central junction box.

"ANFO . . ." The word left his mouth in a gasp, like he'd been punched in the gut.

Valeria darkened. "What is anfo?"

"ANFO," he whispered. "Ammonium nitrate and fuel oil. This load could destroy half the block."

"You piece of shit!" Valeria hit him hard in the arm. Then hit him again for good measure. "How could you, Hugito . . . to my house?"

"I did not mean—"

She froze, eyes transfixed to the barrels and wires in the back of the truck. She grabbed his arm and stepped in tight beside him. Her voice dropped to a husky whisper. "Do you think it might blow up?"

"It did not go off when I drove it here," he said earnestly. "So probably not. See? The wire harness is taped off. Not connected to that other box."

"How do you know so much about bombs?" She punched him again, weaker this time. Her words came out shaky. "And who are these people you are working for?"

"I told you, I do not know," Hugo said. "But we need to go."

"Go?" Still a whisper.

Hugo shut the truck box, gingerly, leaving it just as he found it, and then hustled her back through the screen door.

Both he and Valeria froze at the buzzing sound of a mobile phone dancing across the counter.

He took a deep breath and picked up the phone, index finger up, warning Valeria to hush.

"Is this Sandoval?"

"Yes."

"Do you still have the item?"

The voice was calm, nonchalant. Maybe they did not know after all.

"It is parked in back," Hugo said, willing his voice not to crack.

"We will be there in one hour."

The line went dead without another word. That was normal. Panamanians rarely ended a call with niceties.

"How could you, Hugito?" Valeria started in on him again, tears welling in her dark eyes. "What have you—"

He grabbed her by both shoulders. "Not now! You must pack a bag. Quickly! They will be here in one hour. We need to be gone before they arrive."

Valeria started to protest, but a crunch of gravel out front cut her off. She peeked out the edge of the curtain.

Hugo tried to pull her to him. "You shouldn't stand at the window."

She jerked away.

"It is the police."

Hugo crowded in next to his girlfriend and looked out to see a blue Ford sedan—the kind the National Police drove. It was parked across the street and one house down. They were not here for him. Overwhelming relief washed over Hugo Sandoval. He knew what he had to do.

"Stay in the house," he whispered, and all but

exploded out the front door. He slowed to what he hoped was a more relaxed-looking walk and waved to the officers as they climbed out of the sedan.

The driver smiled and returned the wave as if they were old friends. The man's left arm was missing, the sleeve of his shirt pinned up neatly at the shoulder. He looked to be a little older than Hugo, in his early forties. The passenger was tall and well-groomed, much younger, maybe even a trainee. A wrestler, judging from the fierceness in his eyes and the pronounced cauliflower ear.

Neither man was in uniform. Their sidearms and badges were openly displayed on their belts. Khaki slacks and tailored short-sleeved shirts left no doubt that these men were in excellent condition. Both wore aviator sunglasses that concealed their eyes and their intentions. The driver would be a formidable opponent even with the missing arm.

"**Patrón**," Hugo yelled. It came out choked, like a dying bullfrog. "May I speak with you?"

"Of course," the driver said. "I am Lieutenant Vega, and this is my associate, Agent Pinto."

Hugo's shoulders slumped. He blew out a lung full of air as he relaxed a hair. They really were cops. A promising sign. Still, he could not help but feel like they were looking at him the way an African lion looked at a lone zebra.

Hugo held out the ignition key for the truck before the men could say another word.

"I need to tell you something . . ."

Words gushed from his lips as he told them everything he knew, starting with the ANFO bomb in the truck parked in the backyard and working backward to the unidentified voice on the phone that had offered him the job.

Oddly, neither officer seemed at all surprised.

Hugo motioned for them to follow, all but dragging them with him—a little boy with some hidden treasure he wanted to show.

Lieutenant Vega took the keys and opened the back, clucking when he saw the plastic barrels.

"You were right to tell us," he said. "It looks to be an ANFO bomb. See, Pinto . . . The detonator is there. These wires would run from there to blasting caps placed in those tubes of booster, which would be enough to detonate the ammonium nitrate. A crude but efficient explosive device." He turned to Hugo. "You have done the Republic of Panama a great service."

Hugo gave a sheepish nod. This was turning out so much better than he had feared.

Then, "How long have you known about this?"

"Mere minutes," Hugo said, hoping it sounded as true as it was. "I was not supposed to look inside, but—"

"It is fortunate that you did," Vega said.

Hugo said nothing.

The man went on. "We trust you, Hugito," he said. "If we did not, we would never have enlisted your help."

"What do you mean?"

"You had no way of knowing this, of course," Vega said, "but this is an official Policía Nacional matter. The items in the back of the truck will be used to test the security protocols of the Presidential Guard Battalion of the SPI."

Hugo gave a trembling nod.

The Servicio de Protección Institucional protected the president along with important installations around the Republic of Panama.

"This country needs men like you, Hugo Sandoval," Vega said. "But it would be most embarrassing if any word of this matter leaked to the media. We will, of course, give you a bonus to keep quiet." He chuckled. "The Americans call it hush money."

"Thank you, **patrón,**" Sandoval said. The kettledrum beat of his heart in his ears made it impossible to think. If he'd had a hat in his hands, he would have been wringing it.

Agent Pinto opened the driver's-side door and leaned in, his back to Hugo and the lieutenant.

"I suppose we should pay the man," Vega said to his partner. "Except . . ." He stopped suddenly, holding up his finger and tut-tutting the air.

Agent Pinto busied himself with something inside the truck, hopefully preparing to drive the cursed thing out of Valeria's courtyard.

"I wonder . . ." Vega said to Hugo. "Did anyone else happen to look in the back?" His brow shot up above the aviators. "Your girlfriend, perhaps? Remember, this is official. We need a comprehensive list for our paperwork."

"She was curious," Hugo said. "But she had no idea what she was looking at."

"That does not matter." Vega snapped his fingers. It was surprisingly loud and made Hugo flinch. "Bring her here. I will take a photo of each of you for our files, and then Agent Pinto will see that you are paid."

Hugo called out weakly, half hoping Valeria had fled out the front door.

No such luck. She stepped tentatively outside, letting the screen door slam behind her before she padded across the yard to Hugo's side. She nearly knocked him over, she pushed in so tight.

He wrapped his arm around her shoulders and pulled her close. "It's okay," he whispered. "We did the right thing."

"Thank you for keeping quiet about this matter." Vega said. He took two quick photographs with his mobile phone and then smiled, snapping his fingers again at his companion.

"Agent Pinto," he said. "Pay them their hush money."

"Of course, **patrón.**" Pinto stepped around the open door of the truck cab.

Too late, Hugo saw the agent had attached a black suppressor to the barrel of his pistol.

Pinto's first two shots hit him in the center of his

chest. He was vaguely aware of Valeria's gasping cries as more shots ripped through her.

He fell backward. Unable to move or even turn his head, he stared up at the clear sky beyond the leaves of the lemon trees in Valeria's courtyard. She moaned on the ground beside him.

"Please . . ." he whimpered.

Pinto stepped closer, pointing the black maw of the suppressor directly at Hugo's mouth. The agent's youthful face screwed into a twisted expression of glee that matched the misshapen ear.

"Hush," he said.

24

John Clark had nothing to prove. He'd proved it already. Now it was his job to bring up the new generation—while keeping a toe in the water himself. Men like him did not die in their sleep.

The Campus director of operations stood in the front of the conference room/classroom off the underground range, affectionately known as "the schoolhouse." A leather folio and video remote sat on the table in front of him. Thinning silver hair did little to take away from his looming swagger. He was dressed for function over form—khakis, well-worn desert boots, casual cotton shirt that covered the pistol on his right hip. The stainless clip of his folding Zero Tolerance blade glinted against the right-hand pocket of his slacks.

Located two levels beneath the main Hendley Associates building, the entire area was off-limits to the white-side employees. Very few even knew the space existed. Even so, Gavin Biery, the director of technology, who wore the ESCM (electronic surveillance countermeasures) hat for The Campus, swept the area regularly for listening devices.

Chilly Edwards and Mandy Cobb, the newbies to The Campus, had settled in well, performing as Clark had expected when they arrived—clearheaded and hyperaware of their surroundings. There had been a few hiccups. There always were. In training, mistakes meant the opportunity to learn. In the field . . . well, Clark trained them to keep those to a minimum.

A long oval table of richly polished mahogany occupied the center of the room, surrounded by nine leather swivel chairs. It looked more like something out of a Fortune 100 company conference room than a shooting-range schoolhouse, but Gerry Hendley, a close friend of President Ryan and the "name on the door" of the company, loved good bourbon and fine furniture. A bank of bulletproof windows ran along the far wall, allowing students not on the line to view the six fifty-yard shooting lanes. Everything could be controlled from inside the classroom or on the range itself.

Flat-screen monitors and a large interactive whiteboard covered the head of the conference room. Six wooden chairs lined the wall nearest the door, straight-backed and much less inviting than the padded leather swivels around the table. Had this been a government conference room, these would have been the number two seats, where deputies and aides parked themselves.

Both newcomers had come up in agencies where the old guard hazed their rookies. As Clark expected, Edwards and Cobb took respectful positions in the staff chairs along the wall. Ding Chavez, as assistant director of operations, sat at the head of the table under the whiteboard. Legacy Campus personnel—Caruso, Jack Ryan, Jr., Adara Sherman, Bartosz "Midas" Jankowski, and Lisanne Robertson—spaced themselves evenly in the leather chairs surrounding the table.

Clark surveyed the faces in silence for a time, just long enough to make everyone wonder what he was thinking. The newcomers were attentive, locked on, but Mandy still wore the same look of mild annoyance, along with her khakis, button-down oxford, and green fleece. Clark understood the look. He saw it every day in the mirror when he shaved. Some faces were just made that way.

"Mandy," he said. "You graduated the police academy, endured field training, SWAT selection, FBI selection, and all but the last week of new agent training at Quantico. Correct?"

"Yes, sir," she said. Her eyes shifted, obviously wondering where this was going.

"If you had to pick the worst part?"

"Field training," she fired back immediately.

"And why's that?" Clark asked.

"Because my field training officer was a dick," she said. "He made me go into McDonald's and fill out an employment application every night mid-shift—in uniform—because he was sure I wouldn't make it as a police officer. He and the manager got a big yuck out of it."

"Brilliant!" Midas Jankowski chuckled from the far end of the table. The former Delta colonel was a bear of a man, slightly taller and with a bigger beard than Jack Ryan, Jr., who sat across from him. Lisanne Robertson sat next to Ryan. She leaned forward, her prosthetic arm resting on the table. She'd become so proficient Clark often forgot it wasn't her real limb. Ryan leaned forward and gave Chilly a somber thumbs-up. They'd met before, but the man had, after all, saved his mother's life.

"Here's the deal," Clark said. "We've got no time for hazing, or for treating you like rookies. Cobb, Edwards, move your asses to the table with the rest of us, where you belong."

The legacy operators rolled their chairs sideways to allow the others to grab seats among them. Even Dom and Adara moved apart, though they were an item and were normally joined at the hip during briefings and after-actions.

The newcomers took their seats at the conference table on command, but remained stiff as if sitting at attention.

"We will, of course, train, and we will train hard," Clark said. "But consider yourselves operational as of this moment. Not optimal, but operational. The lion's share of that training will be in the field—together, excelling as a unit." He raised a brow at Jack Junior. "This is not the place for lone wolves."

Junior chuckled. "I thought you said there was no hazing."

Clark ignored him and continued to address the newcomers. "You were chosen because we believe your personalities and skill sets will fit in nicely with this motley crew we have already."

Mandy Cobb leaned back in her chair and heaved a heavy sigh.

"Question?" Clark asked.

"So . . . we're operational as of now?" Her forehead creased. "Does that mean we already have a mission?"

"We do," Clark said. "We're augmenting a team already on the ground in Cartagena. Our part of the op is surveillance only. We'll leave the heavy lifting to the Ground Branch folks." Clark raised a hand before anyone could protest. "I know going out from the jump removes the luxury of a complete training cycle before you go active. But think of it like this: you were days away from graduating the FBI Academy. I can guarantee you that the Bureau would have you hit the ground running. With a senior agent, sure, but everything you did would be real-world. This is that."

Chavez chimed in. "SWAT, the Bureau, you'll both be surprised at the similarities. John and I are big on training, as you will see, but no academy ever gives you enough time to run surveillance-detection routes, covert communication, defensive tactics. You hone those skills by doing them. And you have the basics. Otherwise, you wouldn't be here. If anything, our rules of engagement are . . . less stringent."

"True enough," Clark said. "The point is, you'll learn from each other. Whatever we're working on, we work together."

"Mr. C is right," Midas said. "He works us like rented mules, but we are **a team** of rented mules, all hitched to the same plow."

Clark offered a rare smile. "And that is an excellent place to start introductions. The man with the nice metaphor is Midas. Former Delta . . ."

Each legacy operator introduced themselves to the newest members of The Campus—and vice versa. No one there was a bragger, so intros went quickly—just the facts.

"Let's get the big picture of the targets of this operation," Clark said. "A group of mercenaries responsible for dozens of killings, kidnappings, and coups around the world—including the abduction of the First Lady and the murder of her Secret Service protection detail. They are extremely bad and extremely well trained. They call themselves the Camarilla."

Chilly had firsthand experience with at least two of the Camarilla assholes depicted on the whiteboard. He recognized two of the military ID photos as men he'd clocked through the scope of his sniper rifle during the hostage rescue op where they got back the First Lady. One in a morgue photo was likely his, too, but a 168-grain MatchKing bullet under the eye didn't leave much intact for identification purposes. A Western District of Texas U.S. Marshals mug shot showed a bewildered man holding a placard that said his name was Burt Pennington. He'd been part of the kidnapping, but in the end tried to help Mrs. Ryan escape—the only reason he'd survived the event. Five military ID photos bore diagonal red lines. Deceased.

"These were just the tip of the iceberg," Clark said. "Liberty Crossing has tasked us, along with much of the intelligence community, with identifying the Camarilla's organizational structure."

He clicked the remote and brought up the screen grab of Sabine Gorshkova in her blood-spattered blouse, eyes fierce, looking skyward. "We believe this woman has hired them as her security."

Jack Junior studied the screen. "The Camarilla we've seen before aren't the type to work corporate security. What business is this woman in?"

"Still a lot of questions about her." Clark pressed the remote and brought up the crime scene photos from Bolivia. "But this is an example of her brother's work."

Chilly nearly came up out of his chair when he saw the photos from the bloody scenes in Aviano, Bolivia, and Peru.

"Son of a bitch," Midas said under his breath. "Claw hammers . . ."

Adara spoke next, eyes locked on the brutality of the screen. "If this is her brother, that's the guy I want to go after."

"He's been dealt with." Clark brought up another view of the woman in white, this one from a wider angle that showed the bodies of two prostrate men on the ground at her feet. "Both him and his bodyguard."

Clark gave them a detailed rundown of Joaquín Gorshkov and his sister, Sabine Gorshkova.

Outside, Chilly was a picture of calm—measured breathing, still hands on the table, hyper-focused on the information coming from Clark. Inside, his brain was on overdrive, wondering if he was performing up to snuff. He'd thought they would get some kind of packet with all this intel. Maybe he should take notes. He felt like he should be taking notes. No one else was taking notes . . .

He willed himself to calm down before he entered what his sniper cadre leader called full-bore mental-hyperventilation.

Clark was apparently a mind reader.

"Everything we're giving you is in the file," he said. "I expect you'll all want to read over it again tonight before you leave. Get it set in your mind."

Ryan raised his hand. "This is a screenshot," he said. "Can we see the whole video?"

Clark shook his head. "The Agency hasn't yet

made that available. They don't want it out in the wild, for obvious reasons."

"Still," Adara said. "It would be good to see the whole thing for context."

"Agreed," Clark said. "I'll get with the DNI. I'm sure she'll have the CIA loop us in on everything." He nodded at the screen. "Just looking at the still," he said, "what do you see?"

Dom gave a little shrug. "A targeted killing if it was us," he said. "An assassination if it was someone else."

"It was us," Clark said. "Not The Campus, but CIA."

Targeted killing. Chilly turned the words over in his head.

"So," Jack Junior said. "Gorshkov and his sister are a couple of claw-hammer revolutionaries who have hired the Camarilla?"

"That's the prevailing sentiment." Clark pulled up side-by-side photos of the bearded man behind Gorshkov, one where he was on his feet, frowning at something off camera, the other where he lay on his back with his mouth agape and a hole in his head. "This supremely unlucky guy happened to be directly lined up with Gorshkov. Manuel Ramirez, ex–Chilean SF. He was thought to be on the Camarilla payroll, and if he was, it's a good bet the others are as well. Director Foley has a couple of separate teams mapping everyone in these photos for connections to known Camarilla operatives.

I've got a call with my contact in"—he checked his watch—"two hours. I'll ask her about the video when we talk. Until then, Ding is going to get everyone some time on the line."

"Mr. C," Jack Junior said. "If the CIA's got two teams working on identifying members of the Camarilla, where do we come in?"

"This one." Clark scrolled to the photo of Sabine Gorshkova again. "We're assigned to an Agency team called WINDWARD STATION."

"So we're working for the CIA?" Cobb mused.

"**With** the CIA," Clark said. "But essentially yes. One more thing to keep in mind. The folks we're working with are undeclared. They have no diplomatic cover . . . and neither do we."

C lark stepped away and gave his son-in-law the floor, watching, adding a certain amount of healthy stress with his presence alone.

"All right," Chavez said. "A quick word to our new operators about weapons. In our line of work, a firearm can be essential. But in some instances, going strapped would be more likely to get us in trouble. Your handgun prints on your shirt when you're working in Moscow, for instance, and you go from being a sketchy tourist to an American spy—which lands you in the gulag."

Chavez reached below the conference table and

brought up a cardboard box out of which he took two locking black plastic handgun cases.

"Chilly," he said. "You brought your Glock 43X, right?"

"Yes, sir."

"Mandy, you qualified expert with your Glock 19 at Quantico."

"I did."

Chavez pushed the two cases across the table to the new operators. "Everyone has a favorite setup, but we're going to be a long way from any backup or resupply when we're out, so we customarily carry the same basic kit."

"Except me." Clark tapped the Bill Wilson Combat 1911 on his hip. "But I'm old."

Chavez let that slide like a good son-in-law. "The rest of us have gone to 43Xs so we can all use the same magazines."

"Could I just carry mine?" Chilly asked. "I'm familiar with how it shoots."

"I get that," Chavez said. "But these are ghosts. No serial number to come back to you."

"Or the United States government," Dom Caruso said.

"Exactly. We are deniable, as we explained from the get-go." Chavez nodded to Chilly's pistol case. "This one is set up identically to your personal weapon—Holosun 507K green dot, tungsten guide rod, XS F8 night sights, and a Pyramid Trigger."

"Yeah," Midas chuckled. "Because that doesn't scream 'America.'"

"There is that," Chavez said. "Let's get on guns." He moved his ear pro off the clipboard and consulted the paperwork underneath. "First shooters up are Adara, Midas, Jack, and Chilly. Mandy, Dom, Lisanne, you get to shoot against Mr. C, poor bastards." He gave a sad shake of his head. "Anyway. This course of fire will be from the five-, seven-, and fifteen-yard lines. Smooth and fast. Remember the basics—equal height, equal light. Front sight . . . Press . . ."

The operators looked at Chavez like he was explaining how to boil water.

He grinned. "I'm just shittin' you. You all know the basics. That said, it never hurts to go over them in your head. We're grown-ups here, running a hot line. As you all know, shooting is a perishable skill. In this line of work, if you don't practice, you perish."

The door to the firing line gave an audible whoosh when Chavez pulled it open, pressurized to keep fumes and lead residue safely inside the range itself, where they could be filtered out. The shooters filed through, all grinning at the opportunity to pit their speed and skill against the others.

Like any two sailboats going the same direction, Clark thought. **When shooters get together on the line, it's always a competition.**

Everyone was doing well, better than that, even. But Chilly Edwards was a gunfighter. Clark knew the kid was a talented sniper. He'd taken out three hostiles to save Cathy Ryan, all while under tremendous pressure. But Chilly turned out to be a natural with a pistol as well. He was lightning fast out of the holster, but butter smooth, driving the little Glock as if it were an extension of his hand. The ragged hole in the center of his blue transitional silhouette remained the size of a silver dollar no matter how far out Chavez moved their targets or sped up the course. Clark felt himself itching to get in there and have a run at the kid. He'd been a .45 man for as long as he could remember. John Moses Browning's venerable 1911 had been his choice of sidearm for many a mission during his time as a SEAL with MACV-SOG in Vietnam. He'd stuck with the system after he separated, if you could call it that, using his own Colt to deadly effect on any number of bastards who, if he was honest, simply needed killing. Eventually, the siren song of a "new and better gun" beckoned. He transitioned to a SIG Sauer P220. Double-action trigger, it was still a .45. He loved the gun and would likely still be carrying it but for a run-in with a Russian bastard who'd done a number on his gun hand with the business end of a ball peen hammer. It had taken Herculean effort for Clark just to be able to use his hand again—and he didn't heal nearly as fast as he did when he was young. Extensive nerve and muscle damage made the double-action first shot of the P220 problematic, sending Clark back where he started with a 1911, this time in a Bill Wilson Carry from Wilson Combat. A work of art, the pistol all but disappeared under a light jacket in the outside-the-pants pancake holster over his right hip.

He checked his watch again, a beefy decades-old Seiko Turtle he'd had since his SEAL days. Ding and the first set of shooters were just filing back into the classroom off the range.

Ear pro in hand, Clark led Dom, Cobb, and Lisanne to the door, meeting Chilly as he came out.

"There's still one open lane," Clark said. "Feel like having another go?"

Chilly hooked a thumb at his chest, as if to say, **Who me?**

Clark shrugged. "I understand if you're tired . . ."

"Oh, hell yes," Chilly said. "I mean, hell yes, sir!"

25

The auntie who raised Felix Moncada had often called him a dreamer, describing him as the kind of boy who liked to dress up in costumes and pretend he was someone great.

Now he had a chance to actually be great.

Moncada told his secretary he would be available on his mobile, then put the device on silent and left it in his desk drawer. If things did not go as planned, there would surely be an inquiry after the fact. He saw no point in providing investigators with a detailed map of all his comings and goings.

He'd left his Mercedes S 580 sedan at home, opting for a Ford F-150, which was still shiny and new, but much less conspicuous than a Kalahari-gold sedan. He headed north into Curundú, a rough, poverty-stricken neighborhood where he'd lived with one auntie after the Americans murdered his parents. That auntie had eventually shipped him off to live with her sister on a pineapple plantation west of the city. She'd said it was for his own good, but she'd likely grown tired of him. Even as a child he was self-aware enough to realize he was prone to fits of nervous energy. Still, he went back frequently to visit her and considered the crumbling back alleys and potholed one-way streets of Curundú as much his home as anywhere.

Now he used them to make certain he wasn't being followed, frequently checking his rearview mirror as he drove. He stopped at a fuel station long enough to change into a loose cotton shirt and linen slacks. It would be much too hot for a business suit where he was going.

The pickup had turned into an oven during the time it took him to change clothes and he cranked up the air conditioner as he worked his way to Highway 1, bypassing Casco Viejo, and then exiting near the stadium. He could not help but smile at the high fences and concertina wire of the Ministry of Public Security on his left.

It would do them little good . . .

Moncada wound his way past the Panama Convention Center, whipping quickly into the parking lot of the Biomuseo to check for surveilling vehicles. He released a pent-up sigh when he saw he was free from any tail and committed himself to the Amador Causeway.

Made with the rubble dug from the eight-mile portion of the Panama Canal known as the Culebra Cut, the causeway connected three small islands to the mainland. Other than the way he'd come in, there was no way off except by boat. Oil tankers, container transports, and cruise ships loomed to his left, anchored on a glassy sea, shimmering in mirages of heat as they waited for their appointed time in the canal or dropping off tourists. A flock of what must have been fifty gray pelicans winged along beside him in formation over the water, their grace in the air belying the ungainliness of their great beaks.

Moncada checked his mirrors once again. Sun dazzled the windshields of two dozen cars in the marina parking lot. Heat shimmered off the pavement. Antennas, masts, and radars bristled from motor- and sailboats moored in Flamenco Marina, many of them owned by rich North American expats who came to take advantage of the tax benefits and cheap healthcare in a country they'd once invaded. Moncada shook off the thought and got out of his pickup. Stifling humidity grabbed his lungs and soaked his shirt as soon as he left the comfort of the truck's air-conditioning.

He used the key fob to lock the Ford over his shoulder, hearing the comforting honk of the horn as he made his way toward the harbor. He kept a fifteen-foot Boston Whaler Montauk here under an assumed name. A ball cap and dark sunglasses helped to hide his identity from any passersby. He needn't have worried. Voting was compulsory in Panama, but few could probably identify the president out of context, let alone members of his cabinet or staff.

The 60-horsepower Mercury outboard started on the first crank, and Moncada soon had the little Whaler up on step and flying across the water toward a forty-foot Jeanneau sailboat named the **Bambina,** which was anchored off the point on Bahia Flamenco.

It was a slack tide with no wind, and the **Bambina**'s anchor dropped straight down from her bowsprit, disappearing into the chocolate-brown waters of Panama Bay. Moncada took the Whaler around the sailboat once, slowly, so as not to cause a wake—looking for any signs of trouble.

A shadow passed over him as a large frigate bird flew between him and the sun.

A giant of a man with sandy hair and a week's worth of facial scruff stuck his head up from below and eyed Moncada's approach. He looked as though he could have picked up the Boston Whaler and snapped it in half. Moncada had never met Ian Doyle, all he had was the man's description. **Thick** about covered it. Camarilla operators were camera shy to the extreme. Their leader was rumored to have killed an entire family on vacation in Lagoa, Portugal, for posting vacation photos that had inadvertently captured the shadowy recluse in the background.

Having made the terrifying acquaintance of the Spaniard, Moncada had no doubt that the story was true—and probably softened the details up a bit.

Doyle was expecting his arrival, but the walnut grip of a Browning Hi-Power pistol stuck from his waistband nonetheless. Moncada put the motor in idle and went forward to toss him the bowline.

"Welcome to Panama," he said, wiping sea spray off his hands on to the front of his slacks. "I hope your trip was good."

Doyle said nothing at first, scanning the horizon, not as if he were prey, but like a predator on the lookout for rival killers. He shielded his eyes from the sun with the flat of his hand and looked up at the frigate bird.

"Big son of a bitch," he said, more grunt than words. Moncada hadn't expected the Irish accent.

Seemingly satisfied that they were alone, Doyle secured the bowline to a cleat on the **Bambina**'s rail and then turned toward the companionway.

"How about you run down what you need me to do," he said over his shoulder as he disappeared into the bowels of the boat. His pleasant Irish accent belied the hateful look in his green eyes.

Moncada hauled himself over the lifelines and onto the deck. He followed the sandy-haired giant below, wondering if he was about to be murdered. Doyle found a spot on the settee where he could stretch out his legs. Moncada took his customary spot at the polished teak table. The Jeanneau was a beamy boat, well-appointed with fine wood and soft leatherette cushions. Another man might have been tempted to bring his secretary out here. Not Moncada. He needed an out-of-the-way place for meetings such as this. Besides, his secretary was perfectly happy with their meetings at any of the mid-level tourist hotels downtown.

"I was told you can build the devices we need," he said.

Doyle gave a grunting yawn. "I can," he said. "Provided you have the components."

"That will not be a problem," Moncada said. "Everything in the world comes through Panama." He took a small notebook out of his shirt pocket and slid it and a pen across the table. "Tell me what you need for five devices large enough to, say, destroy a passenger car."

Doyle took the notepad and began to scribble in it. "Five . . ."

"The remainder of your team is—"

"I have that handled," Doyle said. "I understand most are staying near the Ciudad del Saber—formerly Fort Clayton."

"That is correct."

"Very well," Doyle said. "I'll meet them after you and I are done here."

"They know the locations where we want the devices," Moncada said.

"Bombs," Doyle said. "Hell, call them what they are."

"Of course," Moncada said. This man spoke with

such force Moncada had to concentrate to keep from blinking at his every word. "B-bombs. They do not have to be very large, just enough to cause panic."

"Ah," Doyle said. "Panic they will cause. I promise that."

"Good," Moncada said. "So, you have been briefed on the basics of JAMAICA?"

The Irishman leaned back and took a deep breath. "It seems a bit complicated if you think on it too long—"

Moncada started to argue, but Doyle plowed on. "Blow a ship in the canal, set off a series of smaller explosions along with two strategically placed large ones. Throw in a couple of assassinations and some random gunfire. Civilized men will go apeshit and think they are under attack from all sides at once. I understand that when the shooting is over there will be a couple of very important vacancies within your government. Ruskies just happen to be here to smooth the transition to the new flavor-of-the-day government."

Moncada nodded. He didn't like talking so openly about the specifics of the operation.

"Who exactly blows the devices?"

"I will," Moncada said. "To ensure that I am far enough away when they go off."

"That's wise," Doyle said.

Moncada couldn't tell if the man was making fun of him or not. In the end, it didn't matter as long as he did his job. "I can do it by phone, correct?"

"You can," the Irishman said. "I understand the device on the ship is different."

"Ah," Moncada said. "That one is already in place. Your predecessor was concerned about a random radio wave detonating it too soon. He set the GPS so the device will arm when it transits north to south through the first gate of the Cocoli Locks."

"The canal expansion project?"

"Correct," Moncada said. "Once armed, it will blow when it passes through the second set of gates into the middle lock."

"Obliterating any nearby boat pilots," Doyle mused. "As well as any poor gobshites assisting in the transit. What's left of the ship will sink into the locks, blocking that portion of the canal."

"Is this a problem?"

"The body count?" Doyle gave a sardonic chuckle. "I don't give a damn about that." He tapped the ink pen on the table, clicking it while he thought. "Just making sure I have your plan right in my head. There's a hell of a lot of moving parts."

"And fail-safes," Moncada said. His face flushed, unaccustomed to explaining his plan. "Not so difficult. Only a matter of timing and communications."

Doyle laughed out loud at that. **"Señor,"** he said. "Timing and communications are the two elements of any op that are most likely to turn to shit."

"Your boss assured—"

Doyle raised a hand, still chuckling. "Don't get your knickers in a twist. We will do what needs to be done." He cocked his head. "I do have a question about that Chinese container ship. Your country gets a great deal of its revenue from the canal. Blocking it with wreckage seems like a good way to cut off your nose to spite your face."

"Miraflores Locks will remain open for traffic." Moncada had to bite his lip to keep it from trembling. Doyle was not the sort of man to whom you wanted to show weakness. "Do your part and this will work out perfectly."

Mercifully, Doyle didn't appear to respect him enough to take offense.

"I get it," Doyle said. "You take your country apart and then your new Russian friends will help you put it back together, better than it was. That's about the size of it, eh?" Finished with the list of required items, he slid the notepad back across the table, looking Moncada straight in the eye. "If there's anything else I should know, you need to tell me now."

"Maybe," Moncada said. He looked away, staring up and out the companionway, slowly shaking his head as a flock of pelicans winged past. "I can't put a finger on it."

Doyle rapped his knuckles on the teak table. "Hey, we're not going to have another raid by that local **policía señorita** are we?"

"Oh, no," Moncada said. "She won't be a problem. That is being taken care of as we speak."

26

The White House gym, or, more specifically, the President's gym, saw frequent use most weeks, but even more after Cathy's abduction. The job of commander in chief was stressful enough under normal circumstances, but Ryan found himself doing a lot of staring at the ceiling at two in the morning these days. Time in the gym helped. A little.

Special Agent Gary Montgomery jogged on the treadmill beside Ryan's, by his own admission never going all out because he needed to have some left in the tank if the shit hit the fan. That was fine by Ryan. He wanted to talk more than he wanted to run. This was just a way of killing multiple birds with one stone.

Montgomery had been in a cloudy mood since Ryan's discussion with the NSC about heading to Panama. At six feet and a modest one ninety-five, Ryan was no small fry. But Montgomery dwarfed him by inches and pounds. A former boxer for the University of Michigan, his slightly crooked nose added to his mean mug even when he was relatively content. When he was upset, he could frighten children with a glance. If he was well and truly angry, a look from him could make a grown man weep. An upset citizen had once written to the director of the Secret Service complaining that the **troglodyte working the rope line with President Ryan had glared at me with such terrifying, bloodshot eyes** that she was now plagued with chronic diarrhea.

A useful superpower in a United States Secret Service agent.

"You know I appreciate your counsel, Gary," Ryan said. He slowed the speed down to 3.5 to make it easier to carry on a conversation.

"And I have always appreciated that, Mr. President."

There was silence for a time but for the periodic squeak of running shoes on the treadmill belts.

"So, I've made my case for a side trip to Panama," Ryan said. "You've got Protective Intelligence doing a deep dive into the possible dangers. They'll give us a data-driven assessment. As will State and the DoD. I'd like to hear your gut assessment."

"The protests bother me, sir," Montgomery said. "As I said before. Just the right spark will set them off in a hurry." Matching Ryan's pace, Montgomery turned to meet his eye as they jogged. "I'm not sure if you realize this, Mr. President, but you're not only a spark, you're a . . . a flamethrower. You know that bit Secretary Adler said about you making your own weather?"

Ryan nodded.

"He stole that from the Secret Service . . ."

"Is that so?"

"'Jack Ryan makes his own weather,' that's what we say."

Ryan stifled a chuckle. "Is that good or bad?"

"Neither," Montgomery said. "It just is. But beyond your propensity to be larger than life, it's also the office. When the President shows up, those who want to celebrate cheer louder. But those who are angry about something sometimes resort to picking up a stick to make their point."

"I can see that," Ryan said.

Montgomery plowed ahead. "And I've not even mentioned the plot to kill Botero."

"The **foiled** plot," Ryan said.

"Maybe it was foiled. Maybe the PNP just found one cell of many. Assassination plots can be like cancer. If you don't get it all, the leftover cells can prove deadly. Many of my agents and military assets are already staged in Argentina for the upcoming summit. I'll need to move some to Panama prior to our arrival, which means they won't be shoring up security in Mar del Plata."

"You know better than I do, Gary, there are dozens of plots to kill me at any given time. I can't stay locked in the White House during my entire term because someone wants to hurt me."

"No, you can't," Montgomery said. "As much as I would like that to be the case." He pushed the stop button on his treadmill. "You ever mow over a dandelion blossom?"

"Of course."

"What happens?"

Ryan saw where this was going. "They blossom again closer to the ground."

"That's right," Montgomery said. "It makes them harder to find and mow down the next time—and they go to seed much faster. Dandelions have got to be pulled up by the roots." He took a deep breath, choosing his words. "Look, Mr. President, the fact is, my people should have seen San Antonio coming. We failed the First Lady . . . And we failed you."

"I've read the case study," Ryan said. "There was no fault found on the part of the Secret Service."

"That's what the report states," Montgomery said. "But you and I know better. If someone gets harmed or, God forbid, killed on our watch—it can't be anyone's fault but ours. We. Must. Not. Fail. Any other mindset and agents will start a steady diet of excuses every time we have an incident. Zero-fail means just that."

"I get it," Ryan said. "But we'll have protesters everywhere we go."

"That's true," Montgomery said. "But I still have

to advise you of the risks. Due respect, Mr. President, but if it were up to me, I'd have you and your family confined to the PEOC bunker for the rest of your term. You could govern by Zoom."

"Sounds like a Bond villain," Ryan said. "Listen. Here's my thinking. Why does the U.S. have such a shitty reputation in Latin America?"

Montgomery grimaced, obviously not wanting to go there.

Ryan prodded. "Come on."

"Propping up despots, I suppose."

"Right," Ryan said. "Installing dictators to keep communists out. Eisenhower is even on record saying they weren't ready for democracy."

"After they attacked Nixon," Montgomery reminded him.

"True," Ryan said. "But now the Russians are breathing down Botero's neck. This could be our chance to keep communists out by propping up a good man. Seems worth the risk to me."

Montgomery shook his head slowly. "Understood. If you decide to go, then the Secret Service will make it work."

"Of that I have no doubt."

27

Gabriella Canto had no time to go for a run— but knew in her bones that she couldn't afford to skip it, either. Running, from the time she was in primary school, had helped to clear her mind and work through her problems.

And Commissioner Javier Guerra was a problem. The man was up to something. But what? Perhaps she was overreacting, seeing ghosts when there were none. And yet . . .

Canto jogged in place at the corner of Ricardo Arango Avenue and East Fifty-Seventh Street, waiting for a parade of three delivery trucks to rattle through the intersection. With no light or stop sign, conventional wisdom said the vehicle with the most momentum had the right of way. Evening joggers like Major Canto played a dangerous game of **Frogger** every time they crossed the street.

Sweat soaked her gray T-shirt and black running shorts; Canto would have much preferred to get away and run along the causeway or one of the other trails along the sea, but time was a luxury she did not have. Still, her brain needed this and the opportunity to think that it offered. She decided to take her boring usual route in the downtown hotel neighborhood of Obarrio near her apartment. Gleaming skyscrapers of glass and steel, most of them built in the last fifteen years, rose from between run-down businesses and homes with rusting tin siding and orange tile roofs. Bits of black ash floated down from above, remnants of cookfires in the older homes without fancy kitchens like the apartments that towered above them had.

Major Canto cut left down East Fifty-Seventh, alongside a municipal playground and park. The street was dark, narrow, and one way, with what little traffic there was coming at her. She kept to the cracked sidewalk that was really more gravel than concrete. She fell back into her natural rhythm—step, step, breathe. Step, step, breathe. All the while mulling over Guerra's culpability in . . . whatever this was. The man was a pig. There was no doubt about that. He'd been trying to take her to bed since she met him. The thought of it made her want to retch . . .

And then there was the raid.

The killing.

Pulga . . . Flea . . . What had the dead man meant by that? And why had Guerra been so quick to shoot him? To shut him up obviously. Or the commissioner had just been off the street so long he was jumpy on the trigger. **Pulga** could be something innocuous . . . And yet, a man with bombs, Uzi machine guns, and a map to the presidential palace who somehow knew Commissioner Guerra . . . There was nothing innocuous about that.

No, there was too much evidence. The mental gymnastics necessary to believe unreasonable explanations were . . . unreasonable—and it made her head hurt.

Caught up in her mystery, she nearly tripped over a tattered plastic garbage bag full of aluminum cans in the middle of the sidewalk. She looked up in time to note a lone figure emerging from the shadows of a gnarled elm just past the playground on her left. Less than thirty feet ahead, the guy was tall, heavy—and working a little too hard to ignore her. The coal on the end of a cigarette glowed bright orange at the corner of his lips.

Canto glanced around the street. It was getting dark, and what little traffic there was had thinned. She briefly considered crossing to the other side— that's what she would have told her sister to do. There were apartments there, people coming and going. But a section of metal guardrail ran along this portion of the walkway, trapping her between it and the chain-link fence of the park. The railing was short enough to jump, but Canto was a major in the Policía Nacional, not the sort of person to run.

Twenty feet away now.

She was being foolish. Jumpy for no reason. This was nothing.

Wasn't it?

She slowed a half step, letting her right hand swing back so her arm brushed the Smith & Wesson 351 PD AirLite revolver in a belly band holster around her waist. The .22 Magnum wasn't optimum as far as defensive weapons were concerned, but it was far better than tooth and nail—and comforting to know it was there, just in case. The aluminum alloy frame weighed less than twelve ounces and carried seven rounds in the cylinder.

The man ahead turned to face her as she got closer. She knew it was her mind playing tricks on her, but his presence seemed to make the shadows darker, more sinister. She was almost on top of him before she saw the second man, lurking behind the tree. This one was smaller, wiry, with a challenging look on his face that said he didn't give a shit if she knew he was there for her.

Ten feet out. Much too close.

Cursing her own stupidity, Canto put on the brakes and stopped cold in the middle of the sidewalk.

Over a decade of experience on the street and in the gym had ingrained into Gabriella Canto a simple truth about violent confrontations. No matter how strong she was, how much she worked out, in a toe-to-toe fight against a grown man, women were at a severe disadvantage. Two grown men . . . that was a serious problem.

"You boys are scaring me!" she barked, sounding anything but frightened. If the men were impressed by her seasoned command voice they did not show it.

To the contrary, the wiry one called her by name.

"Awww, do not be scared, my little Major Gabilita." The words dripped from a crooked sneer. He took another step from behind the tree, right hand back behind his leg. The arm swung out slightly, allowing Canto to catch the slightest glint of a blade in the shadows. The one with a cigarette had some kind of pistol just visible in his waistband now. A gun and a blade. Canto's breath caught hard in her chest.

Not good. Not good at all.

Neither man made any move toward her, but they didn't step away, either, instead holding their ground as if they expected her to come to them.

A crunch in the gravel behind her sent a rush of adrenaline down her spine. The guy with the cigarette looked up and made eye contact with whoever was coming up from the rear.

The fact that there were three made Canto's decision for her. There was a possibility that they were merely trying to intimidate her, but she didn't have the luxury of waiting to find out. Rather than waste another second on words or orders, she lifted the tail of her T-shirt with her left hand and drew the revolver with her right. She crouched slightly, shoving the gun straight out in front of her.

"Policía!" she barked, and shot the man with the cigarette in the throat as he reached for the pistol in his waistband. Small as it was, the 45-grain projectile did its job, impacting the vertebrae in the back of the man's neck with enough force to drop him on the spot. His body piled up in a heap between his knife-wielding partner and Canto.

Canto adjusted her aim and sent a round toward the man with the knife. Rushed, she swung past center mass. She fired twice, her first shot striking the man's right biceps. The second round took him in the ribs. Wobbled, he dropped the knife, but he was far from out of play.

Another crunch in the gravel caused Canto to spin, revolver held low and tight to her side.

The third attacker was almost on top of her, running, roaring like a locomotive at the sight of his wounded partners. He was a mountain of a man, larger than both the other men put together, much of it fat, but enough muscle to cause real problems in a fight. This one, too, had a knife, a long thin blade for filleting fish, capable of piercing Canto's heart with ease if she let him get close enough.

Conventional wisdom said someone armed with a handgun needed at least twenty-one feet to mount an adequate defense against an attacker with a blade. Canto had less than half that.

Chain-link fence on her right now, metal guardrail to her left, Canto found herself trapped between the wounded attacker behind her and the oncoming giant. Even if she emptied her last four rounds into this man, he could still carve her up with the knife before he realized he was dead. Meeting him head-on was tantamount to suicide. With nowhere to retreat or a good route to move offline, she took the least bad option.

Smith & Wesson in both hands, she dropped back a hair with her right leg, letting it collapse so that she rolled into a semi-controlled fall, staring directly up at the oncoming attacker. On her back and taking care to keep her feet and knees out of the line of fire, she brought the revolver up, squeezing the trigger as the front sight covered the man's groin, then again as it passed his belly button, and a third time as it reached his collar. The steep angle made all three rounds effective, but the last caught him under the chin, taking out his soft palate and ending his fight. He fell close enough to glance off Canto's legs.

Still not out of the woods, she rolled onto her belly, bracing her elbows on the rough gravel, the revolver straight out in front of her. Something brushed her leg behind her. She kicked out blindly, impacting what she thought was the man's face. He cried out and then went quiet.

In front of her, the surviving attacker stooped over his dead friend, pulling the pistol from his belt. Pink blood frothed at the corners of his lips. Canto's earlier shot had punctured a lung.

"Stop!" she yelled. Her words blew dirt and leaves from the path in front of her face.

He ignored her, wrapping his fingers around his dead partner's pistol.

Canto put her last round behind the man's ear. He stiffened, then toppled sideways onto his friend. Flooded with adrenaline, she pulled the trigger again, barely aware that the hammer clicked against an empty chamber. She had no reloads. If there were more than three attackers, she was done for.

A shuffling commotion to her right sent her rolling onto her side, gun up out of habit, though it was empty and useless as anything but a club.

A taxi had pulled to the curb. The astonished driver jumped out and rushed to the rail, a baseball bat in hand.

He stopped cold when he saw the carnage.

"Are . . . are you . . . all right?" he asked.

Canto clamored to her feet, grabbing the metal guardrail for support. "Police," she said, her voice dry and graveled.

"Yes, yes," the driver said. "I will call the police—"

A horrific growl rose behind Canto.

The taxi driver's eyes suddenly flew wide, and his mouth fell open.

Canto spun to find the wiry man on his knees,

swaying zombie-like, his hand again wrapped around the pistol in his dead friend's waistband. Blood soaked his T-shirt and bathed his arm. The angry bullet wound behind his ear oozed fluid as he looked up at her with cold dead eyes like a vengeful doll.

Canto surprised even herself with the speed at which she snatched the wooden bat from the terrified taxi driver. She reached the wiry man with three staggering steps and brought the bat down again and again, shattering his arm. She kicked the pistol out of his reach and then hit him in the head, knocking him off his friend. He gave a rattling breath and fell still, finally coming to grips with the fact that his wounds were fatal.

Panting and drenched in sweat from terror as well as the heat, Canto leaned against the bat, using it as a cane to support her shaking legs. She raised an open hand and gave the astonished taxi driver an exhausted nod.

"I **am** the police . . ."

"Then I will call more police," the man said. He blinked in disbelief at the three bodies along the shadowed sidewalk.

Canto swayed on her feet, suddenly overcome with nausea. "And an ambulance." She swallowed hard. The bat slipped from her grasp, and she sagged against the railing. Even that wasn't going to hold her up much longer.

The taxi driver climbed through the crossbars and rushed to her side. "You are bleeding," he said.

Canto glanced at her arms, both badly scraped. "I know," she said. "I hit the gravel very hard."

"No." The driver shook his head. A dire look crossed his face. "Your leg," he said. "You are cut . . . Stabbed, I think. Bad . . . very bad."

28

Ryan normally used the stairs to reach the second floor of the Residence at the end of a long day, but the debate with Gary Montgomery left him ready to take advantage of the elevator in the old cloakroom. Cathy was waiting in the hallway the moment the door slid open. Agents assigned to PPD were adept at melding with the furnishings, and Nick, the Secret Service agent walking with Ryan, deftly stepped out of the way so the First Couple could have their welcome-home kiss.

Cathy, though, was having none of it. She turned her head and offered only her cheek.

"I saw Gary walk past the Roosevelt Room this afternoon," she said. "He had that little black storm cloud over his head that he gets when you two disagree and he knows he's right."

Ryan didn't even try to demure. It wouldn't have mattered. Cathy had already sussed out the situation in her head.

"Why do you have them around if you're not going to listen to their advice?"

Ryan nodded toward the door. "Let's spare Nick our . . . discussion."

"Good night, Mr. President," Nick said, then nodding. "Dr. Ryan."

Ryan thanked the agent and opened the door for his wife.

He had no problem debating this trip with Gary Montgomery. Cathy was a different story. He needed a minute—

"I thought you had a late surgery."

"The patient had pink eye," Cathy said. "We had to postpone. So, what's Gary's argument? I'm sure I agree with him."

"He doesn't think I should stop in Panama on the way to Argentina."

"You mean the Panama with the stick-wielding protesters marching in the streets and blocking major highways? That Panama?"

"Yep." Ryan tossed his leather briefing folio on the bed and kicked off his shoes. "That's the Panama I'm talking about."

She stared down at her lap now, nodding. "Okay."

Ryan groaned. It would have been easier if she'd argued with him, raised her voice or tried to make a case. But she merely sat there, lips quivering, eyes red. A single tear rolled down her cheek. Her sadness was the strongest argument she could make.

He sat down on the bed beside her, thigh to thigh, and took her hand.

"Look, Cath. I can't possibly imagine what you went through in Texas. But I **can** tell you the best law enforcement and intelligence agencies on this planet are hunting down anyone associated with the Camarilla."

"I'm sure," she said.

"Sweetheart . . ." Ryan took a deep breath, then let it out slowly. He'd been thinking about this for weeks. "If you've had enough, I will resign the presidency tomorrow."

Her head snapped up, incredulous.

"Jack!"

"I'm not kidding," he said. "And I'm not bringing it up to use as leverage. I think you know me better than that. If this were any other job, I'd just do it, not discuss it with you beforehand."

Cathy stared at him, the way she'd looked at the kids when they were growing up and she was waiting for them to "make a better choice." Ryan found it mildly terrifying.

"You're not going to quit," she said, after she let him stew for a time.

"The country would be in terrific hands with Mark Dehart."

"He never even wanted to be the vice president," Cathy said. "He'd curse you until the day he died."

"I didn't want the job, either." Ryan fell back on

the bed and stared up at the ceiling, hands folded on his chest. "I'm serious, Cath. Maybe my run is over. We could both retire and . . . do whatever former presidents and retired ophthalmic surgeons do with all that free time."

Cathy lay back beside him with a low groan. "I'm not ready to retire. And I don't expect you are, either. I know you, Jack Ryan. You were made for this job." She took his hand and moved it down by her hip, fingers interlaced. Shoulder to shoulder, she let her head fall to the side so she was facing him. "I just need time to work through stuff like this. Your adventures in South America haven't always gone to plan . . ."

"I'll give you that," Ryan said, remembering an extremely rough trip to Colombia so many years before.

"And anyway," Cathy said, "this family doesn't hide. I didn't know exactly what I was getting into when I met you, but I knew I was marrying a lace-curtain Irishman with more integrity and drive than any ten mortal men. I'm tougher than I look, Jack Ryan. I just need some time to reset my reality. You know . . . get my bearings."

"I understand."

"You probably don't." Cathy's chest rose and fell as she gave a feather-soft sigh. The corners of her lips perked with just the hint of a smile. "And you know what? That's okay . . ."

29

Major Gabriella Canto lay facedown, sweating against the plastic gurney in the back of an ambulance while a pair of medics clucked over the wound in her leg. Her phone pressed to her ear, she winced and gritted her teeth while she waited for Sergeant Perez to answer her call.

The medics wanted to take her to the hospital, but she forbade it, demanding to stay on the scene until officers she trusted arrived to take custody of the bodies. There was too great a risk that Guerra or someone like him would swoop in and make the bodies and any evidence associated with them disappear. She had little sway over what the medics did or did not do, but the fleshy woman in charge looked as though her shift had been too long and tiring to argue with a blood-spattered major from the National Police.

Canto asked them to leave the rear doors open while they cleaned her wound, saying that the air-conditioning made her shiver. In truth, she wanted to keep an eye on the scene. She'd been clearheaded enough to use her phone to take photographs of the firearms and blades before securing them with two baby-faced PNP officers named Hernandez and Corte, who came in two-up on a motorcycle. Corte, a smallish female riding pillion on the bike, took charge of the weapons, made sure they were clear, and stuffed them in a locking side case. First on the scene, the two officers continued to guard the area until investigators and crime scene technicians arrived. Someone had tried to murder one of their own.

Canto grimaced at a stabbing pain as the overworked medics cleaned and bandaged her wound. She'd asked them to suture it on the spot, but they'd only chuckled dryly and reminded her that they were not in a war zone—or worse yet, Colombia. She would get sutures as soon as she let them take her to the hospital.

Finally, Sergeant Perez answered, recognizing her as the caller.

"Major," he said. "What can I do for you?"

"Fredi!" She choked back a relieved sob, chalked it up to the adrenaline, and gave him a thirty-second rundown of the attack, along with her location.

"I am in my car," he said. "Ten minutes away with traffic."

"Good," she said. "I need someone here I can trust."

"Who could be behind this?" he asked, dumb-founded.

"I am not sure," she said.

"But you have some idea . . ."

"Of course."

"It has something to do with the raid," Perez said. "A relative wanting revenge?"

"Possible," she said. "But I have other suspicions."

"Gue—"

"Do not say the name," she snapped, cutting him off. "We'll talk about this more when you arrive."

"Forgive me for not asking earlier," Perez said. "But are you all right, **patrona**?"

"A bit shaken up." She stifled another sob, cursing herself. "And a small knife wound. It's worse than I hoped for, but not nearly as bad as it could have been."

Her shot beneath the big guy's chin had been a fatal one, but the razor-sharp fillet blade had speared her through the calf when he fell.

"The blade missed any major arteries or tendons," Canto said, "but cut a chunk of flesh that was, according to the medic, the size of a decent filet mignon."

"That's not good," Perez said.

"I'll be fine with a few stitches."

"And a possible skin graft," the lead medic chimed, eavesdropping on Canto's half of the conversation.

Canto ignored that. She had no time for a lengthy

hospital stay. "The commissioner is en route," she said to Perez.

"Who called **him**?" Perez said, surprised.

"I did," Canto said. "He is our boss." She glanced over her shoulder at the medics, who were both listening to every word, though they pretended not to be. Back to Perez. "Just get here as quickly as you can."

Perez arrived first. Guerra had been with his mistress, Josefina, when Canto called him, so he had farther to drive.

Canto asked the two medics to step out and give her a moment of privacy with her bagman. The older female raised her eyebrows up and down and gave Perez the once-over.

"We cannot leave you two alone in the ambulance," she said.

"This is official police business," Canto said, leaving no room for argument. "Give us some privacy."

It was bluster and the medic knew it. She didn't move until Canto promised to let them take her to the hospital the moment she finished speaking to her sergeant.

"Five minutes," the medic said, and climbed down the steps of the ambulance with a grunt.

"You need to watch yourself, Fredi," Canto whispered as soon as the doors slammed shut and they were alone. She was still on her stomach, which would have made her feel vulnerable around anyone else.

"I will, **patrona**." Perez gave a sad shake of his

head and moved to the foot of the gurney. He clucked softly as he perused her wound. "That looks much worse than you described it over the phone. I once found a man who had been dead in his apartment for three days. Left with no one to feed him, his pet dog got hungry and . . . Well, your leg looks like that . . ."

"Thank you for that lovely image," Canto said. "Now move back up here where I can see you, and listen to me. I am serious. For all we know, whoever is behind this could be planning an attack on you as well."

"Are you sure this was not a random mugging?"

"One of them called me his 'little Major Gabilita,'" Canto said. "They knew my name and rank and where I would be running."

"You will need to vary your routines," Perez said.

"And you will, too, Fredi," Canto said. "Something is going on here. Something very bad."

Outside, a car door slammed amid the honk of passing traffic. Commissioner Guerra began shouting orders to everyone on the scene—a seagull, flapping in with a loud squawk and shitting all over everything.

Still on her belly, Canto reached out and grabbed Perez by the tail of his shirt. "Listen to me, my friend. I do not know who we can trust. What I do know . . . What I would bet my life on, is that these men I shot tonight are connected with the men from the San Miguelito raid."

Commissioner Guerra's voice grew louder as he approached the medics waiting outside and demanded to know where his wounded officer was.

"And I would bet something else," Canto whispered. "All three of those dead men were well acquainted with LA PULGA—the Flea. Maybe even on his payroll." She gave Perez a playful smack on the leg. "Now quickly, take out your notepad before Guerra opens that door, and act as though I am giving you something important to do."

30

Hendley Associates' new Gulfstream 550 was fueled and ready to go by the time Campus operatives arrived at the small fixed-base operation at the south end of Reagan National Airport. Blue, red, green, and amber lights of the taxiways and runways behind the plane winked and sparkled in the cool autumn darkness.

The wheels of the Campus-issue duffel grumbled over the tarmac as Chilly dragged it toward the waiting aircraft. It was heavy, full of clothes and assorted camera and recording equipment to add to their legend as documentary filmmakers joining the rest of their production crew already in Colombia.

"Feels like Christmas," he said.

Mandy Cobb looked up from where she walked beside him, pulling her own heavy duffel. "Because of the lights?"

They were dressed like tourists in chinos and loose cotton shirts—she in her green fleece sweater and him in his Schott leather jacket against the crisp fall morning.

"There's that." Chilly shrugged, embarrassed that he'd said anything. "And the anticipation, I guess."

"I hear you there," Cobb said. She slowed her stride a half step, giving them an extra few seconds before they got to the Gulfstream. "Can I ask you something?"

"You bet."

"What do you make of all this, contractors with no diplomatic cover?"

"Not sure yet," Chilly said. "I really didn't know what to expect. It feels right, but . . ."

Clark's resonant voice boomed from the darkness. "This is a lot," he said. "I get it." His luggage was already on the plane and they hadn't heard his crepe-soled desert boots padding up behind them.

"If you were already gung-ho at this point with what little information we've given you, you'd probably not be the kind of people we're looking for." He came up alongside them and stopped, gesturing with a paper sack of popcorn he'd snagged from the FBO flight office. "Look," he said. "As you will see, we are given a hell of a lot of latitude by the CIA and the ODNI, not to mention the White House. We don't want mindless killers. We want thinkers who are, yes, capable of violence, but who have a strong sense of right and wrong. The outside world might see some of what we do as a wobbly moral compass. I do not. There is the law and there is protecting the United States. I may break a few laws, but my moral compass does not waver."

Ding Chavez came up behind them as Clark finished.

"And that, boys and girls, is probably the longest philosophical speech you will ever hear from our fearless leader." He grinned. "Me, on the other hand . . ."

Chilly and Cobb loaded their duffels in the rear baggage hold along with the others. They would have to clear customs when they reached Colombia, making it problematic to bring in some of the items that might become necessary for their mission. Weapons and communications equipment that another government might classify as "spy gear" had been sent ahead via diplomatic courier. If things went according to plan, it would be waiting for them with the CIA ground team that was already in Cartagena.

Sidearms had their place, of course, but in Chilly's mind, a pistol's primary function was to fight his way to a long gun. For this trip, each operator was issued an M4 special purpose rifle with a SIG lower, Sionics upper. The twelve-and-a-half-inch barrel was fitted with a five-and-a-half-inch HuxWrx 3D-printed suppressor that allowed the shooter to fire with or without the suppressor and keep the same point of aim. It wasn't whisper-quiet, but you didn't get nearly as much gas in the face when you shot it. A Nightforce NXS 2.5–10×42 optic and an Aimpoint T-2 red dot mounted at a forty-five-degree angle made it Chilly's idea of a perfect battle rifle. Good for close work, but in the right hands, perfectly capable of reaching out and touching someone.

It was no wonder this whole affair felt like Christmas.

Clark left knives up to the operator's choice. For his fixed blade, Chilly carried a simple Marine Corps Ka-Bar—which drew a quiet nod of approval from Clark. The field of fighting knives was crowded to the point of confusion, but to Chilly, the tried-and-true seven-inch blade was plenty to cut what he needed to cut and stab what he needed to stab. In his pocket, he carried a Zero Tolerance 0357 folding knife with a BlackWash finish—again, more than adequate in the cutty-stabby department. He rounded out his pocket kit with a Zippo lighter, a ferrocerium rod that was part of his key chain, a RATS elastic tourniquet, and a SureFire Titan flashlight, also from his father. When you had a sheriff's deputy for a dad, you got a lot of tactical gear for Christmas.

He had another, brighter flashlight as well as a Leatherman Wave multitool, some paracord, and a personal wound kit in his daypack, but the pocket stuff stayed with him anytime he was wearing pants.

Non-tactical-looking daypack over his shoulder, he stepped aside to let Mandy Cobb go first up the boarding stairs near the front of the aircraft. A low fog scuttled across the black tarmac, combining with the hum of the auxiliary power unit to lend the sleek business jet the look of a rocket getting ready for takeoff.

The smell of new leather hit Chilly's nose as he boarded. He smiled, thinking of a new pickup truck, and said hello to the two pilots in the cockpit to his left. A vast departure from the shabby commercial airliners he'd flown on, the G550 boasted polished teak bulkheads and tables, Corian counters in the galley, and plush leather seating.

The six-foot cabin ceilings meant Clark had to duck just a hair. Chilly, at around five ten, had all kinds of room.

Most of the operators were already on board, exploring. As it turned out, Hendley Associates had only recently upgraded its aircraft and the G550 was as new to everyone else as it was to Chilly and Cobb. The last one of that model off the line.

Chilly couldn't help but feel like the new kid getting on the school bus for the first time with a bunch of returning students who'd already staked out their seats. Fortunately, the cabin offered seating for at least twelve, some in single seats, others in vis-à-vis configuration that faced one another. There were two couches, one midship and one aft near the lavatory.

Clark sat up front, close to the galley and the cockpit. Ding sat across the aisle from him, also in one of the single seats. Midas took a spot behind

Ding, facing aft. Jack Junior sat alone on the aft couch, apparently grouchy because his fiancée, Lisanne, hadn't been able to make the trip. Adara and Dom sat together facing forward at one of the vis-à-vis four places. She motioned for Cobb and Chilly to join them in the two aft-facing seats on the other side of a polished teak table. They started to sit down, but stopped when a middle-aged woman with short auburn hair emerged from the cockpit along with a heavyset man. Both were dressed in navy-blue slacks and white shirts with epaulets.

The man busied himself securing the door, while the woman introduced herself as Helen Reid, the pilot in command. Her first officer was Chester Hicks.

Hicks leaned around the bulkhead after the door was shut and looked at the two newcomers.

"But everybody calls me Country," he said with the hint of a drawl.

Reid looked down at Clark. "I think we're really going to like this bird, John," she said. "The 550 is a heck of a step up. Two Rolls-Royce BR710 engines that together provide us over thirty thousand pounds of thrust. She can take off in less than six thousand feet and land in just a skosh under twenty-eight hundred—getting us in and out of some of the tight spots you like to frequent. We can cram nineteen souls on board and the seats convert to sleep eight. She'll cruise at four hundred eighty-eight knots and give us thirteen honest hours if we need them—which we don't today. Winds are in our favor this morning and the estimated flight time to Cartagena is well under five hours." She gave a friendly nod toward Chilly and Cobb. "Welcome aboard. Any questions?"

Jack Junior piped up from the back. "Same Wi-Fi password?"

"Yep," she said.

The pilots returned to the cockpit and, a short time later, began their taxi roll off the ramp.

"Settling in?" Adara asked.

"I guess," Cobb said as she took her seat next to the large oval window. "This is all sort of a blur."

"Maybe it's better that way," Adara said. "Work is the best stress reducer." Her blond hair was cut relatively short and she reminded Chilly of Olivia Newton-John when she turned badass at the end of **Grease.**

"You think?" Cobb said. "I mean, we're heading to Colombia on a mission, and we've had, what, fifteen minutes of training . . ."

Adara shot a glance at Caruso.

"Dom was FBI—"

"**Is** FBI." Head buried in the latest issue of **Car and Driver,** he tapped the breast pocket of his jacket, which presumably held his creds.

"True," Adara said. "He's on loan, if you want to get technical about it. Gives us someone on the scene with a badge and gun when the rest of us might be hampered in that regard. But make no mistake, he's Campus to the core. The point I was trying to make, Mandy, is that you've got a shitload of training." Adara slid down deeper into the plush leather. "Both of you have chops. John Clark's been doing this for a long time. He doesn't bet on losers."

"She's right." Midas craned his head around his seat and ran a large hand over his full beard. "You're both gonna do great. Besides, we've been needing some new blood for a while. These guys don't ever get my jokes. My advice, sit back and get some rest in this fantastic airplane while you've got the chance. Because if Colombia is anything like it was the last time I was there, the places we'll be staying won't smell like new leather seats."

31

Felix Moncada had switched from his Ford pickup back to his Mercedes sedan and now sat in his assigned parking spot on Eloy Alfaro Avenue down the street from the Palacio de las Garzas. It was a beautiful spot, overlooking the sea, and he sometimes sat there to gather his thoughts before going inside. Today he pounded his fist on the steering wheel and tried in vain to make sense of what was going on. The normally predictable President Botero had suddenly become mercurial, canceling appointments and having closed-door meetings. Moncada was not invited. In fact, few of his regular cohort of advisers were. The American ambassador had come to visit earlier that day. Perhaps that had something to do with it.

Botero was up to something. But what?

As much as Moncada tried to minimize that fact, Operation JAMAICA relied on timing and choreography. Any change in the status jeopardized that. Now was not the time for the son of a whore to make changes. Wheels were already set in motion on machinery that would be difficult if not impossible to stop.

The operation would certainly cost much blood and treasure—but Moncada fervently believed it would be worth the sacrifice. More important, he'd convinced enough others in the government that this could actually succeed despite the risks and complications. His aim was simple enough—to pry Panama away from the **yanqui** grip. The face of things would naturally change if only given a chance.

Moncada's mother and father had been redshirts in Manuel Noriega's Saint Michael the Archangel Dignity Battalion, a guerrilla group formed to assist Panamanian Defense Forces repel a **yanqui** invasion in 1989. But Noriega, who had been an American CIA puppet to begin with, ran and hid at the first sign of U.S. aggression, abandoning the Dignity Battalions as cannon fodder. These Dingbats, as the Yankees called them, proved no match for American military. Moncada was orphaned by artillery fire at the age of four.

The pineapple plantation where young Felix was sent after his auntie in Curundú grew tired of him was nestled in the hills near La Chorrera, west of Panama City. By his early teens the boy found he had a knack for numbers and was soon helping the plantation manager with the books. A degree in finance from the University of Panama got his foot in the door at a legal firm specializing in hiding wealthy people's money. Money got him into politics, which got him more money. It did not take long for him to join that category of successful men who woke up every morning wondering which Rolex they should wear that day. But that wealth also brought a particular weariness, a dissatisfaction with the state of his country.

Operation JAMAICA had been born decades before during the late-night musings of Moncada and his university friends, young and idealistically drunk with nationalism, while actually drunk on Iguana Rum. The others had sobered up and grown up, getting excellent jobs in finance or management with shipping companies that did business on the canal. But the guerrilla blood of his parents still ran through Felix Moncada's veins.

He had no problem with capitalism. He simply hated the United States. Panama was a prize, but far too small to defend herself alone. She needed a big brother, but it would be much healthier for the country if that big brother were farther away.

Some of Moncada's inner circle had dubbed the operation a coup. It was and it wasn't. Botero and Carré would be gone, yes, but Moncada had no intention of installing any particular person into the office of president. He would shake the tree and let nature run her course . . . along with a little help from his friends in Russia. In this case, the czar he did not know was far preferable to the U.S. President he did.

Panama had no standing military, which meant a ruling junta was out of the question. There were, however, several departments within the Public Forces—the National Border Service, the National Aeronaval Service, the National Police, and the Institutional Protection Service. Together these elements of Panama's Ministry of Public Security were charged not only with the security of the canal locks but also with protecting the president, forming what might as well have been a small army. But if something were to happen to throw them into disarray, even pit them against one another, it would be chaos.

Timing was everything—and Botero's action threatened to throw all that off.

Moncada's mobile chirped, drawing his attention away from the murderous thoughts of the moment. The phone was VoIP-encrypted and bounced from server to server, supposedly making it impossible to trace. Still, who could know what new technology the American NSA or CIA had come up with. They were pigs, but they were formidable pigs. Because of that, Moncada rarely used names on the telephone. Only a handful of people had this number. If they called it, he knew who they were.

It was Sabine Gorshkova.

The moonfaced woman's parents had been killed during the 1989 invasion as well, giving her and Moncada a common enemy.

"I am checking on your satisfaction with our response to the recent unfortunate event," she said.

"Your replacement man arrived safely," Moncada said, referring to Doyle. "I believe he has the situation on the ground here well in hand."

"I am happy to hear it," Gorshkova said. "Your dominoes should start to fall at any time. No?"

"Soon," Moncada said. He imagined the explosions. The screaming. The look on Botero's face . . . After that, things would happen in a hurry.

"There is something he's not telling me," Moncada said.

"Who?"

"The president."

"What do you mean?"

"I'm not sure," Moncada said. "It's as if he's had a change of plans. I believe he is making a side trip before he leaves for Mar del Plata."

"Does not the first domino fall before he is scheduled to depart?"

"They all do," Moncada said. "They have to."

"Then do not worry."

"It's a timing issue. He and his number two must be here for this to be successful. If he leaves early for his trip . . ."

"Then do what you need to do at once," Gorshkova

said. "Walk into his office and hit him between the eyes with a hammer. That will certainly tip the dominoes."

"That would be—"

"I am only joking," Gorshkova said, though Moncada was sure that she was not. "My point is that you may be forced to speed up your timeline. Does it really matter if your bombs do not explode in exactly the prescribed order as long as Botero and Carré are dead?"

Yes, it absolutely does, Moncada thought, but he kept it to himself.

"Anyway," she said. "You are paying us a great deal of money and I have a reputation to uphold. If you need more people, tell Doyle. He will give you the price."

"I believe we have enough," Moncada said.

"Excellent," Gorshkova said. "Now, if you will excuse me, Felix, I have my own target to hunt down and kill—and she is proving to be more difficult than I had imagined."

Moncada groaned. Sabine Gorshkova was aggressive and brash, the kind of person who did not care if she used real names on the phone—the kind of person who preferred a hammer to a gun.

32

Sabine Gorshkova finished speaking to the idiot Moncada and tossed her mobile on the desk, picking up her ice-cold mojito. Sweating glass in hand, she leaned back in an overstuffed leather chair, as if she were about to crow.

"Blanca!" she shouted, and then took a long, satisfying drink. "Blanca! You come to visit me and then you hide! I would have thought you would be happy to be someplace other than your wretched apartment! Where are—"

The door to her study opened and her younger sister came in, hands fiddling tentatively at her waist, staring at the floor as if she feared Sabine might bite her head off. She was taller than her older sister by several inches, with Joaquín's slender physique and Sabine's blue eyes and ebony hair—the best of their parents.

Now in her early thirties, Blanca had been a babe in arms when their parents were killed. Sabine had been a child herself, taking care of both of her siblings. It had been hard and she'd had to leave Joaquín in an orphanage for a short time until Uncle Hector had come and rescued them. From the beginning Hector had dubbed little Blanca too weak. He'd proclaimed that she was not cut out for the life he had in mind for the two elder siblings. Even as a child Sabine had seen firsthand how pitiless the old man could be and suspected that had he not been so scared of her, he would have let the jungle have her little sister.

This was no Rudyard Kipling tale. There were no kindly panthers or wolves who might adopt a man cub in the jungles of South America. There were, however, all manner of poisonous spiders and deadly snakes and eels and piranhas, not to mention jaguars that would pick their teeth with an abandoned child. As young and helpless as she was, fire ants would have swarmed her little body before morning.

But Hector had let her live.

Perhaps that had been a mistake.

Blanca had spent much of her life away at boarding schools in Europe and then at the university in Cartagena. Venezuela and Russia were simply too close to home. It also meant changing her name. Blanca Gorshkova became Blanca Pakulova, who was now working on her graduate degree in nursing.

Sabine had worked hard to keep her little sister in the dark, for her own good, but it was impossible to hide the cadre of hardened military men who not only accompanied Sabine everywhere she went but deferred to her as their boss. Blanca was a smart girl, and she was beginning to ask questions. Dangerous questions.

Sabine moved to the couch and patted the cushion beside her. "You are so busy with your studies," she said. "We never get time to talk."

Blanca forced a smile and took a seat, hands folded in her lap. She stared down at her feet. "My university courses are very demanding."

"But no problem for you, Blancacita," Sabine said. "Right?"

Blanca looked up. "I heard some of the men whispering about Joaquín. They stopped when they saw me, but . . . You said he died of a heart attack."

"His heart stopped," Sabine said, a husky catch in her voice. "That much is true. There is more, but you will have to trust me for now."

Blanca gave a resigned nod. Then, as if thinking better of it, sat up, eyes blazing. "What is going on, Sabine? Something bad happened to Joaquín. What is to say that something bad will not happen to you?"

Sabine put a hand on her little sister's thigh and gave it a squeeze. From a distance, it might have looked consoling, but she dug her nails into her sister's flesh hard enough to make a point.

Questions brought pain.

Blanca recoiled, smoothing the fabric of her medical scrubs when Sabine withdrew her hand.

"Nothing bad will happen to me," Sabine said. "In case you have not noticed, all these men are frightened of me."

"Were they not frightened of Joaquín?"

Sabine gave a sad chuckle. "Not as frightened as they should have been," she said. "Not really."

"How long are you staying in Cartagena?"

"I'm not sure," Sabine said. "I have a little business I need to finish up before I return to Russia." She took another sip of the mojito and cocked her head to one side, watching Blanca closely for a reaction. She was too weak to trust with anything important. Pity. They could have made a great team. "Why? Would you like to come with me?"

"No, thank you," she muttered. "My studies. You know . . ."

"Of course," Sabine said. "Will you come back for dinner tonight? I have been told the chef is making empanadas."

Blanca nodded, again not fully committed. "If I am finished in time. My study group and I usually eat at my apartment." She folded her arms as if she were cold. "I don't really need your security men following me. I am fine."

Sabine took a deep breath in a futile attempt to calm herself, then said, "First of all, they are **your** security men as well. These are dangerous times, Blanca. We must not take our safety for granted."

"Okay . . ."

"I will tell them to give you space." Sabine's eyes narrowed. "But you must understand that if something happens to you and they do not stop it, I will personally cut off their balls for not being close enough."

"Sabine!"

"Relax, Blancacita!" Sabine gave her sister's knee a hearty swat. "I am only joking."

She was not.

Blanca gave a visible shudder when Uncle Hector came through the door, dark and silent, like poison smoke from a burning tire. Years of creeping through the jungles and mountains of Latin America had made him as adept at slinking as he was at killing.

Blanca did not know the details of his past, certainly not the blood-soaked violence of his time in Peru's Shining Path, but she'd surely felt his quiet disapproval all her life.

"Please excuse me, dear sister." Blanca kissed Sabine on both cheeks. "I must return to university."

"Suit yourself." Sabine let her hands fall to her lap. "But you are missing out on the empanadas."

Her sister gone, she turned to face her uncle. He might have been a master at creeping through the jungle, but he was not so adept at hiding his emotions, particularly when he had something interesting to share. The old man now grinned like the Cheshire cat.

A Cheshire jaguar.

Sabine moved from the couch back to her chair—
an overstuffed leather thing with rollers so she could
wheel herself across the room to the wet bar without
getting up. As much as she respected her uncle's
business acumen and killer instincts, she did not
particularly want to sit with him on the couch.

"What news?" she asked.

"We pay our friends at customs to let us know of
any aircraft that might pose a threat," he said.

"Right . . . And . . ." She hated it when Hector
did not get to the point.

"He has informed me of a Gulfstream from
Washington, D.C., that is inbound to Cartagena."

"A business jet." Sabine wagged her head. "What
about it?" Business jets came and went from
Colombia's airports many times a week. Some fer-
ried drugs or cash or human cargo, north to south
or south to north, depending on their load. This
was probably nothing to be concerned about—but
Sabine Gorshkova had not remained above ground
and breathing for as long as she had by dismissing
things that were **probably** not dangerous.

"Send someone to see who is on board when it
lands."

Hector gave a smug nod. "Already taken care of,
my dear. The plane will be here within the hour.
Flaco and Annie are en route to the airport as we
speak."

"You are sending Annie?" Sabine asked. "I thought

he was returning to Lima. That was why we did not send him to Panama."

Annie was a former Peruvian soldier, capable enough, if somewhat slovenly in appearance, but Sabine had never come to grips with the fact that Annie could be a given name for men in Peru.

"He did not go," Hector said without further explanation. "He and Flaco will follow the passengers to their accommodations and if they look like they might be a problem, see to it that they are not—"

"It must be done quietly," Sabine said.

Hector changed tacks. "She was asking questions again?"

Sabine nodded. "She was."

"Dangerous," Hector said. "For all of us."

"I know that," Sabine said.

"So . . ."

"I need to think about it," Sabine said.

"She is a threat."

"I said I need to think about it!" Sabine snapped. "Are we clear?"

"Crystal clear," the old man said. "Do not fret about the incoming Gulfstream. Annie and Flaco know how to be discreet and, if they need to be, deadly. That is why I chose them for this job."

33

Chilly woke from an amazingly deep sleep to Adara Sherman's voice as she doled out tourist information about Cartagena—mostly the locations of the most highly rated ice cream joints.

Dom caught Chilly's eye and gave a good-natured shrug. "Ice cream is kind of her thing," he said. "She's got a favorite place just about everywhere we set foot."

"The cucumber flavor in Buenos Aires is the best," Adara said, nodding. "But there's a decent place about three blocks from our hotel."

The Gulfstream banked left on her final approach to Rafael Núñez International Airport on a narrow neck of land in an area known as Crespo between the Caribbean Sea and a shallow inland waterway called the Ciénaga de La Virgen marsh. The city of over a million rose from between the hills and the ocean to the south.

Chilly leaned forward in his seat, getting a bird's-eye view of what was, not too many years ago, a city in one of the most violent countries on the planet—primarily because of Pablo Escobar. Medellín, Cali, and Cartagena flowed with cash and cocaine on the blood of anyone who got in the way of the narcos. The stonework and Spanish influence on the architecture were amazing, even from the air—and so was the poverty. For every high-rise building there were a thousand ramshackle hovels, some of them covered with tin, some with what looked like weathered canvas tarps. Quaint cobblestone streets gave way to uneven dirt roads at the edge of the city. It was as if the planners had run out of money and abruptly stopped with any and all improvements. Rural life with goats and chickens and open cookfires was within spitting distance from the nightclubs and shopping malls of Cartagena.

Adara leaned in, nose to the window, and pointed to the west. "We're staying there, in the old walled city. You guys should come here when we're not hunting bad guys. It's incredible."

"Listen up!" Chavez said from the front of the airplane. "We'll be on the ground in five. We'll clear customs and then link up with our contact. Chilly, Mandy, remind me. Either of you two been to Cartagena before?"

They shook their heads.

"Well, I have," he said. "As you can see out the window, it's a magical-looking place—but it's got a dark side. Don't go anywhere alone. Copy?"

"Something else to think about," Clark said.

"Helen and Country filed a flight plan and notified Colombian customs. Everyone who matters knows we're coming. The politicians, the cartels, even Sabine Gorshkova, if she happens to be here. What they do not know is who we are or what we are doing. We want to be seen joining the production company that's filming a documentary at the University of Cartagena.

"Remember," Clark continued, "rabbits and wolves both survive by keeping their eyes up and ears open. We're not timid, but it's perfectly acceptable to keep your head on a swivel."

"But," Jack Junior said, "be aware you may be tested."

Cobb looked to the rear of the plane at Ryan. "Tested?"

"Could be anything," Jack said. "A sloppy attempted mugging, some idiot trying to steal your watch. If you go jujitsu on the first person to jostle you, it's kind of a clue that we're not a bunch of Hollywood types scouting the best lighting and a decent soy latte."

"Got it," Chilly said. "Head on a swivel, but don't go all jujitsu . . ."

"It gets easier," Midas said.

"It better," Cobb said.

Clearing customs when arriving in a business jet was a straightforward process, much simpler than going through the lines on the commercial side of the airport. Contrary to the cold reception that Chilly expected, the young woman who came to the plane to meet them was all smiles and welcomes. Flying in a sixty-seven-million-dollar airplane did have its perks.

The team emerged from the customs office to find a dusty twelve-passenger van idling in front of the general aviation apron at the north end of the airport, surely running the air conditioner against the heat. A fit-looking Asian man jumped out of the passenger seat as soon as the group made it outside the fence. He embraced each of the Campus operators with backslapping brotherhood hugs, pausing to shake hands with the two newcomers.

"I'm Adam," the Asian man said. "Welcome aboard Windward Productions."

The rest of the introductions would happen once they'd loaded their luggage and climbed in the vehicle.

Under the shade of a drooping banyan tree in the adjacent parking lot, a blocky man named Flaco Rojas sat behind the wheel of a rusted blue Hi-Lux pickup. His partner, former Peruvian Army sniper Annie Suarez, slouched in the passenger seat, an unlit Cohiba Mini cigarillo between his crooked teeth. He wore a stained number 10 Lionel Messi soccer jersey—Barcelona blue and red. Wearing the wrong team's colors could get you killed in Latin America—but this was Messi. Everybody loved Messi.

"Flaco," Suarez said around the cigarillo, "I will give you one million dollars if those sons of whores are really movie people."

"No shit," Flaco grunted as he nestled deeper into his seat, both hands on the wheel and ready to go. His sobriquet meant "skinny," a joke that had stuck with him since his youth. In truth he was almost a foot shorter than his partner, with a square head that appeared to be connected directly to his shoulders with barely the suggestion of a neck—more reminiscent of a fireplug than anything remotely close to **flaco.** A faded green tattoo of crossed arrows and a V-42 dagger graced the copper skin of his right forearm, identical to a U.S. Army Special Forces crest, but instead of **De Oppresso Liber,** the scrolling simply read **RANGER.** An Indigenous Quechua, he'd done three years with the Bolivian Special Forces' 12th Ranger Regiment, getting out after a disagreement with a commanding officer who was **cholo**—of Indigenous and Spanish blood. The CO had ended up in the hospital with his guts on the table beside him and Flaco was thrown into San Pedro prison in La Paz.

The Camarilla let him stew for thirteen months in that hellhole before they finally came calling. Flaco didn't exactly have a ton of marketable skills in the civilian world and the Bolivian economy was in the shitter even if he had. Joining the organization had been a no-brainer.

Eyes on the departing van, Annie Suarez smacked the sun-bleached dash with a rough hand.

"Go!"

Flaco looked sideways at his bossy partner. "You don't have to tell me to do everything."

He waited a beat, just to show he was in charge of driving, and then threw the Hi-Lux in gear.

The Americans turned left on Seventieth, a narrow sometimes three-lane street with whitewashed mom-and-pop stores and residential housing on either side of the road. Flaco stayed four or five cars back until the road curved sharply and became Highway 90A that ran toward the Caribbean—and all the hotels that lined the beaches.

Annie checked his watch and then leaned forward in his seat to give himself room to fish the mobile phone out of his jeans. Cigarillo in one hand, phone in the other, he tilted his head back to stare up at the truck's sagging headliner.

"Let's just kill one or two of them and go. The rest will be scared shitless and get out of Colombia."

Flaco gave a wry chuckle and shook his head. **"Champ'a uma,"** he said. It was his native Quechua for "crazy man"—literally someone growing weeds in their head. **"Patrona** said watch them, not kill anybody. At least not yet. She'll use our guts for sausage casings if we disobey." He looked hard at his partner. "I am not joking."

Annie might not understand the Quechua, but he caught the sentiment.

"It will all turn out the same," he groaned. "That young bastard is a cop, no doubt about it. Probably some of the others, too. The old man has been in the military. I can see it in the way he walks. They sure as hell aren't a bunch of moviemakers."

"Or you are just wishing they weren't so you could try out your new blade?"

"It's not about that," Annie said. "This is a waste of time. That's all. We're going to spend our entire day following these assholes around, find out they are not who they say they are, and then Sabine will tell us to finish them off. I say we skip to the end."

"Then you do not know Sabine Gorshkova." Flaco shivered—meaning it. "Nor should you want to . . ."

Ahead, the van continued southwest, parallel to the sea, working its way through midday traffic.

"They're headed for the Walled City," Flaco said. "Difficult to follow unnoticed."

Annie turned and looked at him, brow up, cigarillo clenched in a sneer. "So you agree," he said. "We should kill them now."

"Champ'a uma," Flaco said.

34

Chilly was mildly surprised when their CIA contact, Adam Yao, didn't even try to run surveillance detection on the way to the hotel. It made sense when he thought about it. Attempting to shake a tail would have been contrary to their cover story.

"You think we're being followed?" Chilly asked, casting a nonchalant glance over his shoulder. He felt naked without a gun.

"Oh, yeah," John Clark said.

"For sure," the man behind the wheel said. "Ratty blue Hi-Lux pickup has been on my ass since we left the airport."

Yao had introduced the driver as Eric Ward, formerly a Green Beret with the 10th Special Forces out of Fort Carson, now assigned to the CIA's Ground Branch—the guys who, among other things, went out and broke the shit that needed breaking.

"Right." Yao turned to Clark, who sat directly behind the driver. "So you know, there's a suppressed

Glock 19 stashed inside the paneling at your feet. Just in case the dudes in the Hi-Lux decide to do anything froggy. Eric's armed. I'm running slick."

"Makes sense," Clark said. He turned to the two newbies in the back. "So, we'll go to our hotel to check in, and then divide into teams that mimic small film production units."

They continued southwest along the ocean until they reached the huge gray wall some twenty feet high that Cartagena's inhabitants had erected around the city in 1586 to protect themselves against frequent pirate attacks. Ward circled the Walled City to the south and then cut back north again to go inside the enclosure on the west side, where the peninsula dropped down toward Bocagrande and the Bay of Cartagena. It was easy to picture fierce battles of locals fighting off pirate fleets as they entered the protected waters.

"This is us," Yao said as Ward wheeled the van into a cobblestone portico that ran between an expansive outdoor seating area and a five-story hotel so yellow it fairly glowed in the afternoon sun.

Mandy Cobb pressed her nose against the window and gave a low whistle. "Midas, I thought you said our accommodations were going to be iffy. They didn't scrimp this go-around."

"Some cover legends are better than others," Midas countered. "We could have come in as NGO aid workers helping dig sewers in the slums. Then we'd be boiling water to brush our teeth instead of drinking mojitos by the rooftop infinity pool." He turned in his seat and gave Cobb a wink. "Once in a great while, things work out in our favor."

Chilly couldn't help but think his lowly rolling duffel looked pretty shabby for a place like this. The Hotel Charleston Santa Teresa was a jewel, lemon-yellow walls tucked amid the narrow cobblestone streets and historic buildings of the Walled City of old Cartagena—ancient as they were colorful.

"There's no parking," Adam said as the van rolled to a stop. "We'll drop everyone off with your gear. Eric will get the vehicle settled a few blocks away and then hoof it back."

"I'll go with him," Chilly said. "If one of you wouldn't mind getting my bag."

Yao looked at Clark, who gave a nod.

"Watch yourselves," Clark said.

Four minutes later, Chilly was in the front passenger seat, rumbling down the cobblestone street with a CIA officer he'd known for all of half an hour in a South American city he'd grown up reading about in **National Geographic** and DEA narco-trafficking reports.

"Where'd you come from?" Ward asked.

"Kind of embarrassed to say," Chilly said. "Considering your Special Forces background."

Ward chuckled. "Let me give you a little perspective. I work for an elite subset of one of the most secretive organizations on the planet. I have code word clearance."

"Cool, cool," Chilly said, meaning it.

"You're missing my point," Ward said. "I know some shit . . . and I'm not a hundred percent sure who the hell you guys actually are. I mean, I recognize John Clark and Ding Chavez. Those men are legends in the intelligence community. People write songs about them . . . And I recognize the President's son, but the rest of you . . . You guys are a mystery."

"Well," Chilly said. "Since you asked, four days ago, I was chasing down speeders on my Harley in Abilene, Texas."

"Ah," Ward said. "You're that guy."

Chilly flushed. "I . . . I guess."

Ward smiled. "No shit? You rode your motorcycle into a shopping mall to stop a couple of active shooters?"

"Seemed like the thing to do."

Ward glanced across the middle console and gave a nod of approval. "You're the sniper who saved the First Lady."

He turned into a private parking lot, three blocks from the hotel, on the seaside of the wall. His eyes flashed to the rearview mirror, suddenly preoccupied. "They're gonna write songs about you, too . . ."

The blue Hi-Lux pickup passed them, then rolled in at the second entrance fifty-five yards down and parked two rows away, closer to the seawall.

"Well hell," Ward said.

"I count two," Chilly said. "One driver, one passenger."

"Yep." Ward passed an empty parking spot and then, putting on his signal, backed in. It was tight, not a particularly easy task in a twelve-passenger van, but it kept the pickup in the rearview mirrors.

"They know we're onto them," Chilly observed.

"Probably," Ward said. "I doubt they care. It's not the way some people think it is. I once had a Chinese spook take a shit in my hotel room while I was at dinner, just to let me know he was thinking of me."

Chilly looked in the side mirror to calm himself. He felt like a rookie on his first day of patrol. Everything and everyone seemed suddenly bent on trying to murder him.

"Took me a minute to get used to it, too," Ward said. "Your guns arrived by diplomatic courier about six hours ago. I'm sure they'll get you jocked-up soon. Walking around all unarmed and shit sucks. It's like playing football buckass naked. Life can be pretty damned cheap in some parts of the world. Easy to eat a bullet even if you maintain your cover—just because some idiot didn't like the way you looked him in the eye. Believe me, we'll all have guns if we go offensive." His voice trailed off as he studied the mirror, fingers on the door handle, ready to bail. "Yeah," he said, almost to himself. "I'm not gettin' the DNI vibe . . ."

"DNI?" Chilly asked. "Director of National Intelligence?"

Ward shook his head. "These acronyms will kill you. Dirección Nacional de Inteligencia. Colombian intelligence . . . Or they could be affiliated with our target." He shot Chilly a side-eyed grin. "Or these two assholes could just be bandits who plan to shoot us in the face and take our van. Gets kind of tricky to figure it out . . . In the meantime, I say we do what the boss said and hoof it back on the double. That guy behind the wheel looks like the only thing he runs after is a donut."

35

A gentle sea breeze carried clipped Slavic voices across the glass-calm water of Panama Bay. Gunner's Mate First Class Mikey Caine stood on the foredeck of the **Munro,** a four-hundred-eighteen-foot United States Coast Guard cutter. He held his breath, a pair of Zeiss binoculars pressed to his eyes. For the first time in his life, he wished he could speak Russian.

The sun had set just minutes before, but dusk went by quickly this near the equator. It was getting dark fast, already the time of evening mariners called nautical twilight, dark enough to see several stars and planets for navigation, but still light enough to make out the horizon. Plenty enough light to see the two Russian warships that glided through the water less than a hundred yards to port going north toward the canal. The 535-foot guided-missile destroyer the bridge had identified as the **Admiral Chabanenko** was in the lead—sleek and

sinister like a long black blade. The 442-foot landing ship **Ivan Gren** sailed along behind.

These assholes were close.

Caine and his one hundred thirty-nine shipmates
had spent the past month running narcotics interdiction between Cuba, Mexico, and the Florida Keys.
Some of the crew called it the Cocaine Triangle,
but from what Caine could see the drug trade had
boundless borders. Now they were going home to
Coast Guard Island in Alameda, California. Just
two hours earlier they'd transited the canal for the
second time in five weeks, this trip north to south,
coming from the Caribbean side, Gatun Lake, the
Culebra Cut, the Pedro Miguel Locks, and finally
through the Miraflores Locks. They were all now
two-time members of the unofficial maritime order
known as the "Order of the Ditch."

As a gunner's mate, the lion's share of Caine's
nine-year career had been aboard cutters, starting
on the 110-foot Island-class cutter **Mustang** out of
Seward, Alaska. For the past eighteen months he'd
served aboard the **Munro,** named for Signalman
First Class Douglas A. Munro, who was the only
Coast Guardsman to ever receive the Congressional
Medal of Honor.

Caine was accustomed to the sea and heavy ship
traffic, but Panama Bay was ridiculously crowded.
It looked as though the **Munro** had been dropped
haphazardly into a life-sized game of Battleship.
They were some thirty nautical miles out from

the mouth of the Ditch and there were still vessels everywhere. Tankers, container ships, sailboats, million-dollar yachts all came and went or sat at anchor waiting for their appointed time to pass through the locks.

And then there were the Russians—the primary reason Caine had come on deck with the binoculars. Under normal circumstances, military vessels from less-than-collegial nations gave each other a standoff of at least three miles—but Panama Bay tended to shove adversaries nearly gunnel to gunnel as they passed in or out of the canal.

By any standard, the Legend-class national security cutter **Munro** was a decent-sized vessel. She was armed with a Bofors MK 110 fifty-seven-millimeter deck gun capable of shooting two hundred rounds per minute and a Phalanx close-in weapon system that could burp out 4,500 twenty-millimeter rounds per minute. There were fifty cals, M240s, shotguns, and sidearms—all of them Caine's domain. Add to that the drones, helos, and fast boats—and the **Munro** was still sadly outgunned by the Russians.

Petty Officer Caine scanned the ships as they passed. He counted a dozen sailors on the destroyer and not quite as many on the deck of the landing ship, all of them doing just what Caine was doing—looking across the water at an adversary. Three of the sailors on the landing ship **Ivan Gren** turned and dropped their trousers, mooning the Coast Guard cutter.

"Assholes," Caine muttered into the binoculars.

"Literally," Chief Boatswain's Mate Sid White-house piped from behind Caine.

Caine gave a little start and then glanced over his shoulder.

"What the hell are they up to . . ."

"They're Russians," Whitehouse said. "Who can tell what they're doing?"

"Shouldn't sneak up on a gunner's mate, Chief," Cain said, and then got quickly back on the binoculars.

A boatswain's mate was the most common and versatile rates in the Coast Guard—as they liked to point out, in this outfit, you either were a boat-swain's mate or you worked for one. At the bottom of the senior NCOs, Whitehouse outranked Caine, who as a PO1 was at the top of the junior NCOs, but they'd been friends for years and spoke freely.

"The **Ivan Gren** transports naval infantry," Whitehouse said, looking through his own pair of binoculars. "Russian marines were probably the ones showing us their ass."

"Yep," Caine said. "As many as three hundred of the bastards. Along with two Ka-29TB assault/transport choppers and about three dozen eight-wheeled amphibious armored personnel carriers. Not a great leap to picture them going all **Red Dawn** someplace."

"Preach, brother," the chief said. "Navy

SOUTHCOM are reporting both the Cuban and Venezuelan navies started joint training about the time we left the area. Amphibious exercises, fire support." He nodded at the Russian ships. "I'm sure these guys are on their way to the far side of the Ditch to join in—and practice that **Red Dawn** shit you're talking about."

With a closing speed approaching forty knots, it didn't take long for the Russian ships to pass and slip into the night among all the other lights on the inky sea.

"Not to worry, though," Chief Whitehouse continued. "SOUTHCOM is sending the **Gettysburg, Farragut,** and the **Boone** from Fourth Fleet to conduct their own naval exercises south of Jamaica— along with the **Wasp,** which will carry a belly full of our Marines. That'll keep the Russians and their Caribbean comrades on their toes. And, they're asking us to hang around until these Ivans are through the ditch."

Caine let his binoculars fall against the strap around his neck. He sighed and looked up at Whitehouse.

"Those shitbirds can be awfully aggressive. You ever think about what we'd do if they did have hostile intent and we were the only ones out here?"

Whitehouse shrugged. "You're the bullet counter. You know how mismatched we would be against either one of those ships."

"Still," Caine said, "you know damn well the skipper would fight if we were fired on."

"Hell yeah," the chief said. "If we were threatened, we'd do our duty and give 'em hell with all we have—thus providing Uncle Sam a bona fide reason to retaliate as we sank beneath the waves . . ."

36

Chilly and the rest of The Campus met in John Clark's room with Adam Yao, Eric Ward, and one other guy from Ground Branch. The rest of the CIA Special Activities officers who made up WINDWARD STATION were already in the field.

Clark's suite was a palatial, two-story affair with spiral stairs, marble floors, and a royal vibe that made Chilly feel like he should take his boots off. There'd been only so many empty rooms in the hotel when Yao arranged accommodations. He'd reasoned that, out of all the sixteen operators now on-site, Clark had spent the most nights sleeping on rocks. He deserved the best room.

"That said," Yao offered when they were all together, "if I'd known what the 'best room' entailed, I might not have been so magnanimous."

Six of Yao's original team, two women and four men, were on-site at the University of Cartagena college of nursing. They had eyes on Blanca Pakulova/

Gorshkova, who was apparently in the middle of a study group for some very important exam, judging by how serious everyone was.

Since there'd been the issue of a tail on the way in from the airport, Yao decided it would be better to leave the team already in place where they were for a few more hours before rotating out with a new team of Campus operators and Ward. He and Clark would run countersurveillance. He tried to yield to Clark for the briefing, but the senior man would have none of it.

Clark leaned back in the chaise longue with his hands folded over his chest, certainly more relaxed than Chilly had ever seen him. "I'm a contractor, Adam," he said. "You're the blue-badge boss. Just point us in the right direction and pull the trigger. We'll be there."

They'd already met Eric Ward. The other CIA blue badge was a stout-looking former SEAL named Lopez, who could have been Ding Chavez's younger brother. The two WINDWARD STATION operators were already familiar with the area, so they would act as de facto leads when the second team rolled out in five hours.

"Remember," Yao said. "At this point, we're only watching, establishing patterns of life, learning if there is anything about this woman that will lead us to her sister . . . Assuming we are correct in that Sabine Gorshkova is her sister."

"Copy that," Cobb said. She sat opposite the

spacious ground-floor room from Clark, sipping from a stainless steel water bottle she'd brought with her. "What's our plan if one of those guys who followed Chilly and Eric decide they don't like the way we look and attempt to make contact with us?"

"I'm not too worried about that," Yao said. "Chances are we've got a lot of work to do before we get into any gunfights."

"We have the Glock 43Xs," Ding said, "but for the moment, it's best none of us get caught with a firearm or anything else that might be construed as spy gear—lockpicks, night vision, thermal . . ." He shot a glance at Yao. "Or killer drones."

"Not to make a deal out of it," Lopez said, "but why the 43X? I'm a SIG 365 guy all the way."

Yao snorted at the former SEAL and rolled his eyes.

Clark gave a rare smile. "Good question," he said. "Simple answer is that we have two new operators who have grown up in this business shooting Glocks. Even if we'd wanted to make this op shooter's choice, we didn't have the time to get the proficiency we need with other weapons systems. Happy to talk firearms choices over a beer with you sometime, though . . ."

Lopez gave a thumbs-up. "Makes sense, chief." Clark was a former SEAL as well. It was a small community and Lopez was obviously familiar with his background.

"The small Glocks are get-off-me guns," Yao said.

"That pretty much sums up all handguns," Midas offered, earning a nod of approval from Clark.

Ding cleared his throat. "Mandy, Chilly, you probably think this next bit is for you alone, but it's not. I give this reminder on virtually every mission—even to myself. Our personalities put us in this line of work. Every one of us in this room is aggressive. None of us can stomach seeing an innocent harmed. But we are here to do a very particular job. Think hard before you try and stop a purse snatcher or—"

"Or thump the shit out of some asshole who's smacking his wife around," Midas said. Then, turning to Chilly and Mandy, he raised his hand. "Guilty as charged. Caught a lot of flak over that error in judgment."

"The point is," Clark said, "we are not law enforcement. We are not peace officers. Our mission is vastly different. Law enforcement officers have a duty to engage. More often than not, our mission is to slip away and not get caught."

"Like I told Chilly," Ward said, "this mission has the potential to evolve rapidly from a surveillance operation to a black bag job—"

"True enough," Yao said. "Now, if we locate Sabine and this op turns into something other than a recce mission, the diplomatic pouch—really a set of Pelican cases—contain the special purpose rifles and a couple of suppressed Glock 19s, and, of course, your slimline Glocks."

The rest of the briefing was short and to the point. **Be aware. Be flexible. Be ready.** They'd link up in Clark's suite in four hours. The intervening time could be used to get some rest and/or study street maps of the area around the University of Cartagena school of nursing, where Blanca Pakulova studied.

Clark and Lopez fell into a spirited conversation about what constituted the perfect deep-cover handgun. Chilly excused himself. A short catnap to clear his head sounded like a good idea.

It wasn't.

He was too on edge to sleep. Not nervous, but hyperaware that he'd been thrown into the deep end of the pool. He knew how to swim, but this was so completely different from anything he'd ever done that his brain was going to need a minute to process it. And the best way to do that was to go for a run.

He considered going out, but since he didn't know the area, he decided to hit the hotel treadmill—not optimum, but at least it would get his blood pumping.

Five minutes later, he headed out the door dressed in shorts, a gray T-shirt with no logo, and a well-worn pair of Saucony runners. He double-checked his pockets for the room key and his phone and then pulled the door closed.

Forty-five minutes and a skosh over four miles later, he grabbed a cup of water from the cooler and trotted out the door feeling clearheaded for the first time since the G550 had touched down in Cartagena. He'd shower, grab a quick bite from downstairs, and then hit the maps, familiarizing himself with the area until it was time to link up with the others.

It seemed foolish to take an elevator to and from a place to exercise, so he took the stairs, making certain the doors didn't lock from the inside. Trotting, he'd made it two flights up, when he heard the door creak open on the floor below, his floor. He slowed to a walk and drifted right, planning to yield to the left if the others were coming up. Male voices echoed in the concrete enclosure, falling silent when they heard the slap of Chilly's shoes on the steps.

Chilly rounded the landing to see two men— the men from the pickup who'd been following the van. They were turned as if to head downstairs, but now froze and looked back over their shoulders to see who was in the stairwell with them. The expressions on their faces said they were just as surprised as he was.

Chilly stood rooted in place, quickly sizing up the men. The taller of the two wore a blue and red soccer jersey with **10** emblazoned on the chest. His partner was shorter, darker, and broader, on the tubby side, but with the muscular neck of a collegiate wrestler—or a fireplug. Chilly instantly identified this one as the greater threat.

High ground was good, but Chilly found himself completely unarmed and wearing nothing but gym clothes. The print of a pistol was plainly visible under Number 10's shirt. At least that told Chilly he was right-handed. For all that mattered if the guy pulled the pistol and shot him before he closed the distance. Fireplug's eyes burned as if he would be happy just using his bare hands. There was no doubt that they recognized Chilly from earlier in the van.

Fireplug shook off his surprise and grabbed a handful of railing, bellowing a string of colorful Spanish curses as he launched himself up the steps. Neither drew a gun, which Chilly took to mean they wanted him alive . . . to torture and interrogate. The photographs of murder victims bludgeoned to death with hammers came rushing back. His dad had often told him it was better to die fighting like hell in the initial attack than to be taken hostage. Cops . . . and now spies . . . didn't fare very well as hostages.

Chilly cast around for any sort of weapon, a fire extinguisher, an axe, a stray broom. Nothing but the walls. That would have to do. Abilene SWAT practiced close-quarters defensive tactics, and he'd rolled plenty of times with the Brazilian jujitsu guys at work, even boxed a little in high school and the Army, but the lion's share of his fighting had been scraps during arrests at work, which, when boiled down, were rarely actual fights, but rather him trying to stop arrestees who just wanted to get away. This was not going to be anything like that.

Three steps down, Fireplug slowed ever so slightly, apparently thinking better of attacking an uphill opponent without some kind of plan. This was happening. There was no getting around it, so rather than try and run, Chilly used the pause to close the distance. Grabbing the rail with both hands to launch himself into a kick that put his feet square in the center of Fireplug's chest.

He might as well have been kicking a brick wall.

Fireplug staggered back a step, but didn't fall— and Chilly landed directly in front of him.

Instead of facing the man head-on, Chilly sidestepped, hooking an arm around the man's neck and yanking backward as he bounded past, intent on dragging him down the stairs. A shout from the landing below drew Chilly's attention to Number 10, who was now bounding up to assist his partner.

Fireplug arched backward, hands flailing as he tried to keep his footing and loose Chilly's arm from around his throat. Chilly put on the brakes and sat down on the steps, using his body weight to wrench Fireplug's neck as he slammed him onto his back, head aimed downhill at his oncoming partner. Chilly had a vague notion of breaking the man's neck, but that wasn't happening. It was a hell of a lot harder to break a grown man's neck than they portrayed in the movies, especially when his body was free to flop around and relieve the pressure. Hurt him, yes. Snap his spine, no. This guy's bull neck looked like it could have taken a blow with a sledgehammer and kept coming.

Chilly let the man slide, heard him groan as he took each stair on his shoulders and spine in a bumpy ride all the way to the landing. He was hurt and probably wouldn't be able to move in the morning, but he wasn't done yet. Chilly would have to deal with him again sooner rather than later. For now, he had a bigger problem. Number 10 bounded past his sliding partner as he smashed headfirst into the landing. Chilly shot to his feet, meeting Number 10 mid-stride, catching him under the chin with the flat of his hand, and driving his head up and over in an effort to send him down the next set of steps.

It almost worked.

Number 10 pivoted and shrugged off the blow, letting Chilly's hand slide by. Overextended and off balance, Chilly caught himself on the rail, driving an elbow in the other man's ribs. Number 10 swung wildly and caught Chilly directly between the eyes with a lucky haymaker. They were all on the landing now, with equal footing. Chilly dished out two more elbows, crosses to the man's neck and face. The first one connected, the second careened off Number 10's shoulder.

Thirty seconds into the fight and Chilly felt himself fading. The four-mile run wasn't helping.

Heart racing, blood thumping in his ears, he didn't hear the stairwell door swing open, but he looked up to see Mandy Cobb standing there, also dressed in running shorts. Fireplug had rolled over, dazed from his bumpy trip down the stairs. He was on all fours now, pushing himself to his feet.

Cobb hauled back and put all her body weight into a brutal kick to Fireplug's ribs, nearly lifting him off the ground. He cried out in surprise as he rolled, a stifled croak with all the wind knocked out of him, and from the sounds of it, a couple of cracked ribs. Still, the thick-necked bastard was far from finished. Cobb kicked him again before he could recover. Chilly had his hands full and didn't have time to observe the results.

Three feet from Chilly, Number 10 recovered from the momentary surprise of Cobb's appearance and let go with a furious growl. He clawed at the tail of the soccer shirt with his left hand, while his right grabbed at a holstered Glock on his hip. His lips drew back in a nasty snarl, like he'd had enough fighting.

The world around Chilly Edwards seemed to slow to a crawl. He was vaguely aware of slurred, disembodied voices—Fireplug's curses, Number 10's threats, Mandy Cobb's barked commands. He launched himself forward, knowing he had to bridge the gap between himself and Number 10. His odds of survival would drop like a stone once the pistol came into play. Chilly figured both of these men were former military, probably very skilled with rifles, and certainly tough as boot leather when it came to hand-to-hand conflict.

But . . .

Number 10's brain was already sending signals that it was time to shoot. In his haste to put an end to Chilly, Number 10 slipped his finger on the trigger before his pistol completely cleared the holster. The gun turned out to be fitted with a suppressor, which made it all the more awkward and time-consuming to draw.

Rather than duck or try to wrest the pistol away, Chilly lunged forward. He slapped Number 10 hard on top of his gun hand, driving the Glock downward against a trigger finger that was already primed for action. The suppressor took the edge off, but the report was still deafening inside the cramped confines of the stairwell. Number 10's yowl of surprise and pain was almost as loud as the shot. Canted toward his own thigh when it went off, the bullet struck him at an angle and destroyed his knee. The gun fell from his grasp and clattered to the concrete. Instead of falling, he hopped forward, grabbing Chilly by the shoulders and administering a brutal headbutt. Chilly latched on and the two men fell to the ground in an exhausted scrum.

Three more suppressed shots split the air. Still in a clench, Chilly felt Number 10 convulse and then go slack, rolling away. Chilly crawfished backward, his brain not quite sure the fight was over.

He looked up to find Mandy Cobb standing over him with the suppressed pistol in both hands.

She kicked a second Glock away from Fireplug, who lay motionless against the far wall. His eyes were open, but unblinking. Two center-mass hits marked the middle of a dark stain on the front of his shirt. She must have picked up Number 10's gun when he dropped it.

Gun up, she looked hard at Chilly.

He saw her mouth moving, but between his own labored breathing and the ringing in his ears he couldn't make out the words.

"Are you hit?" she said, louder this time. She held the gun in one hand and gestured to her torso with the other.

Chilly checked himself, pushing farther away from Number 10. A curved blade fell from the man's clenched fist. He must have drawn it from his belt.

Cobb secured both guns, while Chilly grabbed the knife and used the wall to push himself up on wobbly legs.

"So much for keeping a low profile," Cobb groaned.

"Yeah," Chilly said. "I'm grateful you decided to go for a run when you did." He glanced over his shoulder up the stairwell and then toward the door.

"No cameras," he said.

"None that we can see," Cobb said. "Still, we should get out of here." She passed him Fireplug's

Glock, this one unsuppressed. He was still finding it difficult to breathe, courtesy of what was very likely a broken nose from Number 10's headbutt, but the world had stopped spinning. He press-checked the Glock to make certain there was a round in the chamber in the event these two had friends waiting somewhere, then tucked it under his shirt and started for the door.

"Hang on," Cobb said. "Midas's room is just around the corner, right?"

Chilly nodded, bringing a stabbing pain in his face and tears to his eyes. Yep. The nose was broken.

"Go knock on his door," she said. "I'll wait here."

Less than three minutes later, Midas helped them drag the two dead men into his room. Fortunately, the dead didn't bleed profusely. They left a mess in the stairwell, but Cobb was able to dab away any stray droplets on the tile hall. If there were cameras, it would have looked as though the three Campus operators were helping a couple of drunk friends inside to sleep it off. At least that was the hope.

Midas insisted on a blood sweep, checking them both for wounds. He found the raspberry over Chilly's left kidney.

"You catch a ricochet?"

Chilly shook his head. "That's blunt trauma from a round I took to the vest. Hostage rescue callout a couple of days ago."

Midas gave a tight chuckle. "A couple of days ago . . . From the frying pan to the fire, eh, kid?"

He squatted beside the bodies and looked through their pockets. "No ID." He nodded to Fireplug. "Dagger tattoo on this guy's arm. That's Bolivian Ranger ink. I worked with those guys some when I was in the unit. They're talented operators for the most part. Looks like this one went over to the dark side and signed on with the Camarilla."

Midas stood with a groan and looked at Cobb. She was sitting on the love seat, elbows resting on her thighs, Glock dangling in her hand as she stared at the two men she'd just killed.

"You doin' all right?" he asked.

She gave a slow nod. "I'm fine," she said. "I mean . . . Really, I'm oddly okay." She looked up suddenly to meet his eye. "Is that weird, I mean that I'm not more upset?"

Chilly, who'd been involved in more than his share of officer-involved shootings, heaved a long sigh. "You saved my ass, Mandy," he said. "I'm feeling pretty good about that."

Neither Midas nor Chilly asked her if this was her first. It didn't matter. Every time was different, some easier, some more gut-wrenching. Apart from being prepared for the onset of the shakes or the dazed, slightly disassociated feeling, your first or your latest made little difference.

"You did what you had to," Midas said. "Now we just have to go tell that to Mr. C . . ."

37

The Secret Service agent posted in the West Sitting Hall outside of the President's Dining Room announced the Foleys' arrival at eight p.m. Cathy had insisted on making dinner herself—roast leg of lamb with rosemary, Yorkshire puddings, mashed potatoes, gravy, and peas. Extremely British for a gal named Mueller—and deliciously decadent for a wife who constantly fretted about Jack's intake of fat and cholesterol—but it was a meal she'd grown to love during their time in England.

Cathy hadn't felt much like entertaining since her abduction and rescue. An evening with close friends was a welcome respite from the daily grind of politics and problems. Even so, the prospect of Ryan's trip to Panama the next morning hung like the sword of Damocles over the little group. Cathy was friendly, even talkative, but they'd been married long enough for Jack to know Cathy would bring it up with his director of national intelligence when she felt the time was right.

That time arrived after the main course was cleared and she served a homemade trifle from a clear glass dish designed specifically for this dessert. Layers of sherry-infused angel food cake, vanilla pudding, fruit, shaved almonds, and whipped cream, it was a work of art. Another skill she'd learned in England. Jack couldn't help but notice that she gave him the smallest portion—whether because he'd eaten so many Yorkshire puddings and so much gravy or she was upset about the trip, he wasn't sure. Probably both.

She spooned a generous dollop to Ed Foley, former Moscow chief of station, previous director of the CIA, and Mary Pat's husband. He was retired now, as much as any old intelligence dog could bring himself to retire, still teaching at the Farm and writing the occasional book.

"I understand Mary Pat's going south as well," Cathy said, using a second, smaller spoon to scrape the serving spoon into Ed's bowl. "Are you going with her?"

"Not a chance," Ed said. "I have to stay home and light a fire under the folks at the CIA to clear and approve my latest book before my publisher sends guys in suits to break my kneecaps. Damned thing's already late as it is."

Ed surely knew Cathy was worried, but after four

decades in the intelligence community, he knew a trap when he saw it.

Cathy served Mary Pat, then herself—a much larger portion of trifle than Jack's. Yep. She was upset. The men waited for her to take a bite before they dug in.

She picked up her spoon, but instead of starting, she asked, "Is no one at this table besides me at all worried about this little misadventure to Panama? I read the papers, listen to the news. Russian ships. Labor unrests . . . I mean, come on." The rant was to everyone, but her eyes fell directly on Jack.

Ed glanced at his wife and then down at his bowl. "I know Panama has no army, but they have something like six different law enforcement agencies. We helped train many of them."

Mary Pat looked to the President for direction.

Cathy didn't wait.

"Look," she said. "I know every day is a risk. Honestly, after so many years, I'm usually numb to it. But . . ."

Mary Pat smiled. "This one is important," she said.

"Aren't they all?" Cathy said. "I'm only saying . . ." She put both hands flat on the table, rattling the silverware. "To be honest, I don't know what I'm saying."

"Just so you know," Ryan said. "Gary Montgomery and I have worked out a secret plan for an added layer of security."

"It is a pretty slick plan," Ed Foley said.

Cathy took a deep breath, having said her piece. Her eyes narrowed. "Ed gets to know your secret plan?"

Ryan smiled. "And I'll let you in on it, too, on one condition."

Cathy raised a wary brow. "What's that?"

"That you dig into your trifle," Ryan said. "It looks delicious, but I'm afraid the ghost of my dead father will swoop down and thump my ear if I don't wait for the hostess to take the first bite of her dessert."

38

Colonel Bradley Husberg of the 89th Airlift Wing at Joint Base Andrews banked the Grumman Gulfstream III due south on his final approach. It was just after sunset—18:21 local—23:21 Zulu. The high-rises of Panama City glowed to his left. Lights from countless ships, some at anchor, some steaming their way to or from the Miraflores Locks of the canal, twinkled against the dark void of the bay. A black mote of trees surrounded Panamá Pacifico International. Gear down with less than five knots of breeze on his nose, Husberg lined up on the Pacifico's only runway, 8,497 feet of asphalt that had been part of Howard Air Force Base before it was turned over to the Republic of Panama.

There were three airports within spitting distance of one another serving Panama City. Pacifico was situated to the west across the Bridge of the Americas in Balboa, seemingly carved out of the jungle. A couple of warehouses for humanitarian aid stood out as new, but the rest of it had a retro, Third World feel, as though time had stopped in 1989. Even from the air, Husberg recognized it as a set from an old Bond movie.

It was a near-perfect location for PHOENIX BANNER—a Special Air Mission in service of the President of the United States.

Tail number 60403 was designated a C-20C, a SENEX, or senior executive, version of the G-III with hardened components and upgraded communications equipment. Cutting-edge in myriad respects, the C-20C's avionics remained old-school, making them less vulnerable to the effects of an electromagnetic pulse in the event of a nuclear detonation. Number 60403 was an unremarkable white, as opposed to the more recognizable livery of white and powder blue, allowing it to fly virtually unnoticed into fields all over the world.

The crew tonight was sparse—two Air Force Phoenix security officers, a United States Secret Service agent, an Air Force major from the White House Military Office, who scheduled and authorized every presidential lift, and the two pilots. They were all dressed in khaki slacks and polos. The security officers' pistols were concealed, and their rifles secreted in what looked like oversized tennis racket cases. They came in under cover of darkness one day before the President's scheduled arrival— a secret that everyone fully expected would be leaked at some point. There were a lot of moving parts to a presidential lift. Someone was sure to notice.

Redundancies were baked in for that exact reason—one of them was 60403.

Husberg and his first officer would go to a nearby hotel shortly after they landed, ensuring they got their mandatory crew rest in time for any unplanned egress the following day. The others would remain on board or in the rented hangar space, never leaving the aircraft unguarded. All the military people were cleared "Yankee White," meaning they had undergone strict background investigations in order to work around the President. Every one of them prayed they would never have to, at least not on this mission, in this bird. Number 60403 was a rescue aircraft. If it was designated Air Force One, it would be spiriting the President away from something very, very bad.

A stooped man with a wispy silver beard and a rumpled red Coca-Cola T-shirt stood leaning against his balcony railing with a bottle of Balboa beer and watched the white business jet approach. His apartment at the base of Telegraph Hill was once military housing at Fort Kobbe before the Americans handed it over and provided an unobstructed view of arriving and departing aircraft. The old man had become skilled at identifying airplanes by their silhouettes. Winglets, engine configuration, empennage, taken together they were like a fingerprint.

This was a Gulfstream III. He didn't bother to lift his binoculars while it was still in the air. It was already too dark to see anything of value. He waited until the plane touched down, exited the runway, and taxied back to the north toward the ramp and hangar space. Now he had some light.

No markings. That was interesting in and of itself. Maybe. Not everyone with multimillion-dollar planes wanted to flash who they were with bold paint schemes. The old man wasn't required to find out who owned the plane. His job was to sit on his balcony and drink the occasional beer while he kept track of arrival times, descriptions, and tail numbers.

He shooed away an annoying moth with his beer hand while holding the binoculars to his eyes with the other. A ramp worker rolled out on the tarmac on a tug and towed the plane into a hangar toward the north end of the airport. The aircraft doors remained closed the entire time.

He set down his beer, swatting the bothersome moth to the ground, and opened a tattered green ledger—slightly misshapen from where he stored the stub of a yellow pencil between the pages. Licking the tip of the pencil, he hunched over the book and in meticulous block letters entered the details his employers wanted.

ARRIVAL 6:32 P.M. WHITE GULF-
STREAM III. TAIL NUMBER 60403.
TAKEN IN HANGAR ON ARRIVAL.

In the margin, he made a personal observation—
**Narco-trafficker? Government agency? Maybe
both.**
He closed the book and took another swig of
beer, scanning the skies for another plane. His report would go out in the morning.

39

4:45 A.M.

The white-over-green HMX-1 Sikorsky VH-3D Sea King settled over the South Lawn, lights flashing against the backdrop of the Washington Monument, the Jefferson Memorial, and an indigo sky. It was well before sunrise, but the pilot settled the helicopter's wheels expertly onto circular pads in the manicured grass. He had to keep the head White House groundskeeper happy. The crew chief, a twenty-six-year-old corporal in dress blues, opened the boarding door and stepped out, making certain the rotor wash hadn't blown around any debris that might pose a trip hazard for the President. All clear, the young spit-shined Marine assumed a position of attention beside the boarding door. The first officer, a Marine Corps major who was also in dress blues, sat in the left seat, closest to the White House, and watched. His (or sometimes her) face and not the pilot in command's was the one the media gaggle usually got in their photos. Today, that gaggle was small, just a few diehards, who kept telephoto lenses aimed at the White House grounds twenty-four/seven.

A few steps inside the Oval Office, hidden from the media's stare, Jack Ryan kissed his wife goodbye. The Secret Service agents posted outside in the colonnade kept their backs to the door.

Her blue eyes bright and alert despite the early hour, Cathy wore flannel pajama pants and a faded gray Marine Corps Bulldog T-shirt that made her look sexy as hell.

Ryan kissed her again. "Marine One can wait."

Cathy shot him an impish grin. "I think you're forgetting the Secret Service has pressure pads under the carpet. A rendezvous in here might throw off their system."

"True enough," Ryan grumbled. "I'll be back in a few days, and we'll go someplace where we don't have to worry about pressure pads in the carpet."

Her eyes flashed, all business now. "Just promise me you'll be careful, Jack."

He kissed her on the tip of her nose and then turned to go, but she caught him by both shoulders. "Hang on there, mister. I need to make sure you're camera-ready." She pushed him to arm's length and gave him a quick scan in the dim light of the Resolute desk's lamp.

"Camera ready" was her way of saying he didn't have broccoli in his teeth.

Though naturally self-assured, Ryan would never get used to the scrutiny of being in someone's lens each time he walked out the door. Everyone tripped, made ill-conceived off-the-cuff remarks . . . or walked around with broccoli in their teeth. Cathy did the best she could. Fortunately, the rest of his staff did, too.

Cathy put a hand on his chest. "Got your glasses?"

He nodded.

"Phone? Wallet? Keys?"

He chuckled. It was the same routine they'd practiced since shortly after they married, her giving him a quick "preflight" check before he went out the door—though he hadn't turned a key or bought anything with money from a wallet in years.

"All good," he said.

"Okay, then." She smoothed his shirt under the collar of his green poplin Marine Corps flight jacket, zipping it up against the October chill before she all but shoved him out the door. "Best not keep everyone waiting . . ."

Ryan crossed the lawn quickly, saluting the HMX-1 crew chief and calling him by name. He gave a hearty Marine Corps **ooorah!**—and stopped to chat for a few moments to let the young Marine know he was a vital part of the machine. The HMX-1 cadre was small—just over eight hundred Marines in the whole shebang. The ones who dealt directly with the President—the pilots and crew chiefs—Ryan could keep track of with no problem.

Protocol dictated that POTUS be the last passenger on other than the crew chief, and the first off. Special Agent in Charge Gary Montgomery and five United States Secret Service agents from the Presidential Protective Division were already on board, along with Mary Pat Foley and CIA director Canfield—who happened to be wearing a ball cap and jacket that matched Ryan's.

The crew chief closed the door and let the pilots know they were secure aft. Moments later, the Sikorsky's two General Electric turboshaft engines spooled up and the Sea King lifted smoothly off the South Lawn and into the blue-black darkness above Washington, D.C. Less than two minutes later, Marine One was joined by three more VH-3D helicopters as they crossed the Anacostia River. These four identical HMX-1 White Tops changed positions and directions many times during the quick fifteen-mile flight to Joint Base Andrews. This aerial ballet, sometimes called the "presidential shell game" was meant to confuse anyone on the ground as to which helicopter POTUS was actually in.

The blue and white VC-25 (the military version of a Boeing 747) that served as Air Force One when Ryan was aboard was waiting with members of the Presidential Airlift Group when Marine One touched down. A half-dozen black Chevrolet Suburbans and Tahoes were parked near the rear of the plane. Air Force C-17s with Secret Service vehicles, the presidential Cadillac limo, and a partially dissembled "folded and stuffed" VH-60N White Hawk helicopter from HMX-1 had departed two days earlier and were already standing by in Argentina for the summit.

Ryan and Foley waited while Director Canfield exited the chopper. The crew chief posted outside to greet Marine One was in on the charade, and saluted Canfield as he exited. Canfield returned the salute and headed directly to the airstairs at the forward door of Air Force One, where he got another salute, this one from an Air Force staff sergeant posted at the bottom of the stairs. Canfield and Ryan were close to the same size and anyone who happened to be watching from a distance would see a tall man with a runner's build wearing a Marine Corps ball cap and flight jacket board through the forward door. Even with the lights spilling from the open door of the cavernous hangar, it was easy to mistake D/CIA for POTUS.

Ryan traded his jacket and hat for a black ball cap and blue down jacket that Montgomery had brought with him. The change made, he ducked out of Marine One with Foley and walked quickly into the open hangar. Montgomery and his skeleton crew followed them onto a white Gulfstream III business jet parked inside. A larger cadre of agents would be waiting for them in Panama, at which point two of this crew would split off and accompany Foley to the U.S. embassy, where she had an appointment with the ambassador, FBI legal attaché, DEA special agent in charge, and the CIA chief of station. She was under no illusions that if something happened and they had to set down en route, every agent on the plane would be focused on protecting Ryan.

Admiral Jason Bailey, chief White House physician, was waiting on board the G-III. Looking pink and freshly scrubbed, he was disarmingly alert for such an early hour. Dr. Bailey or one of his staff physicians was always near Ryan when he traveled, remaining just outside any presumed blast radius so they would be able to provide medical care in the event of an attack. On the larger VC-25 version of Air Force One, Bailey had the luxury of a fully equipped clinic, complete exam table, and assorted medications. Traveling on the Gulfstream, he made do with a satchel full of emergency instruments and medications, along with a minifridge stocked with four units of Ryan's blood type.

Ryan greeted the pilots and the lone flight attendant, who all wore Air Force Class A uniforms rather than the more comfortable Nomex flight suits, and then settled in to a forward-facing vis-à-vis leather seat diagonal from Dr. Bailey. Gary Montgomery and four Secret Service agents stooped in the cramped confines to make their way aft. Montgomery was a large man, but these men all dwarfed him. He took the seat directly across from Dr. Bailey, while Foley sat facing aft across from Ryan. The other agents squeezed themselves into seats in the rear and remained on alert while the plane was on the ground.

"Thank you, everyone," Ryan said, buckling his seat belt. "I realize this bird is not quite as spacious as our usual ride."

"As your doctor," Bailey said, "and therefore someone who wants to see you safe and well, I approve of this plan of yours. But I have to ask, Mr. President. Won't pretty much every person in Panama know you're coming as soon as Air Force One lands?"

Ryan grinned. "First off, this is **Gary's** plan. And technically we are sitting on Air Force One right now. But I get your point. The idea **is** for everyone in Panama to know of my visit." He shot a glance at Montgomery, who remained stoic. "Eventually, anyway. A mission that remains secret for the entire trip would negate our purpose for going in the first place. President Botero needs to be able to tout the fact that we're strong allies . . . That I essentially came when he asked."

Foley gave a noncommittal shrug.

Across the aisle, Montgomery raised a brow, but said nothing.

"Gary's plan allows us to be on the ground before anyone knows we're there," Ryan continued. "That should mitigate the worry over pop-up protests hindering the movement of our motorcade."

Dr. Bailey gave a nod of approval.

"So," he mused, "the bulk of your staff and the press entourage flies on what everyone presumes is Air Force One. Do they even know you're not on the plane or that they're heading to Panama?"

"Some of the staff know," Montgomery said quietly, as if he'd lost that argument. "The press gaggle is still in the dark. The rule that Air Force One passengers may go aft of their assigned seat but not forward helps us keep the secret for most of the flight. They're unlikely to find out unless someone from the staff lets it slip."

Ryan said, "The press pool will be briefed just before they land. They're used to changes like this."

"Plus," Foley added, "they all get a scoop of breaking news for headlines and broadcast chyrons. We'll time our arrival to land at Albrook a couple of minutes after the big blue bird touches down at Tocumen International. All eyes should be on the big plane and the decoy team of Secret Service agents waiting for it there."

"HAWKEYE will be waiting for us in slick vehicles at Albrook," Montgomery said. "Along with Airspace Security Branch, and a smaller, less visible detail of PPD agents. Fewer personnel, but a much lower profile."

Sound off, cover, and evacuate was the credo of any executive protection detail. HAWKEYE was the Secret Service code name for its Counter Assault Team, or CAT. This group of highly trained and heavily armed agents specialized in neutralizing any attack if something went sideways, while the main body of the protective detail surrounded the President and got him the hell out of Dodge.

Ryan looked at his watch. "We're looking at about a five-hour flight once we're wheels up," he said. "That puts us on the ground just after eleven thirty local."

"Sounds well thought-out," Bailey said. "Barring any sort of leak."

Montgomery gave a slow nod and turned to look out the window, speaking almost to himself.

"There's always a leak . . ."

40

Felix Moncada woke with the knowledge that today he would liberate Panama, just as Simón Bolívar had liberated Venezuela and Colombia and much of Latin America. It was a gross comparison, vain and high-minded. This, Moncada knew. But it was also true. There would be bloodshed. That was a given. But it would be over quickly, like ripping off a bandage or cauterizing a wound. Best to do it all at once.

One moment Moncada felt as though he might vomit up his breakfast, the next he wanted to break out in song.

And yet, something was wrong. Moncada could not put his finger on what exactly, but it was there, a shadow. His aunt would have called it the wrong kind of wind. She could smell bad omens. He pushed the thought out of his mind as he showered, dressed in his best blue silk suit, and drove his Mercedes to the Palacio de las Garzas—the presidential palace that would very soon become an even more historic landmark than it already was.

Moncada parked in his assigned spot and walked confidently past two uniformed SPI officers guarding the plain wooden barricade that blocked vehicle traffic from the alley toward the employee entrance of the palace.

A black van Moncada had never seen before loitered out front by the seawall on Eloy Alfaro Avenue. There seemed to be more security in the area, including a half-dozen gringos dressed in what American security men always wore in the tropics, khaki slacks and loose short-sleeved shirts to cover their weapons. It was something of a uniform, particularly since the shirts apparently came in only a limited number of colors and patterns. When he asked about the visitors, the guards at the magnetometer told Moncada that His Excellency President Botero was expecting the United States ambassador.

That explained the van out front and the extra gringos. State Department Diplomatic Security and probably a diplomat or two checking the area in advance for their boss. Security personnel had grown jittery after the PNP had unwittingly discovered an apparent plot to kill Botero.

He made his way to the president's office, nodding to the two SPI officers posted in the hall on either side of the entrance. The door to the outer office suite was closed, but Moncada knew that Botero's secretary, a lovely young woman named Dominica, was at her desk inside. He shook his head sadly at the thought of her auburn hair and green eyes. She was innocent and did not deserve the fate that was about to befall her.

But that was the way of things. Sacrifices had to be made.

The U.S. ambassador's visit was a slight hiccup, especially the armed Diplomatic Security agents, but they could be dealt with now that they were accounted for. Protectors, they were not likely expecting anything to happen.

Everything was in place.

The PNP had seized their bombs. But Doyle had made new ones. The embassy bomb would go off first, then the ones near the palace. Moncada checked his watch—today a Rolex two-tone GMT-Master II to celebrate the momentous occasion. Commissioner Guerra would arrive within the hour, followed by Vega and Pinto—two Camarilla operatives Guerra had helped embed inside the Policía Nacional. There would be no turning back. Men of the Camarilla lived for conflict, for violence, finding it at least as important as the money they were paid, probably more so. Moncada had seen it in their eyes. Men like them . . . and now men like **him** . . . they lived for this sort of thing.

With the president and vice president dead,

carnage in the streets and the canal, the surviving ministers would fear for their lives. They would have little choice but to declare martial law.

The Russians, approaching their appointed transit time through the canal, would observe the chaos and do what good citizens of the world would do and help restore order—with no help from the Big Brother to the north.

A coup, but not one to install a military leader. Panama had no military. No, this was a reset to shake up the government and allow it to settle into its natural state.

This was the morning that everything would change.

Two women from the housekeeping staff breezed down the hall past Moncada as if he weren't there. The senior woman spoke in hushed but pointed tones, intent on making certain her younger acolyte understood that every painting, each vase was dusted, and all the rugs and runners were perfectly situated.

Only then did Moncada realize the tiny detail that he'd noticed but not recognized—the smell of a deep clean—freshly waxed floors, polished wood, shampooed upholstery.

Panamanians had a saying—**You sweep where your mother-in-law walks.**

Botero's staff was preparing for a visitor—and presidents did not fret this much for an ordinary ambassador. They certainly didn't shampoo the chair cushions.

Moncada's mobile buzzed in his pocket, causing him to jump. An American agent in the hallway gave him a puzzled look, but he waved it off. Sickened with a growing dread, Moncada retreated to an out-of-the-way spot near the stairs and answered the call. Security recognized him and he was often on the phone, so he was as good as invisible, even amid the hubbub.

It was Guerra.

Moncada cupped his hand over the phone, snapping at the commissioner before he had a chance to get a word out. "I need you and Pinto here at once! Someone important is coming to the palace. You may not be able to get past SPI security if you wait."

"We are on our way," Guerra said. "But there is something you should know."

Moncada held his breath while Guerra told him of the informant's report from Pacifico airport. An unidentified white Gulfstream had landed the evening before and then moved immediately into the hangar, out of sight.

A cold chill washed over Moncada. He'd read about this. It was an American Air Force rescue aircraft. This changed everything.

The President of the United States was coming to Panama.

41

Sabine Gorshkova snatched the diminutive black Beretta from the drawer of her nightstand and depressed the stubby little slide with her thumb and forefinger. The gun reminded her of herself—thick, not that easy to manipulate, and deceptively dangerous. She made certain there was a round in the chamber (though she'd only put it in the drawer a few hours earlier) and then tucked it into the leather holster between the waistband of her white slacks and her right kidney. Hers was not a life that allowed the luxury of digging around in her handbag for a weapon. Certainly not now that the Americans had cut down her brother like a dog. If they were not coming for her yet, they soon would be.

There were better calibers for defensive purposes than the puny .32 ACP, but the Beretta was a gift from Joaquín. She wore it in his honor. Besides, it was small, and she was not, so it concealed perfectly.

Angry with herself for wasting the morning

hours in bed, Sabine smoothed her loose cotton blouse over the pistol and glanced across the bedroom at her head of security and sometimes lover, a muscular South African named De Bruk. She should never have asked him to spend the night. He awakened tender parts of her brain she did not like to face.

Dressed only in a baggy pair of boxers, he held his jeans in one hand and a prepaid mobile phone in the other.

The news he'd just given her was bad.

Sabine opened a tube of lipstick, a color called Gothic Plum to match her nails. "What do you mean when you say they are gone?"

De Bruk dropped the prepaid on the end of the bed and bent over, hopping a little to step into his pants. "The American film crew is still at the hotel, but Flaco and Annie weren't there when Manolo went to relieve them last night."

Sabine shot De Bruk a side-eye in the mirror. "What does that mean . . . they weren't there? Where did they go?"

"I am afraid they have vanished," he said. "Gone AWOL. Nowhere to be found."

Sabine paused, the lipstick grazing her puckered mouth. "What about the Americans?"

"Manolo says they are going about their business as usual, **patrona.**" In bed, she allowed De Bruk to call her **la jefecita,** among other things—but never "Sabine." And the moment their feet hit the floor she was **patrona.** The boss. There was no question about that. De Bruk fastened the button of his jeans over his flat belly as he spoke. "I know there is a girls' college near the Americans' hotel. Flaco has been known to chase—"

Sabine finished applying her lipstick, twisted it back into the tube, and then dabbed an errant fleck off her front tooth.

"If that idiot has left his assignment to bed some fresh piece of Colombian ass . . . I want you to kill him. Slowly. Take his body into the hills and feed it to the pigs."

"Of course, **patrona,**" De Bruk said, his face as passive as if she'd just ordered eggs for breakfast.

De Bruk had made a trip to the pig farm the day before, after discovering that Joaquín's idiot sushi chef had broken protocol and used the same prepaid mobile for a full week, three days longer than he should have.

Uncle Hector had gone along for the ride. He loved the pig farm.

Sabine would have preferred to stay in a more rural area herself—nearer the pigs—but it was too easy to be noticed in sparsely populated places. She'd not stayed anonymous for so long by standing out. Yes, she had security, but what person of substance did not in Colombia, or anywhere in the world, for that matter? Sabine Gorshkova had houses and apartments all over Latin America and

Eastern Europe and even one outside Seville. All of them in affluent neighborhoods where rich politicians and cartel bosses stashed their mistresses. Her two-story faux Spanish colonial in Cartagena was tucked amid the high-rise hotels along the coast of Bocagrande, overlooking the sea and the island of Tierra Bomba to the west. Rich women with designer handbags crawled the streets like insects.

Her uncle had taught her when she was just a child that people's preconceived notions offered more security than a mountain fortress. Who would have believed that Hector Alonso, the wrinkled and stooped Peruvian man, had murdered dozens of men and women with a hammer? Or that Sabine, a pudgy five feet tall with tailored suits and freshly manicured nails, was even more ruthless than her uncle?

"Forgive me for asking," De Bruk said. "But . . ."

"My Blanca problem . . ."

"Yes, **patrona**," De Bruk said.

"I need to think about it."

"Of course," De Bruk said. "I would only point out that she is becoming increasingly unhappy. It appears she has shared with her friends at university how unhappy she is with her family situation. She has not mentioned you by name, not yet anyway, but when people are unhappy, they talk."

"Stupid little . . ." Sabine's voice dropped to a whisper. This was a family affair—and none of

De Bruk's business, no matter how good he was in bed. Blanca did not like her very much. That was clear, but Sabine found it difficult to imagine she would do anything to put her in danger. At least not on purpose. Still . . .

De Bruk spoke again. "Your uncle thinks—"

Sabine raised a hand to shush him. "My uncle has made it clear to me what he wants to do. I told him I need to think about it, and I am telling you the same thing."

"Of course."

De Bruk took his own pistol—a runty Heckler & Koch SFP9 CC—from the nightstand, along with a holster made of stiff plastic-like Kydex. The holster was wide enough to hold the small H&K and a spare ten-round magazine. De Bruk slid the entire affair inside his waistband directly below his belly button, hooking the plastic clips over his belt.

"I will go to the hotel and check on Flaco and Annie myself."

"You do that . . ." Sabine eyed the placement of his holster and pistol. "And be careful with that thing. If you shoot your balls off, then I may as well feed you to the pigs."

He smiled benignly.

"I am serious about this," Sabine said. "What good would you be to—"

Her mobile began to dance across the nightstand, cutting her off. "I am telling you to be careful," she said again and then answered the phone.

She listened for a long moment and then ended the call.

"Patrona?" De Bruk said, concern over the unknown crossing his face.

"That was Minsky in Washington." She gave a slow nod, working through the ramifications of what she'd just learned. "It seems that our Señora Foley arrived at Andrews Air Force Base two hours ago with the U.S. President. She is apparently accompanying him to the summit in Argentina a day sooner than we expected."

"Shall I tell the men to get ready to depart?"

Sabine folded her arms across her bosom. "If I thought for one instant that I would have a chance to get near Mary Pat Foley in Mar del Plata, I would have been in Argentina already." She turned up her nose at the mere mention of the woman's name. "That summit will never take place. Moncada's Operation JAMAICA will kick off at any moment. I have no idea if it will have the outcome that idiot desires, but a few bombs and a little bloodletting in Panama will cause a stir. None of those cowards have the balls to attend a political summit after that."

"Operation JAMAICA . . ." De Bruk mused.

Sabine nodded, arms still crossed, double chin to chest. "Felix Moncada is a buffoon, but his project aligns with our goals." She looked up. "And he pays."

"Forgive me, **patrona**," De Bruk said. "But I

have wondered, why 'JAMAICA'? Is there some significance?"

She shrugged. "Moncada fancies himself as an incarnation of Simón Bolívar."

"The Liberator," De Bruk said.

"Correct," Sabine said, pleased to hear the South African was not completely ignorant of Latin American history. "Bolívar's 'Letter from Jamaica' is something akin to the American Declaration of Independence, asserting the natural rights of Latin Americans. He is—"

Her phone vibrated again.

It was Moncada. As usual, the words gushed out of him like a broken bucket.

". . . a Gulfstream III, one of the planes the Secret Service puts on standby when the President of the U.S. travels abroad . . ." Moncada buzzed like an out-of-tune high string on a guitar. "Do you realize what that means?"

"That Jack Ryan is stopping in Panama," she said.

"It means Jack Ryan is . . . Correct! I do not know when Air Force One departed, but—"

Sabine put the phone on speaker and gave Moncada the information she'd just received from her man in Washington, D.C. Moncada did the math, stuttering as if he might have a stroke.

"Air Force One left Washington at half past six. A five-hour flight . . . He will be here before noon!"

"That is true," Sabine said, her brain already working through her next move.

"But today is the day!" Moncada whimpered. "We cannot . . . I mean to say . . . I trust your men will take care of the American President as well. If he survives after witnessing what we do to Botero, this whole operation will all be for naught—"

Sabine's voice now fell into a soft, mesmerizing cadence—a snake hypnotizing her prey.

"Listen to me closely, Felix Moncada. My men do not engage in suicide missions. I have no love lost for Jack Ryan. But think very hard about what you are saying. U.S. presidents travel with many, many layers of highly trained security, members of their own military, explosive detection dogs . . . And, as you have discovered, extra aircraft. Men of the Camarilla are brave. They are accustomed to dangerous situations and will fight through these dangers if the need arises. My operatives survive by flawless execution of plans that they have rehearsed until they cannot fail. Of course, they may have to bend, adjust to the moment, but this . . . Killing an American president is not something that could be done with a few hours' notice. I will not sanction it. My men will stay in place until after Botero returns from Argentina."

"But—"

"No buts! We will execute your Project JAMAICA at that time. Same outcome, but with far less risk."

"What of the Russian ships?" Moncada gasped, as if it had only just occurred to him. "They were supposed to—"

"Relax, my friend," Sabine said. "Our Russian brothers have drills in the Caribbean, do they not?"

"They do."

"They will have to pass through the canal to go home. I suggest you time Project JAMAICA to coincide with their return voyage."

"Yes," Moncada said, regaining a degree of his normal bravado. "Yes. I can do that. But what of—"

Sabine cut him off. "You have many calls to make. Much to do. We will speak of this at greater length when I arrive."

"What? You are coming to Panama?"

Sabine scoffed out loud. She didn't care if he heard it. It was astounding how a man who found it so difficult to adapt believed he was capable of overthrowing a government.

"I will be there in less than two hours."

"But we are postponing."

"**You** are postponing," she said. "I have a special interest in a little bird traveling with the President. I do not want you to frighten her away before I arrive."

She ended the call and looked across the bedroom at De Bruk, heaving an exhausted sigh.

"I have thought about it," she said.

"Your sister?"

She nodded. "Who is watching her now?"

"Roberto and Gregor."

Sabine checked the time on her mobile. "Ahhh, Blancacita, you will be leaving for classes now . . .

Too many witnesses." She folded her arms again, tapping her foot in thought until an idea came to her. "She planned to visit me this morning. Have Roberto and Gregor break off and wait for her here. They can deal with her when she arrives."

"They should bring her to you?"

"No," Sabine said sadly. "We must leave at once. My sister is . . ." Her throat convulsed, making it impossible to get the words out. She swallowed hard, then looked De Bruk in the eye, calling him by his given name, something she rarely did. "Tell them . . . Tell them to take her to the pig farm."

42

The beautiful woman who was his contact at the Russian embassy had been cordial enough at their earlier meetings, but she still put him on edge. Several inches taller than Moncada with flaming red hair and broad shoulders, she reminded him of a **polianitsa,** the Slavic female warriors of Russian epics. She did not carry a sword, but one would have looked quite at home in her strong hands.

Anya Durova had deferred to him at every turn when he'd arranged a chance meeting on the University of Panama campus to explain the basics of his plan. She'd remained soft-spoken and nurturing even after she'd gotten the Russian Navy involved, acting as though she were on Moncada's side of any question. It was her and him against the powers above. He'd begged her to convince the Russian Navy to send ships and she had taken up his cause like the valiant **polianitsa** that she was and convinced Moscow to send the **Ivan Gren** and the **Admiral Chabanenko.** The warships had an appointment to transit the Pedro Miguel Locks in half an hour on their way through the canal to training maneuvers in the Caribbean with the Cuban and Venezuelan navies. If things had gone to plan, Operation JAMAICA would have begun while the warships were in line for their transit, precipitating a crisis where they could offer their assistance before the United States even knew what was going on. Except now there would be no crisis, no problem in which they could intervene.

Moncada had to ask the beautiful redheaded warrior to release her ships and send them on their way after he'd begged so fervently for her to convince them to loiter in Panama Bay and help when the fireworks of Operation JAMAICA began.

He considered going to the Russian embassy to meet Durova, but decided this was a problem that was infinitely easier to handle over the phone. He put it off as long as he could, then picked up his secure phone and punched in Durova's number. His leg began to bounce faster, making his chair squeak so loudly Moncada was certain his secretary could hear it from the outer office. His stomach felt as if some kind of serpent had crawled into his gut and made a home there, writhing and squirming.

His secure phone hid his caller ID number, but Durova recognized his voice as soon as he said hello.

"Felix, my darling," she said. "To what do I owe this pleasure? We are on a short countdown, are we not?"

"That is why I'm calling," Moncada said. "The ships must go ahead and make their appointed transit times."

"Felix," Durova scoffed. "Surely you must be joking."

Moncada screwed up his courage. "I assure you I am not," he said. "I wish I were. But certain things have occurred that—"

"Felix," Durova said. "How can I put this delicately? Russian warships are like Japanese killing swords. Once they are removed from the scabbard, they must draw blood."

"Even so," Moncada said. "The ships must make their appointed times through the locks. Circumstances have changed."

"You mean the U.S. President has put a fly in the ointment?"

"That is . . ." Moncada stammered. "Yes. That is correct."

"So," Durova said. Moncada had never seen her angry, but it was easy to picture a wild-eyed rant on the other end of the line with each word that spilled out of her mouth. "Are you saying this is the end of it? You asked me to expend untold political clout convincing not one but two captains of the Russian Navy that they should be willing to risk losing their place for transit so they could stand by and wait to render aid to your country. I might add that captains of the Russian Navy are among the most notorious on the planet for being difficult to convince of anything. And now you are . . . How do you say it? Pulling the plug after all this work? You could not have told me this two days ago?"

"This is only a pause," Moncada said. "I plan to be ready for execution by the time the ships pass this way when they return from the Caribbean."

"Another about-face like this and I will be ready for execution."

Durova launched into a stream of white-hot Russian that Moncada couldn't understand. Whatever she said, it was directed at him, and it was not positive.

43

The commander of the 535-foot Udaloy II–class destroyer **Admiral Chabanenko,** Captain of the First Rank Vladimir Rykov, replaced the handset to the secure satellite telephone in his at-sea quarters and made his way forward past CIC—the ship's combat information center—toward the bridge.

The contents of the message were from a GRU major named Anya Durova, but the phone call had come directly from the admiral of the Northern Fleet. The GRU was the intelligence arm of the Russian military, but no matter what they or the pricks at SVR believed, a captain in the Russian Navy did not take orders from the likes of a spy, military or otherwise. Rykov was a fighting man, accustomed to facing his problems in open, honest battle. The very notion of dealing with **spionam**—spies—gave Rykov a gaseous look that frightened his subordinates.

Two **glavny starshinas**—the Russian equivalent

of petty officers—came out of the CIC. The combat information center was notoriously chilly because of the equipment and both men wore poplin jackets. It was dark as well, so it took a moment for their eyes to adjust in the much brighter passage. They spun with their backs to the wall as if pulled by a magnet the moment they realized the captain was walking toward them.

Not quite five feet seven, Rykov appeared to have traded height for muscle when it came to his genetics. A bullish neck and powerful shoulders required extensive tailoring of his uniforms. When he was younger, one of his more senior shipmates had made fun of his size, joking cruelly that he purchased his uniform pants from a children's shop. Rykov had received a reduction in pay for the beating he gave the other officer, but no one ever made fun of his size again.

Now the two sailors coming out of the CIC yielded the ship's passage quickly, acknowledging him respectfully as he passed. **Gangway or sick bay,** the Americans said. A good notion, Rykov thought. He was, after all, the terrible god of their floating world. Beyond that, his shoulders simply did not allow enough room for anyone else to pass without hugging the wall.

Rykov's executive officer, a baby-faced captain of the third rank (equivalent to a lieutenant commander in the United States Navy) named Orlov, announced his presence as he entered the bridge.

He knew about the call, and a raised brow showed his interest in the contents.

The captain gave a subtle shake of his head, invisible to everyone else on the bridge.

"Prepare to get underway as soon as our guest arrives," he said. "Captain Pagodin will receive his canal pilot on the **Ivan Gren** at any moment."

The **Ivan Gren,** a 442-foot Russian landing ship brooded two hundred yards off **Admiral Chabanenko**'s starboard rail. Battleship gray, the broad and bellicose warship carried two Ka-29TB assault helicopters and an impressive array of amphibious landing craft and armored personnel carriers—and two hundred and fifty Navy infantrymen—Russia's answer to the Marines.

There were no new orders to convey. This was exactly what the crew expected him to say. Business as usual.

Both ships waited in the dredged sea approach at the foot of the Miraflores Locks in what was known as the Anchor Line, the spot where transiting vessels stood ready well before their appointed time and waited for word to proceed from maritime traffic control. But for the captain and XO of both ships, everyone expected to pass through the canal in a matter of minutes. The admiral's standdown message meant both ships would carry on the way the crew expected they would all along—passing through the canal to participate in maneuvers with the Cubans and Venezuelans.

And that was just fine with Rykov. He would do his duty the same in the Caribbean as he would have done in Panama Bay. The same way he'd done it for twenty-seven years, the bulk of that serving in Russia's glorious Northern Fleet. Frankly, the sight of land made him uneasy. It had the smell of rot that others equated with the sea. He knew better. The sea smelled . . . well, like the sea. The bustling port of Panama with its prickly white skyscrapers did nothing for him, no matter how new and impressive they were supposed to be.

Rykov lifted a pair of binoculars—Swarovski, not the shitty Russian junk the Navy supplied him—and surveyed the dozen other ships at anchor in Panama Bay, all waiting in the holding area for their turn to transit the canal. Most were container ships, larger than the **Admiral Chabanenko,** but not nearly as formidable. The crew called her **Chernyy Terror**—the Black Terror. The destroyer's sleek line and freshly painted gunmetal-gray hull gave her the appearance of a killing sword. She bristled with weaponry. SS-N-22 "Sunburn" anti-ship missiles, SA-N-9 surface-to-air missiles, twin AK-130 cannons, an AK-630 close-in weapon system, Type 53 torpedoes, and RBU-6000 antisubmarine rockets. Not to mention the two Ka-27 "Helix" attack helicopters.

A black terror indeed.

A commotion on deck drew Rykov's attention to starboard.

"The pilot launch **Boquerón** is coming alongside now, Captain," Savkin, the chief **glavny starshina** of the ship, said. Almost as old as Rykov at forty-seven, he was the equivalent of a senior chief petty officer, the senior enlisted man.

Rykov folded his hands behind his back. What came next was the most emasculating portion of navigating many a foreign port, strait, or canal—turning over control of his ship to a maritime pilot. Had it been up to him, Rykov would have happily sailed around Cape Horn—the tip of South America—and braved all the gales and icebergs the Drake Passage had to throw at him.

He groaned. "Very well. Show the pilot in when he comes aboard."

The ship-to-ship radio chirped. Orlov grabbed the handset, spoke briefly, then hung up.

"The pilot is aboard," he said.

Two hundred yards over the starboard rail, the **Boquerón,** a bright red fifty-foot launch, had finished depositing the canal pilot and now put distance between herself and the Russian destroyer.

"Our tugboats are in place," the XO said.

"Very well," Rykov said, without even attempting to sound like he meant it. None of the men relished turning over the ship to outsiders.

Powerful tugs, one off the bow and another off the stern, would see to it the ships stayed where they were supposed to throughout the transit.

The ship's pilot knocked three times on the hatch,

mainly out of courtesy. The ship was his as soon as he stepped aboard—technically at least. Rykov rankled at the very notion of it. The laws of the Panama Canal Authority might say the pilot was in charge, but the commander of a Russian Navy vessel never relinquished control of his ship. If he did, he ceased to be captain.

Rykov and Orlov pulled the canal pilot aside the moment he entered the bridge, stepping behind the navigation table.

The man introduced himself as Berugatte. An Indigenous Emberá, he had mahogany-colored skin with a broad, squarish face. A bright orange personal flotation vest covered his white uniform shirt, short-sleeved against the sticky heat. The man smiled far too much for Rykov's taste, as if he wanted to brag about a mouth full of exceedingly white teeth.

"Do you speak Russian?" the XO asked, squinting down his nose a little. Probably from the glare of the man's teeth, Rykov thought, mildly amused at his own little joke.

"English," the pilot said. "Or Spanish."

Rykov gave a curt nod. "English."

"Excellent," Berugatte said. "Are we ready to get underway?"

"We are," the XO said. "But we need to discuss the ground rules."

"There are ground rules?" The Emberá man cocked his head. "Is that so?"

"It is," Orlov said. "You may advise the captain

on navigational procedures as required by the canal and harbor authorities, but such advice must be given directly to Captain Rykov by way of suggestions. You may not give him orders."

The pilot closed his eyes and took a deep breath, as if he'd heard this sort of thing before.

The executive officer continued, while Rykov looked on in silence. "On this vessel, only the captain will give the orders to his crew."

Berugatte hid a resigned shrug behind a compliant nod. "Of course." He smiled slyly and looked the XO in the eye. "Permission to speak with the captain directly, since he is standing right beside us."

If one of his crew had been so impertinent Rykov would have had him thrown in the brig, but he didn't want to give the pilot the pleasure of seeing him annoyed.

Instead, Rykov tapped his watch. "Permission granted. It is getting late, Señor Berugatte. I'm surprised you have not advised us to get underway."

44

Chilly Edwards's head snapped up with a start when Mandy Cobb's voice crackled over his earpiece.

Mandy and John Clark had the eye on Blanca Pakulova's front door for the moment, their gray Taurus parked at the other end of the narrow street.

"She's at her mailbox," Mandy said over the radio. "Dressed in hospital scrubs and carrying a small daypack."

At long last, Blanca was moving again.

Chilly sat in the front passenger seat of a beater Volkswagen, stomach roiling from too much coffee, head bobbing from lack of sleep.

Ding Chavez gave a tired chuckle from behind the wheel. "Careful you don't break your neck, bud."

Chilly rubbed his face, wincing when he bumped his broken nose.

Adam Yao's operators had spent the past day following Blanca, assessing risks and establishing patterns of life. They knew which classes she attended, who her professors were, and the location of her modest apartment southeast of campus. They'd watched her stop by a small market a few blocks from the university. She'd come out a short time later with a bottle of whiskey and a bag of **chicharróns**—pork rinds. These were not the puffy version common in the U.S., a female operator from Peru explained, but decadent pieces of fried pork belly.

Her apartment had been dark when she drove her little red Audi TT into the attached parking garage, then lights flickered on when she went inside. By the time Campus operators relieved the original team, the glow of a television cast wavering shadows on the curtains. Chilly envisioned the young woman sitting on the couch, drinking whiskey straight out of the bottle and munching chicharróns from the bag while she binged episodes of some medical drama.

Whatever Blanca had been doing in her apartment, she did it alone. The lights had gone dark again at twenty after ten, leaving the operatives sitting through the long night. They didn't flick on again until six in the morning.

Mandy's voice came over the radio again, filled with dejection. "False alarm. Target just stepped back inside."

Even Chavez groaned at the news. The team had spent the witching hours—when everyone but dogs and drug dealers were asleep—sitting in blacked-out vehicles waiting and watching a dark apartment. **Smoking and joking,** they called it—that dead time after the adrenaline of the day wore off but it was crucial to stay alert, so you told stories, drank coffee, peed in bottles, told more stories, and drank more coffee. Abilene PD had given Chilly plenty of training in that department.

The attack in the hotel stairwell had everyone on the team more than a little jacked, scanning surrounding traffic for another security team or anyone who might be following WINDWARD STATION while they focused on their target.

The previous WINDWARD STATION shift had gotten a good-enough look at Blanca's two-man security team to identify them as among the body-guards on Sorte Mountain when Joaquín Gorshkov was killed. That made them Camarilla, which meant they likely had valuable intel in their heads. Still, considering their situation, both Clark and Yao agreed they should focus on Blanca—for now.

So far, it looked like they were only running a two-man team. Chilly and Ding had the eye on them—a dapper fellow with a pencil-thin mustache and another, smaller man with a powder-blue golf jacket. They'd spent the night outside in front of Blanca's apartment, doing their own smoking and joking, getting out of their white Hi-Lux pickup every hour or so to pee in the gutter.

Pencil-Thin Mustache got out again, did his

business, then gave a little start like something had bitten him. He reached in his pocket for a mobile phone.

Good to see they were jumpy from a long night, too, Chilly thought. He lifted a pair of binoculars to his eyes, hoping to get some read on the conversation.

Pencil-Thin snapped to attention when he answered the call, his mustache twitching a little. Someone important on the other end of the line.

"Now I've got movement with the goons . . ." Chilly relayed what he was seeing over the net, using their shorthand for Blanca's Camarilla watchers.

Golf Jacket climbed out of the pickup and approached his partner, apparently sensing this was an important call.

Pencil-Thin listened more than he spoke, nodding a lot. At length, he lowered the phone and stared at it a moment as if to make certain the call had disconnected, then stuffed it into his pocket. He said something to his partner Chilly couldn't make out. Moments later, they both climbed into their Hilux and drove away without so much as a nod to Blanca.

"Maybe they're going to check on their missing guys at the hotel," Chilly said to Ding.

"Could be . . ."

Caruso, Sherman, and Ryan would rotate in later. For now, they had remained at the hotel, hitting the pool, hanging out at the bar, generally making themselves seen and acting as decoys to anyone who might be looking for the two dead men.

Chilly was still astonished at how quickly Yao had gotten an in-country Agency cleanup team to come to the hotel and retrieve the bodies. They hadn't cut them up or broken their bones to stuff them into bags or anything so Hollywood-gruesome as all that, at least not in front of Chilly or Mandy. The four-man-and-one-woman team was dressed like event caterers and had the dour expressions of people who'd done this sort of thing before, leaving Chilly to wonder just how common an event this was. They made two trips with a room service cart, hauling the bodies one at a time to the basement.

From there . . . Chilly didn't ask.

Clark had offered to let Mandy Cobb bow out of the operation, but she wasn't having it, insisting that she was fine. If anything, Chilly thought, she was more upset about the whole event not bothering her than she was about the shooting. Clark gave Chilly the same option, which he also refused. Clark issued their Glocks almost immediately after he'd been briefed. The attack in the stairwell had changed the parameter of the Campus mission. What had once been a recce mission, a snoop and poop, had morphed into hands-on conflict. Frankly, Chilly preferred it that way. He suspected the rest of the team felt the same.

Twenty minutes later, Mandy spoke again.

"Okay," she said. "This time for real. Red Audi turning right out of the parking garage . . . Blanca driving . . . passing us . . . now."

The team fell into an orchestrated surveillance for the next two hours, leapfrogging, changing positions frequently, staying well back in traffic so as not to be spotted.

The tropical sun was up and beating down with a vengeance, causing the Volkswagen to tick and creak as the metal heated up from the cool of the night. The ancient sedan left a trail of dust as it squeaked over the narrow concrete streets near the University of Cartagena Hospital. Like most vehicles that spent their lives near the sea, the dented sedan was pitted with rust. The decals had been scraped away, but it still bore the faded paint scheme of a Cartagena taxi.

It still smelled like a taxi, redolent of strong coffee, sun-beaten plastic, and stale cigarettes. Chilly didn't mind. It reminded him of early-fall dove-hunting trips with his dad and a neighbor man named Kinsey, who was a retired deputy sheriff from up in Dimmitt. The fall Texas weather was still hot enough to bake the inside of the old pickup and Mr. Kinsey would light a fresh filter-less Camel with the burning stub of his last, one after another all evening long, until it got too dark to see anything but the glow of his cigarette—much less any doves. Not healthy, but a hell of a good time for a nine-year-old boy, listening to the men tell stories—most of which were about hunting out-laws on the Texas plains . . .

A block to the west and three cars behind Blanca's Audi in a twenty-year-old Ford Ranger pickup, Midas and Eric Ward had the eye. Ward called out with their position, prompting Ding to hang a quick right to stay out of their way. The abrupt movement shook Chilly out of the memory.

Ding chuckled again. "You still with us, kid?"

Chilly rubbed a hand over his face, stifling a yawn. "Yep," he said. "All good."

"You should have taken a couple of catnaps when you had the chance," Ding said. "You do this job, you have to learn to grab sleep when you can, where you can."

"I'm fine." Chilly gave in to the yawn with a long shuddering stretch, driving his boots against the floorboard. "Seriously, I—"

Midas's voice came over the net. He always sounded as if he was on the verge of telling a joke.

"I can't tell if our bird is running a surveillance-detection route or just hunting a parking spot."

The previous team had identified the MAC (media access control) addresses unique to Blanca's mobile phone and the Wi-Fi in her car. Ladder-like Yagi antennas attached to tablets allowed Campus opera-tors to track these signals without getting too close.

Slightly ahead and one block farther west, Mandy and Clark paralleled the Audi in their Taurus. The mid-sized Ford was the chameleon of sedans, able to blend into even scant traffic. It had a vanilla look that made witnesses forget exactly what kind of vehicle it was or, better yet, misidentify it as some other make and model.

A whir of wind noise over the radio preceded Adam Yao's voice. "I'll squirt up ahead and get a better eye."

Yao had joined them earlier that morning, riding a Honda Super Cub. The little bike was only a 125ccs, but maneuverable and plenty gutsy enough to zip in and out of city traffic with ease. A motor cop to the bone, Chilly was always happiest when he was on two wheels getting bugs and grit in his teeth. He volunteered for that duty, but Clark decided he had enough to worry about as a new guy running surveillance during the aftermath of a fight without having to dodge Colombian drivers—especially when he looked like he was about to pass out from lack of sleep.

Chilly yawned again. It was probably for the best.

The four vehicles coordinated their movements, leapfrogging frequently so that none of them stayed behind the Audi for more than a few blocks.

"Okay," Yao said against the backdrop of wind noise. "She's getting on Ninety . . . going northwest . . . Everybody, stand by for a heat check . . ."

Boulevards like 90, a main thoroughfare through the city of Cartagena, provided good opportunities for people who thought they might have someone behind them to exit quickly as soon as they got on, forcing an unprepared surveillance team to show their hand. Quick exits, running stale yellow lights, circling a block more than once were all methods of checking for any "heat."

"Nope," Yao said. "She's just getting on the boulevard, heading toward the ocean. I just passed her. Ding, if you want to take the eye . . ."

"Roger that."

"She's heading toward our hotel," Mandy said a few minutes later when the road curved to the left and crossed the tree-choked marshes of Cabrero Lake.

"Maybe," Yao said. "I've already called ahead to let them know where we are. They're saying no sign of her two security guys."

They drove past the Walled City, where their hotel was located. To their left, modest powerboats shared the inner harbor of Cartagena Bay with sleek multimillion-dollar yachts.

"She's going to Bocagrande," Chilly said.

"Copy that," Yao said.

Bocagrande was a narrow L of land that bristled with white high-rise hotels and apartment buildings. Roughly three blocks across at its widest point, it extended out from the mainland toward the less-developed Tierra Bomba Island before jutting back to the east to form the western edge of the "big mouth" of Cartagena Bay.

Clark spoke next. "Target's getting close to the L," he said. "Mandy and I are shooting southeast on

Fifth along the water. We'll turn and approach from the other end."

"Copy," Yao said. "We'll have to stay on her. This place is a hive—"

Mandy spoke up, bonking Yao and garbling his transmission.

She paused, then spoke again quickly when he paused.

"Our white Hi-Lux is on Fifth Street between Ninth and Tenth. Entering the gates of a wonky, stacked-circle high-rise. Wrought-iron fence. Empty boat trailer by the curb on the ocean side. Same pickup, same goons. Looks like one of them is going inside."

"Just one?" Yao asked.

"Yep," Clark said. "We'll get a closer look."

45

Clark drove past the building, slowing just a hair to get a better look. Pencil-Thin Mustache walked toward the door, talking with animated gestures on his phone, moving quickly as if on a mission. The one in the golf jacket was out of the pickup, leaning against the fender smoking a cigarette. Neither of them paid attention to anything outside the wrought-iron fence.

Traffic was light. Morning runners jogged along the path behind Clark and Mandy in onesies and twosies, between the beach cabanas and the street.

"See if anyone meets him at the door if you can," he said to Mandy.

She came up in the seat a little and craned her head as they drove by.

"Nobody," she said. "Looks like he had to punch in a code to get inside."

Clark flipped a quick U-turn half a block down, just past a young woman setting up a motorized three-wheeled cart that sold arroz con pollo. It was the perfect surveillance cover. Clark logged the woman's description just in case and drove on.

"Did Mustache talk into a speaker?"

"I don't think so," Mandy said. "He punched in a code and opened the door."

"Good," Clark said. A coded door wasn't optimum, but at least they hadn't seen any more security outside—yet.

"Mustache looked like a man who forgot his keys," Mandy said. "And he left the other guy outside by the truck. Makes me wonder if they plan to be here long."

"Sensible observation," Clark said.

He waited for a scooter to pass, then made another U-turn before pulling the Taurus along the beach side of the road.

He looked across the center console at Mandy. "I'd really like to get inside that building."

Clark thought he'd done a good job of hiding the concern in his eyes, but she gave him a tight smile and said, "I'll be fine. Really."

He killed the engine and got out, easing his door shut. The clatter of passing traffic and the wind off the ocean across the street would have covered the sound, but with him, quiet was a force of habit. No need to create unnecessary noise, but he didn't want to appear sneaky, either.

"The trick is to act like we belong," he said.

"Gotcha," Mandy said.

Midas called out on radio. "She's making the block on Third Ave and Seventh Street, heading west on Third again."

"Kind of late to start looking for surveillance," Clark said, half to himself.

"I don't think this is an SDR," Yao said. "I just rode past her. She's not paying much attention to her surroundings. I'd guess she's working up her courage."

"Whatever it is," Midas said, "she's turning south onto Fifth . . . Heading your way, Mr. C."

"Copy," Clark said. "We're out of the vehicle scouting."

A warm wind carried the hint of decaying sea life along with the chatter of morning beachgoers from the cabanas along the bay. Palm fronds rattled on the trees along the jogging path behind them. A newer Jeep Wrangler rumbled past towing a Boston Whaler down the street toward the launch.

"Remember," Clark said. "We belong here."

Mandy gave him a thumbs-up—smiling with intensely capable eyes that reminded him of someone else. "Got it."

"Stand on my left and tell me what you see."

"Security cameras through the trees," she said. "One at each corner of the concrete portico overhanging the front door. Both are PTZ—pan-tilt-zoom—controlled from inside."

"Or remotely," Clark said.

"True enough." She looked down the street as

if enjoying the view, but continued to describe the building in front of them. "Rolling vehicle gate is open."

"Front door?"

"Keypad," Mandy said. "The side door is partially obstructed by that jacaranda tree, but it looks like a regular lock. We could pick that. My grandpa taught me how."

Clark smiled at that. "I don't think we'll—"

Midas piped up, cutting him off. "Red Audi coming your way, boss! Passing Seventh Ave . . . now."

Clark motioned Mandy to the other side of the car and directed her attention away from the building toward the beach. An old man and his daughter enjoying the view of the sea and Tierra Bomba Island less than a mile across the water.

"Target's slowing at the gate," Midas said.

"You guys go on past and make a U-turn," Clark said. Yao was technically running the show, but as the person with the eye, he yielded to Clark to make boots-on-the-ground decisions. "Be ready to come in from the south. The rest of you stand by where you are until we see what's going on."

It didn't take long.

The red Audi stuttered forward, rolling and stopping several times as Blanca apparently tried to make sense of why the men who were supposed to have been following her were here before her.

She got out of the car and spoke briefly to the

man, too far away for Clark to make out what they were saying. At length, Blanca threw up her hands as if she was exasperated and then turned to stalk toward the door. Golf Jacket took one last drag off his cigarette and tossed it to the pavement, pushing himself off the fender with a bothered groan that wasn't audible from a distance, but was plain to see.

He barked something, causing the young woman to spin and shoot him a withering look. He opened the back door of the little pickup and motioned her in.

She ignored him and kept heading for the door of her car.

The Camarilla goon strode forward and put a hand on her shoulder. She jerked away like she'd been slapped.

Mandy shot a glance at Clark. "I can go up and act like we're friends," she said. "You know, 'Hey, girl, how you been?' That'll give her some wiggle room if she's in trouble."

"Don't get in trouble yourself," Clark said.

"That's what you're here for," Mandy said. "Right?"

Clark thought back to his time in West Berlin so many years before—and his friends Richard and Lotte Cobb. He gave an uncharacteristic grin. Mandy reminded him more of her grandparents every day.

"Everyone stand by to move in on Cobb's signal,"

he said into the mic on his lapel. Then, turning slightly, eyes still on Blanca and the goon, whispered, "Go."

Mandy sprang forward and trotted across the street, an attack dog let off the leash.

Clark worked his way around the jacaranda tree, staying out of Golf Jacket's line of sight, while keeping an eye on the portico and front door. If anyone was monitoring the cameras, they would have visitors any moment.

Mandy called out before her boots even hit the sidewalk, switching fluidly to Spanish. "I thought I saw you drive past. My man and I are at the Hyatt. It's been so long, sister!"

Blanca looked from Golf Jacket to Mandy, then back to Golf Jacket. Her mouth hung open in surprise and confusion. The Camarilla goon was caught flat-footed, surely unaccustomed to anyone barging onto the property. Still, Blanca was a nursing student and interacted with friends every day. Nothing sinister going on here . . .

Blanca gave Mandy a hard look. "Who are you again?"

Golf Jacket ratcheted up a notch, hand in his pocket. He eyed Mandy as he barked at Blanca. "Señorita Pakulova, we must go. Now."

Mandy's hands were up, her left poised above the belly of her loose blouse, the other slightly lower, canted out, as if she were trying to explain something—or about to draw her pistol.

"Blanca," she said. "Do you want to go with this man?"

"I do not." Pakulova shook her head. "But that does not explain who you—"

"Listen to me, you five-peso whore!" Golf Jacket pulled a small handgun from his pocket and spun to brandish it at Mandy. "You—"

The pistol clattered to the ground an instant before the Camarilla goon did, his words cut short by a 147-grain subsonic nine-millimeter round that struck him to the left of his nose. Clark loved his 1911, but the suppressed Glock 19 was handy for this sort of work. While not exactly Hollywood-quiet, subsonic rounds, a Bowers Group suppressor wet with lithium grease and a slightly heavier recoil spring to slow the slide's action, made the pistol as close to a mouse fart as possible.

Blanca stood rooted in place, frozen at the sight of her former security man's blood pooling on the concrete. She fumbled with her book bag.

Mandy's left hand grabbed the front of her own shirt, while her right drew the pistol out of the holster at her belly. "Do not move!" Then, more calmly, "We are not here to hurt you."

Blanca's face turned ashen. Her head dropped in resignation. "This is about my sister . . ."

The door to the building flew open and Mustache charged out, gun in hand. Clark, still concealed in the shadows of the jacaranda tree, dumped him with two quick shots from the suppressed G19.

"You're not safe here, Blanca!" Mandy snapped. She grabbed the book bag. "You need to come with us."

"Who are you people?"

Ding and Chilly roared up the driveway in the old Volkswagen taxi, skidding to a stop inches away from the dead Golf Jacket.

Chilly bailed out and posted off the fender, facing the gate, while Ding covered the door.

"Get her in the car!" Ding barked. "Pronto!"

Yao, Midas, and Ward watched the street.

Birds chirped. Traffic continued to rumble past. Runners still jogged beyond the trees across the road, oblivious to the two dead men in the driveway.

Clark emerged from the shadows, holding his Glock low and out of sight alongside his thigh.

"Let's go," he said. "We don't know who's inside watching these cameras."

"There is no one inside," Blanca said. "If you're looking for my sister, you are too late. She apparently left a short time ago. These men you killed. They were here for me."

"Where did she go?" Mandy asked.

Blanca stared at her hard, at once terrified and defiant.

Ding waved his hand in a circle over his head, index finger up. "We need to get out of here!" he said. "Details can come later. Mandy, you and the girl are with me."

Mandy took Blanca by the shoulder and gave her a quick pat-down for weapons. "You're sure there's no one else inside?"

"My sister took everyone with her," she said. "Except the two she sent to feed me to the pigs."

46

It gutted Felix Moncada to show his nerves in front of Agent Pinto. Commissioner Guerra was bad enough, but Moncada didn't take him for the bravest of men. Pinto, though, that one was dangerous, just the kind of man Moncada needed. At least the two men had made it to his office before security locked everything down. The humorless Secret Service agents posted beside the X-ray machine and walk-through metal detector had questioned Guerra's business, but SPI security officers explained he was a commissioner and often met with Señor Moncada, President Botero's trusted adviser. The SPI did not wish to offend a PNP commissioner, and the Americans didn't want to offend the SPI. Since Pinto was with him, the Secret Service let both men pass the checkpoint, one of them muttering how this was "no way to run a railroad."

The men were Moncada's guests, so they were

now his problem, camping out in his office while he decided what to do.

They were a distraction to be sure, but he had two immediate problems left to solve—and they were big ones.

Moncada had come to work that morning prepared to watch Agent Pinto shoot his boss in the head. The change of plans forced on him by Sabine Gorshkova gnawed at him. Acid seared his throat. Phone to his ear, he waited in vain for Ian Doyle to answer, his left leg bouncing like a maniacal sewing machine needle. The Irishman was not the sort of man to have voicemail, so the cursed thing just rang and rang and rang. Moncada ended the call and tossed the mobile on his desk.

What good is it to have an experienced man in charge if that man does not answer his phone?

Agent Pinto looked up from his own phone, studied Moncada for a moment like he was a piece of meat, and then returned to playing his game. Guerra read the latest edition of **La Prensa,** a conservative rag that Moncada despised.

Moncada rubbed a hand across his face, breathing into his palm in an effort to keep himself from hyperventilating—or bursting into tears. Today was supposed to be the day. Now the President of the United States had decided to drop by for a visit with his hordes of armed security. Moncada slammed his hand flat on the desk. Months of planning flushed into the sewer. **Postpone,** Sabine had said. What a horrible cosmic joke. It was nothing short of a miracle that he'd been able to achieve the delicate balance of power and finesse that had set the coup in motion this time. The odds of doing it all again . . . Impossible.

Moncada leaned back in his creaky leather chair and stared up at the ceiling, as disappointed as he was frantic. Camarilla operatives were in control of the truck bombs, but he'd kept the detonators for the bombs around the presidential palace himself—to insure he was not inadvertently blown to bits. They were small compared to the vehicle-borne devices, but still capable of turning anyone within twenty yards into a red mist when they went off. The Camarilla men embedded with security staff inside the palace had been quietly told to stand down. Botero was to stay alive, for now.

The Russians were on their way, so that problem was solved. That left the Chinese container ship **Jian Long** an insurmountable problem if he couldn't get in touch with Ian Doyle.

Moncada looked at his Rolex. The **Jian Long** was scheduled to pass through the second set of gates at the Cocoli Locks in less than half an hour, at which point the explosive inside would break it in half at the spine if Moncada was unable to somehow reach Ian Doyle.

A sharp rapping at his office door nearly sent Moncada out of his skin. Guerra and Pinto glanced up from their chairs, surprisingly calm. Moncada's secretary, Sophia, opened the door, literally bouncing with news.

"You will not believe it, Señor Moncada!" she said. "I do not have anything about it in my calendar, but TVN is reporting that Air Force One has just landed at Tocumen airport. The President of the United States has come to visit Panama!"

47

The E-4B running racetracks over the Pacific served as the National Airborne Operations Center, sometimes referred to as KNEECAP— the phonetic pronunciation of the bird's previous Air Force acronym, NEACP, National Emergency Airborne Command Post. A militarized version of a Boeing 747-200, the E-4B would eventually accompany Ryan to Mar del Plata, Argentina, for the Summit of the Americas. For now, it remained airborne, while the much better-known blue and white V-25 military version of the Boeing 747 masquerading for the moment as Air Force One made a direct approach into Tucumen International Airport fourteen miles northeast of the presidential palace.

Grant McCabe, U.S. ambassador to Panama, aware of the charade, was present on the tarmac, along with a hastily assembled delegation of mid-level Panamanian officials and a handful of reporters who'd been listening to aircraft scanners. A ten-piece ensemble from the Presidential Guard Battalion band would play "Hail to the Chief." A small group of demonstrators had seemingly materialized out of the ether beyond the fence, all sporting hastily scrawled cardboard signs demanding the **yanqui President** go home.

A scant five air miles west of the presidential palace, Jack Ryan peered out the large oval window of a nondescript white Gulfstream III banked in a final approach from the north to touch down on Runway 19 at Albrook Gelabert International Airport. Large gantry cranes at the bustling Port of Balboa worked like giant blue ants to the south. Farther to the west the expanded Cocoli Locks admitted huge Panamax ships—vessels too large for the previous locks. The water level rose over eighty-five feet to lift ships going north across the Continental Divide to the Caribbean or lowering them to sea level as they exited the canal into the Pacific.

Most important to the passengers on the white Gulfstream jet was the building to the east, just across the Northern Expressway from the Albrook airport, the headquarters of the Policía Nacional de Panamá. Twenty-thousand strong, the PNP was the closest thing Panama had to an army.

Airport administrators were told they had a VIP coming in, but with the blue and white heavy landing at Tocumen, no one suspected it was the President of the United States.

Could it be a famous soccer player? Maybe one

of the Kardashians? A Russian oligarch? No. Any of those would have been on a far nicer airplane.

A Chevy Tahoe containing two United States Secret Service agents and a senior officer with the Presidential Protection Group had stopped at PNP headquarters an hour prior to the Gulfstream's arrival and folded them into the ruse. There would be no band, but in a matter of minutes, an honor guard of twelve armed National Police officers had convened at the apron of the tarmac.

The Gulfstream landed long, rolling quickly to the end of the runway and turning off on a small apron at the south end of the airport.

Six United States Secret Service vehicles paraded onto the tarmac like a mismatched train set to meet the plane—two Chevy Tahoes, two Jeep Cherokees, a Dodge Charger, and a twelve-passenger van utilized by HAWKEYE—the United States Secret Service's Counter Assault Team that had traveled down the day before. By design, none of the airport personnel had been briefed on the arrival, so two marked Ford F-150 pickups, both belonging to the PNP, ran escort onto the tarmac.

Inside the Gulfstream, the Air Force flight attendant opened the door and folded out the stairs. A Secret Service agent leaned out to visually check that the way was clear before stepping back into the galley and nodding to Gary Montgomery.

Montgomery had been in constant contact with his agents on the ground for the past hour, both here at Albrook and at the presidential palace four miles away.

"We are clear, Mr. President," he said. "I'd ask that you allow me to break protocol and deplane ahead of you. The pilots have turned the airplane to put the fuselage between you and the cameras, but Advance reports half a dozen protesters on the other side of the fence."

"Maybe they don't even know it's me on the airplane," Ryan said.

"Sir . . ." Montgomery took a deep breath and let it out slowly. "There is always a leak."

"You may have mentioned that." Ryan smiled. He nodded out the window toward the neat line of waiting vehicles. "All the different colors are a nice touch."

"We wanted to stay away from the obvious black SUV."

"Wise."

A dark blue BMW sedan rolled onto the tarmac behind the makeshift motorcade. A lanky man in a polo shirt and chinos got out of the front passenger seat, gave the surrounding area a quick scan, and then opened the back door.

"Vice President Carré," Ryan said to himself. "You know, I've met the man on three different occasions, and I don't believe I have ever seen him without that smile on his face."

"I'll make up for it with my mean mug, Mr. President," Montgomery said.

Ryan gave him a grin of approval. "And I'm grateful for it."

The PPD agents who'd been sitting aft moved up the aisle. Three stepped closer to Ryan. The agent who would remain with Mary Pat Foley, a blond, Ken-doll-looking fellow named Brett Johnson, allowed her to go ahead so that he brought up the rear. She stooped to look out just as Montgomery prepared to step off the plane.

Foley turned to Agent Johnson. She preferred to call her agents by their given names.

"I hope we're riding in the Charger, Brett."

"Oh, no, you don't." Ryan chuckled, looking over his shoulder from the boarding door. "I call presidential dibs."

Johnson grinned. "I'm sorry, sir, you're in the gray Tahoe."

"All right," Ryan said and scuffed his toe on the carpet, feigning disappointment.

Foley nudged him in the arm. "You feel that, Jack?" She kept her voice low, conspiratorial, though with everyone bunched up at the top of the stairs, the PPD agents were surely close enough to hear.

"Feel what?"

"That electric vibe." Foley breathed in deeply, as if savoring some delicious aroma. "The live-wire buzz of the unknown. Drugs, guns, dirty money—and a substantial subset of the population that hates our guts. Reminds me of the old days."

Montgomery shot Ryan a dyspeptic look.

"Knock it off, Mary Pat," Ryan said with another chuckle. "You're going to give Gary a heart attack." He didn't admit it, but Ryan knew exactly what Foley was talking about. He could feel it, too, as palpable as the heat and humidity seeping in from the tarmac. He tapped his watch. "We'll meet you at the big plane in three hours. Be safe."

"**You** be safe, Mr. President," Foley said. "No one in this country even knows who I am."

Vice President Carré stood at the base of the boarding stairs, hands clasped at his waist, the ever-present grin on his round face. It was infectious, and Ryan found himself smiling as well.

Gary Montgomery and his detail of PPD agents were apparently immune.

"Welcome to Panama, Mr. President," the vice president said, extending his hand. "Lionel Carré, at your service. His Excellency President Rafael Botero regrets he could not be here to greet you."

Ryan shook the offered hand. "I understand completely," he said. "Better this way. Flying under the radar and all."

"Our thoughts exactly," Carré said.

"I know my Secret Service detail is surprised to have you here," Ryan said. "For the same reasons."

"Not to worry," Carré said. "No one much cares if the vice president comes or goes around here. As you can see, I have only a small security detail. We were able to slip away from the palace without garnering a goodbye, much less a second look."

Montgomery gave a solemn nod at that and took a half step forward, sheepdogging Ryan toward the waiting motorcade.

A tall, square-jawed man in dark aviator sunglasses and the dress uniform of a Panamanian National Police lieutenant stood stoically with the cadre of a half-dozen similarly dressed officers to Carré's left. Missing an arm, the lieutenant's left sleeve was folded up neatly and pinned to the shoulder of his tunic. Already at attention, he braced with an almost audible snap when Ryan stopped and extended his hand.

"Lieutenant Ernesto Vega," the man said. Cable-like muscles tensed along his jaw. "Policía Nacional de Panamá. Welcome to my country, Mr. President."

Montgomery's eyes moved continually, scanning the crowd and beyond as he continued to urge Ryan toward the waiting motorcade like a mother hen. Ryan hated being prodded, but he'd made a deal to listen to Montgomery, so he thanked the lieutenant and moved toward the Chevy Tahoe, inviting the vice president to ride with him. Carré's driver and two SPI security officers would follow in the BMW.

Special Agent Brett Johnson and three agents who'd been on the ground, along with a male-female team whom Ryan suspected were CIA contractors, led Mary Pat Foley to the Dodge Charger. One of the Jeep Cherokees served as the follow car, surely full of heavy weapons and communications gear. Per protocol, Foley's vehicles waited for Ryan's ragtag motorcade to pull away.

POTUS had been on the ground for less than ten minutes and only a handful of people in Panama knew he was there. At least that was the plan.

Gary Montgomery sat in the front passenger seat, speaking in hushed tones to his advance team stationed along the four-mile route to the Palacio de las Garzas. The agent behind the wheel swung the Tahoe wide to clear the aircraft, taking the motorcade past the PNP honor guard.

Lieutenant Ernesto Vega remained at attention. Ryan, a student of human nature, had noted a fleeting look of disdain in the man's eyes during their initial interaction. Now, as the motorcade drove by, Ryan caught the look again, something between a sneer and a frown, like the man wanted to spit.

"Do you know Lieutenant Vega?" Ryan asked the vice president as the motorcade sped through the gates and turned east toward the presidential palace.

"I do not know him well," Carré said. "Most of our interaction is with SPI. You would call it the Institutional Protection Service. We deal more specifically with the Presidential Protection Group within SPI. Lieutenant Vega is PNP—Policía Nacional de Panamá. The poor man apparently lost his arm during a narcotics raid. Some of your Drug Enforcement agents were part of the investigation. It was a significant arrest. A job well done by all involved. Vega received a commendation. His injuries make many of the normal law enforcement duties difficult for him, so he is given other tasks. He is often at the palace. The president's economic adviser has taken it up as a special cause."

Carré's smile flickered, almost fading before coming back even brighter than before, though this time more than a little forced.

Ryan turned and looked out the window, watching Panama City old and new all crammed together go by. Mary Pat had called it, as she always did. He could feel it, too, that live-wire vibe. But was it merely the unknown, or the hum of something more dangerous?

48

LEESBURG, VIRGINIA

Retired CIA director Ed Foley stood at the kitchen counter fussing over a cup of Earl Grey tea and musing about what his wife was up to, when his phone rang. A hell of a boring life for a man accustomed to living in the shadows and operating under Moscow Rules.

Both operations officers for the CIA—much of their careers in denied areas—Ed and Mary Pat Foley had spent the better part of their forty-plus years of marriage wondering what the other one was up to. Both their stars had risen quickly in the Agency, him being promoted to chief of station in Moscow relatively early in his career, her running a number of noteworthy—and dangerous—ops in Eastern Europe during the Cold War. She spoke Russian like a native. The CIA sure as hell leveraged that to the hilt. Sometimes, when she was angry or sullen, usually about something idiotic Ed had done, she could have been mistaken for a Russian—slow to smile and even slower to laugh. But when she did laugh, Mary Pat Kaminsky was the most beautiful creature he'd ever seen.

The life they'd led certainly took a toll on a young couple, frequent moves halfway around the world from parents and grandparents, new schools for the kids, the constant brooding danger. The worst for Ed was the secrecy. Their boys thought he and Mary Pat were cultural attachés until they were in high school. Often, in those early salad days, operational security meant they couldn't even divulge certain specifics of their assignments to each other. Later, the big brains at Langley realized they could wield the Foleys as one weapon, a power couple. It did something to a marriage when you knew that an audio recording of the moment one of your kids was conceived was on tape in some KGB vault.

Now he was retired—and Mary Pat had reached the pinnacle of her career. She was good at her job. The best Ed had ever seen. And still he worried every time she stepped out the door, even with her steely-eyed Secret Service detail.

If she'd been home, where he could see her and know that she was safe, Ed Foley would have just let the damn phone ring.

Leaning over the counter, he adjusted his glasses so he could read the caller ID before he answered. It was a 305 number he didn't recognize, a Florida area code. Probably spam . . . But his tea needed to steep a little longer anyway.

"Hello."

Foley waited a beat, thumb hovering over the end button. He'd resolved long before to hang up on any call if he didn't hear a human voice in the first three seconds.

"Am I speaking to the notorious B.S. Foley?"

Foley hadn't heard that nickname in forever. And even then, from only a handful of people who were with him when he slipped and fell in a snot-slick mound of bat guano during a rainy operation in Mexico. Foley recognized the voice at once as Randell Green, a career intelligence officer he'd worked with many times over the years.

"Randell," Foley said. The sound of his name churned up a torrent of memories. "Great to hear from you. You sort of dropped off the map, bud."

"Yeah, well," Green said. "Old habits . . ."

"How's Paula?"

"No idea," Green said, without offering further explanation. A hell of a lot went unsaid with most retired operations officers, especially if they were clandestine up to the bitter end, but Randell took taciturn to an entirely different level. It was your job as the other half of the conversation to put the pieces together—a maddening trait in a husband to be sure, but a good quality to have in a spy. Foley couldn't help but smile at his old friend's eccentricities.

Green was easily the most observant person Foley had ever met. His true photographic memory was a blessing or a curse, depending on your point of view. It made him a prime candidate to run reconnaissance missions. Absolutely nothing got by him. The problem was that once an image got into his brain, it camped out there for good. Reviewing the vast catalog of information stored in his head left Green little time for exchanging pleasantries. He was always friendly, kindhearted even, but not a conversationalist.

One thing was certain, Randell Green didn't just ring you up to chat about the time of day. If he took the time to actually pick up the phone and call, he had something very important on his mind.

"Looks like you're in Florida," Foley said. "Judging from your cell number. I'm sure that's nicer than it is here this time of year."

"Florida phone," Green said. "My wife and I moved to Panama four years ago."

Foley started to say something else about Paula, but then realized what his old friend had just said.

"Hold on. You're in Panama? Right now?" A cold dread washed over him.

"I am," Green said. "We're in Punta Pacifica, where a bunch of the expats live. Comparatively inexpensive living, good people. Just don't tell anybody. We don't want it to turn into another damned Costa Rica. Anyway, this is probably nothing. I've been out of the business so long my mind is playing tricks on me."

"Okay . . . ?" Foley pushed aside the cup of Earl Grey and listened while he poured a glass of water from the Brita pitcher in the fridge. "What do you mean 'playing tricks'?"

"I'm seeing lots of new faces around here," Green said. "People who don't belong."

"Don't belong how?"

"Well," Green said. "You're gonna think I've lost my mind, but merc types, shooters, young mafia dons. You know, the whole rogues' gallery, like when we were in Moscow and a new gang of Bratva moved into an area. You know the look. Men who have carried a pistol their entire life, been shot at— shot even—and come out the other side. The kind with a shitload of swagger, much of it earned the hard way. There was a guy at the market a couple of days ago that had arms dealer written all over him."

"I get what you mean," Foley said.

These were the kind of wild imaginings that most anyone would blow off if they didn't know Green or hadn't actually observed firsthand how gifted he was. "I'm telling you, Ed, something's going on down here. I just can't put my finger on exactly what it is just yet."

"What does your gut say?" Foley asked.

"I'm not sure," Green said. "Maybe muscle for a new crime family moving in. Drugs, guns, money, human cargo, you name it, it comes through Panama."

Foley looked at his watch. The trip wasn't a secret by now.

"Mary Pat's in Panama," he said.

The line fell silent for a time, then Green said, "I'm sure it's nothing."

"No," Foley said. "I'll give her a call and bring her up to speed on your observations. She'll be grateful to get the insight, I'm sure. It may be a piece to a larger puzzle retired peons like you and me don't get to be privy to anymore."

"Could be," Green said. "You know the 'little green men' Russia sends into countries they want to infiltrate in Eastern Europe?"

"Of course," Foley said.

"Well," Green mused. "This is like that, but Latin American . . . and maybe even a few Russians. I shit you not, Eddie. Something is about to go down. I can't say what or where, but . . . I know I sound crazy . . ." He paused, breathing heavily. Thinking. "Look, I'm sorry to spin you up with Mary Pat down here. Forget I called. I'm just an old man struggling to stay relevant."

"That's rich," Foley said. "You're still relevant enough that I'm about to call the director of national intelligence as soon as I hang up."

"Thank you, Ed," Green said. "Like I said, it's probably nothing, but maybe it'll give her some added intel. Oh, and by the way, I'm catching holy hell from Paula for making you think we're divorced. She's sitting on the couch beside me."

Foley chuckled. "Good to hear. Now I better call Mary Pat with your intel."

"Such as it is," Green said.

"Come see us in Leesburg," Foley said, already thinking about how he was going to word this to Mary Pat.

49

Mary Pat Foley's secure mobile buzzed in the pocket of her slacks while she was still on the airport tarmac chatting with the female CIA contractor who would be in her follow car. Foley took her job seriously as DNI and enjoyed hearing from boots on the ground at all the agencies she oversaw. Agent Johnson was getting antsy to go, but with POTUS on his way, the threat level at the airport had dropped to near nil.

Foley let the phone go to voicemail. Seconds later, it started buzzing again. She excused herself and stepped away from the conversation, shielding her eyes from the sun with one hand while she checked the caller ID. It was Ed. That was strange. Neither made a habit of calling the one who was in the field during an assignment. No matter how much they worried, the house spouse waited for the other to check in. Still, it wasn't like she was behind the Iron Curtain.

As an operations officer, she ran what-if scenarios

and planned contingencies for the worst, often seeing things unfold to the horrible end she'd envisioned. It wreaked havoc on a positive outlook and made any out-of-the-blue call flood her with adrenaline.

Had something happened to the kids? The house? Ed's heart? He wasn't a spring chicken . . .

She steeled herself for bad news as she answered.

A consummate ops boss and seemingly clairvoyant husband, Ed calmed her with the first words out of his mouth, opening the conversation with "Everything is fine."

She ran a hand through her hair and exhaled sharply in relief. "You are incredible, Ed Foley," she said. "To what do I owe this pleasure?"

"Sorry to bug you at work," he said. "Are you with POTUS?"

"I am not," she said. "But I can get in touch with him. Why?"

"Weird deal," Ed said. "I thought you should be aware."

He described the call from Randell Green.

"Randell's always been a squared-away guy," she said after Ed finished his brief. "I'll tell my detail agents and they'll let Gary Montgomery know . . . Better yet. I'll call Gary and tell him to expect your call. He should get the same brief that I do. Too great a chance something would get lost in translation."

Brett Johnson stood a little straighter at Mary Pat's mention of her "detail." She was still on the phone, and he was more concerned about incoming threats, so he didn't make eye contact.

"That's why you make the big bucks, sweetheart," Ed said. "Probably nothing that will affect you, but Randell thought it important enough to call me, so I didn't want to sit on it."

"I'm glad you called," Mary Pat said. "We'll be at the embassy shortly. I'll pass the information on to Claire as well. She may want to talk to Randell."

Claire Nguyen had been a baby clandestine operations officer when Ed taught at the Farm. Now she was station chief in Panama.

"Tell her I said hello," Ed said. "And watch that beautiful ass of yours."

"It's in good hands." She winked at Brett, who gave a somber nod, fortunately hearing only her half of the conversation. "And anyway, if anything happened to me, I'd just sit tight until you flew down and saved me."

Ed did his best Liam Neeson impersonation, which wasn't very good, and reminded her that his particular set of skills was getting a little rusty.

50

At the same moment Mary Pat Foley was speaking to her husband, Major Gabriella Canto of the Policía Nacional de Panamá lay facedown on the clinic exam table, one leg of her camouflage uniform pants rolled up to her knee, when her phone chimed. She ignored the call at first, gripping the paper table cover with both fists, gritting her teeth as the doctor examined the knife wound in her calf. The hospital had wanted to admit her the night before and explore the possibility of skin grafts. She told the doctor to make do with stitches, assuring him she did not care if she had a scar "the size of a mango."

The ER doctor had discharged her, but made her promise to visit her family practitioner the following day. He also made her promise to stop riding her motorcycle. She ignored the latter and thought of ignoring the former as well, but her wound had become angry and red, probably infected, considering the filthy fish knife had sliced nearly to the bone.

She apologized to the doctor and rolled on her side to dig the phone out of her pocket, grateful for the reprieve from all the poking and prodding at the inflamed stitches. The doctor smiled and busied himself preparing a hypodermic needle of antibiotic. He'd known Gabriella since she was a child, so the Glock 19 on her duty belt did not bother or impress him—which was good because, after the previous night, she was not likely to leave home without it. Commissioner Guerra had ordered her to stay home and rest, but he seemed far more interested in having her out of his way than he was concerned about her well-being. She'd decided to put on her uniform and go to work for half a day.

She looked at the number before answering. It was her driver, Fredi Perez.

"Where are you, **patrona**?" He sounded breathless, as if he'd been running.

"The clinic near my mother's."

"In El Chorrillo?"

"Yes . . . Why?"

"Have you not heard? The President of the United States has just arrived in Panama."

Canto sat up abruptly and swung her legs off the table, drawing a concerned scowl from her doctor.

"And we were not notified?"

"I just heard from my friend at headquarters," Perez said. "He flew into Albrook on a small plane . . . under cover. His trip was apparently kept secret until the very last minute. Which means—"

Canto finished his sentence. "Which means he will have much less security. Where is he now?"

"Vice President Carré greeted him at the airport," Perez said. "I assume they are going to the Palacio de las Garzas."

She stood, wincing the moment she put weight on her leg. The doctor shook his head and held up the needle, pointing to her hip just below her belt.

She put the phone on speaker and unfastened her duty belt, leaning over the exam table and supporting the weight of her Glock with one hand while she lowered her pants with the other, just enough to get the shot.

"Where are you?" she asked through clenched teeth, more from the tedium of it all than the pain of the needle or the embarrassment of the doctor seeing her ass cheek. She had things to do.

"San Miguelito Station," Perez said.

"And Guerra?"

Perez gave a grim sigh. "Palacio de las Garzas," he said. "Pinto is with him."

Canto stood and fastened her belt.

"Of course he would be there at this moment . . . I'm minutes away."

"Should we call ahead? Warn someone?"

"Warn them of what?" Canto said. "That the commissioner has come to see the U.S. President? No. Not yet. This may boil down to nothing but the fact that we do not respect our boss."

"But you are going?"

"I am absolutely going," Canto said. "Meet me there as soon as you can. If I see anything of substance, you can be sure I will sound the alarm loud and long."

She ended the call and dropped the phone in her pocket, using both hands to adjust her gun belt so it rode more comfortably on her hips. The doctor tossed the used hypodermic into the "sharps" can and clucked softly, warning that she was about to find herself in a situation that would put her **entre la espada y la pared.**

Literally "between the sword and the wall."

She smiled softly and turned away, speaking over her shoulder as she limped quickly toward the door and her waiting motorcycle.

"I'll be careful with the leg," she said, knowing full well that the wound was not the situation the doctor was worried about.

51

Clark and Yao led their WINDWARD STATION operators on a lengthy surveillance-detection route through the streets of Cartagena. They backtracked and leapfrogged to allow different elements of the team to watch one another for tails. The intelligence they hoped to glean from Blanca Pakulova/Gorshkova was too valuable to risk taking her anywhere official.

Once he was reasonably sure they were in the clear, Yao led them to a second-floor apartment near the airport. The place was quiet and off the main roads, the perfect spot for a CIA safe house. It had to be considered compromised now that Blanca knew its location.

Helen Reid, chief pilot for The Campus, had called with troubling news, raising the stakes even higher than they already were. Someone, almost certainly on orders from Sabine Gorshkova, had shot the front landing gear strut on the G550 with a high-powered rifle. It could be fixed, but would take time.

With Blanca in tow, Clark chalked that up as something to chew on in the back of his mind while he worked on the problem at hand.

Chilly and Midas remained at street level in their vehicles, watching for any rescue attempts, while Clark, Yao, Cobb, and Ward ushered Blanca upstairs. It was all hands on deck by now and the remainder of the CIA blue badgers, along with Dom, Adara, and Jack Junior, circled the area, running countersurveillance.

Inside, Yao and Clark took positions at a rustic wooden table across from Blanca. Ward and Chavez flanked the door behind her, while Mandy sat in the corner, out of sight, robbing her of any calming influence that might come from having another female present in the room. Clark found a dusty glass in the cupboard, filled it from the tap, and passed it to the terrified young woman.

Blanca took a sip of water, her eyes darting from Yao to Clark. She turned to glance behind her, but Yao rapped on the table with his knuckles, focusing her attention on him.

"Look at me!" He spoke in clipped Spanish.

The harshness in his voice appeared to galvanize rather than intimidate her. Clark could see that this young woman had been around enough violence that the implied threat of pain meant nothing.

Her eyes narrowed into dark slits. "Are you the people who killed my brother?"

Yao ignored the question. "Do you know what business your brother was in?"

Blanca scoffed. "My brother was in the business of doing what our sister told him to do."

This was new, but Clark kept his face passive. "And where is your sister?"

"I told you, she left."

"When?"

"I . . . I am not sure," Blanca said. "You killed the men who had that answer." Hands in her lap, she leaned forward, pleading. "I ask you again. Are you the men who killed my brother?"

"That must piss you off," Yao said. "For your sister to abandon you like this."

Blanca stared hard at him for a moment, then laughed. "Abandon me? You are a hilarious man. I do not feel abandoned. I am relieved."

Yao folded his arms, smirking. Not buying it. "You feel relieved?"

Blanca nodded. She stared at her hands, her chin quivering like she might break down at any moment.

"Let's start over," Clark said. "Who were the men at the apartment?"

Her head snapped up. "The men you killed?"

"The men who were trying to force you to go with them," Clark said.

She shrugged. "Roberto and Gregor," she whispered. "I do not know much about Roberto, but I know that Gregor is . . . was from Vladivostok. I think most of the men who work for my sister are former military. Gregor was SOCH. The others did not like him very much. My sister took him in, gave him the lowly job of looking after me."

SOCH was the Russian acronym for willfully abandoning one's military unit. AWOL.

"What I do know is that Roberto and Gregor were weak. Foolish. My sister would never have let you take her like that."

"I see," Yao said. He sat in silence for a time. **Good,** Clark thought. That allowed Blanca to ponder the gravity of her situation.

A full minute of quiet was an eternity in a room full of strangers. Yao waited for all of that and more before scooting his chair forward with a startling squeak against the tile floor. Time to get down to business.

"What is your role in your brother and sister's affairs?"

"Role? What is my **role**?" Blanca's eyes clenched tight, pressing tears. "Sabine would not tell me how my brother died. Do you know?"

Yao knocked on the table to get her attention. "Where is your sister?"

Blanca looked from Yao to Clark and back to Yao. Her entire body began to shake, then something very close to a growl escaped her lips, growing into a shriek. "Did you kill my brother? Tell me!" She slumped in the chair. A string of saliva hung from her bottom lip. Chest heaving, she sniffed. "I need to go to the bathroom."

Yao glanced at Clark, who nodded and glanced at Cobb, tasking her without calling her by name in front of the girl.

"You can't escape," Yao said.

Blanca looked at him blankly and sighed, seemingly exhausted from her outburst. "Escape?" She shook her head. "You people do not understand at all . . ."

52

Moncada had sweated completely through his suit coat by the time Lieutenant Vega answered his phone. In point of fact, the PNP lieutenant had completely ignored Moncada's calls. It had taken a call from Guerra to get him on the line. The commissioner chuckled when he passed his phone across the desk, apparently thinking Moncada's pending heart attack was amusing.

"Has he left the airport?" Moncada asked, perhaps a little too aggressively for Vega.

Silence on the line.

He tried again, more conciliatory. "Is the motorcade on its way, Lieutenant?"

"He departed some time ago."

"How . . ." A calming breath. "How long ago?"

"Minutes," Vega said. "His Secret Service driver is very good. But I am keeping up with him."

Moncada brightened. "So you are with him?"

"Behind him, yes."

"Excellent! We have a big problem." Moncada

started to relate that he had not yet heard if the Irishman Doyle had been able to abort the bomb on the **Jian Long.** It was set to go off at about the time the U.S. President was now going to arrive, which would be in direct contravention to Sabine Gorshkova's orders. Moncada could not believe he was taking orders from this madwoman, but he was too terrified not to. He kept his out-of-control neuroses to himself and said, "I need you to buy us time."

"And how do you propose I do that?"

"Cause an accident," he said. "Radio something suspicious." Yes, he thought that sounded good. He snapped his fingers to get Guerra's attention and repeated himself. Guerra could do that from here.

The PNP looked up from his newspaper and yawned.

Vega shot back, "I am hanging up now."

"Wait," Moncada said. "Where are you—"

His own mobile buzzed across his desk blotter, causing him to yelp in surprise. He'd forgotten that he was speaking on Guerra's.

He ended the call with Vega and picked up his phone.

It was a one-word text from Ian Doyle.

DONE

53

Gabriella Canto made it as far as the checkpoint at Avenue B and San Pablo, behind SPI headquarters and directly adjacent to the presidential palace. Unlike the next street over, this entrance had no fixed gate. What it did have was a bevy of cameras and three dour men armed with long guns, two of them United States Secret Service agents, judging from the enamel five-pointed-star pins on their lapels. She pulled her bike up beside the movable metal barricade and lowered the side stand, prompting the uniformed SPI officer and one of the gringos to step toward her with arms outstretched, palms open, to stop her from coming any closer. The other gringo stood ready with his H&K submachine gun, looking ready, willing, and able to cut her to ribbons if the need arose. Her light jacket had hiked up during the ride and his eye immediately homed in on the pistol at her duty belt.

Straddling the motorcycle, she took off her helmet and planted both feet on the brick street.

"Major Gabriella Canto, Policía Nacional de Panamá," she said. Then to the Secret Service agents, "National Police."

"Credentials," the agent in front said, eyeing her uniform. His partner stayed silent, finger tapping the trigger guard of his MP5.

She passed her ID card to the SPI officer, who studied it for a moment, then handed it back, assuring the Secret Service agents that she was who she said she was.

"Sorry, Major Canto," the lead agent said. "But you could be the chief of the PNP and we couldn't let you in this way. I'm sure you understand."

"My boss is inside," she said. "I need to speak with him. Perhaps someone could get him a message."

The SPI officer gave her a quizzical look, nodding toward the ground. "You're bleeding through your uniform . . . Hey, you're the one who got attacked yesterday."

"I am." Canto gave a sheepish grin, keeping her face calm despite her churning gut.

"Eres una tía dura," he said under his breath. He shot a glance at the Secret Service agent beside him. "Excuse me, but the major is badass."

The agents both suddenly perked up, obviously getting some new information over their earpieces.

"Imminent arrival," the one nearest Canto said for

the benefit of the SPI officer. Then, "Sorry, Major. I'll check on your issue in a moment."

Canto smiled. "I'll call him later," she said. "Sorry to bother you guys. Keep up the good work."

She replaced her helmet and pressed the ignition button on the bike, coaxing it to life with the throttle.

The SPI officer nodded at her leg again. "You should see a doctor."

"I will," she said, flipping down the visor of her helmet and heading west on Avenue B, resisting the urge to speed away too quickly.

The guns, the bombs, the maps to the Palacio de las Garzas, Guerra's quick trigger when the man had mentioned LA PULGA, were all curious indeed—not to mention the attack on her life. Now the President of the United States was here. Ironically, Guerra himself had often warned her in that condescending way of his never to discount the blindingly obvious during an investigation.

But the President's arrival was imminent. How would she explain all of that to agents of the Secret Service before it was too late?

She rolled on the throttle, ignoring the stabbing pain in her leg as she juked in and out of snarled traffic, narrowly avoiding a dark gray Chevy Suburban and waving at two SPI motor officers as she cut north in the narrow gap between cars and buildings on Eighth Street, intent on making it around the block before President Jack Ryan got out of his limo.

Sabine Gorshkova's driver, a snake-hipped former Argentine naval officer named Francisco, slowed the dark gray Suburban to a crawl at the corner of Eighth Street and Avenue B, mere blocks from the Palacio de las Garzas. De Bruk sat beside Sabine on the left, behind Francisco. Uncle Hector lurked alone in the back row. A Toyota Land Cruiser filled to capacity with steady, well-armed men followed the Suburban, rarely on the bumper, but always keeping the boss in sight. Large vehicles were not the norm on the narrow streets and alleys of Panama City's Casco Viejo, but today, dozens of dark SUVs swarmed the area, making the dark gray Suburban fit right in.

Unable to move forward, Francisco rolled down his window and leaned his head out, shouting a pleasant greeting to the uniformed SPI officers, who stood beside their Yamaha motorcycle in the shade of a thick ficus tree. The two officers stood together, a male and a female. Neither looked to be yet thirty. It was a common pairing for motorcycle police across Latin America, the larger officer driving the bike, while the smaller officer, in this case a female, rode pillion. Sabine had trudged the jungles with Colombian FARC and Peruvian Shining Path guerrillas and couldn't help but think the two officers looked like children wearing costumes in their neatly pressed camouflage and polished boots.

As far as Sabine could see, neither was armed with anything more than the Glock pistols on their belts—which they would find woefully lacking if her men decided to play.

Right hand on the steering wheel, Francisco patted the door with his left, keeping both hands visible and putting the officers at ease as they approached. Sabine had chosen the slender Argentine for a driver because he had an easy smile and a soft demeanor that put people, especially police officers, at ease. He was a killer, the kind face notwithstanding. His propensity to violence was simply hidden beneath a boyish grin—like he was just bursting to tell you about the perfect present he'd picked out especially for you. His behavior bordered on flirtatious and sometimes took even Sabine off guard.

Francisco leaned his head farther out the window and flicked his hand disarmingly as he chatted with the officers, both blissfully unaware of the FN Five-seveN hidden under his right thigh, loaded with twenty-one rounds of 5.7x28-millimeter ammo that would cut through their ballistic vests like they were not even there.

Sabine couldn't hear exactly what they were saying from her spot in the backseat beside De Bruk, but she got the gist of it.

"Let me guess," she said when the SPI kids had walked and Francisco rolled up the window. "The American Secret Service says we shall not pass."

"Correct, **patrona,**" Francisco said. "They say it

isn't up to them." He tapped the steering wheel with his thumbs, listening to some silent song inside his head. Of all the men in her employ, Francisco was the only one who put her on edge. He did not try to look handsome or tough or violent. He just was. Sabine liked that. She would probably choose him when she tired of De Bruk.

She pushed the thoughts out of her mind—for now. "Who do we have inside?" she asked, waiting to see who would answer first.

Hector began to rattle off names. "Vega, Gordo, Genovese, DePalma . . ."

De Bruk took out his phone, ready to make a call at her order.

"Gordo," Sabine said. "Tell him I need a situation report."

She'd just thumb-typed the number to Moncada's newest burner, when her phone buzzed with an incoming call.

It was Guerra.

The PNP commissioner worked for Moncada and was technically not in the Camarilla chain of command. Still, he was smart enough to see who was really in charge—no matter who was paying the bills.

"Speak to me, Javier," Sabine said.

"Ryan is no more than two minutes out."

Her response erupted on the heels of a rumbling growl. "And you waited to call me why?"

"I did not wait," Guerra said. "The airport is four

miles away. I called as soon as I had the report from my man."

She snorted, unconvinced. "Are you with Moncada?"

"Pinto and I are with him in his office."

"Give him the phone!"

Moncada came on a half second later, tentative, a cowering puppy waiting to be scolded.

"Felix Moncada," she said in a brassy, accusatory timbre that was known to make people shit themselves. She didn't bother with any unnecessary pleasantries, but let her voice grow in a steady crescendo with each sharply enunciated word. "I am sitting on my ass two blocks away from you. Are you or are you not an economic adviser to the president? I was under the impression you held some sort of sway around here."

"I . . . The Americans . . . They are everywhere. They do not even want us using our mobile phones. I am told Ryan is minutes away."

"So I hear," she snapped. "And what of Mary Pat Foley?"

"Who?" Moncada said.

"Their director of national intelligence," Sabine chided. "What is wrong with you? Did you not have anyone at the airport?"

"Wait . . . Guerra did mention a woman who arrived on the Gulfstream with Ryan. Attractive, nicely dressed. Salt-and-pepper hair—"

"I am not interested in how well she is dressed."

"Of course," Moncada said. "She apparently split off in a Dodge Charger with a small security team of her own."

"Split off?" Sabine snapped her fingers to get her driver's attention. "Mary Pat Foley and her security team have split from the motorcade . . . and gone where?"

"I do not know," Moncada said. "Guerra's man was focused on Ryan, but did say the silver-haired woman went in another direction with her own security—"

Beside Sabine, De Bruk ended his call and held his mobile between them as if it were heavy with news.

"Just a minute," she snapped at Moncada, raising her hand to shush him, even though he could not see the gestures on the other end of the call. It was not a plea, but an unequivocal order. She curled her fingers at De Bruk, beckoning him to be out with the information. "What is it?"

"I just spoke with Gordo, **patrona**," he said. "Ryan's motorcade is turning onto Eloy Alfaro Avenue as we speak."

Sabine's jaw clenched until she thought her teeth might shatter. Her plan had been to watch and learn how the Americans handled Foley's security, follow her to Argentina, and then make a move when she was outside the President's protective bubble. Sabine didn't have an exact notion of how she planned to do it, but trusted something delicious would come to her when she put eyes on the bitch.

Her heart began to drum in anticipation. She could feel the hammer in her fist. She would face the woman who murdered her brother today.

She pounded her leg in thought, cursing her own stupidity as the answer became clear.

"The top intelligence officer of the United States would not waste time visiting the president of Panama," she said. "She would meet officials with cockroach spies of her same stripe. The CIA."

Francisco glanced in the rearview mirror, meeting Sabine's gaze. "She is going to the U.S. embassy." His hand hovered over the gearshift, eyes still filling the mirror. "Shall I take you there?"

Uncle Hector spoke up from the backseat. "Ryan will only be here for a short time. He came in under a ruse in a small, unmarked aircraft. His security apparatus wanted to keep his visit a secret. Now that his secret is out, that same security apparatus will push him to finish what he came to do and move on to Mar del Plata as quickly as possible."

"That is true," Sabine mused.

"Then do something to keep her here," Hector said, a verbal shrug. "Do not forget, the summit at Mar del Plata will have dozens of world leaders, all of them surrounded by layer upon layer of armed security, not to mention the hardened defenses of the venue itself, the Argentine military, and the American armed forces already in place."

A crooked smile spread over Sabine's face as she pondered the possibilities. "And Panama has no army . . . Unless you count mine."

Moncada's pleadings poured out of her phone, no doubt having heard the conversation. She ignored him.

"We would have to contend with the American Secret Service."

Hector leaned forward, chin on the back of the seat like a child asking when they were going to stop for a bathroom break. "But they are a skeleton crew," he said. "That is the price they paid for keeping Ryan's visit a secret. Whatever you do, you need to do it now."

Sabine put the phone to her ear, cutting Moncada off mid-sentence.

"Be quiet and listen," she said. "Blow the explosives as planned. JAMAICA is back on."

"Are you insane?"

"What did you say?"

"I am sorry, but the American President and his entourage will be walking through the door at any moment. Operation JAMAICA is a complicated endeavor. It is—"

"Blow shit up and shoot people," she said. "That does not sound so very complicated to me. Detonate the explosives. Now. I will contact Doyle about the Chinese ship."

Moncada sounded as if he were being strangled. "But the Russians have already passed through the locks. They are probably at Gamboa by now! What will they—"

"The Russians will do what Russians do," Sabine said. "They will break things and accomplish their task—"

The Suburban lurched as Francisco suddenly threw it into reverse.

He shot a glance in the rearview mirror. "Forgive the interruption, **patrona.** Something is going on ahead of us. The men in suits are running, and police are waving everyone back."

De Bruk's phone buzzed. He threw it to his ear, listened momentarily, then snapped his fingers to get Sabine's attention. "It's Gordo. Secret Service K9s have alerted on one of the explosives. They are pulling Ryan back to his limousine."

"Shit!" Sabine said. Then, through gritted teeth, "Moncada, detonate the bombs now. Ryan must not leave."

"And Botero?"

"Do as you planned," she snapped. "Kill everyone in the building, for all I care."

De Bruk's eyes widened in surprise.

"Avoid killing my men, of course," she added. "If you can."

Hector reached over the seat and put a hand on her shoulder. "Very good, child," he said. "Very, very good."

Francisco had the Suburban careening backward on the narrow sidewalk by the time the shock wave from the first explosion rocked them. A half breath later, the car shook from a second bomb farther up the street. Car alarms screamed and honked throughout Casco Viejo. Had Francisco not started rolling backward right when he did, they would have been trapped in the jam of vehicles and pedestrians fleeing the scene before any more bombs went off, and first responders rushing toward the carnage. As it was, he squealed around the corner in reverse and into a vacant alley. He threw the Suburban into drive and sped down the wrong side of the street, scraping building façades and knocking down awnings to avoid oncoming traffic.

"To the U.S. embassy," he said over his shoulder. "Correct, **patrona**?"

"Yes." Sabine hung tight to the grab handle above her door and caught Francisco's soft brown eyes in the rearview mirror, already thinking of feeding De Bruk to the pigs.

54

Secret Service advance agents directed Ryan's motorcade onto Eloy Alfaro Avenue, the red-brick thoroughfare that ran between Casco Viejo and the tidal flats inside the coastal loop known as Cinta Costera. The tide was out, but Ryan noted three police patrol boats stationed some fifty yards to the north in the relatively deep water between the muddy beach and the large parking area along the loop road.

The limo driver, a veteran Secret Service agent named Kennedy, tapped the brakes a hair harder than he intended, causing Ryan to lurch forward against his lap belt. Unlike the Beast, this Tahoe was not armored, and responded differently to what the driver was accustomed to.

"Go around!" Gary Montgomery groused into his lapel mic at the Secret Service agent behind the wheel of the lead vehicle ahead of the presidential limo.

A well-meaning uniformed SPI officer was having a hell of a time keeping left-turning traffic stopped at the intersection with Thirteenth Street. He'd let an old woman selling coconut water roll her metal cart halfway into the intersection.

Special Agent Kennedy smiled grimly at his boss and jigged right, following the lead car around the heavy cart.

"I miss a good POTUS freeze," the agent whispered.

"Yep," Montgomery said, obviously biting his tongue, since Ryan was in the vehicle.

During a "POTUS freeze," state and local law enforcement stopped all traffic along the motorcade route, giving the President's motorcade an open road that didn't require the use of sirens or overly aggressive driving. Police utilized a rolling roadblock of motorcycles and cruisers or just flat blocking traffic for the duration until the President got where he was going. It happened wherever POTUS traveled in the United States and, with proper planning, overseas—as long as the trip was official and out in the open. This off-the-books visit relied on local law enforcement to clear the route as well as they could without telling anyone why. Much of that was done by SPI officers riding ahead two-up on motorcycles and blocking traffic on the fly.

A formal honor guard of six motor officers in blue dress uniforms joined the motorcade from the sea side of the street as they passed Eleventh, roaring out of what appeared to be an underground garage beneath a city park to lead them the last few blocks to the palace.

The Tahoe's windows were not tinted, giving Ryan an unimpeded view of his surroundings—and Montgomery's reactions to them. Dark alleys, milling crowds of pedestrians, and crumbling multistory buildings, many of them only visually secured by the Secret Service in order to guard the secrecy of the visit. It was a fine notion as long as they maintained the element of surprise. Unoccupied cars and trucks were parked along the brick streets and in tiny out-of-the-way car parks wedged between businesses. Montgomery tensed at every vehicle they passed. The whole place was eerily reminiscent of a series of alleys in Colombia during a trip that had not gone well. Ryan's window was rolled down a hair, letting in the smell of seaweed, fried plantains, and spiced empanadas—along with the car exhaust and garbage fumes common to any large city.

Teams from the Secret Service's Technical Security Division had swept the area three times with dogs and digital scanners, but again, not to their normal scrupulous degree of detail. It was impossible to be both meticulous and secret. Easier to keep under wraps, advance PPD agents had driven the streets between Albrook airport and the presidential palace numerous times at different hours of the day. They noted the nearest trauma hospitals, police stations, and high-crime areas, paying special attention to gang graffiti and any street-level drug deals they witnessed going down along the way. This information was fed directly to Montgomery as well as the brains at Protective Intelligence in the upper floors of U.S. Secret Service Headquarters on H Street. These advance agents paid special attention to choke points along various possible routes. Overpasses and bridges provided perfect ambush sites, like where the broad surface avenue that was their main route from the airport went under the tangled interchange of Route 3 and the Pan-American Highway.

The closer they got to the presidential palace, every street and side alley was a potential threat. Fortunately for Gary Montgomery's blood pressure, the uniformed police presence grew exponentially as they continued east past Eighth Street toward the presidential palace.

Vice President Carré, who sat to Ryan's left, leaned forward, mobile phone to his ear.

"Very good." His smile broadened, if such a thing was possible, and he ended the call. He tucked the phone in the breast pocket of his suit and rubbed his hands together. "I cannot tell you, President Ryan, how much this trip means to the Republic of Panama."

"It's my pleasure," Ryan said, meaning it.

Red lights flashing, the police motorcycles continued east on Eloy Alfaro Avenue. Movable metal barricades lined the north side of the street containing a dozen reporters who waited in the shade of three large Cook pines—actually not pines at all, but a variety of subtropical evergreen that tended to tilt toward the equator, no matter where they grew in the world. Ryan had won a bet or two on that little factoid.

The SPI Presidential Protection Group lead car followed the motor officers, allowing Ryan's Tahoe to roll to a stop between the twin pillars in front of the steps leading up to the red-carpeted entrance of the Palacio de las Garzas. The white three-story presidential palace's triple-arched portico was guarded by four police officers. This honor guard wore dark blue tunics with white uniform pants and white covers. At first glance, they could have easily been mistaken for United States Marines. Each man held an M16 rifle with bayonet out in front of him, perpendicular to the ground, rendering courtesy to Ryan as he arrived.

His Excellency President Rafael Botero stood at the top of the steps between a Panamanian and a U.S. flag. Flanked by two members of his Presidential Protection Group, hands clasped at the waist of his dark blue suit, he bounced slightly in place, obviously ecstatic that Ryan had come when he asked.

A single United States Secret Service agent stood curbside with his hand extended, marking the exact spot he wanted the Tahoe's bumper to stop. Other agents worked the north side of the street, ensuring that the media stayed behind their flimsy barricades. At least two Secret Service agents—Ryan suspected there were more—stepped out from under the shadows of the portico at the motorcade's arrival. Ray-Bans shielded their eyes.

Montgomery didn't exactly relax, but the wrinkles in his brow grew slightly less furrowed now that Ryan was sandwiched between boots-on-the-ground advance agents, his protective PPD bubble, and HAWKEYE—the van full of Counter Assault Team agents and their heavy weapons.

Montgomery exited the Tahoe as soon as it stopped. He stood next to the rear passenger door, touching the handle, but keeping his eyes up, scanning the area for threats. Four other agents piled out of the follow car, taking up their positions with Montgomery and the on-the-scene advance agents to form a modified diamond with which they would surround Ryan when he got out of the car. Only when these agents were in place and Montgomery got an all-clear signal from his agent inside the palace did he open the Tahoe's door.

Vice President Carré's security met him on the left side of the Tahoe, waiting on Ryan to exit before they opened the door for their boss. The two men walked up the steps together, at which point Carré stepped deftly to one side, giving the cameras an unimpeded view of the two presidents.

"May I present His Excellency President Botero."

The two leaders shook hands, pausing for photos before turning to move their meeting inside. The most important of Botero's aims had been accomplished: the media knew he had the political juice to get Ryan to visit when called. Inside, they would have lunch and speak as the friends that they were.

The entryway was tight even with the wrought-iron gates wide open, and the Secret Service diamond was forced to compress into an elongated spear with two advance agents in the lead directly behind President Botero, while Gary Montgomery walked within arm's reach behind Ryan's right shoulder. The remainder of the detail would follow through the door two by two.

Ryan was not quite through the doorway when a commotion arose outside, somewhere down the street.

Inside the main entry hall, Felix Moncada stood to the side of the staircase sweating bullets as he listened to the madness from Sabine Gorshkova pour out of the mobile phone. This was not the way he had envisioned this moment, and yet, here it was thrust upon him. Guerra stood to his left. Agent Pinto, slightly behind him, hidden by

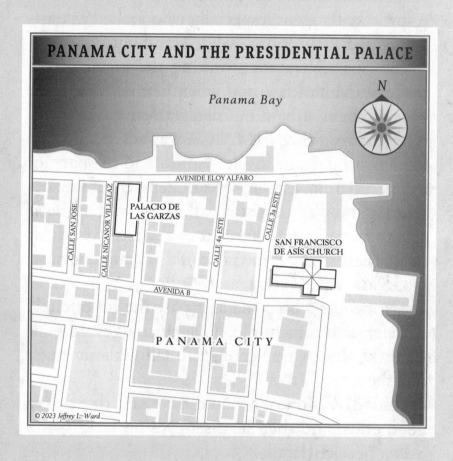

PANAMA CITY AND THE PRESIDENTIAL PALACE

N

Panama Bay

AVENIDE ELOY ALFARO

PALACIO DE
LAS GARZAS

CALLE SAN JOSE

CALLE NICANOR VILLALAZ

CALLE 4a ESTE

CALLE 3a ESTE

SAN FRANCISCO
DE ASÍS CHURCH

AVENIDA B

PANAMA CITY

© 2023 Jeffrey L. Ward

Guerra and Moncada. SPI protective officers would not question the presence of Botero's economic adviser or a ranking commissioner with the Policía Nacional de Panamá at an important visit like this. A lowly PNP agent, especially who looked as dangerous as Fabian Pinto, would stand out.

The two contractors working the metal detectors gave Moncada a nod when he met their eyes. One of them, a balding man named Gordo, had received word that JAMAICA was again a go and informed his team inside. Gordo and his partner were Camarilla, as were several members of the secretarial and cleaning staff, all of whom had been able to sneak in handguns over the past week. All in all, there were seven Camarilla operatives inside, plus Moncada, Guerra, and Pinto.

Ten people who'd made it past the inner circle of defense to foment a coup against a government that was already ripe enough to fall without much of a shove.

Yesterday, Moncada would have said those were good odds, and then he'd set eyes on Jack Ryan's Secret Service detail.

The big one—they were all big—but the one in charge who stood directly behind Ryan suddenly perked up as they stepped through the door. He reached to tap the President on his shoulder, asking him to pause.

This whole thing was turning into a shitshow.

A Secret Service explosives detection canine had

discovered one of the devices. Packed in roast coffee beans and sealed in layer upon layer of plastic, the bomb had been placed by an electric light in the crotch of a lower limb of one of the Cook pines across the street, higher than any dog handler would usually search.

Moncada could see Gordo on the phone now, probably getting a blow-by-blow from another operative posted outside and then relaying the information to Sabine.

The foyer inside the palace was large once through the entrance, giving Lionel Carré and his detail of two SPI agents plenty of room to come up alongside Ryan.

President Botero continued toward his office, while Ryan slowed, then stopped, presumably to return to his idling motorcade and speed away to his waiting 747.

Sabine screamed her order into Moncada's phone.

Guerra and Pinto edged toward the center of the hall on a course to intercept Botero and his SPI detail.

Terrified of Sabine's scolding threats, Moncada reached into his jacket pocket for the detonator, toggled the safety/arming switch, flicked up the protective hood on the right side of the device—and depressed the button.

Botero's men, too, had gotten word of the Secret Service bomb dog and were already pulling their president toward his office.

Ryan's detail, who had been intent on ushering

him quickly off the premises, suddenly found the exterior of the palace an extremely hostile environment.

A second device was above the gas tank of Moncada's Mercedes sedan, which was parked mere yards from Ryan's motorcade—and the Secret Service CAT vehicle. It would eliminate, or at least stun, the Secret Service tactical unit hiding in the van. There was no question that the blast would kill most of the motor officers, who would have been standing with their bikes, absent even the protection of a thin metal car body. Moncada knew some of them, respected them, had even met their children. He pressed the second button anyway, consoling himself with the belief that if those men were patriots, they would be happy to give their lives for Panama.

55

The overpressure from the explosion slammed into Ryan like a sledgehammer between the shoulder blades.

Montgomery took the brunt of the blast wave and stumbled forward. He barked into the mic pinned to his collar, using plain talk. This was no time for code words.

"Ambush! Ambush! Ambush!"

His fist twisted the fabric of Ryan's suit jacket at the shoulder, nearly lifting him off the ground.

Tires squealed outside as the limo backed into position. HAWKEYE—the CAT—would be moving to cover Ryan's egress to the motorcade, and then the vehicles themselves as it spirited him out of this danger zone.

Ryan felt himself being dragged backward in an iron grip.

"Make a hole!" Montgomery yelled—over the radio and to any of his agents within earshot.

A second blast cut him short, driving him forward

again. This one close enough to send a wave of debris flying past the doorway.

The street outside the palace turned into a riot of squealing car alarms and frantic screams.

Still held by the shoulder, Ryan was pushed forward, the way cleared by two Secret Service agents ahead of him and Montgomery. Both the agents had suddenly sprouted short MP5K submachine guns from beneath their suit jackets. Not much bigger than a large handgun, these personal defense weapons carried thirty-round magazines—and had a cyclic rate of nine hundred rounds per minute.

Vice President Carré jerked away from his own security officer and staggered up beside Ryan. He shot a glance at Montgomery.

"This way!"

The nearest advance agent, familiar with the interior of the palace, nodded, agreeing with Carré's suggestion.

Ahead, through the melee of staff and security personnel, Ryan caught a glimpse of Rafael Botero being dragged by a uniformed police officer toward what was presumably the same secure room.

Gabriella Canto reached the corner before the first bomb went off. As horrific as the blast was, the confusion of car alarms, acrid smoke, and mangled bodies opened a path for her like the Red Sea parting before Moses. With everyone running away, none of the officers took more than a passing glance at her offered badge and ID card, assuming she was there to help.

It was a law of human nature: act like you belong and everyone assumes that you do.

She made it inside the portico just moments before the second blast, the shock wave shoving her through the doors. Ears ringing, barely able to breathe, she staggered into a knot of stunned Secret Service agents that surrounded the President. With Panamanian and American authorities alike brandishing weapons and looking for a threat, she kept her badge handy to keep from getting shot. She made it past the metal detectors just as SPI and Secret Service personnel set up a rear guard behind her.

She limped forward, everyone naturally assuming she'd been wounded in the blast. Commissioner Guerra rounded the corner ahead. She'd yet to locate his lapdog, Agent Pinto, in the milling crowd. Both men were connected to all this. Canto didn't know how, but she intended to find out. She ran past the President and his security men, intent on getting to Guerra before they did. It didn't matter that she was in uniform. Any second, the Secret Service or SPI would order her to stay away.

Fifteen seconds after the last explosion Ryan moved as if borne by an ocean wave, half cajoled, half shoved by Gary Montgomery and the ring of five PPD agents that had closed in around him to form a human shield. Carré and his two security men moved beside them in an unstoppable shuffling scrum.

They rounded the corner as two popping shots came from the side office—into which they'd been heading.

Montgomery pulled up short, lifting Ryan off his feet to get him to stop. Four more rapid-fire shots cracked in the confined space.

The two advance agents immediately put themselves between the gunfire and the President.

"Taking gunfire in the center hall!" Montgomery yelled, training his pistol on the door while he dragged Ryan sideways. "HAWKEYE! Get your asses in here!" He turned Ryan down a side hall with Carré.

One of the vice president's two bodyguards stumbled, then fell face-first onto the marble floor. Montgomery slammed on the brakes again. The SPI officer had been shot in the neck with some kind of suppressed weapon. The bomb blasts had stunned Ryan's hearing, leaving him with a constant ringing whine over the clatter and screams of his surroundings. Even the earlier pistol shots had sounded muffled and surreal.

A half step later and Carré's second SPI guard slumped to his knees, as did the Secret Service agent who'd moved forward to take the advance spot. The other agents formed a wall of bodies between the President and the previous gunfire.

Ryan, who was slightly ahead and nearer to Carré, saw the man with a misshapen ear a split second before Montgomery. He was wearing a uniform. Green, different from the SPI. Retreating into an alcove off the hall, the man raised a suppressed pistol directly at the vice president's head. Carré saw it, too, a fraction of a second after Ryan, and flinched as a shot split the air. This one was close and much too loud to come from a suppressed weapon.

"Gun left!" A Secret Service agent rushed past Ryan and Montgomery toward the threat— a Panamanian female wearing the same camouflage green uniform as the man she'd just shot behind his misshapen ear. Her nameplate said her name was Canto, a major in the National Police.

"Friendly!" Montgomery barked. This woman had clearly saved Lionel Carré's life.

More gunfire clattered behind them, punctuating shouted orders from harried Secret Service agents, telling people to get down.

A third device exploded outside, rocking the building as if it had been hit by artillery fire. Ryan crouched out of instinct. Bits of paint and dust shaken loose by the blast rained down around him.

Gunfire at the president's office in front of them and behind them on the street, Ryan and his remaining group of agents found themselves with few options.

"Crash! Crash! Center hall!" Montgomery said again, instructing HAWKEYE to fight their way to the President at all costs.

Then a deeply resonant voice rose above the noise in the hall ahead. Ryan, who was surprised by little in the world, chanced a look over his shoulder at Montgomery, who screwed up his face in grim determination at the words.

"¡Los americanos han asesinado al Presidente Botero!"

The Americans have assassinated President Botero!

56

"**M**ierda!**" Gabriella Canto cursed. "That is Guerra. He is behind all of this."

Montgomery didn't waste time quizzing her. He called again for HAWKEYE, half of whom had been caught up in the third blast. The remainder were pinned down at the door in a standoff with SPI Presidential Protection Group agents and uniformed Presidential Guard Battalion officers, who all apparently believed they were under attack by the United States.

"Mr. President," Montgomery said. "We need to move. Now!"

Carré shook off the shock of nearly being assassinated and pointed through the alcove into what looked like a small chapel. "In here," he said.

Montgomery paused, still gripping the shoulder of Ryan's suit. "Is this a dead end?"

"Dead end?"

"Is there a door out?"

Carré took a deep breath. "Of a sort," he said. His voice was tight. A trickle of blood ran from a gash below his ear. "But you must trust me."

The gunfire from President Botero's office grew closer and more intense, making the decision for them.

Montgomery spun Ryan around, handgun up, entering the room first behind Carré to make certain they weren't walking into another ambush. Major Canto followed along with the remaining Secret Service agent carrying an MP5K. The agent, a youngster named Galbraith who'd been assigned to PPD for less than a month, turned to post at the door.

"I've got this, boss," he hissed to Montgomery. "Go!"

Carré moved quickly to a life-sized statue of the Virgin Mary and then pushed the center of the plaster wall behind her. A four-by-eight-foot panel slid inward, just a few inches at first, but enough to reveal a set of stone stairs leading down into the darkness in the dead space behind the wall.

"This way!"

Montgomery called out on the radio, "HAWK-EYE! Status?" A pause, then, "Shit! They've got one of our radios."

It was Ryan's turn to balk.

"What?"

"Someone's talking on our comms," Montgomery said. He cursed again. "They're listening to everything we say." Almost in the same breath, he whistled to get Galbraith's attention. The younger agent had heard the strange voices on the radio as well.

"Tell the detail my radio's down, but I'm taking the President down the hall out a west exit."

"Got it," Galbraith said, snapping to the plan without further explanation.

Vice President Carré took the lead, using the light from his phone. Ryan went next, followed by Montgomery and then Major Canto.

Montgomery slid the wall panel half shut and then whistled to Galbraith again. "Make the call and then get your ass over here with us!"

"Go, boss," the young agent said. "Someone needs to stay."

Major Canto moved to return to the chapel. "I will stay—"

The clatter of gunfire grew louder. Whoever was shooting was almost on top of them.

Galbraith fired down the hall, leaning back to speak over his shoulder.

"Just go," he said. "Shut the door now!"

Gary Montgomery cursed some more, yanking Major Canto inside the hidden passage, not to save her or bring her into the protective bubble. Ryan was his only concern. But he needed to close the wall panel and she was in the way.

A string of shots stitched the air moments after the panel hissed tight. Harried voices spoke quickly, demanding in Spanish to know where the American President was. To Ryan's relief, Special

Agent Galbraith answered that, as far as he knew, the Secret Service had taken the President out the west side of the palace.

"Guerra!" Canto whispered, chest heaving, head shaking with fury.

Carré held a finger to his lips and mouthed the words **If we can hear them, then they can hear us . . .**

The group shuffled down the narrow steps, following the cool, ozone smell of earthworks and cool stone to a pitch-black passage that Ryan estimated to be eight or ten feet below the chapel. Nests of cobwebs and a thick layer of dust said it had not seen use for a very long time.

"Who is this Guerra son of a bitch?" Ryan asked, furious at what he'd heard after they'd gone through the wall.

"Commissioner Javier Guerra," Major Canto said, grimacing in the shadows as if she wanted to spit. "He is my boss with the Panama National Police—and the reason I am here. To warn you, Mr. President. I fear you have walked into the middle of a coup."

More shots popped above. Muffled by masonry and thick timbers, it was impossible to tell if they came from the chapel or somewhere more distant. Ryan said a little prayer for Special Agent Galbraith.

Relatively safe for the moment, Montgomery grabbed the President by the shoulders and turned him from side to side to perform a blood sweep, checking for wounds. Many a man had bled to death without realizing he'd been hit.

"I'm fine, Gary," Ryan said.

Montgomery turned his attention to Vice President Carré. "Tell me this leads us out to the street."

"Honestly," Carré said, "up until today, I had only heard of these tunnels. They are said to go in several different directions."

Montgomery nodded, listening for a moment to his radio. "My guys are still engaging hostiles on the perimeter anyway, and who knows how many more bombs . . ." He turned to scan the passage behind them. "How many people know about this place?"

"That I do not know," Carré said. "The palace was built in 1673, so there has always been an assumption of secret rooms and whatnot. Botero was told by the previous president, and he told me. Presidents are always fearful of coups—for obvious reasons."

"Would the Protection Group know about them?" Ryan asked.

"That is highly unlikely," Carré said. "Historically, presidential guards are the most likely culprits in a coup. I imagine these tunnels were built to hide from pirates, but over time, I believe they became a place for presidents to hide from their own men. Either way, it is good to keep those hiding places secret."

"I am sorry for your Secret Service agent," Canto said. "I should have been the one." She flinched at the sound of more gunshots and muffled thuds through the floor above, then put her hand on the stone.

"Entre la espada y la pared . . ."

Ryan spoke enough Spanish to understand.

They were indeed between the sword and the wall.

57

LEESBURG, VIRGINIA

Ed Foley was not one to be tethered to his cell phone twenty-four hours a day. In fact, he usually left the damned thing charging in the kitchen when he sat down in his study for one of his inspirational power naps. He was just beginning to drift off in his recliner, when the distant sound bumped his ears. It was extremely faint, like the scrape of a branch on the kitchen window screen or a cat scratching at the back door. Except they didn't have any pets, and Foley had trimmed the bushes around the house himself. He sat up, straining to hear, or rather, straining to filter out the hum of the refrigerator, the tick of the furnace, the background noises common to every house. Russian apartments were the worst. They came with screams. Sometimes from the water pipes, sometimes the neighbors.

He glanced out the window at the big oak in

the front yard. A tire swing he'd hung up for the grandkids swayed in the breeze. Autumn leaves skittered down the street. Convinced the new noise was just the wind, Foley relaxed and settled into the La-Z-Boy again. He breathed in the comforting smells of his study—books, leather, pipe tobacco from a periodic indulgence when Mary Pat was away. It was the perfect place for a quick snooze.

Foley had started taking catnaps in his seventh-floor office at Langley during his tenure as director of the CIA. He'd read somewhere that both Salvador Dalí and Thomas Edison found inspiration when they were awakened during the moment of transition into sleep. Foley found that it was a simple matter of leaning back in his recliner while clutching a small brass Buddhist scepter called a **dorje** that he'd picked up on a trip to Lhasa with Mary Pat. Edison had held a small metal ball. Dalí utilized a heavy key. The trick was to hold the object in a fist so that it fell from your hand and clattered to the floor the moment you fell asleep, waking you in a sudden moment of clarity and inspiration. Foley found that it worked more often than not, allowing him to suss out the answers to many complicated issues, though it scared the hell out of Mary Pat. The first time she saw the **dorje** slip from his hand when he drifted off, she assumed he was having a stroke.

Today, it was Mary Pat's situation he was thinking on as he clutched the little brass scepter and settled deeper into his chair. He was missing something important. Some world event in Panama. The call from his old friend, Randell Green . . . Something . . .

The scratching noise came again, slightly louder now, followed by a low creak.

Ed set the **dorje** on the small table beside his chair, gingerly as not to make a sound.

A footstep creaked on the hardwood floor above.

The problem with alarm systems was that they tended to make people feel more secure than they actually were. Most people, but not Ed Foley. He knew better. All the tremble pads and glass-break sensors in the world wouldn't stop a determined intruder. Glass was, well, just that. Glass. A fragile suggestion of security. That's why residents of so many other countries (and some U.S. cities) bolted bars to their windows. Sure, an audible alarm might frighten off a junkie looking for jewelry or guns to sell for an easy score. Someone coming in to cause harm—the kind of person who invaded the home of the director of national intelligence and a former director of the CIA—that kind of person did what they came to do despite a security system. Alarms were not a moat or a thick castle wall. They were a warning, not protection. And even then, only if the intruder wasn't smart enough to disable the system. It was a moot point. Ed rarely armed his during the day. It was too much of a hassle.

Another soft creak. This one came from the top

of the stairs. Whoever this was must have used a ladder in the backyard and then come through the upstairs guest room.

There was only one from the sound of it, Foley thought. He could handle one . . . But then, his hearing wasn't what it used to be. The noises were spaced, creak . . . quiet . . . creak . . . quiet. Foley pictured the guy moving slowly, getting the lay of the land. Hunting. The stairs were at the end of the hall, a fair distance to cover in a house big enough to hold all the grandkids when they came to visit. Foley figured he had a minute, maybe less.

In the movies, former spies had safe rooms, surveillance systems, walls o' guns . . .

Ed had his wits and a few odds and ends that any world-traveling grandfather/intelligence officer might have lying around.

He eased out of his chair and got to his feet. No point in just sitting there and getting shot . . . or garroted, or whatever this intruder intended to do. He cast around the study, looking for something to use as a weapon. He had a shotgun and an old Beretta pistol, but they were upstairs in the bedroom safe. A fat lot of good they would do him there.

His Jaguar XF was parked in the driveway out front. He left the detached garage for the lawn mower and Mary Pat's Land Rover. The keys were on the end table beside his chair. He thought of hitting the Jag's car alarm, but decided against it, for the moment at least.

Whatever he used to defend himself, it was going to have to come from here in the study. He'd spent his entire adult life spying around the world and had accumulated a few knickknacks over the years— a leather slapjack favored by the KGB, a Russian saber (that actually belonged to Mary Pat), a black-thorn walking stick, a Zulu spear. He decided on the stiff rhino-hide quirt called a sjambok from the mantel. Springy as steel and over three feet long, it was capable of flaying skin in the hands of someone who knew what they were doing. Ed Foley did not, but he could do some damage anyway.

Probably.

Mary Pat had a Secret Service detail, but they were portal-to-portal, meaning they didn't hang around and guard the house when she wasn't there. The Service had installed duress alarms in the bed-room, the bathrooms, and the kitchen, but Ed had told them not to bother with his study.

Shit. No gun. No panic button. No phone. He'd resorted to a rawhide stick he barely knew how to use, and his arthritis was acting up so bad he could hardly snap his fingers.

Then he remembered something Mary Pat often told clandestine officer trainees at the Farm.

There weren't too many fights that couldn't be won with a good pair of running shoes.

———

The Russian paused at the top of the stairs, listening, trying to figure out where Edward Foley was. The breeze was kicking up outside and he still wore the Washington Nationals ball cap against the chill. The Russian, really a Belorussian named Minsky, had been watching the Foley home all morning from a surprisingly good vantage point in the swale of a nearby park. A camera and a slow-moving dog gave him a plausible reason for being there. The animal shelter hadn't asked many questions when he'd shown interest in one of the older, arthritic mutts. If anything, they pushed him out the door before he could change his mind.

Ed Foley was home. Minsky had seen him walk past the kitchen window less than ten minutes earlier. He'd scoured real estate websites, studying similar homes in the area to get an educated idea of the interior layout. Foley was likely still on the first floor. That was good. Minsky would be able to come in from above and get the drop on him before he had a chance to go for a gun. These days, almost every American he knew had one.

Minsky brought a suppressed Glock 26 in nine-millimeter, stubby, thirteen rounds with his extended magazine, and relatively hush. Sabine had made it very clear that she wanted Foley done with a claw hammer. Twisted, yes, but Minsky didn't mind. He would lead with the Glock, then move on to the Craftsman that was tucked into his belt. Sabine wouldn't know from the Polaroids that he shot Foley first and then worked him over with the hammer while, or even after, he let the bullets do the heavy lifting.

The sleepy Leesburg neighborhood was made up mostly of working couples with kids in school. There were very few nosy neighbors at home this time of day. Even if they were, the Foleys' backyard was shielded by a privacy fence. The wind gave Minsky cover to get up on the roof. As an added precaution, he wore dark blue coveralls like those worn by utility workers. Americans tended to think that it couldn't happen to them, especially not in this quiet neighborhood. If anyone did happen to notice a guy on the roof, they would assume he was with the electric company.

An ice pick, aluminum foil, and some electrician's tape had taken care of the window alarm. Crepe-soled chukka boots dampened his steps, but gave him the traction he'd need to run or fight if the need arose. This was not, as the Americans said, his first rodeo.

Minsky took two tentative steps down the stairs, then stopped and held his breath to listen. Nothing. That was odd. People weren't quiet in their own homes—unless they were trying to hide.

A telltale scrape pulled Minsky's attention down the hall to his right. Then Foley had a little coughing fit, as if he were trying to clear his throat. He sounded relaxed, blissfully unaware. Good. It was midday. The time for old men to curl up on the sofa and have a nap. Foley suspected nothing.

Minsky padded swiftly down the stairs. Maybe he would start out with the hammer after all.

He made it to the end of the hall in four quick strides, stopping just outside the door to what looked like a study. Maybe even a gun room. He reconsidered his bravado from moments before and drew the suppressed pistol, leaving the claw hammer in his belt. The smell of pipe tobacco rolled out into the hall. Pleasant, Minsky thought, considering the circumstances. A faint rattle coming from inside the room made him freeze. It was a familiar sound, but . . .

The rattle suddenly intensified. His stomach fell as he realized it was the sound of miniblinds shuffling in the wind—an open window. Minsky cursed, chancing a quick peek around the corner. He checked the direction opposite the window first so he didn't get brained with an ashtray or shot in the back of the head. Experience taught Minsky it was advisable to enter a room quickly rather than hang out at the door. The only other place Foley could be was behind the desk. He wasn't there.

The conniving old prick must have used the coughing fit to hide the noise of opening the window—

An engine roared to life in the driveway. Minsky

dove through the window, rolling to his feet on the grass. Pistol up, he strode quickly across the driveway to the idling Jaguar sedan, putting two quick rounds through the door. Someone was sure to see him, but it didn't matter. Sabine Gorshkova would feed his head to the pigs if he let this asshole get away. Foley must have seen him coming and ducked down to stay out of sight. Minsky put another shot through the door before moving up to administer the coup de grâce.

The Jag was empty.

A horrific noise jerked Minsky's attention to his right. It took him a split second to realize Edward Foley had crashed through the garage door and now barreled directly toward him behind the wheel of a white Land Rover.

Conniving old prick indeed . . .

Rather than throwing the man into the air like Ed thought it would, the Land Rover's high bumper had slammed him into the ground like a hammer, knocking him completely out of his crepe-soled chukkas and, from the looks of his skull, killing him instantly. The pistol he'd been holding ended up in the front yard a good twenty feet away from the body. Ed left it there, thinking it better not to have a weapon in his hand when the police arrived.

The 911 operator wanted to keep him on the line, but he hung up anyway, eager to check in with his wife. He'd been retired awhile. If someone wanted to kill him, odds were, they were trying to kill her as well.

58

Clark and the others were on their feet when Cobb led Blanca out of the bathroom.

The young woman's face was flushed and wet with tears. Her chest convulsed with periodic sobs.

Cobb put a hand on her shoulder and gave it a light pat.

"Come on, Blanca," she said. "Go ahead. Tell them what you told me."

Yao started to speak, but Cobb threw up her hand. "Give her a sec."

Blanca gave a sad shake of her head, hand to her chest.

"You think that I . . . I play a role in my sister's lunatic bloodlust? You want to know what kind of hammer did I use?" She tugged at the collar of her scrubs and then patted her chest as if to illustrate her point. "I am a nurse. I help people."

Yao raised a brow.

"Bloodlust?"

"She thinks I did not know." The young woman wagged her head. "But I am not a fool. I heard things. I found their photographs and videos." Her eyes glazed. She winced as if she were picturing the terrible images all over again.

"Please sit," Cobb said. "Before you fall down." She shot a look at Clark that said, **I've got this.**

Clark and Yao resumed their spots at the table, but Cobb stayed beside the trembling young woman as she took her seat.

"Go ahead," Cobb prodded.

"My brother was a bad man, but he was bad because he was weak. Oh . . . but Sabine . . . My sister is on an entirely different plane." Blanca blinked repeatedly, as if coming out of a trance. "I assume that's why you are after her and, by extension, after me." She looked at Clark and then Yao, wanting to get both their attention. "I will tell you this. Sabine has eyes everywhere, so she must know you are here. I feel certain that is why she left so quickly."

"And it doesn't bother you that your sister abandoned you to the authorities?" Yao asked.

Blanca stared back at him.

"My sister murders innocent people with hammer and axe. Abandoning me would not exactly be such a great stretch for her. I suspect our uncle Hector sent Roberto and Gregor to kill me. Or perhaps Sabine sent them. Neither she nor my brother ever had much use for me."

Yao gave a slow nod. "Your brother was—"

Exasperated, Blanca cut him off. "My brother was a simpering fool. He hid behind expensive clothing and rich food, pretending he was a great and powerful man of mystery. In truth he was a pawn who followed our sister's orders. If those orders were to bludgeon women and children to death, then he did it, no questions asked. Frankly, I am surprised Sabine did not kill him herself for being so bourgeois. If I were not her sister, she would have killed me a very long time ago." Blanca gave a little sigh. "I expect she's gotten around to the idea of it now. Love and hate are all snarled together in her head, the same emotion, really. I do not think she ever loved our brother so much as she hates those who ordered his death. No. Joaquín was only the face of things, insomuch as anyone was."

"I'll ask you again," Yao said. "Where is your sister right now?"

She shot a glance at Cobb.

"Panama."

Clark had to force himself to remain stoic. Foley didn't make a habit of briefing him about Ryan's travel plans, or her own, but she'd mentioned their secret trip to Panama the day before, soliciting any usable intelligence The Campus or WINDWARD STATION might have uncovered while they were in Latin America. Clark hadn't had any—until now.

The President's schedule was need-to-know, so he'd not shared it with the rest of the team. Cobb had no idea how vital her information was.

Yao, who'd been briefed about the travel, pushed himself up and over the table, startling even Cobb. "To do what?"

"Knowing her, she has gone to murder someone," Blanca said. "You must understand, killing comes quite naturally to Sabine. She sees her actions as a crusade. Ridding the world of the bourgeois, just as the inquisitor Torquemada cleansed the world of heretics."

Yao lowered himself to his chair, slowly, eyes locked on Blanca. "She called your brother Torquemada?"

"Oh, you people!" Blanca rubbed her face with both hands, as if it pained her that her interrogators were so dense. "Sabine sees **herself** as Torquemada. Her men call her 'the Spaniard.'"

Clark tried to call Director Foley, while Yao arranged transport for Blanca with the members of his WINDWARD STATION team who would stay behind. Whether they were able to find Sabine today or not, the girl had a wealth of knowledge in her head that she probably didn't realize she had.

Panama was less than a two-hour flight away, but it might as well be on the other side of the world the way things were looking.

Clark got nothing but a fast busy, so he hung up and tried again, this time getting the **all circuits are busy** notice. He tried Arnie van Damm's direct line. Again, he got a fast busy. Shit! The harried voices at the Secret Service's protective ops and the CIA's Ops Center both told him to hold before promptly cutting him off.

Chavez came in with Jack Junior and Midas.

Yao burst into the room with Ward, slightly out of breath. "Okay," he said. "Myrna should have us a ride by the time we get to the airport."

Clark grabbed his pack and followed Caruso toward the door.

Mandy Cobb hustled along beside him, chewing on her bottom lip. "I didn't know the President was in Panama."

"You wouldn't have," Clark said. "It's a wonder I even knew." He cocked his head. "Excellent work with Blanca. Nice job convincing her we're the good guys."

"Oh," Cobb said. "I didn't do that. She's not interested in how good we are. I had to promise her we wouldn't arrest her sister."

"That's not an option—"

Cobb shook her head. "I had to promise we would kill her."

59

Blow the ship, don't blow the ship . . .
Moncada wanted one thing. Sabine wanted another. He was the client, but she was the boss—and in Doyle's business, you went with the boss, especially when she was so fond of a ball-peen hammer. It wasn't even that Doyle was scared of her. On the contrary. He could have put a bullet in her most any day of the week.

Probably.

But it was hard not to respect the hell out of someone who could be so batshit crazy and at the same time remain so strategically savvy. Besides, Sabine Gorshkova was the golden goose for men like Doyle. Her organization allowed him to do what he was born to do—fight and get paid for it. Doyle just wished the crazy bitch would make up her mind.

He'd just stopped for a cold Pony Malta at the Terpel Va&Ven, a convenience store on Omar

Torrijos Herrera Avenue, when she called with her hair on fire and gave him new orders.

Doyle checked his watch.

He'd defanged the device less than twenty minutes earlier on the vessel's approach to the Cocoli Locks from the south. That gave him ten minutes at most if he wanted to be sure it was reactivated while still inside the third and last chamber.

Doyle left the soft drink on the counter and ran back to his car, driving as fast as he could without drawing attention. He parked in the same parking spot he'd used before under a small copse of trees, easy to miss by passing traffic, but not as if he'd intended to hide it. He grabbed a daypack from the backseat and plunged into the tick-infested grass. He hopped a rusted four-strand barbed-wire fence and crashed through more jungle until he reached a clearing that overlooked the entry lanes to the Miraflores Locks—and gave him a clear line of sight to the Cocoli Locks just under a mile to the southwest.

The **Jian Long** was passing from the second chamber to the third and final lock. Had Doyle not deleted the earlier coordinates, it would have already blown.

"Well, Señor Moncada," the Irishman said under his breath. "You'll get what you get . . ."

The original plan had been to blow up the ship in the middle of the locks. The third lock would have to do.

Doyle set the daypack in the grass at the base of

a gnarled tree and thought about the people he was about to kill while he unfolded a gunmetal-gray off-the-shelf quadcopter drone not much larger than his open palm.

The container ship was a Post-Panamax, 1,181 feet long and 144 feet wide. Massive, but with systems so automated Doyle doubted there were even a dozen crewmen on board. The concrete walls of the lock were fifty feet thick in spots. The blast wave from the explosion would be contained by those barriers and would be directed fore and aft, sweeping the piers of anyone unlucky enough to be standing on or around them. The pilot, linemen, tugboat operators, even people running the control center, would be within the kill zone. The magnitude of damage depended on what kind of material was in the shipping containers that surrounded the device. Certain chemicals, when exposed to enough heat, would foment secondary explosions and raging fires. A fertilizer ship, sugar, wheat flour . . . he'd seen—and caused—some hellacious explosions in his time.

Doyle wasn't blind to the pending deaths. His unscientific guestimate put the butcher's bill between ten and thirty, maybe more if the ship happened to be carrying a gob of magnesium engine parts. But war meant killing, and he'd signed up for war, even if it wasn't a conventional one. He thought about it a lot during the day, but still managed to fall asleep just fine the moment his head hit the pillow most nights, so he reckoned he didn't need a headshrinker just yet.

Or maybe that was exactly what he needed.

Either way, he was hella good at his job.

Arias had set the safety so the bomb would arm as soon as the ship passed the first set of gates—which it had done twenty minutes before. Doyle could do nothing about that. Originally, a GPS controller had been set to touch off the detonator when it reached the middle chamber. Doyle had deleted those co-ordinates, essentially leaving an armed bomb with no detonate command—a cocked gun just waiting for a finger to find the trigger. Buried deep in the row upon row of stacked shipping containers, the bomb's antenna was not especially sensitive by design, ensuring against accidental detonation by a randomly similar frequency. Detonating the device was not difficult. Doyle just needed to be within range, while not getting so close as to get himself killed. That's where the drone came in.

The little quadcopter lifted off from his hand, tilting forward slightly to zip across the water. It disappeared quickly against the frenetic backdrop of ships and cranes and blinding blue sky. Doyle watched his phone screen instead, getting a bird's-eye view of the approaching locks while he waited for the green light that indicated it was ready to relay his signal. Drones were forbidden around the locks, but that didn't matter. This one would be obliterated by the blast before anyone had a chance to pick up a phone.

60

Captain Vladimir Rykov was born and raised in the village of Pevek on the northern coast of Siberia's Chukotka autonomous region, a place of cold and wind and more cold. Sweat plastered his uniform to his body in the most inconvenient places. His maternal grandmother was Siberian Yupik, more accustomed to fur parkas and bitter winds off the Chukchi Sea. He'd inherited her short stature, blocky build, and her tendency to wilt and grow drowsy in the heat.

As much as Rykov despised the Canal Authority pilot assuming control of his destroyer, he had to admit that Berugatte's moderately interesting factoids at least kept him awake. The man still smiled like a fool, but Rykov learned to ignore the man's annoying teeth and listen to his excellent descriptions of their transit.

In the most basic terms, the Panama Canal was simply a series of water chambers used to lift maritime traffic the eighty-five feet above sea level needed to clear the Continental Divide and reach the level of Gatun Lake, the man-made reservoir formed by damming at least three great rivers and flooding thousands of hectares of Indigenous land.

But there was nothing simple about the engineering marvel that was the Panama Canal.

Señor Berugatte had guided the **Admiral Chabanenko** from the approach lanes of the Pacific into the first of the two chambers, or flights, that comprised the Miraflores Locks. Of special interest to Rykov as a naval war fighter, the canal's designers had situated the first set of locks inland and around a dogleg corner to guard against torpedo attacks from the Pacific—in the days when torpedoes only fired in a straight line.

Each chamber was one hundred and ten feet wide and one thousand fifty feet in length. Once the ship was inside, operators in the central control room located on the upper flight of the locks used controls on a scale model that mirrored the lock system to close huge gates, seven feet thick and, in the case of the Miraflores flights, eighty-two-feet tall, to allow for the drastic Pacific tidal changes. Canal Authority crews on the sides of the lock tossed light snagging ropes to sailors aboard the ship that, once caught, were used to pull heavy lines that secured the ship to the gray electric locomotives that were Mitsubishi-built with Kawasaki electric engines. The **Admiral Chabanenko** would provide her own propulsion in and out of the chambers. These "mules" helped the ship stay in position during the transit—two on each side, both fore and aft, for a total of eight, running on broad tracks fixed into specially strengthened concrete. Ships steered by passing water over the rudder. This required speed, which was in short supply inside the confined space of the lock. Beefy tugboats helped with the centering.

The gates shut and the ship secure, the controllers opened fourteen massive culverts, each eighteen feet in diameter. The system utilized gravity to fill the chamber with over twenty-six million gallons of water in less than ten minutes and raise the ship. When the water level between chambers was even, the gates in front opened and the ship sailed into the second lock, where the behemoth gates closed behind it and the filling process was repeated. One mile inland, they did it again at the Pedro Miguel Lock, altogether lifting the Russian destroyer a total of eighty-five feet above sea level.

Five hundred thirty-five feet in length, the **Admiral Chabanenko** took up almost half the usable space inside the first chamber. At four hundred forty-two feet, the troop transport ship stayed one chamber behind to allow for spacing. Both Russian captains were happy not to have their vessels trapped together in the same concrete prison if something were to go awry.

The Culebra Cut came next, the narrow 8.75-mile

trench that snaked its way through the Continental Divide past the town of Gamboa.

Ninety percent of the canal's original construction was still in use a century after it had been built. Marveling over the incredible feat of civil engineering, Captain Rykov invited Señor Berugatte to join his senior officers in the officers' wardroom when they reached the Chagres River arm of Gatun Lake. The pilot demurred at first, insisting that he stay on the bridge. Rykov assured him that there was a redundant radar screen in the wardroom, insisting that his new friend join him and the ship's senior leadership. Whether it was the offer of premium Beluga Gold Line vodka, or Rykov's powers of persuasion, Berugatte complied and participated in the four traditional Russian Navy toasts—first to the fleet, second to Mother Russia, third to the sea, and finally to the sailors' wives and sweethearts.

Señor Berugatte grew more familiar after four **stopka** of vodka—ten mil larger than an American shot glass. He lifted his arm to show the jaguar bracelet and gave a nod to the amulet on the captain's wrist.

"May I ask the significance, Captain?"

Rykov considered the question a moment. No one from his crew was likely to be so forward, which was a shame really.

"Arrluk," he said. "It is Siberian Yupik for 'orca,' hunters of the sea. This was a gift from my grandmother—"

The ship's intercom blared, extremely loud in the cramped confines of the wardroom.

"Captain to the bridge, please. Captain to the bridge."

The tremulous voice belonged to the officer of the watch, Senior Lieutenant Vasyli Stepanov. The flighty boy had once spied a harp seal lounging in the water and thought the ship was being boarded by pirates. He spooked at everything, and they were, after all, at least twelve miles from the sea in a lake surrounded by jungle. This was not a likely location for a naval emergency. Even so, Rykov rose to go address young Stepanov's problem, but he took a moment to finish explaining the amulet to Berugatte.

"My grandmother's people believe orca change into wolves in the winter and then back to whales in summer. Both are powerful hunters who help man when he is worthy. If she were here, she would have had me make a small offering of tobacco over the side of the ship as a gift for **arrluk**—also her pet name for me."

Berugatte opened his mouth to speak, but stopped when the **Chabanenko** gave an almost imperceptible shudder—more a muffled sound than actual movement. It would hardly have been noticeable to a landsman, but every seaman in the wardroom heard it . . . felt it. The shock waves of an explosion.

Sound traveled roughly four times faster in water than through air, slightly less in this heat. The ship's sonar had surely picked up the blast and Senior Lieutenant Stepanov had called to let the captain know. At twelve miles away, the audible wave would be some fifteen seconds behind.

Rykov shot a glance at his first officer. Neither man said it out loud, but they had just heard the container vessel **Jian Long** explode.

The captain lifted a handset from the wall below the intercom speaker, connecting him directly to the bridge.

"This is Rykov," he said. "I am on my way. Prepare to come about. Advise the **Ivan Gren** of our intentions."

He felt certain Captain Pagodin had come to the same instantaneous conclusion he had.

Berugatte's face, already red from the vodka, flushed a strangled purple. "Captain! What are you . . . This is madness—"

"Come with me," Rykov snapped. "I am going to need your help."

"But why?" The man's voice rose in pitch, like one of Panama's infamous mosquitoes. "We do not even know what caused . . ." He cocked his head at the captain. "You know what caused the explosion, don't you?"

Rykov stopped at the hatch and turned slowly to face Señor Berugatte. He looked past the flustered pilot, directly at his first officer.

"Mr. Orlov, place this man under guard. If he resists, order one of the infantrymen to shoot him."

Captain Rykov spoke in English to be certain the pilot understood every word, cold and dispassionate as cracking ice. "Señor Berugatte, I am turning this vessel around. I can do it with you or without you. The choice is yours."

The pilot pawed at his face with both hands, as if trying to wake from a bad dream or get some awful image out of his head. "What was it, Captain? What was the sound that could make you thumb your nose at international law?"

"You flatter yourselves," Rykov said. "Panama's bureaucratic timetables have hardly risen to the level of international law." He gave a little shrug, as if this conversation were beneath him. "And even if that were the case, this a ship of war. It does not sail away from the sound of a fight."

61

Arnie van Damm briefed Vice President Mark Dehart as they walked, giving him everything he knew before they even made it to the tunnels that connected the Eisenhower Executive Office Building to the White House and the underground Presidential Emergency Operations Center.

Unfortunately, **everything** he knew did not amount to much.

"The situation is unfolding rapidly," the CoS said. "I was already in the EEOB, on the cell phone with my counterpart in Botero's office. There was an explosion . . . and then gunfire . . ." Van Damm slowed, getting choked up. "I could hear brass hitting the ground, then the line went dead." He shook it off and picked up the pace.

Dehart glanced sideways at Special Agent Keenan Mulvaney as they walked. "And your people on the ground?"

"Our radios have apparently been compromised.

Cell signals are being jammed. The first report of an explosion came in at 12:09 local."

Dehart checked his watch. "That's six minutes ago."

Deputy National Security Adviser Robby Forrestal met them in the tunnel halfway between the EEOB and the PEOC. Tablet computer in hand, the Navy commander turned to match the vice president's stride, filling him in on the latest.

"The President is still unaccounted for, and the Secret Service is still under fire," Forrestal said.

"And the local police are just standing by?"

"They appear to be the ones shooting at the Secret Service. We believe Botero has been killed. It appears President Ryan has walked into a coup."

"Son of a bitch!" Mulvaney slammed a fist into his open palm as he walked. He apologized immediately.

"You're right," Dehart said. "This is a shitshow." He rolled his hand at Forrestal bidding him to continue.

"I understand there are Russian warships in the area."

Forrestal filled him in on the two ships in the canal.

"They left Panama Bay this morning, heading north," he said. "But they are now stopped near Gamboa at the entrance to the lake."

"Stopped." Dehart nodded, taking that in. "Do they have aircraft?"

"Four attack helicopters at most between them,"

Forrestal said. "The **Ivan Gren** would normally carry at least a company of Russian Naval Infantry. We're not sure at present."

"What assets do we have near Panama?" Dehart asked.

"On the Caribbean side," the commander said, "the Fourth Fleet is conducting naval exercises south of Jamaica. The **Gettysburg, Farragut,** and the **Boone**—a guided-missile cruiser, destroyer, and a frigate. The LHD **Wasp** is a little farther north with two companies of Marines. On the Pacific side, the **Abraham Lincoln** carrier strike group is abeam the southern tip of the Baja Peninsula."

"Damn it!" Dehart spat. "I thought we were having them loiter closer than that."

Forrestal looked at his tablet. He held up a finger, asking permission to read something coming in in real time.

"Sir," he said. "The Russian destroyer appears to be turning around."

"In the canal?"

"Yes, sir," Forrestal said.

"Can they do that?"

"They've already done it," Forrestal said. "They're in the Cut, heading toward Panama City."

"Arnie," Dehart said. "Let's get the president of the Russian Federation on the line as soon as we reach the PEOC." He shook his head, overcome with the urge to punch something. Someone. "If Russia is involved in this, it's an act of war."

"Mr. Vice President," Commander Forrestal said, "the U.S. Coast Guard national security cutter **Munro** is right there."

"Right where?" Dehart asked, sounding unconvinced.

"At the Port of Balboa . . . the southern opening of the canal, in a perfect position to greet the Russians."

62

Captain Rykov hove to, allowing Pagodin to pass with the **Ivan Gren** before he ordered the one-hundred-and-eighty-degree turn. He wanted the destroyer in the lead—and Pagodin had another mission to fulfill.

Moments after they'd heard the distant rumble, a junior lieutenant manning CIC noted a priority incoming call from the commander of the Northern Fleet. Rykov opted to take it from his at-sea cabin off the bridge. As he'd suspected, the container ship **Jian Long** now lay on the canal floor with a broken back, completely blocking the Cocoli Locks. Intelligence operatives from SVR—Russia's answer to the American CIA—reported a growing death toll and panic along the waterway. At first Panamanian authorities had hoped that the blast was an industrial accident, but word soon came in that at least three more devices had detonated in and around the presidential palace. This was an act of terrorism. With no way of knowing how many more bombs were in place, the Canal Authority and the SPI, who handled security on the locks, had shut down the Miraflores approach as well.

Until they had answers, the Panama Canal was closed. The government itself appeared to be under attack, possibly even by the Americans. Of course, Admiral Kozlov had been briefed by Anya Durova and knew exactly what was going on, but one never knew who was listening in on this sort of "secure" call. Some GRU intelligence puke on routine monitoring duty could decide he'd uncovered a conspiracy—which would have been troublesome, but right on the nose.

Captains Rykov and Pagodin were ordered to return directly to the Port of Balboa, which was exactly what they had already decided to do. They would offer their assistance and support to the poor embattled citizens of Panama, not as invaders, but as saviors, good citizens of the world who happened to be passing by when the trouble started.

Admiral Kozlov was an abrupt man, long on desired outcomes, but extremely curt on specifics of how to reach them. He left the details to his men in the field—and then brought them up on charges if they made a mistake, ending careers—or worse. Rykov preferred it that way. He would much rather live with the consequences of his own decisions than deal with the day-to-day idiocy of a fat-assed admiral who had forgotten port from starboard. It would not have mattered anyway. Captains were responsible for their ships in the event of a failure. Unlike the British Navy, Russians did not, as Voltaire put it, think it "wise to kill an admiral from time to time to encourage the others."

Captains, however, were left to luff in the wind for the errors of their crews.

Señor Berugatte could hardly keep still. At the moment, he rocked back and forth like a penguin with no place to go, staring out the window, white bubbles of spittle at the corners of his mouth. His left eye twitched and fluttered as he grunted his instructions directly to the helmsmen, dispensing with the previous formality of making suggestions to the captain first. Rykov didn't object.

Before, Berugatte's role had seemed largely a matter of regulation, as if Rykov did not know how to pilot his own vessel through a muddy ditch. Now he needed the man's expertise to keep the destroyer centered in the recently dredged channel. The helmsman took note of the instructions and used a combination of reverse screws and a bow thruster to spin the stocky vessel and get her back on a southerly course.

"You understand, Señor Berugatte," the captain said. "Your countrymen are in need of our assistance."

"This you told me," the pilot said. "But bombs, gunfire? How? Why? None of it makes sense."

"Events of this nature rarely do," Rykov said. "The point is that Russia is here to provide whatever assistance is necessary."

"Forgive me, but I fail to see how reversing course against my orders helps anything," Berugatte said.

Rykov raised a wary brow. "Your orders?"

Berugatte threw up his hands. "Regulations, then. And if, as you said, there is shooting at the presidential palace, what can a Russian warship do to help?"

"You would be surprised, **señor,**" Rykov said. "And anyway, my vessel is not alone. I feel sure you will soon receive a call from your counterpart aboard the **Ivan Gren** informing you that it is stopping in Gamboa to disembark two companies of our finest naval infantrymen with amphibious fighting vehicles." He put a hand on the pilot's shoulder, addressing him by the given name on his badge for the first time, at once consoling him and letting him know who was in charge. "You see, Alejandro, I said Russia is here to help and help is what we will do."

Approximately five hundred feet to stern, in the wide and sluggish Chagres River arm of Gatun Lake, Captain Pagodin was performing an identical one-hundred-eighty-degree turn on the **Ivan Gren,** likely against the express will of a pilot who was just as disturbed by the action as Alejandro Berugatte. Once the transport ship was again headed south, it would proceed to the port of Gamboa, where two hundred naval infantrymen from the 155th Separate Marine Brigade would take their fighting vehicles up the muddy banks and race down the road toward Panama City ahead of the ships, ensuring compliance from Canal Authority lock controllers when the warships arrived, before rolling through Panama City. It was mostly for show, but what a show it would be. Rykov was not usually prone to spectacles, but even he had to admit that the next few hours were going to be glorious.

Señor Berugatte took a half step away from the console and gave a shuddering sigh as soon as the destroyer's new heading was established.

"I know you say you are here to help," he said. The poor man's chin trembled as if he might burst into tears at any moment. "But I must tell you, Captain, this endeavor is extremely dangerous. By this time, many other vessels would have already passed through the locks prior to the container ship's explosion."

Rykov looked at the radarman, who gave a nod to the display in front of him. "He is right, Captain. I am showing AIS signals from six vessels in the Culebra Cut. The largest appears to be the Greek container ship **Apelles.**"

Berugatte gave an excited nod, believing he'd gained an ally. "See! It would be extremely dangerous to meet any large vessel in the Cut. The **Apelles** is beyond large, a Neo-Panamax, over forty meters wide!"

"He will move out of our way," Rykov said, his certitude surprising even himself.

The pilot put a hand on his forehead. "Captain! We are speaking of a narrow canal. There is no place for another ship to go!"

Rykov leaned forward, studying the electronic chart. **"Apelles..."** he mused. "What is her beam?"

"Forty-two meters, Captain," the young radar-man said.

Rykov glanced up at the pilot. "How wide is the Culebra Cut?"

"A little over one hundred ninety meters on the straightaways," Berugatte said. "Slightly more on the curves. But that does not—"

Rykov cut him off. "We are comparatively slender at only nineteen meters. That is only sixty-one meters in total." He scoffed. "Leaving us with . . . one hundred and twenty-nine meters to spare. That is over four hundred feet."

"Forgive me for saying this, Captain," Berugatte said. "But you are dead wrong. The Cut is plagued by frequent mudslides. Ships must stay in the dredged portion, well away from the banks." His eyes fluttered as he did the calculations in his head. "Giving both ships plenty of standoff . . . and accounting for their individual beams . . . that leaves us with forty-five meters between the two vessels as they pass—at best, a mere one hundred and fifty feet."

"You assume I care if the **Apelles** runs aground." Rykov snatched a microphone from the control panel and passed it to the pilot. "Then you must warn your pilot counterparts on the oncoming vessels to give us the road."

Berugatte broadcast the situation, instigating a flurry of cursing. The arguments were predominately in Spanish, but Rykov thought he got the gist of them.

"Well?" he snapped. "Will they yield the passage?"

"There is nowhere to yield to." Berugatte shook his head. "By law, each of those vessels have the right-of-way. Santos, the man piloting the container ship **Apelles,** is a friend of mine. If he were in my shoes you would have to shoot him before he complied."

"Then he is fortunate he is not on my ship," Rykov said.

"Captain," Berugatte pleaded. "Santos is extremely stubborn, especially when he is in the right. He was a Navy captain himself when Panama still had a military. You will not intimidate him."

Rykov darkened. "What does he say, exactly?"

"He says **Apelles** is so large it has right-of-way by tonnage."

Captain Rykov gave a contemplative nod. "What are you afraid of?"

"What?"

"As a Canal Authority pilot," Rykov said, "what

are you afraid will happen when we pass the container ship?"

"I fear the sloughing banks will force us to pass much closer than one hundred and fifty feet. You are no doubt familiar with the Bernoulli's principle regarding fluids and pressure."

Rykov nodded. "You think the water will be slower between our passing ships, decreasing the pressure and . . . sucking the hulls of our ships together."

"The danger of that happening is real," Berugatte said. "Especially if we are forced to pass closer than we hope."

Now the captain darkened. "But if the **Apelles** is not moving, we will sail by with little decrease in pressure between the two vessels."

"But she **is** moving," the pilot said.

"She won't be." Rykov snatched the mic from the console. "Captain to CIC, make ready for Moskit missile launch."

The weapons officer answered immediately, just as Rykov knew he would.

"Aye, Captain."

"Mr. Orlov, get me a firing solution for the **Apelles.** Provide your findings to CIC. Advise them to fire on my command."

"Aye, Captain," the first officer said, moving to the electronic chart at the helm as calmly as if Rykov had just asked him to check the water temperature.

Berugatte began to hyperventilate.

"Captain, what are you doing?"

Rykov looked up from the screen, darkening. "In less than one minute, my sailors will be ready to launch what the Americans call a 'Sunburn' anti-ship missile. It is a glorious weapon, traveling at some twenty-eight hundred kilometers per hour . . . **Apelles** is . . . a breath away. We will see who has right-of-way by tonnage when the Greek container ship is an island of smoldering metal."

"Captain, you would not—"

"Yes," Rykov said. "I absolutely would, and it is your job to convince your friend Santos of my sincerity."

The pilot took a deep breath and exhaled slowly, finally coming to grips with the fact that he had no choice.

"We should be able to pass the **Apelles** safely enough," he said. "But I assure you, there is **no** room for error."

Rykov gave the terrified pilot a rare smile.

"Then see that we make no errors."

63

Mary Pat Foley's two-vehicle motorcade had just crossed Friendship Avenue, the boulevard that cut through the five-hundred-acre Metropolitan Park, when the first reports of trouble poured in over the Secret Service radios. The U.S. embassy was just over a mile to the north. Brett Johnson, the special agent leading the detail, ordered the driver to punch it and make a run for the gates.

The order given, he turned to look over his shoulder from the front passenger seat.

"We're not sure what's going on yet, ma'am. Reports of gunfire and bombs. That's all we know."

Foley stifled a scream. She wanted to throw her phone through the window. Every tower and cell circuit in Panama was busy. She couldn't get through to Ryan, the embassy, anyone.

She wanted to ask for Brett Johnson's satellite phone, but he was using it, and at this point, his need to coordinate security trumped her desire to know what was going on.

"Nobody's answering you, either?" she asked.

"No, ma'am," he said. "Everyone's priority is the President."

"As is mine," she said, sounding harsher than she wanted to. "Sorry. Do we know where he is?"

"No, ma'am. We were just told to stay off the air as much as possible. Sounds like someone has access to one of our handhelds."

Foley's heart sank. Secret Service agents didn't just give up their radios. If an agent had lost theirs . . .

Feeling caged and helpless in the backseat, she looked to her left in time to see a huge ball of fire and smoke roll skyward beyond the trees to the east. The south entry locks to the canal lay in that direction, maybe three miles away.

"That was a big son of a bitch . . ." she said under her breath. "Holy shit!"

Her phone began to buzz in the front pocket of her slacks. She fished it out, hoping it was Jack letting her know he was safe.

It was Ed.

She answered, intent on keeping the call short.

"Sweetheart," she said. "I don't know what you've heard, but I'm okay. I really can't talk—"

"Mary Pat!" he snapped. "Listen to me. You could be in danger."

"Wait," she said. "What?" She kept the reports of gunfire and bombs to herself. "What do you mean?"

A deep breath came from the other end of the line. Then sirens. Tires skidding to a stop.

Sirens?

She forgot about her own problems and focused on her husband.

"What the hell, Edward?"

"Someone just tried to kill me," he said. "Pretty sure he planned to use a claw hammer."

She leaned forward, plugging her ear with one finger to block out the background noise.

"Are you okay?"

"I am fine . . . and the bad guy is dead. Don't worry about me. Remember what Randell Green said? Something is going on down in Panama. I'm afraid my incident could be connected to you."

"I'm afraid so, too," Foley said.

The Dodge suddenly shook, as if grabbed by an unseen fist. Startled, Foley gasped in surprise as another fireball rolled above the trees ahead at the entrance to embassy housing.

Brett ordered a one-eighty. The driver, a tall, Tarzan-looking thirtysomething named Reed Parker, had obviously trained ad nauseam in evasive driving. He dropped the transmission into second, then cranked the wheel hard to the left, forcing the Charger into a controlled skid. The rear end broke loose and slid around, pointing the nose back south, the way they had come. He threw the car in high gear again and punched it.

"Yes!" Brett said. "Take us back to Albrook airport now."

Ed had to have heard the squealing tires loud and clear over the phone.

"Are you okay?"

"Yes," Foley said. "And no."

She brought him up to speed with everything she knew, which wasn't much. "I'm in good hands," she said.

"And Jack?"

"Unknown," Foley said. "Listen, I have to—"

The driver tapped the brakes a split second before Brett yelled, "Ambush! Ambush! Ambush! Ma'am! Keep your head down!"

Foley slid down in the backseat, but not before she caught sight of two SUVs blocking the road in front of them. At least two men with guns stood beside each vehicle.

Her driver slammed on the brakes, skidding to a stop before throwing the Charger in reverse and then punching the gas to accelerate backward to the north. He avoided executing a one-eighty right away so as not to put the rear of the Charger, and therefore Foley, directly in the line of fire. The Jeep Cherokee follow car, still heading south, shot past, putting itself between the ambush and the Dodge Charger. Only then did Foley's driver turn the car around, this time in a perfectly executed J-turn at fifteen miles an hour in reverse.

It was Foley's turn to say, "Yes! Way to go, Parker!"

This guy deserved a medal.

Still low in her seat, she heard the pop of distant gunfire, like a stick smacking a tin shed. She knew her agents and the CIA team in the follow Jeep had MP5s. But these shots came from larger rifles. AKs maybe. And the volume of the blasts said they were pointed in her direction.

"Son of a bitch!" Brett said through clenched teeth.

Pumped with adrenaline, it took a moment for Foley to realize that though the Charger had recovered from the skidding J-turn, it still wobbled. Something was wrong.

The driver cursed. "The tire's come off the rim!"

More gunfire cracked behind them.

The driver glanced sideways at Brett, obviously listening to radio traffic over his earpiece that Foley wasn't privy to.

"They're being overrun, boss," he whispered.

"Just drive!"

The car began to shimmy violently, then a second tire blew, sending the Charger careening into the ditch.

Brett turned, half leaning over the seat.

"What kind of shoes are you wearing?"

Stunned, Foley blinked back at him. "What?"

"Shoes!" the agent snapped.

"Flats—"

"Good," he said. "We need to run for the trees."

"Brett, I—"

"Ma'am," Brett said, "our agents in the follow are taking fire from six armed individuals. They have a limited supply of ammunition. Our vehicle is dead in the—"

"Got it," Foley said. "I'll follow you."

Reed Parker bailed out of the Charger, leaving the driver's-side door open wide, offering conceal-ment, if not actual cover from oncoming gunfire.

"Get her out of here," he said, taking a position with his pistol behind the A-pillar between the door and the windshield. "I'll hold here."

"Bullshit," Brett said from behind the wheel well, where he shielded Foley with his body. "Cover us until we reach the wood line, then haul ass to the trees."

"Roger that," Parker said. "I'm right behind you."

Brett looked down at Foley. "Ready?"

She nodded. "I wouldn't mind a gun."

Brett gave her a Glock 42 from his ankle. "There you go. Now stay low."

It was only after they'd crashed through the waist-high saw grass and elephant's ears that Foley realized she still had Ed on speaker in her pocket.

"Can you hear me, hon?" she said, running be-side Brett Johnson into the dark jungle shadows.

"I hear you," came the reply.

"We're in the Metropolitan Park," Foley said as she ran, making herself heard and understood as best she could between panting breaths. "North of . . ." She glanced over at Brett Johnson.

He filled in the blank. "Friendship Avenue."

"North of Friendship Avenue, across the road,

but southeast of the embassy. Taking fire from at least six assailants. Not sure, but I think I got a look at Sabine Gorshkova. We could really use some help here . . . I need to call John Clark."

She heard the sickening series of beeps from her pocket, letting her know the call had dropped.

"We should keep moving," Johnson said. "Put as much ground between them and us as we can."

"What about Reed?"

Automatic gunfire rattled through the thick foliage from the direction of the road. Monkeys screamed in the treetops. A flock of startled parakeets exploded skyward.

Brett Johnson checked the magazine on his MP5, chewing on his bottom lip. "Director Foley," he said. "I can't worry about Parker right now. I can only worry about you."

She fished the phone out of her pocket. No signal. She cursed. "We need some help."

"Yes, we do," Johnson said, gathering himself up to run again. "But everyone else is busy looking for POTUS."

"Maybe not," Foley said. "That is, if my husband got my message."

64

It was three hundred miles from Cartagena to Panama City, and Clark wanted to be there yesterday. Myrna Chaman, one of Yao's WINDWARD STATION operators, had been working full-time to find the teams transport since Clark learned the G550 was down. It sounded like she'd found two aircraft that could make the trip in less than two hours—still far too long, but it would have to do.

Clark drove while Yao navigated the quickest route through traffic to the general-aviation side of Rafael Nuñez airport, on the other side of the runway from the Hendley Associates' wounded G550.

As far as WINDWARD STATION was concerned, Blanca Pakulova/Gorshkova was the best lead they'd had since the sushi chef. She was beyond cooperative, but surely had countless details in her head that she didn't even know were relevant. She needed to be debriefed, but in order to do that, they had to keep her safe. Sabine was the primary target, even more so now with the new information about her leadership position in the Camarilla. Even so, she was in the wind, where Blanca was a bird in the hand—and her life was in danger. Five of Yao's operators stayed behind to get her to the U.S., while Yao, Ward, and Lopez from his team accompanied the Campus operators to Panama to begin the hunt for Sabine in the middle of . . . whatever it was that was going on.

Cobb and Midas sat in the back of the Taurus. The others piled in the van with Eric Ward.

Clark looked in the rearview to make sure Midas was paying attention and then spoke over his shoulder, double-checking the important stuff.

"Dom, Jack, and Adara grabbed the guns from the hotel?"

"They did, boss," Midas said. "It's all in the van. Junior's ready to invade Panama, if you get my meaning."

Clark glanced over his shoulder. "Is he good to go?"

"Jack?" Midas said. "Yeah. He's channeling his anger. But I wouldn't want to get in his way right now."

"I know how he feels," Clark said.

Yao lifted his phone, checking the route, and then told Clark to make a left. "These are small planes," he said. "Space is limited."

"Understood," Midas said. "They left the toiletries, clothes, and all that other unimportant shit at the hotel." He turned to Cobb. "And that, my friend, is why we never put our names on our skivvies. We abandon shit overseas all the time."

"Myrna's got us a Beechcraft Baron and a Piper Navajo," Yao said. "Lopez tells me they'll cruise around two hundred and thirty miles an hour and change. That gets us to Panama in a little under ninety minutes from wheels up."

"That's cruise speed," Clark said. "I'm not concerned about saving fuel as long as we get there fast."

"Agreed," Yao said. "Lopez is a hotshot pilot. I'll tell him not to spare the horses."

Mandy Cobb leaned forward from the backseat. "Who's your Navajo pilot?"

"Not one of my team," Yao said. "CIA does business with a couple of charter companies in Central and South America. Myrna says this is one of those."

"Narco . . ." Clark mused.

"It's better not to ask if we want to get out of here today," Yao said.

The general aviation fixed-base operation where Myrna had chartered the aircraft was on the east side of the Cartagena airport in the middle of a stony plain of sun-bleached ground. Bits of tattered garbage hung on dessicated shrubs, baking in the glaring heat of the sun. Clark pulled over at a small guard shack with a Yamaha 250 in the shade out front. Yao gave the security guy two hundred U.S. dollars and bypassed the requirement to sign in. Clark got the idea that the unofficial fee was on a sliding scale. A Taurus might pay less than a Mercedes, but Americans paid a premium no matter what they were driving.

Myrna Chaman arrived first and opened the gate so they could pull out to the ramp. Clark breathed a sigh of relief at the sight of six planes, single engines and twins, on tie-downs in front of a modern glass and concrete office. Yao's description notwithstanding, he'd expected something like a ratty biplane held together with duct tape and haywire. Here, everything was clean squared away—a reflection of the U.S. government contracts (and narco-trafficking dollars) that kept the business flush.

Myrna met Clark and Yao at the office door and whistled over their shoulders at the rest of the team, who were hurriedly stacking guns and gear from the vehicles by the aircraft. She waved her hands, warning them off the twin-engine Piper Navajo.

"That one's a no-go," she shouted. "The pilot's got issues, so we're down to one plane." She turned to Yao. "Sorry, boss. He seemed fine over the phone."

A thirtysomething man in chino shorts and a white polo stepped to the open door and leaned against the jamb. Bloodshot eyes and a sappy grin revealed the issues Myrna was talking about.

"I'm good," the kid said, licking his lips and squinting at the sun. "I'm not drinking."

Clark stifled the urge to throttle him. "The hell you say."

"No," he said. "Really. Microdosing some ketamine for anxiety. That's all. I'll be good in a jiff."

"Yeah," Yao said. "That's not happening."

Clark looked out at their pile of gear. They'd trimmed it down to nothing but necessities, but it was still a stretch to think about cramming it and eleven operators on two aircraft. One plane was a shitshow.

Yao took a step forward, crowding the man, obviously pissed. "No other pilots?"

"The bookkeeper can fly the One Seventy-Two," the pilot said, blinking, as if he were trying—and failing—to focus. "It needs a prop, though . . ."

Lopez and Cobb trotted over to see what was going on, catching enough of the conversation to see what was going on.

"I can fit myself and five passengers in the Beechcraft," he said. "Let me know who and we'll get her loaded."

The rest of the team came up, knowing that some of them were about to get cut. Jack looked like he might break the micro-dosing idiot in half.

Cobb faced outbound, studying the neat line of parked aircraft. She turned quickly and pointed to a sleek single-engine low wing on the south end of the apron.

"What about that one?" she asked the microdoser.

He leaned out to get a better look. "The Malibu? She's fast."

"Is she for rent?" Cobb asked.

"It's a moot point," Yao said. "Unless you know how to fly it."

"I do," Cobb said. "My dad owns a percentage of one with three friends. I've got about eighty hours in it."

Chilly, standing in the back of the group, gave a little gasp. "No shit," he mumbled. "You fly a plane, too."

She gave a humble shrug. "It'll hold six including the pilot. We should be good to go."

Clark looked at Chavez and gave a nod.

"You heard her," Chavez said. "Let's get loaded and haul ass!"

The kid sucked air through his teeth. He hadn't microdosed so much that he couldn't smell a profit.

"That's an expensive plane. Pressurized. Retractable gear, it's considerably more expensive than the Navajo."

"No," Clark said. "It's not." He took the dizzy kid by the shoulder and gave a firm squeeze, enough to convey his intentions. "Let's go get the keys."

Clark and Yao rode in the Beechcraft Baron with Lopez, Chavez, and Adara, wanting to use the time to strategize. The others flew in the Piper with Cobb. It was a faster airplane by roughly ten knots, so it made sense they carried the heavier payload.

Myrna Chaman was staying behind to help guard Blanca Pakulova, so she took care of the payment and last-minute paperwork so the others could get on the road.

Traffic was light with most of the country sitting in front of televisions or surfing the internet, trying to find out what was going on in the neighboring country. Cobb took off first, bringing up the Malibu's gear soon after rotation and then banking to the south in a smooth, sweeping arc. If she was nervous, it didn't show from the ground.

Lopez took off moments later, as soon as he got clearance, and fell in behind the Piper. Lopez pushed his normal cruise speed of two hundred thirty-six miles per hour a hair closer to the Piper's two-forty-five.

"Where'd you find this kid?" Yao asked. "I might try to snatch her away from you for the Agency."

Clark started to answer, but his phone buzzed. Hungry for news, he fished it out of his pocket.

"John?" the voice on the other end said—measured, but out of breath, like he was in a hurry. "It's Ed. Ed Foley."

"This is John. I hear you, Ed." Clark shut up after that. Interjecting or finishing other people's sentences was anathema to good intelligence work. When someone called to brief, you let them speak without interruption.

"MP's in trouble in Panama!" Foley said; bottom

line up front. It was no wonder he was strained. "As of . . . fifteen minutes ago, she was in Metropolitan Park in Panama City north of . . . Friendship Avenue. I was on the phone with her. It sounded like her detail was run off the road on the way to the U.S. embassy. She says at least six shooters, one of them is a . . . Sabine Gorshkova."

Clark resisted the urge to ask questions. Ed was retired, unaware of most of the intel Mary Pat was privy to. He would certainly be familiar with the existence of the Camarilla. They'd made the news many times after San Antonio. Sabine Gorshkova was probably new to him.

"There was gunfire in the background," Foley continued. "I could hear Brett Johnson's voice, so she's still with her Secret Service detail. I don't know where you are, but she told me to call you, then the call dropped."

Clark waited a beat in case Foley had anything else.

Then, "We're leaving Colombia for Panama City," he said. "Sounds like the shit's hit the fan down there. I'm sure the phone circuits are jammed. Call me back with any updates when you get in touch with her again." Clark smiled, hoping it showed in his voice and gave the man a little consolation.

"John," Foley said, more than a little tentative.

"Go ahead."

"This thing at the presidential palace . . . I'm watching it on the news right now, cell-phone video from someone across the road by the seawall. It looks bad. Entire front portico has collapsed. Do you know if Jack made it in?"

"I do not," Clark said.

"Okay, it's just that . . . everyone in Panama is going to be focused on nothing but finding the President."

"Not everyone, Ed," Clark said. "Not everyone."

Clark used the satellite phone to contact his boss as soon as he ended the call with Ed Foley. Hendley had nothing new from his end, but Clark brought him up to speed on their situation and asked him to provide the information to anyone and everyone up the chain, including Langley, the FBI, and the Secret Service. With any luck someone else would reach Mary Pat long before they made the flight across the Caribbean. Not only did they have to fly there, but they had to land, procure vehicles, and then get themselves to Metropolitan Park, which, from what Clark could glean from the Web, was a jungle. Phone circuits were overloaded, but he busied himself arranging rental vehicles over the internet. If there weren't any cars when he got there, they would steal what they needed.

Yao, in the aft-facing seat across from Clark, was having about as much luck. It was impossible to get through to the CIA or anyone at the embassy on the phone. Yao knew the station chief, Claire

Nguyen, well enough to have her personal cell. The line wouldn't connect long enough for him to leave a voicemail. He sent a text about Foley's predicament and the new information about Sabine, on the off chance that it would get through. Next, he contacted the WINDWARD STATION operators with Blanca and asked them to send a cable with the same information. So far, they'd heard nothing.

Panama Station had gone dark.

Yao was able to reach someone at Langley. He chatted with them for a few minutes, growing animated with each passing word. He ended the call and put on his green David Clark headset.

"Change of plans," he said over the intercom so Lopez could hear. "Adjust your course for Colón instead of Panama City."

"Roger that," Lopez said, turning a hair to the north. "I'll let Mandy know."

"Turns out we have some assets in Panama after all," Yao said. "Fort Bragg Security Assistance Training command had some TAFT guys work with Panamanian law enforcement to carve out a little spot in the jungle at what used to be Fort Sherman."

TAFT was a Technical Assistance Field Team, U.S. Army soldiers who trained foreign counterparts in their areas of expertise, often drug interdiction, riverine, and jungle operations.

"Fort Sherman?"

"On the Caribbean side," Yao said. "Across the mouth of the bay from Colón. The fort was a jungle operations training center back in the day. There's a little marina there now, but the jungle's reclaimed most of the grounds since we turned it back over to Panama. At least it had until our guys carved out their little training nook. The administration is trying to make it permanent, but they haven't gotten a deal papered yet."

"Hang on," Clark said. "You said 'had.'"

"The Bragg guys were there for nearly a year. Most of them rotated out three days ago."

Clark rubbed his eyes, feeling a whopper of a headache coming on. "They're not going to be much good to us, Adam, not if they left three days ago."

"Most of them left," Yao said. "A couple of guys married Panamanian wives during their tours. They volunteered to stay behind and get the equipment squared away."

"Okay . . ."

"One of those guys is a pilot," Yao said. "Flies their MH-6 Little Bird . . . which is still on-site. They have two, but only one pilot . . . And anyway, you know helicopters. It takes three in the inventory to keep one working bird in the air."

"Colón's what, fifty miles from Panama City?"

"Not even that," Yao said. "Pick your best shooters and we'll go get Director Foley."

Clark gave a slow nod.

"And take care of Sabine Gorshkova in the process." A sudden thought occurred to him. "That is, if this pilot is there and we can find him and the choppers haven't been crated for a C-130 . . ."

65

FIFTEEN MINUTES AFTER THE FIRST DETONATION

Vice President Mark Dehart's wife, Dee, was already in the PEOC sitting quietly with Cathy Ryan when he and van Damm arrived. The First Lady was remarkably calm, but sat hunched over slightly, leaning on her knees, clutching what looked like a square of heavy wool fabric between her fingers. Dee gave her husband a quick kiss—she knew it would calm him.

"How's she holding up?" Dehart asked his wife.

"Better than I would," Dee whispered. "She got ahold of her two eldest kids. Her daughter's on her way here now."

"Very well," Dehart said. "Thanks for taking care of her."

"You bet," Dee said. "Now go do your thing."

She left Dehart where he was and escorted the

First Lady into the President's quarters, away from the hubbub of what was essentially a military communications center—an underground version of the Situation Room. Both were known as the "Meat Grinder" for good reason.

There were few situations more volatile than an "out of pocket" President after a bombing. Many of the National Security Council principals had beaten Dehart to the bunker and were already seated around the conference table. Live feeds of what looked to be cell-phone footage played on the flat-screen monitors along the wall above them.

Secretaries of Homeland Security, Defense, and State, along with the attorney general and the chairman of the Joint Chiefs all stood until Dehart took his seat at the head of the table. It was a place he'd hoped never to sit again.

The Secret Service would normally wait outside the Situation Room during this sort of meeting, but under the circumstances, the special agent in charge positioned himself near the door so he could keep his protectee in sight.

"Where are we?" Dehart asked.

CIA director Canfield entered the room next with his Latin America desk division chief, Lexi Glazier. They heard the question and Canfield gave a nod to Glazier.

"If I may, Mr. Vice President," she said. "Our latest reports say the shooting has stopped inside the palace, but Panamanian authorities have yet to allow the Secret Service entry."

SecState Scott Adler spoke next. "Ambassador McCabe has requested a meeting with the minister of foreign affairs, but his office says he is not reachable. He could be stalling, or they could be telling the truth. It's virtually impossible to reach anyone in Panama at the moment, even on a landline."

"Damage?" Dehart asked.

"Here's what we've pieced together," Canfield said. "Mostly from local news reports and internet feeds. Two explosive devices in front of the presidential palace. The detonation wasn't captured on video, but our EOD personnel believe it was a car bomb from the aftermath. It was close enough to the building that it collapsed the portico and blocked the main doors—which blocked Secret Service CAT from making entry. Many of them appear to have been injured in the blast." Canfield shot a side-eye at Mulvaney and the two agents beside him. "Unknown number of casualties at this point. Three larger vehicle-borne devices were detonated within minutes of the two palace bombs. One in front of the Ministry of Public Security, one in a small shopping center adjacent to the U.S. embassy. A third much larger device destroyed the Chinese container ship **Jian Long** while it was inside the newer locks of the canal. There are unconfirmed reports that President Botero has been shot and killed. Vice President Carré and President Ryan both remain unaccounted for."

Dehart loosened his tie and gave a nod to the secretary of defense.

"Bob?"

"The USS **Abraham Lincoln** is on the Pacific side, still too far away, but the **Theodore Roosevelt** carrier strike group was heading toward the east coast of South America when the events occurred. They were meant to provide a measure of security during the upcoming summit. At this time they are in international waters off the coast of Venezuela, eight hundred sixty nautical miles northeast of Panama City. A division of four F/A-18 Super Hornets is launching from the **Roosevelt** as we speak. Panama has no Air Force to be concerned with, but the Russian ships **Ivan Gren** and **Admiral Chabanenko** are both outfitted with advanced air defense systems. One of the Hornets is a Growler. It will be able to jam the Russian's guidance systems, but they will see that as an act of aggression."

"Good," Dehart said. "I want them to see us and hear us."

"Absolutely, sir," SecDef Bob Burgess said. "Their presence will be felt by everyone in Panama. I guarantee it."

"I'm not a fighter pilot," Dehart said. "But eight hundred miles is a stretch for an F-18 isn't it? Do we already have a tanker in the sky down there?"

"One is in route," Burgess said. "But you're right.

Some of the Super Hornets on the **Roosevelt** are set up with buddy system fueler capability. These 'tanker' F-18s will launch first, fly with the division for roughly three hundred miles, top them off, then return to the ship. They'll repeat the process, meeting the division en route on their return trip."

The attorney general was next with his report. A former special agent with the FBI, Dan Murray and Jack Ryan went back decades. The strain in his voice was palpable.

"Mr. Vice President, FBI HRT and Delta are both spooling up for imminent departure. It will, of course, take time, but SOP is to get them moving immediately."

"Agreed," Dehart said. "I don't know exactly what we're dealing with here. But if this is, as we suspect, a coup, I'm really concerned about civilian casualties if we go in hot."

"No doubt," Murray said. "I spoke with the HRT commander just before your arrival. He understands."

"Same with CAG," Burgess said, referring to the 1st Special Forces Operational Detachment–Delta, commonly referred to as Delta Force or Combat Applications Group.

Dehart checked his watch.

"I read nineteen minutes after the first detonation," he said. "You should be commended for getting so much rolling so quickly. Now keep it going."

An Air Force major working comms approached

the table. "Mr. Vice President," he said. "I have Russian Federation president Yermilov on the secure line. The interpreter is standing by."

Dehart took a deep breath. The last time he'd sat in for Jack Ryan, he'd had to bully the president of China. "Let's have him, then."

Thank you for taking my call, President Yermilov," Dehart said. "As I imagine you are aware, we are more than a little concerned about President Ryan."

"Of course, of course," Yermilov said in accented English. "We, too, are worried for our good friend Jack Ryan."

"We are also concerned about the effect of these events on Panama."

"**Da** . . . as am I . . ."

"My advisers reminded me a moment ago that the USSR joined as the thirty-sixth signatory to the Treaty Concerning the Permanent Neutrality and Operation of the Panama Canal in 1988. I assume that holds sway with Russia."

"It does," Yermilov said. "We would have it no other way. Protection of the canal is paramount. That is why my ships are returning to the Pacific port—to ensure stability and peace. The U.S. would be doing the same thing if you happened to be close by."

"We look forward to working together with you in this regard."

"I believe we have it . . . as you say . . . handled."

"I disagree," Dehart said. "Respectfully. Nothing has been handled until President Ryan is safe and secure."

"I will tell my people to keep an eye out for him," Yermilov said. It might have been his second language, but the remark came across a hair too flippant for Dehart.

"We would not only appreciate that," Dehart said, "we would require it. Let me ask, Mr. President, have you ever plowed a field with a tractor?"

"Have I . . . what now?"

There was a mumble on the line as the interpreter filled him in.

"I have people to plow my fields," Yermilov said. He was apparently over being diplomatic.

"So the answer is no?"

"It is."

"Well, I have, thousands of acres in fact, and I will tell you, if you want straight furrows, you must focus on a single point at the end of the row—your objective. You cannot get caught up by all the distractions around you."

"That makes sense," Yermilov said. "But I do not think this is the time for stories."

"Or the time for subterfuge and ruses," Dehart said. "So I will be blunt, President Yermilov. I am not a politician. I am a farmer sitting in a politician's chair. I do not know how to bluff or posture. I have no other objective at this moment than getting President Ryan back unharmed—and I will obliterate anything or anyone who gets in my way." He took a breath, held it for a count of four, and then calmly said, "I look forward to working with you to resolve this matter peacefully."

He ended the call before Yermilov could respond.

Adler tapped the table with the end of his pen. "Due respect, but those will be construed as fighting words."

"Good," Dehart said. "What's next?"

66

York and Long, the United States Secret Service agents behind the presidential palace at Avenue B and San Pablo Street, had been standing post with SPI Presidential Guard Battalion officer Gomez since long before the President's arrival—long enough for them all to show pics of their families, the fish that they'd caught, to start telling jokes.

It was hard to point a gun at someone you'd been joking with for the past hour and a half, let alone shoot at them.

While SPI Presidential Guard Battalion and Presidential Protection Group officers were engaged in a tense standoff and sporadic gunfire, York and Long and Gomez stood together at their barricade, firearms at the ready, but certainly not pointed at one another—and tried to figure out what the hell was going on. All the radios were either tits up or compromised. There was no way to either get through or to trust what you heard if you did. Gomez thought he recognized a Russian accent, but since it was a Russian accent speaking Spanish, neither York nor Long clocked it. Word had come over the Secret Service radio that POTUS had made it out. Then someone else said that was a lie (the supposed Spanish Russian accent). An English voice none of them recognized advised all "special Secret Service agents" to report to the front of the palace on Eloy Alfaro Avenue. Apart from the shit syntax, Long and York knew that was wrong. No way any Service brass would call everyone off post at this point in the game. Still another voice over Gomez's radio warned SPI officers that a secret American kill squad was liquidating anyone who might have witnessed His Excellency President Botero's assassination.

One thing was for sure, someone wanted the two factions to fight in a bad way.

It sounded like the building had collapsed, and if they could believe it, the director general of the PNP was on his way to "sort things out."

A soft voice drew the men's attention down the street. A uniformed PNP officer approached from the west, where he'd coasted up on his motorcycle. His duty weapon was holstered. He held his hands high over his head.

"May I approach?" he said, pausing twenty feet out. He repeated himself in Spanish and English.

York looked at Gomez, who shrugged. "He could have come out shooting."

Long kept his MP5K low, and his finger along the trigger guard, but watched the newcomer for any sudden moves.

He introduced himself as Sergeant Fredi Perez, special assistant to Major Gabriella Canto.

"No way," Gomez said. He looked at the Secret Service agents. "That's the badass who was just here. She stopped a plot to kill the president one day and then killed three dudes trying to murder her the next. Badass." He looked up at Sergeant Perez. "She was just here maybe . . . what?"

"About a minute before all hell broke loose," Long said.

"It's very important I find her," Perez said. "She suspected something like this might happen. We believe one of our superiors might be involved."

"Who?" York asked.

Perez rolled his lips. "I'd rather not say. I don't want to add to all this confusion if we are wrong."

"That's the smartest thing I've heard all day," Long said.

"What I would like to do is go in," Perez said. "Confront him myself . . . And find Major Canto if she is still alive."

"You'll probably get shot," Gomez said.

"Maybe," Perez said.

Long and York stepped aside, looking at Gomez.

"Up to you," York said. "But someone needs to do something."

Vice President Carré led the others through the tunnel, using the beam of Gary Montgomery's flashlight to find his way. Ryan followed with the hulking agent right by his side, ready to yank him out of the jaws of whatever subterranean troglodyte they happened to encounter. Major Canto brought up the rear, adding her own light to the mix when the tunnel turned or doglegged. Otherwise, she saved her battery. Half an hour in, Ryan decided he needed to start carrying a flashlight, and a knife, and possibly a gun, considering the way this was turning out. Gary and Cathy would have fits if he even joked about that. No. He was past that. Others would do the shooting of things that needed to be shot.

"The church should be this way," Carré said as the tunnel began to angle downward, gently at first, then steep enough that they needed both lights to keep their feet on the moist stone. "Though I must admit, it would be very easy to become turned around."

"Wherever it comes out," Ryan said, "we need to get you in front of a camera as quickly as we can. If President Botero is dead as we suspect, and you are missing, the country will be in limbo."

"Who is next?" Montgomery asked.

"No one," Carré said. "At least not specifically.

Our constitution states that the cabinet must appoint a new president in the event both president and vice president die."

"And with the bombing," Ryan said, "they will need a leader more than ever."

Montgomery darkened. "I'm not comfortable getting you outside before we know what's going on out there."

"Understood," Ryan said. "We'll play by your rules when the time comes."

Montgomery said nothing, but gave Ryan a look that said there was no question that they were going to play by his rules.

Major Canto took a few steps forward, playing her light across the wall ahead where the tunnel made a sharp turn. For a split second, Ryan thought it was a dead end. When they rounded the corner, he realized that's exactly what it was—just not the way he'd thought.

Guerra ordered two SPI contractors he knew to be Camarilla to accompany him as he searched the interior of the palace. In truth, he asked them nicely. Camarilla operatives did not take orders from the local PNP, even if he was a commissioner. The younger one, about thirty, had a goatee. The other one, probably in his mid-forties, was taller, well-muscled, but had a substantial gut. Maddeningly they insisted on addressing him as LA PULGA.

Guerra called them Goat and Fatty . . . in his head.

Apart from the grand entry hall, the inside of the building was cluttered, but not burned or structurally damaged. There was blood, lots of it, from the many dead, both American and Panamanian.

Guerra did not care about the death toll. He was only interested in certain bodies—the vice president's and now, by necessity, Jack Ryan's. Guerra could not be sure, but he thought he'd seen the delicious little piece of pie Major Canto in the great hall just before the roof collapsed.

He'd just finished putting a bullet in Botero when someone, likely Major Canto, murdered Fabian Pinto. While the men were not friends per se, Pinto worked for him, so Guerra took his death as a personal insult and returned to the room next to where he was killed. The Secret Service agent they'd found hiding there had told them nothing—so far, anyway. Guerra would see to that shortly, after he had a look around.

Apart from being a horrible leader and a man of deeply flawed morals, he was a talented investigator. It didn't take him very long to find what he was looking for.

A tiny ridge of debris along the back wall.

The rooms had been thoroughly cleaned, the tile polished to a high gloss in anticipation of the **yanqui** President's visit, but the explosive concussion had knocked dust from the walls and ceilings of the three-hundred-and-fifty-year-old building.

He stared hard at the tiny trail of dust, letting it tell its story. Hardly noticeable and barely wider than a hair, it ran diagonally at a forty-five-degree angle from the wall. He gave the wall a firm shove, and as he suspected, it moved.

He motioned the SPI officers over and gestured to the opening with his chin. "Where does this go?"

Both men shrugged.

"I will go and get reinforcements," Goat said.

"If Carré and Ryan are down there," said Fatty, "then they have Secret Service with them and Protection Group."

"Not many," Guerra said, "if you count the bodies in the hall. And we need them both dead, not taken prisoner. If you bring more SPI, there's too great a chance this will end in a talk instead of gunfire." Guerra peeked inside the dark passage. It smelled like mildew and sewage, and . . . something else he could not put his finger on.

He drew his sidearm, more to demonstrate his commitment than in response to danger. "Get some lights and rifles. Hurry. We must not let them get out of the palace."

67

Felix Moncada made it out the west door of the palace while the shooting was still going on out front. Unlike members of the SPI, he didn't worry about the Secret Service agents shooting at him. They had no bad intentions.

He'd run the three blocks to the Ministry of Government building on Central Avenue, knowing this was where the various ministers would convene to sort out this assault on the nation's sovereignty.

All the secretaries had fled at the sounds of bombs and gunfire, so he had no gatekeepers to contend with outside the conference room. Confident that he had a plan all the ministers would agree with, he marched past the empty desks and knocked on the great wooden door, not as much for permission as to keep from getting shot by any of the ministers who might have brought a pistol with them under these circumstances.

There were six ministers present—public health, foreign relations, trade, public security, government, and justice. Moncada made his case for martial law, engaging the assistance of their Russian friends to secure the canal from the chaos of this unknown threat.

Three of the men voiced some level of agreement that a deal with the Russians would teach the United States a lesson in humility, but none of them were nearly as ruffled as Moncada imagined they would be, not even the minister of public security, who'd had a truck bomb blow a crater the size of a small lake in front of his building. If anything, the man was the most even-keeled of anyone in the room.

When Moncada took a breath, waiting for his words to be not only accepted but praised for their insight and forward thinking, the minister of foreign affairs looked up from his notepad, where he'd been preparing a list of world leaders to call, and said, "Who are you again?"

68

wo oncoming vessels had politely—and wisely—yielded the right of way to the Russian destroyer **Admiral Chabanenko.** They were making excellent time, even throwing up a nice wake in the ditch behind them when there were no other ships to contend with. All was going well but for Señor Berugatte's constant whine, which was getting on Rykov's last nerve.

"I cannot guarantee they will open the locks for you," the pilot said.

Rykov and his first officer both chuckled at that.

"Oh, I can," Rykov said. "I told you, behind us, **Ivan Gren** has by now shit out two hundred of our highly trained Naval Infantry troops. These men are moving ahead of us, ensuring the cooperation of your canal controllers at Miraflores and Pedro Miguel. Not to mention the Ka-29TB assault helicopters that will support them from the air. So you see, my friend, the locks will open for us, one way or another. If you would like, you could call and

warn your friends manning the gates, for the sake of their health."

"Yes, all right," Berugatte said, giving up. "But there is still the matter of the **Apelles.** I have looked at the charts and the best place to pass them would be after the Empire Reach. The channel widens slightly before the next straightaway we call the Culebra Reach."

The helmsman gave a slight shake of his head. "**Apelles** has already passed the Culebra Reach," he said. "It is one kilometer dead ahead and closing."

Rykov gave a resigned shrug. "It seems that ship has sailed, so to speak."

The Greek container ship hove into view less than five minutes later, well before the point Berugatte called Empire Reach. A collective gasp went up from the crew on the bridge. Even Rykov had to work to control his breathing.

The monstrous bow was a wall of steel that looked as though it blocked the entire passage. She sounded her foghorn, the sound waves rattling the windows and bulkheads of the sleek destroyer.

"Our speed is twelve kilometers an hour, Captain," the helmsman said, no doubt checking to see if Rykov wanted to slow a bit. "**Apelles** is holding at eight."

"That is much too fast!" Berugatte said. "We must—"

Rykov raised a hand, as if to strike the sniveling pilot.

Two hundred meters ahead and closing, the **Apelles** loomed larger by the second, leaving only the tiniest sliver of canal available for the destroyer to slip by.

"Steady as you go," Rykov said.

"Captain, **Apelles** is slowing," the helmsman said.

Rykov could feel the irresistible pull of the Greek ship as the **Admiral Chabanenko,** the Black Terror, plowed into the shadowed gap between the oncoming behemoth and the sloughing southern bank of the canal.

Berugatte began to pray to the Virgin Mary, loud and fast. Rykov was truly afraid the man might vomit or soil his pants.

The rumble of both ships' engines reverberated between them.

"If you are going to pray," the captain said, as much to himself as to the trembling pilot, "then address your prayers to Saint Nikola. He is a doer, not an intercessory. There is no time for a saint to beg God to get involved."

69

ONE HOUR AFTER DETONATION

Every time Mary Pat Foley pushed an elephant ear or palm frond or hanging vine out of her way, she either drew chides from a troupe of monkeys or sent a flock of birds wheeling above the canopy, squawking and crying as if to say, **Here they are! Here they are!**

They'd crossed several trails, two wider and more groomed than the others, but decided to keep to the jungle rather than venture out and face strangers, who might draw unwanted attention. Five hundred acres was almost one square mile, plenty of room to get lost. With luck and a little care, Foley hoped it was enough to stay lost long enough for help to arrive—if it was coming at all.

Johnson had holstered his sidearm. Foley had stuffed the little .380 in her pocket. They found they needed both hands to keep the thick vegetation from shredding their arms and faces. They moved slowly and methodically, trying to keep from leaving a clear trail in the undergrowth and using the sun filtering through the trees to keep them from going in circles and walking into the arms of Sabine Gorshkova. Every step kicked up a centipede or sent a snake slithering over dead leaves. Foley calculated she had inadvertently eaten at least three spiders and wore the homes of at least a dozen others in her hair.

Johnson, in the lead, slowed enough to gingerly clear a web, and the silver-dollar-sized spider hanging with it, out of their path.

"What's the difference between a jungle and a tropical rainforest?" he whispered.

"I don't know . . ."

"If you know what you're doing," the agent said, "it's a rainforest. If you don't, it's a jungle."

Affability under extremely harsh conditions was apparently Johnson's superpower.

Screaming monkeys and tattletale birds, or possibly some deadly viper, would be what got them killed, but in the meantime they had to contend with all manner of itchy creatures—chiggers and ticks and sand flies that were, at the moment, competing with a cloud of mosquitoes for every drop of Foley's blood. It was some kind of blessing that she would not survive long enough for malaria or dengue fever to manifest.

The foliage thinned some, hardly noticeable unless you happened to be bushwhacking through it.

"Maybe we should try to find high ground," Foley said. "So I can make another call."

A flock of unseen birds chattered out of the canopy somewhere behind them.

"These guys are professionals," Johnson whispered. "And we don't know what's going on with all the explosions. We may be in some kind of **Red Dawn** situation right now." He caught Foley's eye and shook his head. "And I'm not joking about that, ma'am. It might be better to hunker down and keep you—"

His head snapped upward, as if he'd gotten a sudden shock. Foley thought he'd been bitten by a snake, until the crack of a gunshot filtered through the trees a moment later.

Johnson hunched forward, favoring his left arm. He'd been shot. Foley tried to see where he was hit, but he threw his right arm around her and pulled her into the underbrush, disappearing into the jungle shadows.

She hoped.

70

I am certain I got him, **patrona**," De Bruk said when they reached the clearing. Two of the other three men with Sabine Gorshkova fanned out, scanning the jungle for threats. These Secret Service agents were not pushovers like some child at a Bolivian clinic. They fought back. The bastards at Foley's motorcade had taken out four of Sabine's soldiers before they'd been cut down and, even then, only because the agents carried just enough ammunition for a gunfight they thought **might** happen, where Sabine and her men brought enough for the gunfight they **knew** was inevitable.

De Bruk pushed aside leaves and shrubs, searching for any evidence that could redeem him. His once handsome face bore a weeping diagonal gash from above one eye to the bottom of his chin, where a branch of some thorn tree had whipped back and caught him unprepared. Sabine had been the one to let the branch go prematurely, but no one, least of all De Bruk, mentioned it. A thorn had scraped

one eye, deeply from the looks of the tears wetting
the man's bloody cheek.

An excited cry escaped his chest. It would have been
endearing had she still carried any feelings for him.

"Tracks!" he said, idiotically triumphant.

"Or the tracks of a tapir," Sabine said. "No one
saw them but you."

"Here, **patrona.**" Francisco gave a similar cry
as De Bruk. "Blood," he said.

On one hand, Sabine was happy to know that
De Bruk had actually hit one of the Secret Service
men. On the other hand, it annoyed her that he had
been right and Francisco had taken his side.

"It is probably tapir blood," she groused. "But we
will follow it anyway."

She unfolded the antenna on the satellite phone
she'd brought with her from the car and turned back
and forth to get a signal under the thick overhead
canopy, while her men searched the detritus on the
jungle floor for enough tracks to give them a direction
of travel. Blood or no blood, her men would not have
survived if they'd been after a more worthy opponent.

Miraculously, she got a signal . . . And Ian Doyle
actually answered.

"Where are you?" she snapped. This was no time
for celebrating just because a phone call decided
to connect.

"Miraflores," Doyle said. "Near the locks, watching the show."

"Good," Sabine said. "I have a job for you."

71

Deep in the tunnels beneath Palacio de las Garzas, Jack Ryan hunkered in the moist darkness beside Montgomery, Carré, and Canto. They'd heard something. A distant groan. At first, Ryan thought it was the blast of another bomb. Or possibly thunder. But it did not go away. Rather, it grew louder, more intense, like an oncoming train, or . . .

Ryan checked the luminous face of his Explorer and did the math. Yes, he thought. He knew exactly what the sound was.

They were right on time.

Less than two hours after the first bombs detonated in front of the presidential palace, a division of four F/A-18E Super Hornets of the Blue Diamonds/Strike Fighter Squadron 146 crossed into Panamanian airspace. If the USS **Theodore Roosevelt** was a big stick for American diplomacy, the Diamonds were the spiky, barbed-wire-wrapped end of that stick. They came in from the east, two sections of two, wing-on-wing, less than five hundred feet over the treetops at seven hundred miles an hour. Low and loud. Powerful vortices left tornadoes of leaves and dust and debris in their wake. Windows shattered; car alarms screamed.

Their mission was not to bomb or fire missiles, although they could if the need arose. Everyone in Panama (and, the pilots thought, likely Costa Rica and Colombia) knew the Americans were here—and they wanted their President back.

The smoldering hulk of a huge ship lay in the canal locks to the west.

"How we looking?" the flight leader said.

The strike fighters had been in the Russian destroyer's MEZ, or missile engagement zone, for several minutes.

"We're good," Grizzly One, the E/A-18G off the leader's wing, said. Modified Boeing F-18s, the two "Growler" electronic warfare aircraft in this division, worked in concert to tactically jam radar and guidance systems on the Russian vessels, spoofing their electronics into thinking they were bouncing all over the place—or blinding them entirely.

A line of troop carriers rolled along like ants on the Gamboa Road parallel to the canal. Three camouflage Russian attack helicopters landed in a clearing to the north near what looked like a dilapidated prison.

"Got 'em," Grizzly Two said.

The procession stopped and the line of Russian soldiers looked skyward as the jets roared overhead. Some shook their fists. Most clamped their hands on top of their helmets and watched with open mouths, no doubt wondering if this was the last sight they would ever see.

W e are blind, Captain," the targeting officer in the CIC reported over the intercom.

Rykov looked out the starboard windows at the rough concrete walls that surrounded his ship and slammed an angry hand down on the chart table.

The container ship **Apelles** had come to a stop in the narrow cut, allowing the warship to slip by unscathed, thanks to Saint Nikola and, clearly apparent to Rykov, his iron will.

Now, in the locks, his ship might as well have been a fish in a barrel.

Ivan Gren's Naval Infantry had performed their mission flawlessly, bullying the canal controllers into opening the gates at Pedro Miguel. Passage through the first of the two chambers at Miraflores had been uneventful as well. The American Super Hornets had overflown them, as the water level quickly dropped over fifty feet to compensate for the falling tide of the Pacific Ocean on the other side of the massive gate. Only the top of their electronic array peeked above the top of the lock.

The rest of the ship sat stuck in a concrete tomb. There were still missiles, of course, but the priority message from Admiral Kozlov, commander of the Northern Fleet, had done more to preclude a missile deployment than the American Growlers. It had absolutely gutted Rykov and Pagodin to order their attack helicopters to stand down.

The burbling-over on the surface subsided as the water leveled off with the ocean.

"They are refusing to open the gates," the radioman said.

"Refusing!"

"An American ship has moved into the canal approach on the Pacific side."

"It would have the right of passage, Captain," Berugatte said, innocently holding up his watch. "Traffic is northbound this time of day."

"Shut up!" Rykov snapped.

"Captain," the seaman at the radio said. "The American ship is hailing us."

Rykov ordered him on speaker.

"Good afternoon, Russian destroyer **Admiral Chabanenko,**" the American said, butchering the pronunciation of the ship's name. "This is Captain Cody Marsh of the U.S. Coast Guard national security cutter **Munro . . .**"

The Coast Guard captain fell silent while the cursed jets made another booming pass, seemingly close enough to rake the antennas off the destroyer.

For the first time in two hours, Berugatte was a picture of calm.

"Sorry about that," Captain Marsh said. "Made me lose my train of thought."

"Suka!" Rykov said under his breath. This idiot sounded like someone from an American cowboy movie. He half expected the man to say **shucks.**

The American did not disappoint in that regard.

"Anyhow, I've been authorized by my government to thank you and your marines for assisting us in helping the Panamanians restore order during this turbulent time. As you can imagine, we are under a great deal of stress. I was under the impression that you were going to wait for us to join you in Miraflores Lake, but I was obviously misinformed."

A Coast Guard cutter, Rykov thought, **against a Russian missile destroyer?** The Black Terror would pick its teeth with the bones of this puny puddle boat.

Two more strike fighters thundered overhead.

"So . . ." the cowboy said. "Pardon my confusion. I'll reverse course now and yield the way so they can get you outta there."

Rykov licked his lips, considering his options. His first instinct was to blow this American imbecile out of the water. But with the Super Hornets overhead, he had little choice. He snatched up the microphone.

"Good day, Captain Marsh," he said. "As always, Russia is glad to assist . . ."

Señor Berugatte beamed.

"Am I correct in assuming that since Russia is to the west," the pilot asked, "you will likely continue in that direction?"

"What?"

"I assume you will not need my guidance in making another transit through the canal on this trip?"

"You are correct in assuming you may get off my vessel before I have you thrown off!" Rykov wheeled. "Mr. Orlov, the bridge is yours."

"I think it would be best if you disembarked," Orlov whispered.

"And I will," Berugatte said. "With great pleasure, as soon as I see you out of the approach."

Rykov bit his tongue as he exited the bridge for the silence of his cabin—and wondered if his career was over . . . for simply following orders. Maybe. Chances were, neither Admiral Kozlov nor anyone else would ever speak of this again . . . Except for the Americans.

Those cowboys would crow about this day for decades.

72

"Anything on the radio?" Ryan asked.

Montgomery monitored Secret Service traffic through his earpiece. He shook his head, his wide face an eerie orange from the glow of his flashlight.

The group had stalled, a fifty-foot lake of black water blocking their way forward and unknown dangers to the rear. Time, Ryan thought, was their friend . . . up to a point.

"The Panamanians need to be the heroes," he said. "With you leading the charge, Lionel. We have got to get you out of here and in front of a camera."

The distant thunder of fighter jets roared somewhere above, muffled by stone, but still exhilarating.

"But the people need to see that we are friends," Carré said. "And that I know for a fact the Secret Service had no part in President Botero's assassination."

"Guerra . . ." Major Canto said. "He is behind this."

"He is part of it," the vice president said. "But he is not the mastermind. I believe he is working with one of Botero's advisers . . ."

Carré's voice trailed off. He cocked his head toward the water, then turned quickly back toward the dogleg turn, fifteen feet behind them, the way they'd come.

"The jets?" Canto whispered.

Carré shook his head.

Montgomery cupped a hand over his flashlight so that it gave only the slightest glow. He rose quietly for a man of his size and then switched off the light completely as he moved toward the turn.

Inky, palpable blackness overwhelmed the tunnel. Their breathing the only other sound but for a periodic drip of water.

Then a deafening crack. Men's voices growled. Barked orders in Spanish boomed against stone walls. Another gunshot brought a cry and then a hiss of breath, like the air leaking from a tire.

Ryan rolled toward Carré, covering him with his body.

Major Canto aimed the beam of her flashlight past Montgomery, low, so as not to blind him. They had discussed this eventuality. She fired twice, but Ryan, draped over the vice president, couldn't see her target.

The tunnel came alive with gunfire and blinding orange flashes. A bullet slapped the path beside

Ryan, showering him and Carré with fragments of stone.

"Gabriella!" a man's voice cried out. **"Soy Fredi!"**

A friendly, Ryan thought. That would make little difference to Montgomery, who had no idea which of the people in the tunnel were shooting at him.

A feral growl erupted from the corner as a shadow barreled out, crashing into Montgomery and driving him backward. Ryan heard a pistol clatter to the ground.

"Light!" Montgomery shouted, muffled against the body of his attacker.

Major Canto switched on her flashlight, illuminating the Secret Service agent and a tall, sandy-haired man in a PNP uniform. The one she'd called Commissioner Guerra. Two SPI guards lay dead on the ground.

Montgomery stepped offline to gain distance, fists up, circling. A lightning jab materialized out of nowhere, snapping Guerra's head backward so that he was gazing at the ceiling. Montgomery hit him again, twice, before he had a chance to look down. In truth, it was over before it started, but Montgomery, who spent most every waking hour in front of a multitude of cameras resisting the urge to punch someone, sent a devastating right uppercut to a staggered Guerra's chin, shattering teeth and breaking his jaw.

Montgomery had to drag the unconscious man out of the water, grudgingly, so he wouldn't drown.

Unconscious or dead, all the attackers were hand-cuffed behind their backs. Fortunately, with Fredi Perez's arrival, they had three sets of cuffs.

The sergeant rushed to Canto's side, which drew a look from Montgomery, but the major assured everyone he was friendly.

"You are bleeding," Perez said, pressing a hand against the bloodstain blossoming quickly across Canto's calf.

"The stitches," she said.

Vice President Carré groaned, dusting off his suit as he climbed to his feet.

"What news do you have of the palace?"

"Still very dangerous inside," Perez said. "I am not certain who the conspirators are—or if we will ever know."

"We will know," Carré said. "Commissioner Guerra will tell us. What about outside?"

"The director general of the PNP has arrived with truckloads of at least five hundred officers. He is bringing everything under control, but it will take time. Still too dangerous for you to go back."

"How do we know he's not part of the coup?" Montgomery asked, putting words to Ryan's thoughts.

"He is my uncle," Carré said.

"So now we wait here for how long until he settles things?" Ryan said.

Perez played his light across the water. "Or we can go this way."

"Go where?" Canto asked.

"I believe we are almost to the Church of San Francisco de Asis, at the water's edge."

The light fell on what looked like the top of a doorway peeking above the water's surface. It had not been visible minutes before.

"Look," Perez said, moving the beam along the wall. "Eyebolts."

"Ah," Carré said. "I see. In addition to a place of refuge, this was once a prison chamber."

"Tide torture," Perez said. "My father reads about all things pirate. In the old days, city leaders would imprison pirates and other reprobates to tide torture, forcing them to endure endless cycles of rising and falling waters, freezing in the darkness, not knowing if the next tide would be high enough to drown them."

"Or hoping it would be," Major Canto quietly offered.

"Anyway," Perez said, brightening the mood, "we can go through there in a few minutes. See? The water level is dropping quickly." He looked at his boss. "You should ride on my back," he said. "So your wound does not get infected." He held on to her hand to steady her, among other reasons obvious to everyone around except perhaps Major Canto.

Carré smiled at the two PNP officers. "I want to thank you for saving my life."

Both Canto and Perez dipped their heads.

"Your Excellency."

Carré turned to Ryan. "And you, Mr. President. You and Agent Montgomery. I am in your debt . . ."

Twenty minutes later, the water level dropped low enough for them to wade across and reach the door, the timbers of which had long rotted away. Ryan slipped his suit coat off.

"What is it, boss?" Gary Montgomery said. The big man's voice rasped from near complete exhaustion.

Ryan held up the coat, his finger sticking through a bullet hole that had punched neatly through the fabric beside the bottom front button. "Better than getting gut shot."

"How did that happen?"

"When I was on top of Carré," Ryan said. "My suit coat was kind of splayed out, I guess. I heard the bullet smack the rocks. Didn't realize it was that close."

"Yeah," Montgomery said. "About you shielding Carré . . . Are you trying to take my job?"

"Someone needs to," Ryan said. "Director Howe advised me last week he plans to retire. I was thinking you'd be a good fit for that one . . ."

"Director of the Service . . ." Montgomery looked like he might fall over. "I like the job I have."

"I wouldn't be arguing with you all the time," Ryan offered.

"There is that," Montgomery said.

"At any rate," Ryan said. "Think it over. The offer's on the table. Honestly, I can't think of anyone else."

Ryan put a finger through the bullet hole again and then dropped the coat on the ground.

"Mr. President," Montgomery said, shining the flashlight on the crumpled coat.

"It's better if Cathy doesn't find any more bullet holes in my clothes." Ryan paused before stepping into the water. "About me arguing with you . . . I know it was your advice all along that I shouldn't come on this trip. If you want to say I told you so—"

"All due respect, sir," Montgomery said, "Jack Ryan has to be Jack Ryan. We all know that. To steal a line from Charles de Gaulle's security man—'It's my job to guard the President of the United States. It's your job to **be** the President of the United States.'"

73

Chilly Edwards was still breathing out of his mouth from the broken nose courtesy of the fight in the hotel stairwell, but he didn't let that slow him. He felt his stomach rise in his throat as United States Army Chief Warrant Officer 3 Rick "Seldom" Wright flew his Boeing-Hughes MH-6 Killer Egg nap of the earth—skimming the canopy of the jungle below.

The transition had gone much more smoothly than Chilly had imagined.

Chief Wright had been on the tarmac in his flat-black Little Bird, waiting to pick the team up as soon as their two planes had touched down in Colón. Panamanian law enforcement, having received stand-down orders from their new president, but still trying to make sense of what was going on, stood back as they bailed quickly out of the fixed-wing aircraft and, already jocked up with gear and guns, sprinted across the field to the waiting chopper.

Before they even landed, Clark and Yao tapped four operators to ride the benches over the skids—Lopez, Midas, Dom, and Chilly. The MH-6 normally flew with a two-person crew, but no one had expected this bird to go out again before it was folded up and shipped home. Chief Wright's copilot had returned stateside. Clark and Chavez clearly wanted to go, but yielded the front seat to Yao. He was, after all, the man who'd set up the move.

Chilly sat on the starboard side of the helicopter, straddling the commando board over the skid. The bird had no doors and he was inches away from the pilot. Midas sat on the bench behind him. Dom and Lopez took the port side.

Chilly's SPR, special purpose rifle, felt particularly familiar in his hands, calming even in the one-hundred-sixty-mile-an-hour wind outside the Little Bird that was skimming treetops close enough he felt like he could drag a boot through the leaves.

Chief Wright pushed the envelope, and they made the fifty-mile journey over the Continental Divide to the northern edge of Metropolitan Park in a matter of minutes.

"Heads up, boys," Yao said over the intercom. "Ninety seconds out."

Chilly's cheeks hurt from grinning as the chopper dropped even lower. He thought of his buds at APD and his team sergeant's well-meaning counsel that he would not be happy sitting behind a desk.

He was right . . . And oh so wrong.

———

Bullets thwacked the trees and skittered through the foliage around Mary Pat Foley's head. She clutched the little .380 Glock in one hand—down to one round from trying to hold off her attackers. The other hand held her phone to her ear, hissing directions to Adam Yao. He was supposedly on his way in a chopper, though she couldn't hear anything but ricochets and the screeches of what had to be every bird and monkey in Metropolitan Park.

Mary Pat and Johnson had crawled through the tangled vines and thick undergrowth to reach a clearing at the top of a hill for a quick pickup when Yao arrived, but now it looked like that clearing might get them killed.

The Secret Service agent sat propped on the back of a tree off the trail, left arm clamped to his side in an effort to stop the bleeding. He'd taken what they thought was a handgun round under his arm. The bullet had entered from the front and lodged (they thought) under his shoulder blade. A rifle round would have been much more devastating, but Foley worried that if he didn't get medical care soon, what kind of gun it was wouldn't be an issue. There was no way to put a tourniquet on a wound like his, and direct pressure wasn't cutting it. She imagined he was in great pain. She'd been shot herself and it was . . . Well, it was horrible. But Johnson sat stoically while holding his Glock in his right hand, obviously working hard to control his labored breathing.

The way things were looking, if the cavalry didn't get here soon, everything would be moot—at least to Foley and Johnson.

"Adam!" she said. "You guys better haul ass!"

A hail of bullets pattered the leaves around Foley like a driving rain.

"Hey! Maaaaary! I got something to say to you!"

Foley ducked around the tree, away from the sound of the voice. She'd never heard the woman's voice, but she knew this was Sabine Gorshkova.

"Maarrry! Come on, Maary."

It was the stuff of nightmares.

More gunfire. This time coming from her right.

Foley held the phone closer. "The bastards are flanking us, Adam!"

She could see two of Sabine's men now, creeping toward her from out of the jungle. They must have been given orders not to shoot. One, a tall blond man, barked commands to the other in accented English. Maybe South African, Foley thought. She looked to her left, where Sabine strode toward her, head back, pistol up, throwing caution to the wind.

Ten yards out, the South African raised a rifle toward Brett Johnson, but Sabine quickly put up her hand and he lowered the barrel. She took a hammer out of her belt and passed it to the man, grinning, urging him forward.

"Nope," Johnson said, and shot the South African in the chest as he approached.

Sabine screamed for her men to advance.

They never heard her.

The air in the clearing grew suddenly dense, or perhaps it just felt that way to Foley, when the little egg-shaped helicopter popped above the tree line, rotor tilted forward as if beating the jungle into submission. It had been remarkably quiet until it rose above the foliage, silent if she hadn't known it was coming.

Two operators sat on each strut, bringing a total of four guns to bear.

Sabine gave up on her hammer plan and went back to guns, rushing toward Foley at a dead run. Johnson fired again, but the shot went wide. Foley waited a beat, firing her last round when Sabine was less than ten feet out.

The shrieking woman stumbled, but kept coming, pistol up.

"Maaaa—"

Two quick shots from the hovering chopper took her jaw, silencing her for good.

All three of her men fell in a hail of bullets.

Once the Little Bird appeared, it was over in less than five seconds.

Adrenaline surging, Mary Pat realized that this was the woman who had ordered the hit on her husband. The evil thing who had murdered so many around the world. She stifled the urge to crawl over and bash in what was left of her skull with a stone. Instead, she rolled to Brett Johnson and pressed her hand to the wound under his arm.

He arched his back, grimacing. His eyes fluttered closed.

He reminded her of her son.

"Brett," she said. "Come on, buddy."

He opened his eyes. "I'm going to be fine. Seriously." He gave Foley a loopy smile as if to demonstrate. Then said, "Man, was that bitch scary or what . . ."

74

Ian Doyle heard the thump of boots up on the **Bambina**'s cockpit. He nodded to himself, waiting quietly at the polished teak table, wishing he had a cigarette.

Felix Moncada about shit himself when he dropped down the companionway and found the big Irishman on his sailboat.

And he hadn't even seen the gun.

"I . . . You are here . . ." Moncada forced a smile.

"I am," Doyle said. "Where are you off to?"

"I . . . Nowhere," Moncada stammered. "I was . . . You know, the same thing you are, I suppose."

"I doubt that."

"You are very good at your job," Moncada said, as if he were about to make an offer of employment.

"Indeed, I am." Doyle raised a suppressed pistol and put two in the man's chest.

Moncada staggered backward and fell against the steps of the companionway. It took him a few gasping seconds to die. Unlike his whack-job boss, Doyle wasn't about watching people suffer, but he didn't want to get blood all over everything, either. He rolled the body in a plastic sheet he'd brought for that purpose.

He left the body and went topside, shaking out a Carrolls Number 1. He lit it while he watched the sunset.

Sabine was dead. They hadn't named her on the news, but Doyle knew it was her they were talking about. The mission had failed. Most of the people he knew were gone or in prison.

He finished the cigarette and flicked it into the sea.

At least he'd gotten a boat out of the deal.

His Excellency President Lionel Carré insisted on making his televised speech to the people of Panama in front of the ruined Palacio de las Garzas.

The director general of Servicio de Protección Institucional—along with every government minister in office—insisted even more strongly that he give his speech in a secure studio surrounded by vetted security personnel. Jack Ryan had returned home, wisely choosing his wife's well-being over a photo opportunity with Panama.

As agreed during tense trilateral meetings between Panama, the U.S., and Russia, Carré closed his speech with a heartfelt thank-you to President

Yermilov for their help during the almost successful coup. It allowed the Russians to save a modicum of face on the world stage, and in return, the Kremlin would turn over the extensive files they kept on members of the Camarilla.

75

Clark asked Mandy Cobb to meet him in the CIA Museum at Langley—getting special dispensation from Mary Pat Foley to tour. An amazing place full of things that brought a hundred memories rushing back. It was invitation-only to anyone outside the CIA and was billed as the most interesting museum you'll never get to see. Clark was sure it struck him differently than visitors who'd had no part in any of the operations on display.

Cobb stopped by the exhibit on the Enigma coding machine from World War II. Appropriate, Clark thought, considering what he had in mind.

"Fantastic work," he said. "From everyone on the team."

"I'm still . . ." She paused, as if trying to work out what she wanted to say. "Mr. Clark . . . John, from the time I was a little girl I have always wanted to be a part of something bigger. But . . . it's just that . . . I have plenty of confidence in my abilities, but I am also self-aware. I'm not quite sure I'm elite enough for this group."

Clark reached behind a glass display next to the wall and retrieved a black Pelican briefcase. "I have some things for you."

She gave a soft groan. "Okay . . ."

"Gear issue of a sort," Clark said. "More like returning something that rightfully belongs to you. I didn't want it to color your judgment during our first meeting at Quantico, but the truth is, I knew your grandparents. A very long time ago."

"You were in Berlin before the Wall came down?"

"I was," Clark said. "Did you know much about them?"

She shrugged. "Oma Lotte died before I was old enough to remember her. But I knew Grandpa Rich. Like I said, he taught me how to pick locks. Always thought that was weird for a grandfather."

"Do you know what he did during World War Two?"

"He never talked about it," she said. "And I'm not sure my dad knew very much. Do you?"

"OSS." Clark nodded to the museum exhibit. "Forerunner to the CIA. Your grandmother was a resistance fighter against the Nazis inside Germany. The two of them worked together, doing some of the same type of things we do at The Campus. Interdiction, sabotage, looking for high-value targets . . ." Clark gave another rare grin, picturing Lotte Cobb, Mandy's grandmother. "You know, spy shit. They were both older by the time I met them, working without diplomatic cover during the Cold War. I am not exaggerating when I say I have never met anyone as fierce as Lotte Cobb."

Mandy's mouth fell open. "No kidding? My grandparents were spies?"

"In the purest sense of the word," Clark said. "During the coldest part of the Cold War. The bad guys were different back then. On the surface, it was a gentleman's game—but beneath the civilized veneer the Soviet KGB and East German Stasi were as bad as the Nazis. Your grandparents made many trips deep into East Berlin. Some of them I was fortunate enough to be a part of."

Mandy heaved a long sigh. "It's hard to believe my sweet little grandpa was a spy . . ."

Clark flipped the latches on the Pelican case and opened the lid. "A long time ago, well before you were born, your grandparents literally took a young spy in from the cold of Berlin. I'd just been in a . . . Let's just say a dustup with a couple of KGB thugs and needed a place to recuperate. Rich and Lotte were my contacts, a refuge in a dark and dangerous place."

Clark lifted a vintage Fairbairn Sykes dagger out of the Pelican case and slid the long stiletto blade across the glass museum case. It was still in its original leather sheath. "This was your grandfather's."

Next, Clark took out a Browning Fabrique Nationale 1910 pistol chambered in .32 ACP. He opened the slide to show Cobb it was empty and then pushed it toward her on a shearling wool pad. "And this was your grandmother's. Not to be too dark, but I think it's important for you to know both these things were put to good use."

Clark pushed the case to Cobb, shooting a furtive glance over his shoulder. He smiled. "You'll need this to get those out of here."

"You think the museum would want them?"

"Hell yes, they would want them," Clark said. "But that's up to you." He stepped back, a tremendous weight that he'd been carrying for a very long time finally off his chest. "They gave these weapons to me when I needed them. And now I'm getting them back where they belong."

A tear ran down Mandy Cobb's cheek.

"Your grandparents were part of something bigger," Clark said. "And so are you."

Mind if we swing by the post office?" Chilly said, opening the pickup door for Mandy Cobb. A hell of a lot had happened in five days. They were on their way to Founding Farmers, a restaurant in Tysons Corner that Midas had told them about. It was supposed to be amazing. Something about a Jefferson donut. Chilly didn't care. He just wanted to compare notes. As newbies to The Campus, he and Cobb had a lot to talk about. It wasn't a date.

He assured her of that. But she sure looked good in her green fleece and ball cap.

Cobb checked her phone and navigated him to the post office drop box on the way to the Tysons Corner Center.

Chilly pulled his pickup close and rolled down the window.

"Abilene PD," Cobb said, noting the address on the eight-by-eight cardboard box. "That's cool. Mailing a present home."

"Something like that," Chilly said, and dropped his badge in the slot.

ABOUT THE AUTHORS

TOM CLANCY was the author of more than eighteen #1 **New York Times** bestselling novels. His first effort, **The Hunt for Red October,** sold briskly as a result of rave reviews, then catapulted onto the bestseller list after President Reagan pronounced it "the perfect yarn." Clancy was the undisputed master at blending exceptional realism and authenticity, intricate plotting, and razor-sharp suspense. He passed away in October 2013.

MARC CAMERON is a retired Chief Deputy U.S. Marshal and twenty-nine-year law enforcement veteran. He is the author of the **New York Times** bestselling Jericho Quinn thrillers and the Arliss Cutter mystery series; his short stories have appeared in **The Saturday Evening Post** and **Boys' Life** magazine. Cameron is a certified law enforcement scuba diver and a man-tracking instructor, and holds a second-degree black belt in jujitsu. An avid sailor and adventure motorcyclist, he lives in Alaska with his beautiful bride and BMW motorcycle.

LIKE WHAT YOU'VE READ?

Try these titles,
also available in large print:

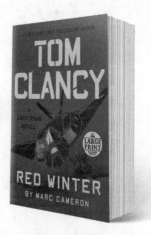

**Tom Clancy
Flash Point**
(by Don Bentley)
ISBN 978-0-593-67654-7

**Tom Clancy
Weapons Grade**
(by Don Bentley)
ISBN 978-0-593-74382-9

**Tom Clancy
Red Winter**
(by Marc Cameron)
ISBN 978-0-593-63276-5

For more information on large print titles, visit
www.penguinrandomhouse.com/large-print-format-books